DESPERATE GROUND

DESPERATE GROUND

BY JAMES R. BENN

Quiet Storm Publishing • Martinsburg, WV

Published by Quiet Storm Publishing
PO BOX 1666
Martinsburg, WV 25402

www.quietstormpublishing.com

Cover by : Georgiana Goodwin

ISBN: 0974408484

Library of Congress Control Number: 2004100099

Printed in the United States of America

For my father,

S/Sgt. Harold J. Benn

A soldier of World War II.

When you leave your own country behind, and take your army across neighboring territory, you find yourself on *critical ground.*

When there are means of communication on all four sides, the ground is one of *intersecting highways.*

When you penetrate deeply into a country, it is *serious ground.*

When you penetrate but a little way, it is *facile ground.* When you have the enemy's strongholds on your rear, and narrow passes in front, it is *hemmed-in ground.*

When there is no place of refuge at all, it is ***desperate ground***.

On ***desperate ground,***
proclaim to your soldiers
the hopelessness of saving their lives.
The only chance of life
lies in giving up all hope of it.

-Sun Tzu, The Art of War
ca 500 B.C.

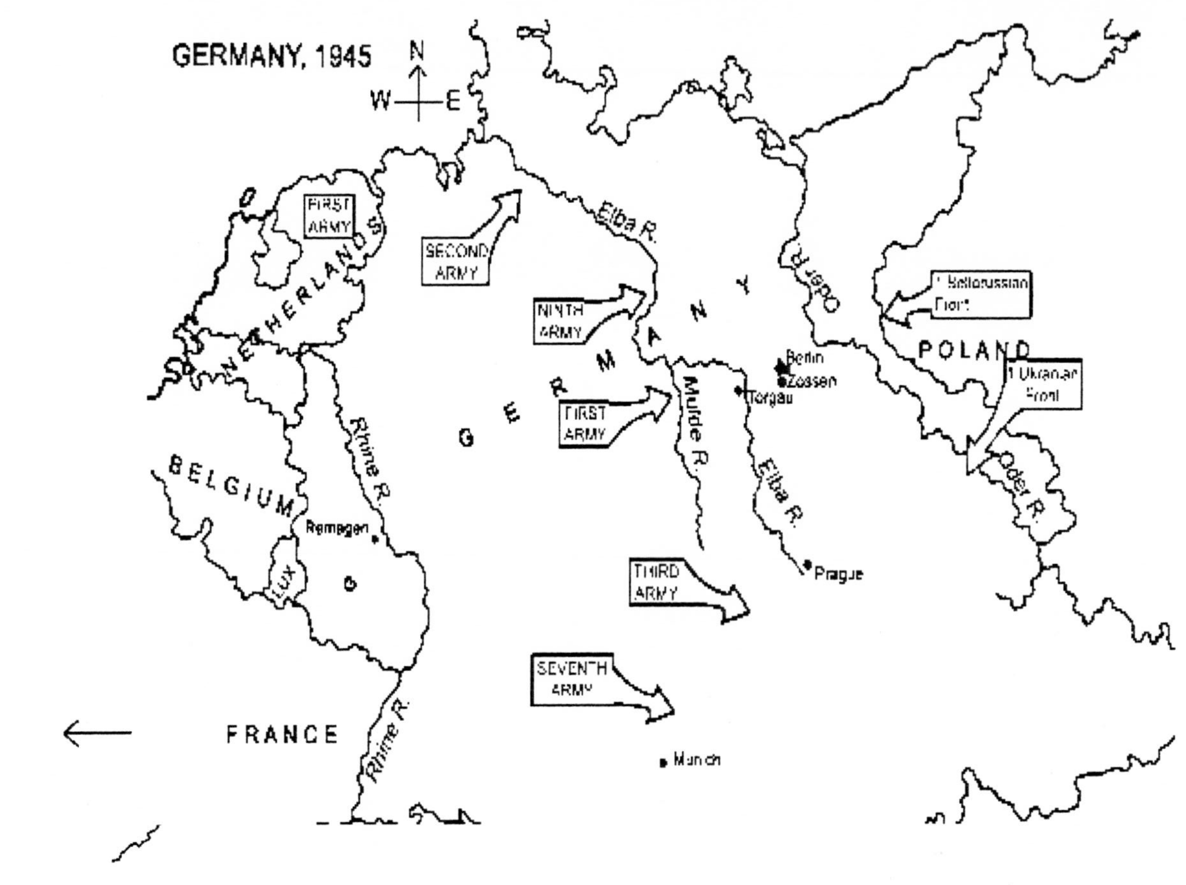
GERMANY, 1945
N
W
E
NETHERLANDS
FIRST ARMY
SECOND ARMY
Elba R.
NINTH ARMY
FIRST ARMY
THIRD ARMY
SEVENTH ARMY
GERMANY
BELGIUM
LUX
Remagen
Rhine R.
FRANCE
Mulde R.
Torgau
Berlin
Zossen
Prague
Munich
Oder R.
POLAND
Front
1 Ukranian Front

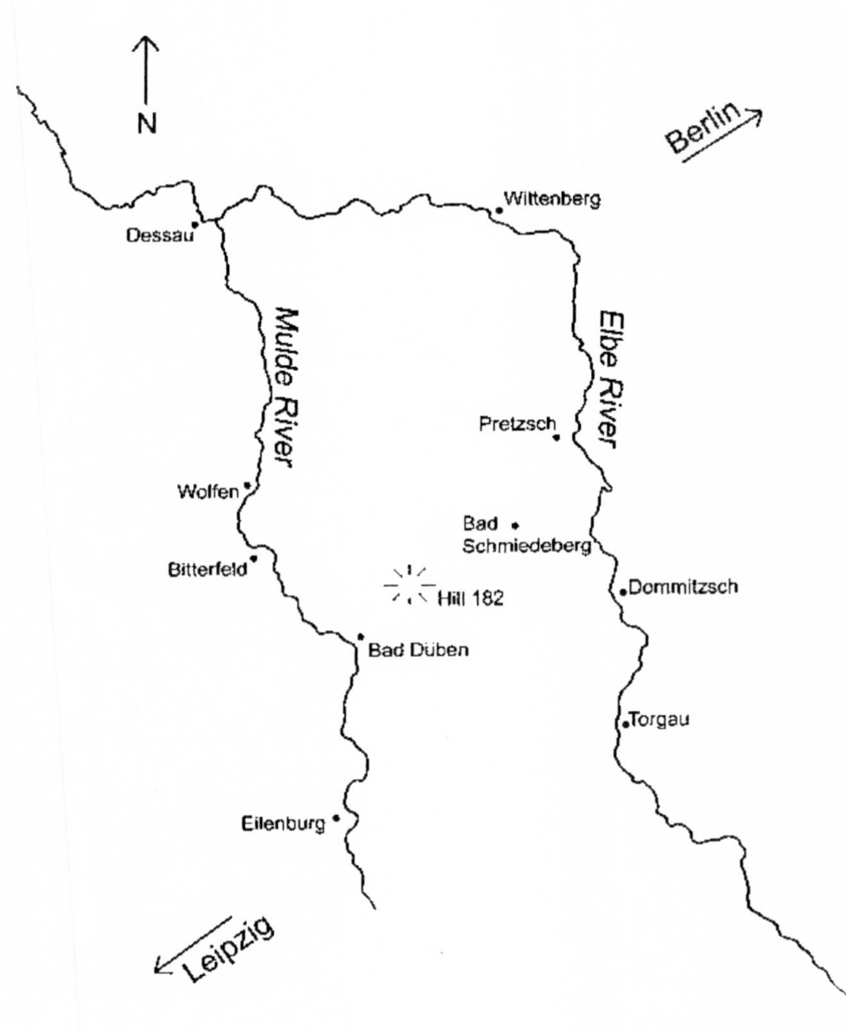
N
Berlin
Wittenberg
Dessau
Mulde River
Elbe River
Pretzsch
Wolfen
Bad
Schmiedeberg
Bitterfeld
Dommitzsch
Hill 182
Bad Düben
Torgau
Eilenburg
Leipzig

PROLOGUE

10 May 1940
Dutch-German Border

Leutnant (Second Lieutenant) Dieter Neukirk jumped from the back of the lead truck as the convoy pulled to the side of the road. He could see a group of officers moving like shadows inside the railroad station, the feeble lamplight struggling to illuminate the predawn night. He yawned and straightened out his stiff back, sore from the long, dark ride from Dusseldorf. For a second, all was quiet except for the sound of wheels braking on the gravel road.

Now it begins, he thought to himself. Suddenly the moment's stillness was broken by shouted commands and the heavy sound of booted soldiers laden with gear hitting the ground one after another as they disembarked and formed up along the roadside. The door of the railroad stationmaster's office slammed open and light spilled out, framing the form of the officer in command of the operation. As always, Major Erich Remke physically dominated all others around him. He strode down the steps with a focused purpose as junior officers and two civilians in leather trench coats followed him, quickening their pace to keep up with the long stride his six-foot athletic frame allowed. He went straight to Neukirk.

"Report, *Leutnant*!" Remke demanded.

"Brandenburg Special Detachment 55 is forming up, Sir!" Neukirk responded as he stood to attention, bracing for the intensity of Remke's scrutiny. "We will be ready for boarding in five minutes."

As if in mechanical response to his report, the locomotive on the far side of the station released a great hiss of steam, moving forward on the tracks, closer to the men who were pulling their ragged line into order as they spied Major Remke eyeing them. He looked back at Neukirk but said nothing as he pulled off his gray German officer's greatcoat and threw it towards his aide without looking away from the younger officer. Remke, like all the men of Special Detachment 55, was not wearing the gray-green uniform of the German Wehrmacht, but rather the green tunic and pants of the Dutch Army.

"Let us inspect our Dutch soldiers, Neukirk," said Remke with a slight smile. He walked down the line of men, more than 100 strong, all arrayed with Dutch uniforms and weapons. Neukirk's non-commissioned officer, *Feldwebel* (Sergeant) Jost Brunner, fell into step to the right of him.

"Everything ready?" asked Neukirk in a whisper.

"Damned well better be," grumbled Brunner in his broad Bavarian accent. Neukirk relaxed just a bit, doubting that the Major could find anything to fault after the months of training and practice that had brought the Detachment to this place, moments before the German invasion of France and the Low Countries.

Major Erich Remke and his men were all members of the Brandenburg Regiment, a special military formation attached to the German Secret Service – the *Abwehr*. Men were recruited into the Brandenburg organization from all branches of the service based upon a set of very special skills. Most could speak several languages, one well enough to pass as a native. They were trained in the operation of weapons from every army in Europe, as well as radio communications, explosives, and other deadly skills. Their training in hand-to-hand combat and the varied and stealthy methods of killing made them one of the most efficient, lethal, silent, and secretive units operating in this first year of the Second World War. Ironically, the need for specialists in foreign language with military backgrounds, combined with the intense secrecy in which they operated, provided the Brandenburg Regiment with an ethnic mix that would not have been tolerated in any other of Hitler's formations. There were Czarist Russians and Polish adventurers, fascist Frenchmen and Italian monarchists, all united by a common strain of German blood and military service, and by some a desire to right a wrong that had been inflicted on their family in another part of Europe. It was even rumored that some political opponents of the regime had found refuge in the Regiment, where the secrecy that surrounded those who were accepted into its ranks protected them.

Brandenburgers had infiltrated across the Polish border in 1939, hours before the German invasion. Dressed in Polish uniforms and led by their Polish-speaking comrades, they seized strategic crossroads and ambushed Polish troops as they came unawares toward the front.

Poland was only a dress rehearsal. Today the Brandenburg Regiment was sending groups of soldiers across the frontier in advance of the infantry and Panzers, which would constitute the ground invasion force of the Low Countries. In order to speed up the drive across Holland and Belgium, Brandenburgers in enemy uniform would again infiltrate into enemy territory. This time, the move was bolder than in Poland. Much bolder, and much more of a gamble.

Special Detachment 55 was a group of Dutch speaking German soldiers, outfitted exactly as a company of Dutch infantry. Their assignment was to capture a critically important bridge across the Maas River, less than ten kilometers on the other side of the border. Between German forces and the bridge was the small city of Venlo, and if resistance there held up the main forces, all hope of capturing the bridge and speeding across the river into the interior of the southern Netherlands was lost.

It was Major Remke who had come up with the plan. His men, dressed as Dutch infantry, would ride on the outside of a train made up of a locomotive and half a dozen cars. They would smash through the border crossing and head down the rail line straight through to Venlo. Once in the city, a Dutch troop train moving towards a strategic bridge would excite little comment, especially since by then German air attacks would already be underway against Belgium, the Netherlands and Luxembourg. The initial paralysis that a sudden attack causes would be their ally. They would bluff or shoot their way down the line to the Maas. There they would seize the bridge, aided by two reinforced Wehrmacht heavy weapons companies concealed inside the train cars. With their machine guns, anti-tank guns and mortars, the 300-man battle group would dig in and hold at both ends of the bridge, while the Brandenburg engineers dismantled the explosives, which the Dutch would certainly have in place. Unless the first wave of Panzers met with heavy resistance, Remke expected his force would be relieved by noon on that first day.

Remke completed his inspection. At the last man in line, he turned on his heel and barked at Neukirk.

"*Leutnant*!"

"*Herr* Major!" Neukirk responded nervously, expecting a reprimand for some overlooked detail. Instead, Remke nearly smiled and tilted his head slightly to the waiting locomotive, now building a head of steam and seeming to strain forward towards the frontier.

"Shall we board the morning express to Venlo, Deiter?"

It was the first time he had ever addressed his subordinate by his given name, and the first suggestion that beneath the driven, highly focused exterior there might be humor and humanity. Neukirk could almost hear Jost gasp just behind him. For three months, since *Leutnant* Neukirk had been given his first important assignment as the officer in charge of Special Detachment 55, he had seen rigorous and even dangerous training under the demanding Major Erich Remke, who had command of all troops involved in Operation En Passant. Remke was an accomplished chess player, and the idea of an oblique capture of his target while moving behind the front line appealed to him.

Neukirk now saw an excitement in Remke where there had only been a calm exterior before. He felt honored and exhilarated to be part of this daring and dashing undertaking. He broke through his nervousness and attempted to match Remke's bravado.

"*Jawohl, Herr* Major. I have an appointment in that direction myself this morning."

He could see Remke appreciated the comment, but was soon back to the business at hand.

"The heavy weapons group is in place. Mount your men by squads- we leave in ten minutes," said Remke as he glanced at his watch.

Lt. Neukirk turned to his sergeant, but *Feldwebel* Brunner had already heard and anticipated the order.

"First Squad take positions on the engine!" he bellowed, although the men were all close enough to have heard him whisper. He walked down the line and directed the squads to their positions on the top of the cars, up front on the locomotive and at the rear of the last car where a machine gun was set up to discourage pursuit.

Neukirk watched the activity all around him. Everything was going smoothly, just as it had every time they had practiced it. He was proud, nervous, excited and scared, and couldn't tell which emotion he was feeling at any one moment. He just knew he didn't want his men to see anything but confident pride.

He walked up to the locomotive and prepared to take his position along the narrow walkway above the steel wheels. As the opening rays of the dawning sun lit the train, he suddenly noticed something different. In all their training drills, they had used the same locomotive and cars so they would know them like the back of their hand. This was the same train, but the ornate paint job identifying it as a German Rail steam engine and freight cars had been painted over. It was now a solid, deep black with no telltale identity markings. Steam from the engine was released and a great cloud of it rose up in front of Neukirk as the shrill sound of the whistle assaulted his ears. Through the steam he could hazily see his men swarming over the dark and powerful form of the engine that would carry them into the conflict. He stood for a moment as if rooted to the ground, feeling a sudden stab of unexpected terror grip his heart. If they rode this dark beast over the border now, would they ever return? Neukirk knew with a certainty that his life was about to profoundly change, and that nothing would ever be the same. He also knew that he had never even given that thought a moment's consideration before.

Above them all stood Remke. He was perched on the front of the engine, standing with his arm lazily wrapped around the searchlight on the face of the locomotive.

"Come *Leutnant*, it's now or never," challenged Remke. Neukirk shook himself and mounted the engine as he had been trained to do. He knew everything that would happen next, until they journeyed beyond the exact memorized moves of their training procedures and into the unknown, just over the border beyond the next hill.

Jost was at the last car, and signaled ahead that all was ready. The "Dutch" soldiers were at their stations and the regular Wehrmacht *Landser* were hidden inside. Every man was ready.

"Forward!" yelled Remke and drew out the word as he brought his arm down and held it pointed ahead. The train lurched forward as the massive wheels moved beneath Neukirk. He held on to the handrail tightly as the train picked up speed and the wind began to whip up around them.

Once the train got up to speed it took under ten minutes to bring the Dutch border station into sight. Neukirk squinted his eyes against the wind and dust and could see no unusual activity. He had scouted the border crossing every day for the past week, and he knew the routine. There were two Dutch soldiers in front of the gate lowered across the tracks, two in a machine gun pit on the north side of the tracks, and several more within a small guard shack a few meters down the line.

As the train grew closer and did not slow down, Neukirk could see the guards start to wave their arms, probably assuming the engineer would hit the brakes any moment. The whistle let out a long blast and the train increased in speed. The wind was more powerful now, causing Neukirk to shield his tearing eyes while at the same time tracking the movements of the enemy. He drew his pistol.

Suddenly the train flew through the barrier. Wood splintered and Neukirk could hear yells as the Dutch tried to react to the surprise. An explosion boomed on the opposite side of the train as grenades dealt with the machine gun emplacement. Neukirk turned quickly as the engine pulled the cars through the crossing. Several Dutch soldiers on his side of the train had come to their wits and were running alongside, unslinging their rifles. They were receding in Neukirk's vision as he heard a burst of fire and saw the Dutch drop dead in their tracks. They were the first dead men Neukirk had ever seen. They crumpled completely, as if the bodies had evaporated and left nothing but green rags and a rifle to fall to the ground.

He saw a helmet roll down the embankment and then everything vanished, as if it had never happened, as the tracks veered to the right.

Neukirk's mouth was open wide and his heart was beating furiously against his chest. One hand gripped the railing and the other clenched his pistol, unfired. He felt frozen in place, confused and half blind as the wind blew tears sideways across his face. He could hardly take in what had just happened, so suddenly and violently.

He looked up at Major Remke, looking for guidance or some sense of control. What he saw chilled his soul. Remke was high on his perch, staring straight head as the wind blasted him. He did not look back, nor to his men. He held his gaze calmly on the horizon ahead, and no squinting, tears, or movement marred his face. His eyes were like stones.

CHAPTER ONE

31 December 1944
Rozan, Poland
Behind Russian Lines

Some days were better than others now for Colonel Erich Remke. There were days when he didn't think about it for hours. There were occasionally nights when he actually slept without nightmares, and once in a while he might wake up without thinking about it first thing in the morning.

Today was not such a day.

Remke crawled forward, slowly and carefully, so his weight against the snow wouldn't make the scrunching sound that signaled a heavily armed soldier pressing down on over a foot of freshly fallen snow. He stopped, lowering his face into the cold snow, trying to shock himself back to reality.

No, not now! Not here!

He lifted his face from the snow. Frozen crystals fell from his cheeks as he shook off the snow that had melted from his body heat, then instantly froze again among the tears he hid from his men. Remke took a deep breath and slowly, deliberately, turned his head. He saw his two men, clad totally in white, crawling just behind him. Even their weapons, StuG 43 Assault Rifles, were wrapped in white cloth, as were their boots. The only non-white item they wore was the warm Russian fur cap, the best headgear for prolonged periods in the freezing cold. Even these were covered by the hoods of their white parkas. Lying still in the snow, they were practically invisible.

Satisfied with their pace, Remke thought of his mission, the responsibility calming and focusing him. They still had a long way to go and he couldn't allow his emotions to take over. He exhaled in relief that the moment passed, careful to not send a plume of telltale frozen breath sailing into the air. He moved on, crawling at an agonizingly slow pace, moving very deliberately, aware that the slightest abrupt motion could be picked up in the peripheral vision of an alert Russian sentry.

Remke knew that the pressure was just under the surface, barely contained. It had been that way for months, since he had received the news. News that he had hoped would never come. But it had, with a vengeance.

Remke came from East Prussia, the eastern-most province of Germany, on the Baltic coast. His family was among the minor nobility, living among the Prussian forests at the outer reaches of the German border. Anna, his fiancée, came from a nobler but slightly impoverished family from a neighboring estate. They had been inseparable as children, playing each summer in the fields and gardens of their family homes. As they grew, they fell deeply in love and looked forward to a life together, amongst their families and the familiar green hills of East Prussia. Remke could still smell the freshness of Anna's long blond hair in the sunshine.

The war came, and delayed the grand wedding their families had planned. At first, it seemed like the war would be brief, victory certain, and a young decorated officer would return a hero to claim his bride and his lands. Then defeat in North Africa followed defeat at Stalingrad, and the fates seemed to laugh at the young lovers. There was no wedding, and no return home except for one short leave and later, recuperation from wounds. During that visit, Remke had begged his parents to leave East Prussia before the Russians got too close. They wouldn't listen. They had lived through the Great War, they said, and would live through this one too, on the family estate. Remke remembered pleading with Anna to convince them, but she couldn't. Her parents were just as stubborn.

Remke crawled to the base of a large pine tree, its limbs coated with thick white snow. He signaled to his men to rest for a minute under the cover of the low branches. He sat up and looked back from where they had come. It was beginning to snow now, and even a light coating would hide their tracks.

Excellent, he thought, enjoying the cat and mouse game of this reconnaissance behind enemy lines. He could hear the sound of engines coming from just over the next ridge. He knew they were close to their objective. He tried to relax, knowing the short distance to the ridge would be the most dangerous part of the approach. He looked around, taking in the stark beauty of the green firs rising up from the snow-draped landscape. *Just like home.*

As soon as the innocent thought slipped out, Remke knew it was a mistake. Memories of Anna in winter played out in his mind, joyful and alive against the pure white snow. He knew he couldn't quiet them.

Please, no...

The last time he had seen her was in winter, late in the season, with the coming of spring and the Russians both a certainty. Her parents were ill, suffering badly from the cold and the lack of proper food. She wouldn't leave them. He ordered, argued, begged and pleaded. She would not think of leaving without them. When she kissed him good-bye and told him not to worry, he smiled and promised to come back for all of them when they were well. They both knew his orders might not allow it. They pretended it was true, holding hands at the railway station until the train started to move and Remke jumped on, looking into Anna's blue eyes until a blast from the engine threw up a cloud of steam and she was lost.

Remke tried to shake off the vision of Anna at the station, vanishing in the white cloud. He didn't want to think about what happened next. He signaled to one of his men to stay at the fir tree, to provide covering fire in case they needed to beat a hasty retreat. He crawled out from under the branches, his body tense and alert for the sounds of sentries on patrol. His eyes darted over the landscape as he tried to stay focused on the mission and keep the agonizing thoughts of Anna at the hands of the Russians at bay.

The certain knowledge of what happened to Anna burned in his brain. He would have guessed enough in any case, as he had about his own parents after they failed to get out in time. One household servant from Anna's family had escaped, found Remke and told him everything. How the Russians had shot Anna's parents in their sickbed, how they had kept Anna for days, raping her repeatedly until she broke free and found the only escape possible, jumping through a fourth story window to the cobblestone drive below. How she had called for him, screaming his name in the night when they came for her.

Sometimes, Remke could hear her calling out to him. It happened often in his dreams and it was starting to happen when he was awake. It happened now. A gust of wind blew through the branches of the fir trees behind him. In the low murmur of pine needles he thought he heard the mournful sound of Anna calling his name, over and over again. He stopped and pressed his hands to his ears. He still heard her. Lying prone in the snow, far behind enemy lines, Remke fought a battle in his mind, struggling against the demons that plagued him, spoke in Anna's voice and now came whenever they wished. It took all of his willpower to start moving again and not cry out Anna's name into the wind.

He finally made it to the top of the ridge, mentally exhausted and feeling the tension course through his body. He felt like he might explode. The mission. He had to stay focused on the mission. He signaled his companion to come forward. Silently, the other man crawled up, nodded at Remke and pulled a camera from inside his parka. His eyes widened when he saw what lay before them.

In front of them was a small valley, running between two ridgelines. A roadway was plowed out, and camouflage netting was set up on either side of the road. Rows and rows of artillery pieces were parked there, invisible from the air. There were trucks and ammunition crates, Katyusha 132mm rockets, and towed artillery of all sizes, including powerful 152mm howitzers. Camouflaged anti-aircraft emplacements ringed the valley.

Remke had been certain the Russians were building up for an offensive in this area. Here was the proof. This artillery park held enough firepower to shatter the German line at any point. He nodded to the other man, who began taking pictures as Remke counted the artillery pieces. He made notes of the number of each type, estimating what he could not see beneath the netting. As soon as he was done he gave the photographer a look, silently asking if he had enough pictures. He got an affirmative nod, and they both began crawling backwards down the ridge, to the relative safety of the cover beneath the fir trees.

Remke felt an initial joy and relief at finding his objective. It was quickly tempered by the thought that he would have preferred to be wrong. Once the Russians unleashed this offensive, it would be the beginning of the end. The rest of Germany could soon expect the same treatment as Anna and his family had received in East Prussia. He wished he could do something to stop it all, but the end seemed inevitable.

Occupied with the slow and methodical crawl through the snow, Remke took a minute to realize that the voices were gone, and thoughts of Anna were not torturing him. The intensity of the last few minutes had washed it all away, at least for now. He felt clear-headed, alert, and in control. It was a blessed relief.

Minutes later, they re-grouped with the man on rear guard and caught their breath. Remke watched the fat snowflakes coating the trail they had left. In less than an hour there would be no trace they had been here. He smiled and nodded his head to each man, a job well done so far. They followed him out, towards the German lines.

Soon they made it back to where they had hidden their snowshoes. Remke judged they were far enough away from the artillery park to speak in a whisper.

"Karl, is the camera safe?"

"Wrapped up like a baby inside my parka, Colonel."

"Good. Stay between us. Wilfred, take the lead. We need to make good time. I want to make it back to our lines before dark." It was already past noon, and the winter darkness would descend in a few hours.

For the first hour, they made good time. They moved through stands of pine trees and skirted open fields, keeping to the low ground. It felt good to move after the hours of agonizingly slow crawling, and they were all in good spirits at the thought completing their mission.

Fatigue started to set in, and the dull, repetitive trudging on the snowshoes began to wear on Remke. It allowed his mind to wander and linger over memories he had once cherished but now feared for what they brought. Anna's face began to appear in his mind, beautiful and smiling, gazing into his eyes. Then she would see something, something he couldn't see, and the smile would turn to anguish and then she would scream, scream out his name, screaming for help, then for mercy, and finally it was just a scream that went on and on.

Remke gripped his Assault Rifle until his hands shook. He tried to tell himself the screams weren't real as he looked around, as if Anna were somewhere close by, and if he only ran to her he could save her…

"Do you hear something, Colonel?" Karl had turned around to see Remke swiveling his head, looking in every direction.

"No…I thought I did…but no, it must be the wind."

"Quiet as a church in these woods, Colonel."

"Yes, it is."

Remke let his grip on the weapon loosen. He was breathing hard, stunned that he had nearly asked Karl if he heard the screams.

I must be losing my mind. God help me, what should I do?

Colonel Erich Remke was a decorated professional soldier. He was a hard man when it came to combat. He never saw any reason for softness or half-measures when it came to a mission or his men. He prided himself on his planning and execution, both of which were aimed at success with the least possible cost to the men in his command. Often that meant inflicting the highest possible cost on the enemy, with ferocity and sudden unexpected violence. He had killed often, many times close enough to smell the sweat and fear of the other man. He knew how to put away the feelings and emotions he saved for Anna and his family, how to close them off so he could win and live on the battlefield. This hard man now walked behind his two men, tears streaming down his face, a face filled with fear and shame that he was about to go absolutely, totally insane.

As always, the demons receded. Remke felt a calm rationality inside of himself, as if his mind was compensating for where it had just gone.

Wilfred had just signaled a halt, and was kneeling down behind some boulders. Remke went forward.

"Look there, Colonel." Wilfred pointed towards a clearing beyond the rocks. There was a road with a staff car pulled over to the side, its hood open. Two Russian soldiers were bent over it, working on the engine.

"Should we go down the road and work around them, Colonel?" Wilfred asked in a whisper.

Remke pulled out his binoculars. He looked at the men and the car. He saw at least one figure inside. Then he looked at his watch. He turned and summoned Karl.

"There's at least one officer inside. We could use a prisoner, especially if he's high ranking. There's enough time to make it back with him before dark."

Remke watched his two men. He hadn't given the order yet, and wasn't completely sure they should take the risk. He wanted their reaction.

"There's enough time if we take him quickly and if he can make it through the snow," offered Karl.

"We are close, though, only about three kilometers. I wouldn't want to try sneaking up on our lines after dark though, password or not," stated Wilfred. The German troops manning the line on their approach route had been notified that a long-range patrol was due back, and passwords had been given. That didn't mean someone wouldn't get nervous, especially after dark.

"Alright, it's too good a chance to pass up. We're far enough away from the artillery park that they'll never suspect we've seen it. Take your hoods off so they can see the Russian fur caps. We'll just walk down the road like we own it. They'll think we're one of their patrols heading out."

They circled the boulders and came to the road out of sight of the car. They took off their snowshoes and slung them over their backs. Remke hoisted his Assault Rifle over his shoulder and carried it behind him, so the Russians wouldn't immediately see it was a German weapon. He pulled out his Walther P-38 pistol and checked the safety, stowing it in his pocket for easy access.

"I'll go first. My Russian is better than either of yours," Remke said.

"Lead on, Comrade Colonel," Karl said with a laugh. Remke smiled, glad his men were willing to try this at the end of a long mission. He still felt in control and was clear-headed. He wouldn't have tried this if he wasn't, and he thought about how in action, the voices seemed to leave him alone, as if they knew their own survival depended on it. He wondered when they might change their mind.

They rounded a corner and saw the car. Remke walked ahead in the middle of the road, Karl and Wilfred behind him, one to each side. They looked nonchalant, as if they were indeed behind their own lines. With their Russian caps and nondescript white camouflage suits, Remke was sure they wouldn't arouse suspicion. He was right. One of the Russians working on the engine looked up when they were about thirty yards away, said something indistinct and then bent his head back to the task, cursing the engine and the mother of the man who designed it.

Remke walked up to them and stopped about six feet away.

"Comrades," he said, addressing them in fluent Russian, "do you need any help?"

As he spoke, Karl and Wilfred moved past him, staring inside the car, affecting a dumb curiosity that would not be out of place for a peasant Soviet soldier.

"Nothing we couldn't handle if it was a tractor engine," said one of the soldiers. "But this engine is a little more complicated. I doubt the Comrade Major and Comrade Colonel would want to walk back to headquarters, but you might ask them. Maybe they want a car sent back. You must be headed there, right?"

"Yes, we're just coming back from patrol." Remke nodded slightly to Karl and Wilfred. A Major and a Colonel would be quite a catch, just the thing to top off their mission. He put his hand in his pocket, grasping the Walther and taking one last look around. No one else was in the area.

Then he heard it. A scream from inside the car. A woman screaming. The soldier working on the engine stood up and looked at Remke, leering at him and nodding his head toward the inside of the car.

"Want some, Comrade? She's a nice fuck, I've had her once myself after the officers got done with her."

"Damn officers, they take all the blond girls first," the other man said. "By the time we get a hold of them there's not much left."

The screaming went on. Remke looked at Karl and Wilfred, but they were just standing there, waiting for him. He couldn't believe it. The two Russians were laughing at him now, their rough red faces lit up with frenzied lust.

"Erich! Help!"

It was Anna's voice. It was impossible. A million thoughts ran through his mind as he pulled out his pistol. He lifted it up to the face in front of him and squeezed the trigger. Could she still be alive? How could she have survived? Brains and blood splattered against the open hood. He turned the pistol on the second man, who was still grinning at him, as if he knew.

"A really nice fuck, Comrade."

He shot him twice in the face, then turned toward the rear door. Karl and Wilfred already had their Assault Rifles out and aimed at the door.

"No!" Remke cried out, fearful they would shoot. "Anna! Anna!"

He worked the latch and threw open the door. A fat Russian officer almost flew out, his hands held up, gasping in shock and falling to his knees. Remke stuck his head inside, and saw another man, holding a young girl's head by her blond hair, forcing her to suck his penis. He held a gun to her head.

"She's a really nice fuck, Comrade. You want her? We can share."

Remke couldn't understand the man's attitude, and he couldn't see the girl clearly. Her long blond hair fell down over her face.

"Anna?" Remke could feel someone pulling at him, pulling him out of the car. He resisted.

"Anna?" He screamed at her. "Anna, is that you?"

She pulled back her hair, not seeming to care there was a pistol to her head. She looked up at him, caressing the Russian's penis.

"Erich," Anna answered, "Am I a really good fuck?"

Suddenly everything exploded as a bright flash illuminated the inside of the car, and then Remke's ears were shattered as someone fired an Assault Rifle into the car.

"Anna!" Remke bellowed as he turned, shaking off whatever was holding him. In slow motion, he saw Karl firing into the car, the spent casings arcing into the air, the muzzle blast spouting death a dozen times over for Anna. He was enraged. He threw off the person holding him and fired his pistol until Karl stopped shooting.

He could hear someone calling his name, but it wasn't Anna.

"Colonel, stop!"

He stooped to look inside, crying out Anna's name. The inside of the car was thick with the smell of cordite, and hazy with smoke. The windows were red with splattered blood. He tried to make out what was inside, but between the smoke and his tears and the blood everywhere he couldn't see anything. He pulled his head out of the car.

"What have you done with Anna?"

"Colonel," Wilfred said shakily, "you've killed Karl!"

Remke didn't know who this man was, except that he was the one who pulled him away from Anna. His Walther was still in his hand, and before he knew it he was pulling the trigger and emptying it into Wilfred. It hardly mattered. He threw it away and pulled the Assault Rifle from his shoulder. The Russian officer was still kneeling on the ground, his hands up and shaking.

"What have you done with Anna?" he asked, in Russian this time. No answer. Remke wiped at his eyes and looked back into the car. The smoke had cleared. Slumped against the opposite door was another Russian officer, a pistol in his hand. No Anna.

Remke felt something fall away inside of himself. He had crossed a threshold that he never imagined existed. He knew that it had been the work of the demons. As he stood in the blood of his own men he knew that they did it for a purpose, to show him the way. He felt cleansed, changed and confident. He looked at the Russian officer, still holding his shaking hands up. Remke understood it was over, since he didn't leer at him or say anything about Anna. He had a different part to play.

Remke stood over him, and pictured Anna in his mind. Not the trick of the demons inside the car, but Anna as she had been, innocent and beautiful. He pulled the trigger. The automatic weapon pulsed in his hands as a burst of bullets smashed into the Russian's chest, slamming him on his back. Remke emptied the clip into him. He stood over the ruined body, and thought of Anna. There were only pleasant thoughts.

He stood there for a minute, enjoying the feeling of peace as the snow and mud in the road absorbed the blood flowing around him. He walked over to Karl and retrieved the camera, thankful that one of his shots hadn't damaged it. He understood now that Karl had been firing at the Russian who was about to blow his head off with that pistol, and that Wilfred had pulled him back just in time for the shot to miss. He regretted the loss of Karl and Wilfred, but he saw how critical it had been for him. He couldn't have let them live, after they saw him in that state. No one could know about Anna. It was too bad, really.

Calmly, Remke put on his snowshoes and headed towards the German lines. He had a lot to do. He had to make his report and then get out into the field again. Something about how easy it was to fool the Russians with those fur caps tucked itself away in his mind. It just might be useful.

This was the day Remke marked as his turning point. He was no longer afraid of going insane. He understood too much now. The demons would extract their price from him, he knew. But they had shown him the way, the way for all of them.

From that day on, Erich Remke never wanted the war to end. He never wanted to stop killing Russians.

CHAPTER TWO

5 January 1945
Saint Alban's Military Hospital
Darbyshire, England

White. Everything was white. Every morning when he opened his eyes he saw white walls, white sheets, the white uniforms of the nurses as they hurried by, and the white coats of the doctors as they gathered at the foot of his bed and murmured among themselves. His bandages were white; it seemed his entire life was now swathed in freshly laundered whiteness.

Then he would close his eyes and the only white he saw was dirty white snow. Tank treads churning up mud and splattering it against the snow banks as they accelerated and turned in the forests of the Ardennes. The snow soon turned shades of brown from the dirt and black from explosions, leaking oil, smoke and struggle. Then the red blood would start seeping out from the wounded and dead until the white snow absorbed it all and the landscape was all reds and blacks and explosions and dead bodies falling on top of him…

"Jesus!" Billy Boyle gasped and woke up gulping for breath. "Goddamn sonuvabitch! Jesus H. Christ on a crutch!"

"Captain Boyle!"

Billy looked up with his mouth gaping open and eyes wide. He closed his eyes and flopped back into his pillow. *Oohh noooo*, he thought. *I can't take anymore of this shit!*

He opened one eye, hoping that the owner of that voice would be gone as he focused on the figure in the doorway to his private room. Unfortunately, he saw the face of Doctor Reginald Cuthbert-Hewes, a full

Colonel in His Majesty's Medical Service, a distinguished pre-war psychiatrist, and his keeper in the whitewashed prison that was St. Alban's.

St. Alban's had opened in 1922 as a private hospital for the upper classes. Specifically, for the rich upper classes with "nervous" disorders and other undisclosed aliments that required that they spend their stay safely away from public view. The location outside Darbyshire was perfect. The small town did not even have a train station and the road leading to the hospital was unmarked. Gently rolling wooded hills provided both serenity and seclusion. The hospital building was designed in the art deco style popular at the time, and each private room had been decorated with polished teakwood furniture, paintings and hand-woven Persian carpets. All of which was now in storage, having been replaced by military beds and desks when the British Defence Ministry had taken over in 1940. The hidden and little-known facility was perfect for the recovery and recuperation of personnel engaged in top security operations. Spies, commandos, generals and secretive foreigners from occupied nations had all recovered from their physical and emotional wounds within these walls. Or least on paper they did. Battle fatigue, neurosis, and loss of nerve were on occasion "cured" ahead of schedule when it was necessary to return a patient whose file was marked "Priority Personnel" to active duty.

Billy knew that Doctor Cuthbert-Hewes prided himself on his rate of return. He felt it his duty to get the highly trained soldiers and spies who came into his care back into the fight against Nazism as soon as possible. He knew Cuthbert-Hewes believed that since Billy had volunteered for hazardous duty, it was only logical to put him back together in body and mind as efficiently as possible and return him to the fight. It was just that Billy felt exactly the opposite about himself- he wanted out. He had wanted out in the worst way since he had shown up at St. Alban's with a severe concussion, shrapnel wounds all over his body, a nervous twitch, night tremors, a wise mouth, and "Priority Personnel" stamped on his file.

"I see we're still having those nasty nightmares, Captain," said Cuthbert-Hewes as he tapped his pencil against the clipboard he always carried. "Perhaps we need to increase our little talks to three a day. Got to get you in tip-top shape, body and mind, don't you know! There's still a war on, so we must press on until you're rid of those nasty visions."

Cuthbert-Hewes smiled and Billy wondered how his mouth could smile like that while his mustache stayed in a straight line. He was staring at the doctor intently trying to figure it out, tilting his head slightly in either direction so he could see the upward turn on each side of Cuthbert-Hewes' ridiculously smiling face. Misunderstanding the look on Billy's face, the doctor turned solicitous and spoke as if to a small child.

"Now don't worry too much, Boyle. My therapeutic techniques are quite advanced. I've just gotten a Royal Commando sergeant who came in here with two broken legs and screaming bloody murder about never going up in a glider again, to volunteer for active service! What do you think of that, Captain?"

The smile went up further as Cuthbert-Hewes recounted his success. The mustache was still exactly straight, parallel to the floor.

"I think that shows a lot of control. Stiff upper lip," said Billy as he struggled to keep a straight face. Baiting Cuthbert-Hewes had been one of his favorite pastimes since he had met him after regaining consciousness six days ago.

"Why yes, exactly my point, old chap..." Cuthbert-Hewes was about to launch into one of his lectures but halted as Billy started laughing loudly and hysterically.

Through the open door, Billy could see Doctor Chester Fielding, casually know as "Doc" by all his patients at St. Alban's, ambling down the hall, concentrating on chewing the unlit cigar jutting from the side of his mouth. He brushed past Cuthbert-Hewes who was muttering to himself as he nearly parade-marched out of the room, muttering something about "damnable colonial".

Billy wiped his eyes as he studied the rumpled, tie-less American uniform and disheveled appearance of Doc Fielding, a direct contrast to the efficient and well-tailored Cuthbert-Hewes. As a medical doctor, Doc focused on healing the physical wounds of his patients, but his kindly and humane nature allowed him to reach out to them in ways that the psychiatrist could not. Billy got along with Doc, even though Doc was charged with the same mission as Cuthbert-Hewes; to heal the wounded and get them back on their feet so they could once again try to cheat death within the hidden world of secret missions, spies, and assassinations. The difference between the two was that Doc Fielding genuinely cared about those who were in his care, while Cuthbert-Hewes saw them solely as valuable tools in service to the war effort, tools that had to be repaired and returned to service within the shortest possible time.

Doc chuckled to himself as he stood at the end of Billy's bed. "Well, Billy, you must be feeling better today," he said, chewing on his cigar. "I've never seen Reginald in such a high snit."

"He's too easy a target, Doc. Can't let an opportunity to get under his skin go by," said Billy. He smiled deliberately as he relaxed back into his pillow and linked his hands behind his head. The shock of waking had worn off, and he felt his usual confidence beginning to return. He tried to hurry the process by appearing more relaxed than he really felt. The recent memories of blood and snow were still playing across his mind's eye, receding but not yet loosening their grip. He struggled to remain composed. A shudder ran through his body and he fought to not let it show. He kept the smile on his face and prayed Doc wouldn't see through it. He wanted to get out of St. Alban's as soon as possible, assuming that now, finally, he could go home.

"So Doc, tell me. When can I get out of here?"

"Well, young man," said Doc Fielding as he flipped through Billy's medical chart, "Your shrapnel wounds were minor and are healing fine. The concussion was serious, and I wouldn't want you to get another like it anytime soon, but you're coming along well. It's your nerves we're worried about."

"Aw, Doc, I'm OK," Billy protested. "Just a little shook up from the Bulge. Everyone gets a little nervous in the service now and then. There's nothing wrong with me that my Mom's cooking won't cure as soon as I get home."

Doc looked at him with a frown. He threw down the chart and pulled a chair up to Billy's bed.

"OK, Captain, I'm going to give it to you straight. You're not going home, not right now anyway."

There was silence. Billy struggled to comprehend what he had just been told. He worked his mouth but nothing came out. It was like he had been punched in the gut and was gasping for air.

"Wait a minute, Doc," Billy finally gasped, grabbing the other man's arm and raising his voice. "I've been hung out and wrung dry half a dozen times in this war. I've been getting the shit end of the stick since I left the States in '42, and it's gotta stop!"

"Now son, every guy thinks he's special. Remember, lots of boys have been over here that long. And they're not on SHAEF headquarters staff either," Doc said with a firm reprimanding look at Billy, "where many obviously have some vital role to play, although in your case I can't figure out what that might be."

Billy let go of Doc's arm and wearily sank his head back onto his pillow. "Well, I used to be a cop before the war, in Boston. Got promoted to Detective and was pretty damn good at it, too. I was supposed to be assigned to a security detail at the War Department in Washington, but they sent me here instead with General Eisenhower." He discreetly left out the fact that his family had secured his appointment in Washington to keep him safe and away from any combat zone. All that had changed when the General was sent to London in 1942.

"So you lucked out and got a job tagging after Ike," Doc said. "That doesn't tell me why you think you deserve a ticket home."

"Uncle Ike didn't want me to tag along after him."

"*Uncle* Ike?" Doc said incredulously.

"Sure," answered Billy. "I think we're actually third cousins once removed or something like that, but I just took to calling him Uncle. Only when we were alone, of course. He didn't seem to mind. I think he likes having some family around."

"Get to the point, Billy."

"Uncle Ike used me to report back to him on what was going on whenever he thought he needed some inside dope. Sometimes he thought he was getting snookered by the brass and wanted someone to take a quiet look-see and let him know what was really going on. Mostly verifying intelligence info at the front. There were a few times when some high-level officers were doing some black market business, or worse. And some other stuff I'm not supposed to talk about."

"Which is why he wanted a cop, and was glad to get someone with personal ties to him, someone he could trust," Doc offered.

"That's my guess. He told me I didn't have to do any of this, that it was all on a volunteer basis. But every time I tried to say no thanks, he would just start talking and then I'd find myself with his arm around my shoulder, walking me out of the office, thanking me and telling me I was his favorite nephew." Billy paused, trying to explain the relationship with his uncle, who also happened to be the Allied Supreme Commander.

"You know, when Uncle Ike starts in on you, you think everything he says makes perfect sense. You want to be part of the team. You want to help out. Then when you're out in the hallway and his door shuts behind you and you realize what you just signed on for, you can't quite remember exactly why in Hell you said yes."

Doc grinned. "He is an expert at running the war while keeping the Brits, the French, a handful of minor European allies, and the Pentagon happy. After that, a single young officer already beholden to him wouldn't be too tough to convince."

"That's why I have to get out of here and get my ticket home punched. I've been on too many of these special missions for my own good. The last one almost got me killed, as you can see," said Billy, gesturing angrily at the bandages on his head.

"I figure I've done my share by now. I've seen more action that nearly all those desk jockeys at SHAEF, and damn more than I ever thought I would back in Boston. The little jobs Uncle Ike gives me usually involve getting close enough to the front to get shot at. Once by our side, but that's another story."

"Well, Billy, I appreciate you telling me all this. But, I'm sorry to say your injuries are not bad enough to send you home, especially since SHAEF has called twice already to see when you can be released.

Otherwise it would be a close call, but with important Priority Personnel like yourself..." Doc gestured helplessly.

"They're sending a car for you in a couple of days. I told them you'd be ready."

Billy felt the shudder go through his body again.

What are you worrying about, he thought, trying to calm himself. *The war's almost over, what could happen now?*

CHAPTER THREE

6 January 1945
Outside Breslau, Poland
30 Kilometers east of the Oder River

The winds howled, reaching 30 kilometers per hour that night on the frigid Polish flatlands. The temperature was below freezing. With winds drifting snow into lines of banks higher than a man, it would be a frozen death for anyone to lie down to sleep or rest. The remnants of the once-formidable Brandenburg Division now staggered westward in retreat, hoping to take up positions behind the Oder River before the Russian tanks caught up with them. The long-awaited Russian offensive was pushing the Germans back into their own territory now, closing in for the kill. The Brandenburgers had been assigned rear-guard duty, to allow as many German units as possible to escape over the Oder. Now it was their turn to pull out. The only difference was that now there was no one between them and the advancing Soviet armor. They had to make it to the river or die on this freezing plain.

They had been marching for fifteen hours, and the men had to sleep. There was no shelter on the open landscape, nothing but hard frozen ground and snow banks drifting into long lines as if they would oppose the march of the division. The men formed into small groups of six or eight, huddled together in a circle, and leaned inward until their heads nearly touched. Leaning on their rifles in the snow, they soon fell asleep standing up, supported by their weapons and each other. The combined breath of the group of weary men provided a small pocket of warmer air, a small, pathetic oasis of life in a wintry hell.

The wind swirled around them and coated their backs with pelts of snow. The area on either side of the road, visible only through the tracks in the snow, looked like a farmer's field in early winter. Human haystacks stretched as far as the eye could see in the dark night. The feeble reflected light of the full moon, blurred by gusts of snow, showed occasional and agonized movement as men stirred, awoke, or fell to the ground dead asleep.

First light came early. *Hauptmann* (Captain) Dieter Neukirk stumbled as the man next to him collapsed forward. He reached out and steadied himself, at the same time pulling up the fallen soldier.

"Jost, get up you clod! Get the men ready." Neukirk shook the snow from his back and reeled back and forth on unsteady legs.

"Sir…it's not Jost…he was wounded a month ago, remember?" Hans von Schierke took his commander's hand and pulled himself up. He looked into Neukirk's eyes and whispered, "Dieter, are you alright? Dieter, pull yourself together!"

Dieter didn't know if he was still asleep or awake. Images swam in front of his eyes and he saw Jost Brunner, his faithful and sturdy sergeant who could always be depended upon to get the men moving, even in the worst circumstances. But he knew Jost had been wounded and evacuated weeks ago…he wiped his gloved hand against his face. The feel of the hard cold cloth brought him to the present, and he saw his friend Hans looking with concern as the snow blew between them.

"Hans…yes, I…I know". He broke contact and turned away towards his men. He knew. He knew how desperate the situation was. The Oder River was their goal, and he didn't know if they could make it. He thought of Napolean's army making this same retreat in the last century. This time, it wouldn't be Russian cavalry pursing them and nipping at their heels. Russian T-34 tanks were behind them to the east. To the west, the Oder River provided a line of defense just in the front of the German border.

He churned through the snow and moved from group to group, urging the men to form up and get moving westward. He spoke to them in both German and Russian, for the many Hiwis that now filled the ranks of the Brandenburgers. Hiwi was short for *Hilfswillige* (volunteer help) and was the term used for Russian volunteers who served with the Wehrmacht. Hiwis came mainly from the vast pool of Russian prisoners of war, some actual volunteers, many drafted from POW camps to serve as auxiliary laborers and support personnel. As German losses mounted, Hiwis began to be used as combat replacements. In some cases, they were motivated by genuine anti-Communist beliefs. Others fought because they were told to, but they all fought well. Hiwis were bound by a similar fate if captured by the Soviets- instant execution.

As his men moved towards the road, several groups left behind still forms in the snow, those whose last ounce of energy was spent marching to this point and no farther. By the time the troops were back on the road, drifting snow had buried those left behind and nothing could be seen except a receding line of defeat heading west, away from the rising sun, coming up blood red in the winter sky.

As the sun rose into the thin, cold air, the winds calmed and the bitter snow lessened. By mid morning the gray heavy clouds had rolled to the north and a brilliant blue sky was uncovered slowly, hesitantly, until the new white snow sparkled with reflected light. Dieter turned to the east and shielded his eyes against the bright sunlight.

"Hans, can you see anything?" he asked.

Hans von Schierke pulled his Zeiss field glasses from his case and handed his rifle to a nearby soldier. There was a small ridge along the road and he scrambled up it, plowing through a snow bank. The little rise gave him a vantage point from which to scan the flat terrain as he slowly and methodically studied the land along a 180-degree arc to their rear.

Dieter had counted on Hans in many situations since he had joined the Brandenburgers when the unit had been expanded from a Regiment to a Division following the fall of France. Dieter was one of the few people who knew Hans had dropped the "von" from his name on the enlistment papers, hoping it would throw off the Gestapo as they went through their systematic investigations and purges of those suspected of anti-Nazi activities. Many officers in the Brandenburg Division with "von" in their name had automatically been arrested or transferred out to penal battalions after the unsuccessful plot to kill Hitler on the previous July 20th had shown how deeply many of their aristocratic class had been involved.

Even though he was without rank, von Schierke's natural leadership ability and bearing could not be hidden. The men accepted him as an equal, but as a very unusual equal, one who sometimes led them and other times faded into the line as just another rifleman. Just now, necks craned to watch him scan the horizon, as if they were waiting for a general. Even Dieter was impatient.

"Well, do you see anything? Damn, man, tell us what you see!"

Hans continued to scan slowly, methodically, not responding the demands from his captain. Suddenly he froze, and adjusted the binoculars, keeping them trained on the southeastern horizon.

"Armored cars," he said tersely. "Six…no, eight moving slowly. Headed southeast." He returned to his scanning of the horizon.

"Shit! More armored cars, on this road! BA-10s." The BA-10 was a fast but lightly armored Russian reconnaissance vehicle, well armed with a 45mm cannon and two machine guns.

"Get down," Dieter said and signaled with his arms for everyone to flatten at the same time.

"Schmidt!" he called out to a group of nearby men, "Get your Hiwis up here! *Panzerfausts* forward!" Sixteen men in white camouflage smocks, each carrying a *Panzerfaust*, a one-shot version of the American bazooka, and their pockets stuffed with grenades, ran up in a crouch. *Feldwebel* Schmidt knelt next to Neukirk and passively waited for orders.

"Schmidt, there's a group of BA-10s coming down the road straight at us. They probably haven't seen us yet, but they must know we're close. There's another group of them off to the east, probably trying to cut off our route to the Oder."

Schmidt knew what was coming, but he was a veteran non-commissioned officer, and he never volunteered. Not even his opinion. He just looked down the road and back to *Hauptmann* Neukirk.

Von Schierke crawled over to them. "There's only six coming at us. No infantry, no Panzers. But they can't be far behind, otherwise they wouldn't send those others to get behind us," he said, gesturing with his thumb towards the southeast.

"Right. We've got to deal with them quickly. Schmidt, take half of your Hiwis and place them in that drainage ditch that we crossed about 200 meters back down the road. Hans, place the other half behind this rise, along the road. You hit them as they cross the ditch," he said, pointing at Schmidt. "Hans, hit them again here. I'll come forward with the rest of First Company and finish them off."

Schmidt spat into the snow. He shrugged and said, "Just don't forget us in that ditch after the Ivans cross over." He quickly jogged down the road, signaling for half his men to follow.

Hans assembled the other group and they hid themselves along the small ridge. Dieter pulled the rest of the men back. He instructed the *Leutnants* in charge of the Second and Third companies to continue double-time down the road. It was critical that the other armored cars not get across the road and block their retreat.

Dieter didn't try to hide his men as they spread out in combat formation and continued down the road. He wanted the BA-10s to see them and be drawn to the bait.

Within five minutes Dieter could hear the tracked vehicles coming up the road, their engines straining at a top speed of about 50 kilometers per hour. He knew they had been spotted. Calling to his men to halt and spread out in a defensive arc across the road, he knelt with his Schmeisser

MP40 submachine gun at the ready. Everybody was in place. As usual, Dieter felt his heart racing in the few minutes before an action, when there was nothing left to do but wait.

Dieter watched the thin line along the ground that marked the drainage ditch and Schmidt's hiding place. The lead armored car came within 50 meters of the ditch and pulled off to the left. The next one followed, two more turned to the right, and the last two came up abreast in the middle on the road.

"Damn!" Dieter smashed his fist into the ground as the line of armored cars opened fire from their stationary position. He had miscalculated. The Russians were going to pound them from a distance with their cannon before closing in for the kill with their machine guns. Rounds began to explode in front of his exposed line of men, and he knew it would only be a matter of minutes before the shells burst among them.

Schmidt, hidden at the bottom of the ditch, had heard the vehicles spread out and halt just short of his position. As soon as he heard the first salvo, he knew the original plan was not going to work.

"Well, boys," Schmidt said loudly above the din, "let's take a long shot." Without speaking, each of the Hiwis nodded to Schmidt and readied themselves.

"Now!" bellowed Schmidt as he rose and placed the *Panzerfaust* on the edge of the ditch. In a split second he found his target, aimed, and pressed the trigger. The rocket blasted toward the right-hand car and hit it square on the turret. There was an explosion, followed by another as the ammunition blew up, ripping the lightly armored vehicle apart, spreading flame over the snow and sending black acrid smoke skyward.

There was a brief, surprising moment of silence as the BA-10 crews oriented themselves to this new, closer threat and as the six Hiwis aimed their *Panzerfausts*. Suddenly the air exploded as rockets launched and turrets turned and depressed their cannon, firing wildly at the forms rising up in front of them. Machine guns began to chatter, sending spouts of snow and dirt flying in every direction.

Two BA-10s exploded in bright flame. Another took a hit just in front of the front right wheel. Two other *Panzerfaust* rounds exploded harmlessly beyond their targets.

One Hiwi was slower than the others getting back under cover, hesitating to watch his round hit home.

"Aleksandr!" Schmidt yelled, reaching up to pull him down. As Aleksandr heard his name he froze, eyes wide in disbelief as machine gun rounds stitched a straight line in the ground in front of him. The last two bullets hit him in the upper chest, forcing him back against the ditch wall.

He slid lifelessly down, coming to rest next to Schmidt with a look of utter surprise on his face.

The unhit armored cars suddenly accelerated at the same time, moving towards the edge of the ditch from where they could fire down towards Schmidt and his men, leaving them with no cover and less hope.

The stationary BA-10 was smoking, but its turret and guns still operated. Shells slammed into the back of the ditch wall just behind the men, showering them with rocks and clumps of frozen dirt.

"Follow me," growled Schmidt, and crawled towards the point where the two armored cars would crest the ditch, a grenade in each hand.

Machine guns opened up as the two BA-10s began to seek out their targets. Schmidt tossed both grenades and the remaining Hiwis did the same. They held their hands over their ears as the grenades exploded. Schmidt waited for the sound of secondary explosions. He heard only the roar of two engines and continuous machine gun fire as the armored cars began their final approach to the lip of the ditch. Schmidt scrambled to pull another grenade from his pocket, knowing that once the got into the ditch, either of the BA-10s could massacre them. Then he saw the front wheels and cannon barrel above him. One of the Hiwis screamed.

The universe exploded around them. Schmidt waited for death to come, but he could only hear explosions. He looked up and saw a pillar of flame ascending from the turret of the BA-10. He heard yelling and the launch of other *Panzerfausts*. Hans von Schierke jumped into the ditch and landed in the midst of Schmidt and his Hiwis.

"Hello, boys," he said with a smile as he caught his breath, "we thought you'd like a hand." An explosion punctuated his sentence as the reinforcements dealt with the last BA-10.

Dieter walked toward the ditch, now churned up from explosions, metal and fire. He had watched as von Schierke led a charge to stop the BA-10s from gaining the ditch. As he and his men jumped down from the ridge and ran forward to gain a position from which to fire their *Panzerfausts*, one of the BA-10s had taken notice and turned twin machine gun fire on them. One of the Hiwis had been killed and another wounded. He walked by the sprawled form lying face down in the reddening snow.

Dieter stopped at the edge of the ditch and saw Schmidt kneeling beside a still form. He was holding Aleksandr's hand. Dieter was startled to see tears in the eyes of the grizzled veteran.

Schmidt looked up at him. "He was a good boy, sir…I told him to get down." He shook his head sadly. "He was such a good lad." The other Hiwis gathered around and some placed their hands gently on his shoulders. Suddenly, he looked very old and tired.

"Come, Schmidt," Dieter said gently. "There's not much time." He swung his MP40 over his shoulder as he turned on his heel and resumed the march westward. The men, still dazed by the fight, slowly pulled themselves together and followed their officer down the road, leaving Aleksandr with his young lifeless face gazing skyward.

As Dieter trudged onward, he looked at the men around him and thought about how few were left from the early days. He thought about his first action at the Maas River and how nervous he had been, how stunning the sudden violence had been. It was now routine, just a part of every day. Dieter idly wondered what had become of Erich Remke.

I wonder what he's up to now, if he isn't dead already?

CHAPTER FOUR

7 January 1945
Alderhorst
Hitler's Western Field Headquarters
Bad Nauheim, Germany

Colonel-General Heinz Guderian stood at the edge of the map table, holding his hands locked behind his back and rocking slightly on his heels. As Chief of Staff of the *Oberkommando des Heeres* (OKH), Guderian was, on paper at least, responsible for the operations of German forces on all fronts. The enormity of the situation on the map of the eastern and western fronts jumped out at him. He felt as if giant jaws were closing in on him, which in fact they nearly were.

There had been a time, during the invasion of France in 1940, when Guderian was known as "Hurrying Heinz" for the rapidity with which he maneuvered his XIX Panzer Corps. Not only had he out-fought and out-maneuvered the French, he had provocatively disobeyed a direct order from the *Führer*. Hitler had ordered him to halt his troops, fearing he was becoming overextended. Guderian knew the situation to be otherwise and blithely ignored the order, to the credit and success of his Corps.

Now he neither hurried nor disobeyed. The head of the German General Staff waited and begged. He waited for Hitler to see him and begged to move troops to effectively meet the encroaching threat from the East. Since November, Hitler had been deeply involved in the planning and execution of the Ardennes Offensive, sending vast quantities of men and material into the Ardennes. The ruined remnants of that force were now struggling back into Germany through the snow and ice, the

Americans pressing the salient back and thoroughly in control of the military situation. All Guderian could see was the wasted opportunity in the East. Far fewer troops could have dug in defensively and held the Americans and British off during the winter, with the remainder sent to the Eastern Front to stem the red tide now flowing towards the German border.

Since Hitler had finally admitted the defeat of his Ardennes Offensive, Guderian hoped to bring some sanity to the situation. He looked up from the map at the officer opposite him, General Reinhardt Gehlen, intelligence chief for Foreign Armies East, responsible for gathering military intelligence on Soviet plans and intentions. He was reporting to Guderian to prepare him for the upcoming briefing with Hitler.

"So, *Herr* General, all indications point to a massive Soviet offensive at several key points along the front, here, here, and perhaps here," stressed Gehlen, as he sketched three red arrows on the situation map, all pointing ultimately to Berlin.

"Do you trust your sources? Are you sure the Russians are not feeding you misleading information?"

"Everything we based our conclusion upon has been verified. Prisoner interrogation, radio traffic, aerial reconnaissance, all techniques are used to confirm what we discover. We have our own reconnaissance units on the ground, coordinating with our troops in the area. My own men often bring back first-hand information," said Gehlen with a tone that said he could imagine no further questioning of his conclusions.

Gehlen snapped his fingers and one of his officers brought a stack of photographs to the table. They were of a Russian artillery park, showing lines of camouflaged heavy artillery and transport hidden in a small valley. As the officer laid the photos out, Guderian saw the *Deutsches Afrika Korps* cuffband and the Knight's Cross with Oak Leaves at his neck. Guderian knew instantly that this tall officer was likely the type to bring back such information first hand.

"The offensive will commence no sooner than one week and no later than two. Our line troops and reserves are completely inadequate to hold off the offensive in more than one location." Gehlen paused and added, "The line will break."

Guderian felt this statement like a hammer blow. He struggled not to let the effect it had show.

"Very well. Return to your headquarters at once. Keep me informed daily." The General looked past Gehlen to the officers standing behind him and scanned their faces.

"One of your officers will be detached to my headquarters as liaison. You." Guderian indicated the DAK officer.

"Very well *Herr* General," Gehlen said, "allow me to introduce Colonel Erich Remke."

Remke accompanied Major Bernd Baron Freytag von Loringhoven, Guderian's Adjutant, to the radio section to set up procedures for establishing daily radio communications between Foreign Armies East and Guderian's mobile headquarters. Remke provided the code keys to be used when receiving Enigma transcripts from Foreign Armies East. Enigma was the coding device used for top-secret communications. As they walked back from the radio room, Freytag observed Remke carefully. He did not know the officer and was eager to gain an understanding of him before they met with Hitler the next day. Meetings with the *Führer* were difficult enough and he did not want his Chief dependent upon information from an officer who was an unknown factor.

"Colonel, we will need a final report on any changes or new developments by Noon tomorrow. The *Führer* briefing is scheduled for the afternoon."

"I will be fully prepared, Major," Remke said, stressing the last word to remind Freytag of his lesser status. Although Remke out-ranked him, Freytag's position as Adjutant to the powerful OKH commander put him in a position to deliver instructions to many generals, and a mere Colonel did not impress him.

"Glad to be transferred out of the Eastern Front, Colonel?"

It was a simple question, but Freytag thought the answer might reveal something of the officer's character, outlook, and politics. Remke glanced sharply at the Major and picked up his pace to show his displeasure. Freytag, just as tall as Remke, had no difficulty keeping up.

"I am glad to be wherever I can serve the Reich best, Major, even if it is in a comfortable post." Remke spoke with a sneer showing on his face as he deliberately stared at the immaculately clean and well-tailored uniform of aristocratic adjutant. "But I do regret leaving my comrades behind at the front. My hope is the information we've gathered will help the *Führer* decide how to best strike back at the Bolsheviks."

"Colonel," Freytag said as he turned in front of Remke to stop him and look directly at him as he spoke, "information will mean little at the *Führer* briefing if it is not presented in exactly the right manner. You must let General Guderian do all the speaking. Stand to the back of the room and speak only if directed to. If asked, do not offer any opinion, simply the facts requested."

"Don't worry, Baron," Remke said derisively, "I won't embarrass your General. I managed not to embarrass Rommel when the *Führer* presented me with the Oak Leaves to my Iron Cross. Now stand aside!"

Late that night, Guderian and Freytag sat in front of a warm fire with glasses of Cognac. Maps and troop data had been prepared and they were as ready as possible for the session tomorrow. Guderian relaxed, took a drink and stared into the flames.

"So what have you found out about our new intelligence officer, Freytag? It's not that often anymore that one sees a veteran of the *Afrika Korps.*"

"That's the least of it, sir," said Freytag, picking up a dossier. "He graduated at the top of his class at the officer's training academy, after getting his degree in foreign languages at Heidelburg University. Speaks Russian, English, French and Dutch fluently, Arabic passably. He was recruited into the Brandenburg Regiment in 1939 and was involved in top-secret Abwehr operations. He made a name for himself in the invasion of the Netherlands- Operation En Passant…"

"That was Remke?" Guderian interrupted. "That was a fine coup. Without that bridge we would have lost days, tanks and men at the Maas."

"It did get him noticed. After that he requested a transfer out of the Brandenburgers so he could see more front-line action after the fall of France. He took command of a reconnaissance unit with the 10th Panzer in North Africa, and ended up on Rommel's staff with his intelligence unit. Decorated personally by Hitler. He was wounded and invalided out of Tunis before the end. He spent time recuperating in France, and was sent for 'light duty' at von Rundstedt's headquarters in Paris for six months, duties unspecified," Freytag noted with a raised eyebrow, "that's unusual."

"Probably something with the Gestapo or those SS bastards. They probably had him shipping paintings for them out of the Lourve!" Guderian snorted into his drink.

Freytag shrugged and continued. "In early '44 he was transferred to the Eastern Front. Served with 2nd Panzer for a time and then was attached to Foreign Armies East." He stopped his reading and looked up at Guderian.

"What is it?" asked the General.

"His family estate in East Prussia is on the eastern border. The Russians overran that area early this year. His family and fiancé were all killed. It was just after that when he requested transfer to Foreign Armies East. He developed his own special operations group and carried out a number of special intelligence-gathering missions."

"Interesting. Let's see how he bears up tomorrow. Perhaps his extensive military experience has steeled him to survive a briefing with Adolf!" Guderian smiled ruefully at his little joke, and then his smile faded and his face darkened as the firelight played upon it.

"We must prevail, Freytag. We need reinforcements in the East, or else all is lost..."

Guderian's voice trailed off as he stared into the bright fire. The fire leapt up from the logs and he saw red flames everywhere.

The *Führer* briefing the next day began quietly enough. Guderian presented Gehlen's intelligence findings, all pointing at a massive Soviet offensive before the end of the month. Hitler started to argue with details of the report, constantly seeking to frame them in a positive light. Guderian, one of the few generals who would stand up and argue with Hitler, would not give in. The dispute became heated.

Remke had never seen anything like it. Hitler screamed into Guderian's face, his veins pulsing red and sweat beading on his pale skin. Remke felt a sense of frustration as he saw the clash between the two men halting any serious discussion of how to stop the Russian advance. He longed to be back at Foreign Armies East, where he could strike back instead of enduring this useless briefing. Strike back at those who ruined his life, who killed Anna...he felt the familiar agony and anger rise in his throat. Coldly, he put away those thoughts, knowing they would come again, later, when he was alone.

Remke listened as Guderian sighed loudly in frustration and tried to get Hitler to focus on the report one more time.

"My *Führer*, if you will just look at these reports from Gehlen, there can be no doubt..."

"Nonsense!" Hitler swept the report off the map table and slammed his fist down. Colored pencils danced over the map of Germany. "Those responsible for this report should be placed in a lunatic asylum!"

"If Gehlen is crazy then so am I," shot back Guderian.

"My *Führer*," he began again, motioning to Remke to step forward, "please listen to this officer. He comes to us directly from the Eastern Front. As you can see he is a highly decorated officer. The hero of the Maas River Bridge is not one given to flights of fancy."

Guderian watched as Hitler took in Remke and his decorations. He now knew that he could not persuade the *Führer*, but hoped that a combat veteran fresh from the front could more easily convince him.

Hitler's demeanor changed instantly. He was no longer argumentative, but rather solicitous.

"Remke, isn't it?" Hitler asked. Remke snapped his heels and did a slight bow.

"Yes, my Führer. I had the honor of receiving my Oak Leaves from you in 1942."

"Of course, yes. I remember the occasion well. So, they have you counting Bolsheviks now. Do you share General Guderian's opinion that all is lost?"

Remke quickly understood how both Hitler and Guderian had maneuvered him. He desperately sought an answer that would please both men. An idea flashed in his mind as he glanced at the map. It was a bold, simple move. Perhaps too simple? He decided to wait and think it through.

"The numbers General Gehlen presented to General Guderian are correct," Remke began, quickly adding "but numbers are not everything in this struggle. With your leadership and the iron will of the German soldier, we will turn the Soviets back."

Hitler spread his arms and turned to Guderian, gesturing towards Remke.

"How little faith in me you generals have! The younger men believe where you do not. Guderian, remember, our reserves in the east have never been stronger. Soon we will have jet aircraft and other wonder weapons rolling off the assembly lines. Hold on at the Oder River!"

"How can we hold?" Guderian responded, but with little hope of a rational response. "There are no useful reserves; less than 12 divisions along a 1200 kilometer front!"

Hitler did not even hear the question. Remke's answer had allowed him to build a wall of disbelief around himself. Hitler looked toward the end of the table, where SS *Reichsführer* Heinrich Himmler sat quietly. He had not moved or spoken throughout the briefing. Himmler looked up at his *Führer*, ever obedient and eager to please. The *Reichsführer* was the second most powerful man in the Third Reich and head of the dreaded SS and Gestapo, but he was also possessed by a pathetic need to please Adolf Hitler and was in physical agony simply being in the *Führer's* presence when he was contradicted.

"So, *Reichsführer*, what do you think of this so-called Soviet offensive?"

Knowing exactly what his *Führer* needed to hear, Himmler affected indifference to the threat. He shrugged his shoulders as he removed and polished his prince-nez glasses. Putting them on calmly he looked into Hitler's eyes and finally spoke.

"It's all an enormous bluff, of course."

The briefing was over.

"We failed, Freytag." Guderian slumped into his chair in front of the fireplace once they returned to their quarters following the briefing.

"No, you made the best possible argument, General." Freytag then turned to Remke who, along with several other staff officers, provided an informal debriefing audience. "But you, Colonel, what did you expect to gain with that drivel about leadership and iron will?"

Remke ignored the statement, and instead commented on Freytag's response to Guderian.

"It could not have been the best possible argument, since it did not convince the *Führer*. Therefore you are correct and it was a failure."

The room was silent, as Guderian leaned forward in the chair and turned his head to look at Remke. He gave a short, sharp laugh and said, "Our friend from the east speaks the truth. Not helpful, but truthful."

"*Herr* General," Remke stepped forward in front of Guderian. "I could have helped earlier in the discussion if I had been prepared. First I was instructed by Major Freytag not to offer any opinions during the briefing, and then I'm thrown in as a last-ditch attempt to change the *Führer's* mind. It was already too late."

"What do you suggest, Colonel?" asked one of the junior officers, a bit defensively. Remke carefully considered his answer. He needed to think his idea through quietly. He decided to wait.

"I am not yet ready to make a concrete suggestion. However I do know that extreme measures are called for to save the Fatherland. I also know that any plan must acknowledge the greatness of the Führer. Nothing will be accomplished by questioning his strategic vision and inferring his troop dispositions are faulty."

"In other words, make him think it's his plan." Freytag said cynically.

Remke had been looking straight at Guderian and held his gaze as he answered.

"Yes."

Guderian shrugged, dismissing the topic.

Remke's mind wandered. He thought about Russian fur caps and wondered just where the Brandenburgers were right now. They held the key to the plan churning through his mind, and he would need them, if enough were left alive.

CHAPTER FIVE

16 January 1945
SHAEF Headquarters
London, England

Captain Billy Boyle sat still in the back seat of the taxi as it pulled to a stop in front of SHAEF (Supreme Headquarters, Allied Expeditionary Force) Headquarters. He looked out of the side window at the stone steps to the front door, flanked by sandbags and guards with Thompson submachine guns at the ready. The wind blew intermittent raindrops, thick with forming sleet, across the sidewalk and against the main door.

"Here you are, Gov," said the cabbie as he rang up the charge on his meter. He turned to look at Billy, who continued to sit motionless, staring at the building.

"You alright, are you Gov?"

Billy flinched suddenly, as if he had been slapped. He fished some coins out of his trench coat pocket. "Yeah, I'm fine. Here you go."

Billy then opened the car door and grunted as he got out and stood up stiffly. As he shut the door he felt the pain and strain on his shoulder from the worst of his shrapnel wounds. After a moment of dizziness, the pain passed. The doctors at St. Alban's had proclaimed him fit for duty just two days ago, after he had received his sealed orders to report to SHAEF HQ within forty-eight hours. Billy knew the two events were not coincidence, and that if SHAEF required it he would have been delivered here bandaged and bleeding.

Damn, he thought to himself. He then turned and tried to improve his own attitude with a smile for the MP as he handed him his papers, including the orders. The MP Sergeant, half-frozen in the hard rain, was not receptive to any kind of smile from some kid officer.

"OK, see the lieutenant at the desk inside. Straight down the main hall."

"Yeah, Sarge. I've been here before. I know the drill."

The lieutenant at the duty desk reviewed his orders, logged him in on the HQ roster, and directed him to see Lieutenant Colonel Samuel Harding. Harding worked for the SHAEF Assistant Chief of Staff, G-2 (Intelligence), and was responsible for liaison with the U.S. Office of Strategic Services, the British Special Air Service Regiment, various governments-in-exile, and numerous Allied committees that analyzed intelligence data. Harding was also a BIGOT. BIGOT was the code name denoting those few senior officers who were aware of and had access to one of the greatest and best-kept secrets of the war. The Allies had broken the Enigma code and had been decoding and reading German radio transmissions since the start of the war. The Enigma device coded messages before they were sent and decoded them once received. Due to the complexity of this primitive but still powerful computing engine, the Germans had complete faith in the security of their coded radio transmissions. They were dead wrong. An Enigma device was smuggled out of Poland in 1939 and had been brought to Great Britain, where it was studied by a brilliant group of scientists at Bletchley Park, using their own computer to decode the transmissions.

Inadvertently, Hitler by-passed the Enigma system in favor of written orders for his Ardennes Offensive, due to his mistrust of the General Staff and concerns about security. The fact that without Enigma data, the Allies were taken totally by surprise in the Battle of the Bulge and dealt a deadly blow, was not lost on Colonel Harding and other G-2 staff as they watched Allied forces move into German territory.

Billy had never heard of Enigma, and didn't know of the ultra top-secret BIGOT designation. BIGOTS were not allowed in combat areas, due to the chance of capture and the potential for revealing what they knew under torture. He did know that Col. Harding was highly informed and connected with multiple intelligence sources. He also knew that from time to time Harding revealed to him, on a "need to know" basis, some startling intelligence data. Billy was also certain there was a highly placed Allied spy somewhere in the German High Command, and Harding did nothing to dissuade him from that notion.

When Billy first arrived in London in 1942, he was directed by Eisenhower to coordinate security arrangements with the Norwegian government in exile for a meeting to discuss resistance activities in their country. When a Norwegian official ended up murdered, Billy was forced to conduct an investigation that led him to German-occupied Norway. He made it back alive and Ike gave him a pat on the back and sent him to London to work for Sam Harding until he needed him again. Billy was to return to Harding and his G2 staff on temporary duty, with the understanding that he reported to the SHAEF Commander directly.

At first, Harding thought Ike had foisted a relative on him with the intent of providing him a safe sinecure, and he treated him accordingly. Billy had actually enjoyed the easy duty at first. It wasn't long though, before he began to resent comments about "Nephew Billy". This was made worse by the fact that his Norwegian mission was top secret, and that he had been strongly warned about the consequences of violating the Official Secrets Act.

The next two years were filled with a wide variety of duties, some for Harding and others directly for Ike. There were crimes in high places that needed to be investigated discretely, with justice duly tempered by military and strategic requirements. Eisenhower wanted to keep any Allied dirty laundry firmly under his control and behind closed doors. At the same time he believed no one, regardless of rank or status, was to be beyond justice. Billy was his secret weapon, his personal emissary, conducting top-secret investigations throughout North Africa and Europe, in pursuit of those who thought their position, military prowess, or power would allow them to bend regulations or break the law with impunity. These cases sometimes led to the front lines, or behind them. The enemy often had a way of getting involved, sometimes accidentally and other times after Billy discovered there was more to the matter than met the eye. While less of a reluctant hero now than when he first arrived in England, Billy had always felt he justifiably combined duty with a healthy sense of self-preservation.

With several years of history between them and a grudging respect for each other, Billy and Sam Harding faced each other across Harding's paper-strewn oak desk. Billy sank into the comfortable leather chair at the corner of the desk. A large, detailed map of Germany was hung on the wall. Billy avoided looking at it, hoping it was not a sign of his next destination.

Harding glanced at the clock on the mantle over the fireplace, where a low coal fire glowed and helped to warm the room against the January chill and gloom.

"Just about five, Billy. How about a toast to your return?"

"A drink is an excellent idea, Colonel, but I think we better drink to something more pleasant. Still drinking Bushmills?"

Billy appreciated the fact that Harding preferred the Irish whiskey, whereas most of the other SHAEF officers kept a bottle of Scotch in the desk drawers. Billy knew that the WASPish Samuel J. Harding must have some Irish blood in him.

"Got a fresh bottle of Black Bush right here," said the Colonel, pulling an unopened bottle and two glasses from a bottom desk drawer. Harding poured for each of them and handed Billy his glass. He looked up to the map and held his glass out.

"To the Endgame, Billy?"

"To the end of the war, Colonel," Billy said coldly. As he brought the glass to his lips he noticed that his hand was shaking and the lip of the glass rattled against his teeth as he drained it in a single, thankful gulp. Harding took only a small drink of his. They both sat in silence, and Billy waited for what he knew was coming. He didn't know exactly what Harding had in mind, but he knew something was up as Harding eyed the map between sips. Billy drummed his fingers on the arm of the chair and fidgeted in his seat. Finally he spoke.

"OK, I can't stand the suspense. What's up? What do you mean exactly by end game?"

Harding smiled. "Endgame is a chess term, Billy. It refers to the last phase of the game, when forces have been reduced and checkmate is in sight."

They both looked up at the map at the same time. On the eastern front, red arrows pushed towards German territory as a result of a major Soviet offensive launched just a few days ago. To the east, the remnants of the Bulge still showed in southern Belgium and Luxembourg. Along the rest of the line, British, Canadian, American and French armies stood roughly along the German border.

"Patton's due to begin cutting off the Bulge in a few days. Once we eliminate the escape route for the remaining German forces there, we'll start pushing east all along the line," proclaimed Harding.

"It always amazes me how easy it is to move units around a mapboard at headquarters," answered Billy, remembering the howling, freezing wind and life at the front, living outside in unbearable conditions.

"I know, Billy," Harding answered soberly. "As a matter of fact, that's one of the reasons we wanted you back here so fast. You know what it's like at the front and the kind of information we need here. We've got a job for you, but no behind the lines rough stuff. A nice staff job. We need to be sure the intelligence we're getting is up to the minute and matches the reality at the front."

Billy was suspicious. It seemed too good to be true, and he was wary.

"Tell me more," he said cautiously.

"Ike will tell you all about it. We're having dinner with him tonight."

Billy felt his gut tighten. "Can I have another drink?"

Two hours later Colonel Harding and Captain Boyle were having drinks at Eisenhower's residence, Telegraph Cottage, outside of London. Lord Tedder, Marshal of the Royal Air Force and Eisenhower's deputy commander at SHAEF, was in attendance as were three other officers and two American journalists. Kay Summersby, Ike's British driver and confidante, circulated among the men, refreshed drinks and provided a subtle feminine influence on the gathering.

The two journalists had cornered Eisenhower and kept him involved in an off-the-record conversation, so he had been unable to greet Billy when he saw him enter the room. Kay had noticed and intervened to steer the reporters to the bar, allowing Ike to escape and move across the room toward Billy.

Ike looked trim and fit as he usually did. He wore his trademark short "Ike" jacket and finely tailored trousers. Except for dark lines under his eyes, he looked relaxed. Billy knew that those lines hid a tremendous amount of stress and responsibility.

"William!" Ike exclaimed, flashing his famous toothy grin and calling Billy by his proper name, as he always did.

"Uncle Ike, how are you?" asked Billy as they shook hands. Eisenhower made it a rule that these gatherings at Telegraph Cottage were informal affairs, devoid of the military correctness he pursued in public. Unless they were alone and talking about family, this was virtually the only place where Billy addressed Eisenhower in this manner.

"Just fine, my boy. Good to see you up and around, William. I had a bad moment when I heard you were wounded. Glad you're OK."

"I'm fine, sir. Just glad to be on my feet and in one piece."

Billy had planned to tell Ike about his injuries and his early release from the hospital. As he faced him, he couldn't bear to add to his Uncle's burdens by complaining. He had been ready to tell Eisenhower that he needed two weeks, or maybe a month's leave to recover properly. As soon as he saw his Uncle's smiling face surrounded by deep stress lines, his resolve weakened. It totally vanished as Ike praised him for his mission in the Ardennes.

"You did a damn fine job in Belgium, son. It would have been a disaster if word had leaked out that one of our own generals looted art treasures in an allied nation he was supposed to be liberating. Or, if he got away with it. Too bad it had to be in the middle of the German offensive though," Ike said sadly, his hand on Billy's shoulder. Out of the corner of his eye, Ike saw one of the reporters heading for their small group.

"Let's step into the study for a few minutes. We won't be able to talk freely here or at dinner." The SHAEF commander led Harding and Billy into his comfortable study and shut and locked the door behind them.

"William, as you well know, we got caught with our pants down in the Ardennes," Eisenhower began, "you saw the effect that had and I don't intend to let it happen again." He paused and tapped his fingers hard on the edge of his desk.

"Never," Eisenhower said flatly, his eyes boring into Billy. "I'm not going let our boys get chewed up by another surprise. I want to know *everything* that's happening out there."

"Sir," Billy interrupted as he looked at his uncle and Harding, "what does this have to do with me? How can I tell you more than all the G-2 staffs out there, from every division at the front up to Army Group?"

Eisenhower nodded to Harding, indicating he should continue.

"Captain, we have more intelligence data coming in here than we know what to do with," Harding stated. "The more we get, the harder it is to sift the wheat from the chaff. We need eyes and ears at the front, where the intelligence comes from, to tell us the difference between what's really going on and what each level of military bureaucracy tells us they think we want to hear."

"Or what they wish was going on," Ike said with a tired grin.

"Right," echoed Harding, "by the time reports get to SHAEF, they've often gone through too many layers of wishful thinking and brown-nosing to be of any use."

"But what about your other sources of G-2?" asked Billy. "I know you don't get everything from the front." His mind raced to find a way to talk them out of this, to stop the seemingly endless flow of logic that he knew would end up with his life at risk. He caught a quick exchange of glances between the two men.

"Let's just say we have a variety of sources, and leave it at that," said Harding. "The main point is, we need to combine every source into a discernable whole in order to understand the full picture. To do that, we absolutely need fresh, unfiltered information from the front."

"Direct from the front, Colonel?"

"Relax, William," Eisenhower interjected. "I know you've just come through a rough time, and we've worked you pretty hard the past few years. This assignment should make up for that, and contribute to the successful conclusion of the war."

Eisenhower pulled open a bottom desk drawer and withdrew an envelope with the SHAEF shield on it. He handed them to Billy.

"These are your orders, William. You are to proceed to First Army headquarters, where you will be attached to their G-2 Intelligence Section. The orders make it clear that you will report to Colonel Harding, and through him to me."

As Eisenhower paused, Billy could only think that this arrangement would hardly make him popular at First Army HQ, where he'd probably be seen as a SHAEF spy. It then occurred to him that this was exactly what Harding and Ike had in mind. He leaned forward and directed his question to Eisenhower.

"Uncle Ike, are you asking me to *spy* on First Army for you?"

"No, Captain," Harding cut in abruptly. "You will have access to all First Army G-2 and other readiness reports. What will be different is that we will also provide you, via courier, with summaries of all intelligence reports received here, from all G-2 staff in Northwestern Europe. It will be your job to then compare that data with the situation in front of First Army."

"I want to hear from you directly, William," Eisenhower said, "and I want to know how the current situation at the front stacks up against the reports we're getting. If Army Group G-2 tells us that the enemy is weakening and running away in droves, I want you to tell me what the GI's in First Army are seeing."

"What's so special about First Army?" asked Billy. "What about Patton's Third Army?"

"We're sending liaison officers out to Third, Seventh and Ninth Armies as well," Ike explained. "But I choose you for First Army because I'm especially concerned about their area of operations. They'll be proceeding along a line of attack that will ultimately bring them south of Berlin. This puts them astride the route between Berlin and this Alpine Redoubt we've been hearing about."

Eisenhower was referring to the rumors of a Nazi stronghold in the Bavarian and Austrian Alps, where Hitler could hold out for an extended period of time and cause immense Allied casualties. There were German troops retreating from Italy, the Balkans, Russia, and the western front, and all of them could possibly end up in the Alps, where Allied troops would have to fight for every pass and mountain top.

"Be on the lookout for any surprises as the Wehrmacht pulls back to defend Berlin, or for indications of large-scale troop movements into the Alps."

Harding tapped the sealed envelope Billy held.

"These orders give you full access to all the resources you'll need to get the job done, including the use of a Reconnaissance Platoon from First Army's Headquarters Company. General Hodges has been notified of your assignment, and General Eisenhower has personally asked him to extend you every courtesy."

"I understand," Billy told the two men. Mentally he surrendered to the inexorable. Everything had been planned for him. Generals were waiting for him. After the Generals were the GIs. Then the Germans. "When do you want me there?"

"Transport has been arranged for the morning," Harding concluded.

"Gentleman," Ike said with a smile, "shall we join the others?"

Billy felt less like smiling than his uncle. He followed Ike out of the room, placing the sealed orders in his inside tunic pocket. As he did, he could feel his heart beating rapidly and the sweat soaking through his shirt. He suddenly felt afraid, and the now familiar shudder ran through his body. They had not asked him if he wanted to go, or if he felt he was up to it. Or even if he wanted to spend his last night out on the town, instead of spending the evening making small talk with staff officers and journalists. He followed them meekly, feeling weak, used, and foolish. After all he had done and endured for them, they were blithely ordering him to the front again.

Billy sat through dinner and the conversation seemed to drift past him. The other guests ignored him as they engaged in the witty chitchat of the powerful and the sure. They spoke with the certainty of those who knew they would not spend a single night in a freezing foxhole or ever be far from a warm meal or a cocktail hour. The orders in his tunic pocket pressed against his skin and reminded him that another, far different and uncertain world awaited him. He drank heavily and it did not help.

CHAPTER SIX

22 January 1945
Saint Ludwig's Hospital
Berlin, Germany

Sister Anneliese walked up to desk of Elsa Klein, her gray nurse's uniform flapping with purpose. She carried a clipboard thick with patient charts, her mouth set in a stern frown.

"Elsa," the sister said, "where is *Feldwebel* Jost Brunner today? He is supposed to be in physical therapy for his leg this morning."

Sister Anneliese tapped the file with her pencil as she lifted her eyebrow at Elsa. Elsa Klein worked at St. Ludwig's as the hospital's Chief Social Worker, responsible mainly for the needs of poorer patients, following discharge from the charity wards. St. Ludwig's was a Catholic hospital, and nearly every nurse here was a nun. Sister Anneliese was the Head Nurse, and a formidable figure in every sense of the word. She came from sturdy northern German peasant stock, and her wide, strong form towered over the desk where Elsa sat.

"I only have three Sisters to work in the physical therapy ward, *Fräulein* Klein. When a patient doesn't show up for his appointment we waste time. Do you know how many men with leg wounds we have here?"

Elsa knew very well. Since 1943 the hospital had been taken over by the Wehrmacht for military use. In November of that year, the hospital had been notified that except for an emergency room and an outpatient clinic, all beds were to be reserved for military casualties. All civilian patients were to be transferred out within two weeks. Elsa's job had changed from social worker to rehabilitation specialist, but not until she had overseen the discharge of hundreds of patients, many not yet ready to leave without medical care.

As the sister waited for an answer, a group of doctors and a high-ranking SS officer walked by. The SS man had been slightly injured in last night's bombing raid, and the Chief Surgeon and his assistant were giving him a tour of the facility before he left. The white sling holding his left arm contrasted sharply with his black uniform and boots.

Elsa looked into Anneliese's eyes and meaningfully glanced to the SS officer, to insure the Sister took notice of him.

"Sister, I apologize for the error," Elsa said, somewhat formerly. "*Feldwebel* Brunner had greatly improved and I took him off the list for therapy. Perhaps the typist missed it. In any case, I thought a long walk with his cane would help build up his strength. He offered to pick up some extra rations for us."

Anneliese let a discrete gasp escape her lips as she took in the hidden meaning behind Elsa's words. Wehrmacht soldiers on temporary leave from the hospital, but not discharged from it, could draw their own rations from the local Berlin garrison commissary. Some did this to supplement the hospital menu, and once in a great while a good man like Jost Brunner would do it for an entirely different reason.

Before the two women could exchange any further words, *Herr Doktor* Hubert Kappelen walked over to them, accompanied by the SS officer.

"Sister Anneliese, *Fräulein* Klein, may I introduce *Sturmbannführer* Otto Hettstedt? The *Sturmbannführer* was injured last night in the terror bombing." *Sturmbannführer* was the SS rank equivalent to a major in the regular forces.

"Heil Hitler!" snapped Hettstedt, as he clicked his heels and gave a lazy half-armed Nazi salute with his good arm, and bowed slightly towards the women. He was a short, pudgy man and the finely tailored uniform did little to hide his well-fed form.

"Heil Hitler!" responded Sister Anneliese, loudly and with her substantial arm fully extended, as Elsa stood up from her seat. "I trust the *Sturmbannführer* was not seriously hurt?"

"No, Sister," Hettstedt said, as he looked directly at Elsa. A smile crept up on the sides of his mouth as he let his gaze wander from her light brown hair falling across her forehead, to her bright blue eyes, over her full mouth, and downward to her breasts. Elsa willed her breathing to be calm and returned Hettstedt's look as if it were completely normal.

"As a matter of fact, *Fräulein*," Hettstedt continued, as if Sister Anneliese was not there, "I was just returning from a late night meeting at *Prinz Albrecht Strasse*." At the mere mention of the combined SS and

Gestapo headquarters, he puffed out his chest and looked around at the effect it had on his listeners.

"*Sturmbannführer* Hettstedt is in the Reich Security Main Office," (*Reichssicherheitshauptamt*, or RSHA) *Doktor* Kappelen interjected. "Amt IV, I believe you said?" Amt IV was the department entitled Investigation and Fighting of Enemies. *Doktor* Kappelen already knew that Hettstedt worked out of Amt IV, Section B1. Section B1 investigated "Political Catholicism", and Hettstedt was responsible for activities in the General-Government area of occupied Poland. He thought it a great joke that he had been brought here for his injury.

"Yes, and I am sure you must not be enemies of the state, otherwise I would not be walking out of here!" Hettstedt laughed at his own joke, and the others joined in dutifully. Having center stage with his small audience, Hettstedt gave his version of a morale-boosting speech, keeping his eyes fixed on Elsa.

"You are doing heroic work here. Healing our comrades from the front and allowing them to once again defend the Reich is a holy duty, a duty for which St. Ludwig's is ideally suited."

Elsa half listened as Hettstedt droned on. She thought how much his soft, fat body contrasted with the rail-thin, consumed men that came to the hospital from the front. She imagined them walking out of the hospital and directly into the trenches as the front lines moved closer to Berlin. She looked to her left at Sister Anneliese and could see her hanging onto every word with rapt admiration.

"And so, I must not detain you any longer. You have done well to return me to my work so quickly. The Reich thanks you. Heil Hitler!"

This time Hettstedt gave the full-armed salute, perhaps not to be shown up again by Sister Anneliese's enthusiastic response. The group all followed with the required salute. Hettstedt withdrew his arm a moment before the others and grabbed Elsa's outstretched hand and kissed it in what he undoubtedly saw as a romantic flourish.

"Until we meet again, *Fräulein* Klein. Sister, *Herr Doktor*."

The *Sturmbannführer* turned on his heel and left the room, full of self-importance and certain he had inspired the medical staff. He mentally made a note to return again, perhaps in his official capacity. It would be good to demonstrate to his superiors that Catholic organizations under his jurisdiction were actively contributing to the war effort. That nun certainly would be a good example of how a religious person should respond to the war effort. She saluted like stormtrooper. And the *Fräulein*...he would like to see her again also, in a more private setting. Despite the pain in his shoulder, Hettstedt left the hospital humming as he considered the benefits of his office with the *Prinz Albrecht Strasse* address. It certainly made the young ladies tremble, which is just how Otto Hettstedt liked them.

As Hettstedt cleared the door, Elsa muttered a quick excuse and ran to the women's washroom. Once inside, she leaned back against the door and tried to calm herself, looking at her shaking hand. Suddenly she felt dizzy, then she retched violently into the sink.

"By the Holy Father, Sister, you laid it on thick with that one," *Doktor* Kappelen said, half in admiration and half in disbelief. "I couldn't wait to get rid of him, especially after our new guests arrived late last night."

The doctor quickly glanced around the room to be sure no one Elsa was listening, a reflex action by now. St. Ludwig's harbored a dangerous secret, one that in these trying days would earn all concerned a bullet in the back of the head, at best. St. Ludwig's Hospital of Berlin treated Jews. Hidden Jews. Throughout the city, by ones, twos and small groups, sympathetic friends, opponents of the regime, or religious conspirators, hid Jews. No one knew exactly how many, but there were enough that at any one time there was likely to be a need for medical treatment. With the increased bombing that the city had seen over the last year, the hidden Jews now often needed treatment for wounds, burns and broken bones as well as normal illness and the effects of malnutrition. With food rationing restricting the diets of Germans with official papers, there was very little food for the undocumented Jews.

No one could remember how it started. At first, in early 1943, there were whispers among the sisters of secret visitors to the sealed tuberculosis ward, an area of the hospital certain to stifle the curiosity of those who could not be trusted. As some of the sisters and staff realized what was occurring, they offered their help to Sister Anneliese. Elsa was among them. They provided medical care, food and emotional support. Those who came to them were often paralyzed with fear at being outside their safe havens without papers.

As the bombings brought more civilian casualties to St. Ludwig's, Elsa conceived of a plan. She took identity papers from those who died and saved them for someone who matched their age and appearance. It was a slow process, but Elsa had provided eleven hidden Jews with Aryan identity papers by the time the Wehrmacht took over the hospital. Then she had her great inspiration.

There were over three hundred civilian beds to be cleared within a very short time. Not all the patients could be discharged under their own care, and many were not healthy enough to recover in wartime Berlin. Elsa had gone to the Wehrmacht officer that had delivered his orders to the hospital and demanded transport to the country for one hundred priority civilian patients. She had informed him that they would not survive in Berlin in their condition and that they must be taken to the countryside. At great expense to the hospital she would assign each patient a nurse's aide to accompany and care for them. These aides of course must also be issued priority travel. If the Wehrmacht would not cooperate and was willing to let her patients, some who were Party members, die, then she would have to inform the appropriate authorities.

Within a matter of days Elsa had priority travel papers for one hundred patients and one hundred nurse's aides. Word went out quickly through the underground network of hidden Jews for able-bodied women to come to St. Ludwig's for a chance to get out of the city. If some of the nurse's aides were painfully thin and white-skinned, no one noticed in the confusion of the move. The Bavarian countryside was soon home to one hundred recuperating Berliners and their novice nurse's aides.

Following the military takeover of the hospital the Gestapo ran security checks on the entire staff. One doctor and one janitor disappeared. They had never been involved with the care of hidden Jews, and no one knew what had happened to them. Then one of the nurses denounced a doctor for "defeatist" comments. He was taken away for three weeks, returned with a limp and spoke to no one. This had a chilling effect on Elsa and her circle of conspirators. The euphoria they felt at getting so many out of the city vanished as they slowly realized that death not only came for them from enemy bombers in the sky but from their countrymen's grip on the ground as well.

Elsa returned to Sister Anneliese and the doctor, wiping her mouth with her hand. She was as pale as a ghost. "Come with me," she beckoned to the sister.

The two women walked through the emergency ward, still full of those being treated after the night's bombing raid. They entered a corridor and went into a room marked "Supplies". Elsa pulled a key from her pocket and opened a cupboard door. The inside was empty. She knocked twice, sharply, on the wall. Grabbing the molding along the edge of the wall, she slid it sideways. Inside, the meager light from the supply room revealed two huddled forms. Each shielded their eyes against the light. They were shivering in the cold of the unheated hiding place.

"Don't worry," said Elsa to the two girls. She turned to Sister Anneliese and explained, "Twin sisters, thirteen years old- their apartment was bombed out and everyone else in it was killed. Their hiding place was destroyed. What should we do?"

The older woman knew exactly what to do. She pushed past Elsa and opened her arms wide.

"Children," she whispered. They fell into her arms sobbing and she rocked them back and forth.

Of course, Anneliese. You always go to the heart of the matter, Elsa thought to herself. *But what will we do tomorrow?*

With the two girls in the Sister's care, Elsa walked back lethargically to her office, drained by the events of the night and the morning. She nearly ran into a smiling Jost Brunner as she turned a corner.

"Elsa, wait 'til you see what I brought! Sausage, cheese, and chocolate!"

Jost stopped as he looked into Elsa's weary face.

"What's the matter, child? Why so sad?"

"Oh, Jost, I don't know how much longer I can go on." She leaned forward and hugged him, arms around his broad chest and a tear slowly drifting across her cheek.

"There, there, now," he soothed, patting her on the back with his one free arm while the other held his sack of rations.

"Now let me tell you one thing. That fiancée of yours has gotten us all out of some pretty tight spots. He won't get caught out there," he gestured with his arm. "And my leg is doing much better. As soon as you send me back, I'll be sure let him know he needs to get back home," Jost said with a smile.

"I worry that you're not there to look after him," Elsa said with a smile, wiping her tear away. "I wouldn't want him to do anything stupid or heroic. Dieter can be so stubborn!"

"My dear, I will not get in between a lover's quarrel," Jost said lightheartedly. "If you defame my commanding officer any more, I'll have to return to my unit and inform him!"

He turned and walked with her down the corridor, limping slightly and with an arm around her shoulder.

"Now I spent all morning drinking awful ersatz coffee with a supply sergeant just to talk him out of these extra rations. You'd better take this chocolate and give it to those kids you've got stashed around here somewhere."

CHAPTER SEVEN

13 February 1945
Reich Chancellery
Berlin, Germany

In the month since his assignment to Guderian's OKH staff, Colonel Erich Remke had made himself invaluable, preparing detailed and up to the minute reports on Russian strength and intentions along the Eastern Front. He also spent many late night hours working alone, pouring over maps and writing in a notebook that he stored in a safe during the day. When asked by other staff what he was working on, Remke simply declined to reply.

Such behavior had not earned Remke many friends, and his caustic tongue and confident belief in his own opinions did not make him a desired companion for the few off-duty hours the officers were allowed. Everyone at the OKH headquarters in Zossen, just south of Berlin, was overstressed and overworked, and few cared to spend any more time than necessary with Remke. They were a close-knit group, intensely loyal to General Guderian, and Remke was too much of a loner to become part of the General's informal family. Remke could see that for himself in the travel arrangements in the two large staff cars taking them to Berlin. Guderian rode in the first car with his Chief of Staff, General Walther Wenck, along with his adjutant, Major Freytag. Remke traveled with *Hauptmann* Boldt and several junior offices in the second car.

The previous day, Remke had asked Guderian for a transfer back to Foreign Armies East. Guderian told Remke to get back to work, and that although the Reich would be better off with fewer soldiers at headquarters, they were all stuck here for now.

"Tomorrow that may change, at the *Führer* briefing," Guderian had said, "we're going to put everything at stake, risking all our heads."

Guderian had been furious when he heard that Hitler had appointed SS *Reichsführer* Himmler to lead Army Group Vistula. This army group, hastily formed from units of every type in northeastern Germany, was to block Russian forces from East Prussia to the Oder River. Army Group Vistula was already under heavy attack, and Himmler's lack of combat experience and near command paralysis was sure to bring about a disaster. Guderian planned to demand that General Wenck take over command of Army Group Vistula, as Himmler's Chief of Staff. To get Hitler to admit that his SS commander needed assistance from a regular Wehrmacht officer, thereby publicly embarrassing the *Reichsführer*, might be nearly impossible, but Guderian steeled himself for the attempt.

The mid-day sun was bright and the February sky, usually gray and overcast, was a brilliant blue. As the cars left the Zossen countryside and entered the Berlin city limits, the sky began to be obscured by lingering smoke and clouds of dust from recently collapsed buildings. As they drove north on *Potsdamer Strasse* into the central city, it seemed as if night had fallen at two in the afternoon. Wind blew dust and debris through the streets, and some fires still burned while workers dug out the rubble of bombed buildings. At a main intersection, the cars halted for several fire engines racing from one burning building to another. Remke looked out of the car window. On the right-hand side of the street, in an area cleared of debris and rubble, ten bodies were neatly laid out, yet to be covered. Three men, five women and two children. The men were older than the women, to be expected when all available manpower was at the front. Four of the women were middle-aged, and the younger woman was probably the mother of the two children; one was laid out on either side of her. She still had on her apron, as if about to make breakfast for her little boy and girl.

"My God," murmured Boldt. "When will it all end?"

"If briefings and staff reports could win wars, it would be over tomorrow," Remke said.

"I know you hold this staff work in low regard," Boldt replied, "but it must be done. General Guderian needs our support to put his ideas before the *Führer.* Where else could you contribute so much to the defense of the Reich?"

The last of the fire engines cleared the intersection and the staff cars pulled forward, leaving behind the row of corpses.

"Where else, indeed, Boldt," said Remke, half to himself, "where else indeed?" Remke stared out of the window, his thoughts flying to another woman, dead at the hands of his enemies. Remke felt his right hand tremble as he thought of Anna and willed it into stillness. Stuck at a headquarters office, he had no occasion to find any relief on the battlefield, and the stress was beginning to tell.

The car drove on, the occupants in silence. Through the *Tiergarten*, along the canal, towards the Spree River, everywhere there were signs of recent and previous bombings, lines of refugees coming in from the east, destruction everywhere. The British had bombed Berlin the night before, and the Americans had struck in the early morning, insuring they would be over the target and home again in good weather. This meant that the city could be certain of no further bombing until later that night. Even with ruined buildings still smoldering from the last raid, there was evident relief on the faces of some Berliners. Those who had escaped injury appeared to enjoy the prospect of a full day not spent waiting for the air raid warning. Perhaps because of this, it had been announced that today's *Führer* briefing would take place above ground, in Hitler's undamaged study in the Reich Chancellery.

The lead staff car stopped as SS guards stood in the center of the road, just one block from the Chancellery. They motioned the cars to pull over and park. Guderian and his officers stepped out and faced the SS officer in charge of the detail.

"*Herr* General, you and your staff will have to walk the remaining distance. The streets are all blocked by bomb damage. The south entrance to the Chancellery is just around that corner."

"Very well," acknowledged Guderian. He and his party of officers gathered up their maps and briefcases and began a winding, single file walk through rubble-strewn streets. The nearby buildings and the smoke billowing up from them blocked the feeble sunlight. Remke shivered from the cold as the acrid smoke bit into his nostrils. The group approached the Reich Chancellery entrance coughing and breathing through handkerchiefs held over their faces.

"Papers please, *Herr* General!" a guard standing by the massive doors barked, the "please" sounding more like an order than a polite request of a general staff officer. Guderian beckoned Boldt forward and he withdrew documents for each member of the party from his briefcase. One by one, the guard checked the papers and motioned each individual inside. The SS men of the *Leibstandarte* Adolf Hitler, the *Führer's* personal bodyguard, displayed an open arrogance when it came to Wehrmacht general officers. Following the July 20th plot against Hitler, salutes and basic military courtesies had vanished. SS guards took pleasure in treating Wehrmacht generals as if they were common soldiers.

Once inside, the group was brought into an anteroom furnished with only a long table. The walls were faced with green marble, and dusty light came from several large windows along the outer wall. A central staircase ascended from behind the table, and then split in either direction underneath a huge Imperial eagle grasping a swastika in its claws. Remke could not help himself from scanning the room as if it were a trap. SS guards on the staircase above them held Schmeisser submachine guns at the ready. The guards in the room with them were arranged so as to be clear of the field of fire from the staircase.

"Briefcases and sidearms on the table!" announced the SS *Scharführer* (non-commissioned officer) in charge of the guard detail. Each officer placed his briefcase on the table and opened it. Silent guards went through their contents with practiced dexterity. Maps were unrolled, files opened, and identity papers checked once again for each officer. Receipts for sidearms were given to each officer, visitors not being allowed to carry weapons in the *Führer's* presence. The officers had to open their greatcoats and allow the guards to check them for hidden weapons. The *Scharführer* searched Guderian himself, and even he seemed uneasy with this personal intrusion of a respected military figure.

"Everything is in order, *Herr* General. Please follow me."

The group headed up the staircase, past the steady gazes of the guards, and followed behind the *Scharführer* as he led them down a long hallway with offices on each side. Everything looked normal until they turned a corner and wind blasted them from the outside. Bombs had fallen along the street next to the Chancellery, and the outer row of offices had been blown out. Doors were shattered and windows nonexistent. The wind blew papers and debris from the ruined offices out into the hallway. Memos and maps swirled around the feet of the group as they walked by, shoulders hunched against the cold shock of air.

Their route was a roundabout one due to bomb damage. Remke had time to remember his last visit here, when the walls were adorned with artwork and tapestries, and expensive carpets were soft underfoot. Now the walls were bare and cracked in places. Fire damage was evident, and in places the ceiling had caved in. Soot and dust were everywhere.

"I didn't know how bad things were here," said Remke, to no one in particular. He had not been in Berlin for more than eight months. While he accepted the destruction and death war had brought, he had never thought the German capital itself could be punished so harshly. His methodical military mind, informed by all the latest intelligence, saw no alternative to the steady advance of the Allied forces toward this very spot.

Unless someone did something. Something unexpected. Which was just the kind of idea that was slowly and surely taking final form in Remke's mind and detailed in his notebooks.

"What did you say, Remke?" asked Freytag, just ahead of him.

Remke did not answer. His thoughts were speeding ahead of them all. After a final identity check, they were shown into the *Führer's* large outer office, the last room before his private study, where the briefing would take place.

Remke was astounded at the difference between these rooms and the shattered city outside the Chancellery walls. Here, paintings decorated the walls and fine carpets stretched out before them. Everything was clean and sparkling. Tables were set with food and drink. Real coffee, schnapps and an abundance of sandwiches and pastries were arranged for the officers as they waited to be brought into the inner sanctum. Remke glanced at the dust covering his boots from the walk into the building and felt out of place.

The room was already filled with others attending the briefing. Field Marshal Keitel, chief of the High Command and his Chief of Staff General Jodl, stood chatting and drinking coffee. Before anyone could say anything, Hitler's adjutant, General Burgdorf, opened the doors to the inner study and said, "The *Führer* would like you to come in."

The study was a huge, cavernous room. The ceiling was gilded and very high, with decorated chandeliers hanging across it. An enormous pastel carpet covered the floor. At the far end of the room Hitler's desk, decorated with swastikas and snakes, stood against the wall. Standing alone in the middle of the room, his left arm limp at his side and his head shaking slightly, stood Adolf Hitler.

Reichsmarshal Hermann Goering, as the highest-ranking officer, led the group into the room, others following in order of rank. Single file, they all approached Hitler and received a soft, silent handshake. Various officers arranged themselves around the huge red marble map table that ran half the length of the long wall. Freytag and Boldt arranged the maps to be consulted during the briefing. Remke watched as junior officers stepped back and positioned themselves behind their seniors. Himmler and Goering stood by Hitler.

SS *Brigadeführer* (Brigadier General) Hermann Fegelin came up to Remke and stood beside him. Fegelin was Himmler's personal representative to the *Führer*, mainly because Fegelin was married to the sister of Eva Braun, Hitler's mistress. Fegelin had known Remke in Paris in 1944, and was curious as to why he was there. The briefing was about to begin, but Fegelin just had time to whisper to Remke.

"My dear Remke, what brings you to a *Führer* briefing? Who are you here with?"

"Guderian."

"Well then, I should excuse myself," said Fegelin with a sly smile, who knew the confrontation that was brewing between their respective bosses.

"Never mind, Fegelin, I need to stand behind my general," Remke said as he moved away toward the end of the map table where Freytag and the others stood behind Guderian. Remke had gotten to know Fegelin well during the brief period in Paris. He actually admired the man, for being so open about his political ambitions. With so much deceit at the highest party levels, Remke found it refreshing that a charming, unscrupulous cad like Fegelin had actually risen to this level, even if only through marriage and flattery.

Remke found his spot at the end of the table. Keitel and Jodl began the briefing with an overview of the situation on all fronts. Their carefully worded reports avoided any reference to defeats or withdrawals. Even with the Allies approaching Germany's borders, they made it sound like victory was just around the corner. Jodl droned on, describing the defense of the Colmar Pocket on the western front in glowing terms, even though he knew all German forces had already surrendered or been overrun. The *Führer* would have to be prepared for that news very carefully.

Remke looked around the room as he waited for Jodl to finish. His gaze wandered to the glass doors opposite Hitler's desk. He remembered the colorful, extensive gardens outside when he was here in the springtime. He took one step to the left to get a view past the officer in front of him.

With a shock, he was suddenly reminded of the devastated world outside. The garden was no more. Piles of rubble were heaped up on the sides, and bomb craters had disgorged circles of smoking dirt where this morning's bombs had hit.

An aide saw Remke staring outside and quietly walked to the glass doors, pulling the curtains shut and absolving the room from the vision of the ruined garden. Remke blinked his eyes and looked around at the others in the room. Here in the sea of gold braid, shined boots and elegantly pressed pants with general staff red stripes down the side, nothing seemed out of place. Yet destruction lapped at the edges of this very room; how much longer could it be kept at bay?

Remke made a silent vow to do what he could to prevent it, no matter what it took. He had to find a way, a way to continue the war and make the Russians pay for what they did to him. And to Anna. He felt his anger rise, and realized his fist was clenched. He forced himself to relax, to regain control before his emotions got the best of him. *Not here, not now!* As he did so, Guderian stepped forward and began his report. Remke stiffened and readied himself. Guderian wasted no time in describing the Russian attacks and the need for a counter-attack within two days.

"It cannot be done," exclaimed Himmler. "Army Group Vistula needs more fuel and ammunition brought up to the front lines. Two days is impossible." Himmler removed his prince-nez glasses and polished them furiously, a sure sign of nervousness.

"The *Reichsführer* knows the situation of Army Group Vistula better than anyone," Hitler said, "I agree with his assessment."

"We can't wait until the last can of petrol and the last shell have been issued!" Guderian responded, "By that time the Russians will be too strong!"

"I will not allow you to accuse me of procrastination!" yelled Hitler.

Guderian ignored him and went to the heart of the matter.

"I want General Wenck appointed as Army Group Vistula chief of staff. Otherwise there can be no guarantee the attack will be successful." Guderian told himself to stop there but could not hold his temper. He gestured toward Himmler, still polishing his glasses.

"The man can't do it. How *could* he do it?"

"The *Reichsführer* is man enough to lead the attack on his own. How dare you criticize him!" Hitler's voice rose even higher and he shook his good right hand at Guderian.

"I must insist that General Wenck be transferred to the staff of Army Group Vistula to lead the operation properly."

"Never!" shouted Hitler, and the argument continued to rage. Junior officers started, in their practiced fashion, to slip out of the room. Himmler remained silent, as accusations about his personal bravery flew about the room. Hitler raged at Guderian, shouting into his face, spittle spewing from his mouth. Suddenly, the argument ended.

Hitler walked over to Himmler and out of the blue said, "Well, Himmler, Wenck is going to Army Group Vistula tonight as chief of staff." Turning to Guderian, Hitler said in a charming voice, "Today, the general staff has won a battle."

The briefing ended shortly after that. Guderian and Wenck left immediately to prepare for Wenck's departure to Army Group Vistula. Himmler also left immediately, stung by the *Führer's* withdrawal of his support. Fegelin struck up another conversation with Remke, stopping him from leaving with Guderian.

"Remke, join us over here. The *Führer* likes to unwind after these briefings. He likes you, do you know?"

"I am honored, Fegelin. But are you sure I am welcome? I don't wish to appear presumptuous."

"Not at all. The *Führer* likes new listeners, and you impressed him with your comments last time. Are you worried about not chasing after

Guderian?" Remke bristled and Fegelin knew he had hit home with his comment.

"You know I don't chase after anyone, Fegelin. I may have some more comments today that the *Führer* may find interesting. Lead on."

Fegelin led him to the soft leather chairs grouped around Hitler's desk. Goering, Martin Bormann, Burgdorf, and several other aides were already seated. Hitler was describing the V-2 rockets being fired at London, Paris, Antwerp and Brussels.

"The V-2 is just the first generation of rocket weapons we will unleash on the Allies. The A-10 model is being developed with a range of 4,500 kilometers. We will be able to attack New York City and bring the war home to the Americans. The A-10 will carry a version of the V-2, and once in flight, it will launch the V-2 from the stratosphere. These and other terror weapons will shake the mongrel Americans with fear. They could never withstand the punishment the German people have taken. Or the British people for that matter."

"Quite right, my *Führer*," Bormann said. Martin Bormann, Nazi Party Chief, was always ready to say whatever his leader needed to hear. He had made himself indispensable by doing whatever Hitler needed and by agreeing with him totally.

"The English are close to our Aryan race, but the Americans have allowed too many inferior breeds to intermingle with them. They could never share the mastery of the world with us," Hitler continued. He relaxed into his chair and appeared to focus on something beyond the vision of those in the room. He spoke as if global victory was just within his grasp, and the ruined gardens and city beyond these walls were just an illusion.

"My *Führer*, I was just saying the same thing about the English to Colonel Remke," Fegelin blurted, introducing Remke to the circle and ingratiating himself with Hitler at the same time.

"This morning a report came in from one of the British prisoner of war camps near Danzig. It was being evacuated to move the prisoners out of the...the, ah," Fegelin stumbled over his words, not wanting to acknowledge directly that Russian forces were approaching so close to this eastern German city, "...operational area of the city's defenses." The evident relief on his face at having come up with such a non-descriptive turn of phrase made Remke smile.

"And one entire barracks of prisoners volunteered to join us in the fight against Bolshevism! Can you imagine, a British SS unit fighting alongside other Europeans against the threat from the east!"

"My dear Fegelin," Hitler said, "we hear these flights of fancy repeatedly. This is probably an exaggeration brought on by a handful of prisoners motivated by nothing more than the prospect of extra rations."

"This report is real. With your permission, I can investigate further and formulate a plan to recruit Allied prisoners of sufficient Aryan background. It would electrify the world to hear of former enemies united against the Communists. It would be a true European bulwark against Bolshevism- we already have Frenchmen, Danes, Norwegians and many others fighting with the SS. Colonel Remke has fought alongside many of them in the Brandenburg Division."

Now Remke understood why Fegelin brought him into the *Führer's* post-briefing circle. He had a plan to propose and wanted to offer Remke's experiences to back him up. He knew the *Führer* would reject the Brandenburg Division as an example because of its past link with the traitorous Abwehr. But the *Führer* liked Remke, and that might allow Fegelin a moment's consideration.

Hitler folded his hands in front of him and slowly nodded his head. The room was silent as all assembled waited to hear which way the *Führer* would decide. Fegelin fidgeted with his hands, clasped behind his back, hiding his nervousness. He desperately wanted permission to leave Berlin, preferably headed west, away from the Russians. A tour of POW camps might just do the trick.

"It would be a magnificent moment," Hitler said somewhat dreamily, "but I refuse to be tempted by the statements of half a dozen Englishmen. If you can bring proof of more men willing to fight with us, Fegelin, then perhaps we can do something."

It was a characteristic Hitler response. He did not say yes or no, but left the idea open in case it could work. Fegelin would now have to prove his case, and could count on no other support from the powerful men in the room, as none would wish to ally themselves with an idea the *Führer* might discount in the near future. They had not earned themselves a presence in these comfortable leather chairs, surrounding their beloved leader, by sticking their necks out.

Fegelin was about to open his mouth, trying to figure out how best to respond to his own advantage, when Remke spoke for the first time.

"There is another way to bring about that magnificent moment."

In combat, there were times when Remke could see clearly and exactly what needed to be done to carry the day. No matter how loud the explosions or how fierce the enemy fire, he could find the exact moment to act. He knew without hesitation that this was one of those moments. The chance would not come again. He knew exactly what to say next.

"I can make it happen."

Fegelin moved back a half step to look at Remke, astounded by the calm pronouncement. Goering let out a sharp laugh, and Bormann never took his eyes off of Hitler.

"So a colonel will win the war for us?" Goering asked sarcastically.

"Only the *Führer* can win the war for us," said Remke, looking directly at Hitler. "But I can put a plan in his hands to hasten the day."

Remke stood still and waited. Hitler looked up from his seat and studied him, his eyelids heavy and hooded over his dark eyes.

"Tell us your plan, Colonel Remke."

"Of course, my *Führer.* As you have pointed out, it would change everything to have the British and Americans engage the Russian forces in combat. We also know that recruiting volunteers from POW camps is a fantasy that will gather nothing but a few malcontents."

"Remke, I must protest!" Fegelin shouted, waving his arms in frustration.

"Quiet, Fegelin!" At his *Führer's* remonstrance, Fegelin visibly winced and shrank back.

"Remke is correct. We should not expect anything from efforts to recruit these volunteers. Now, continue."

"If the British and the Americans will not come to us to fight the Russians, then we must bring the Russians to them."

"Are you seriously suggesting we allow the Allies' forces to join together?"

"Not precisely. Instead of dreaming about British volunteers, we simply need to look to our own forces for ample Russian troops. We still have large numbers of *Hilfswillige* serving with our divisions on the eastern front. I propose we select a sufficient number of Hiwis, led by German officers and train and outfit them as Russian troops. This will not be difficult, since they are already familiar with Russian weaponry."

"And these Russians will engage the British?" Burgdorf asked.

"No. The Americans." It was Hitler who answered, anticipating the response.

"Exactly my *Führer,*" Remke smiled. "That is the only area of operation where we have the required room to maneuver."

The others in the room were confused, but Hitler seemed to be reading Remke's mind.

"Show me," Hitler said as he jumped to his feet and approached the map table. Remke now considered his next move very carefully. The central point of his plan was to channel the American and Russian forces to a near meeting, which meant that Hitler would have to agree to a strategic withdrawal along both fronts. He had fired generals for suggesting much less, and shot them for not much more. Remke began to build his case.

"My plan is only a last resort, my *Führer.* It will take advantage of the Allies' momentum if the Wehrmacht fails to hold the borders of Germany, and strike them in a manner they will never suspect. As you have said, the Allies are a weak coalition, and sooner or later they will come to blows."

"When I attacked Poland in 1939 and the Soviet Union in 1941, I left the western defenses nearly empty. I knew the French and British would not attack, but it was a gamble! I was willing to gamble when all my generals spoke against me! The greater the prize, Remke, the greater the gamble. Now tell me what we would gain by cutting Germany in half." Remke saw his opening, drew a deep breath, and continued.

"If the Russians approach Berlin, I know it will be stoutly defended. Every German will do his duty, and the Russians will break themselves upon our defenses. As with every strong defensive point, enemy forces tend to bounce off of it. Russian armored units will probably circle around each side of the city, heading roughly northwest and southwest."

This was elementary military strategy, and Remke could see all his listeners were in agreement. Heads nodded and all eyes studied the map laid out on the table.

"North of the city, there are numerous lakes which break up the terrain. We will strongly defend the coastal cities on the Baltic Sea, and Russian units may focus on those. To the south though, there is about 140 kilometers of flat land between Berlin and the Saxony mountains. That is where we should channel a limited advance of Soviet forces."

"How far would you allow them to penetrate?"

"This area is opposite the current line of the American Ninth and First Armies. If they do not change their approach, it is likely that Patton's Third Army will turn southeast towards Bavaria and Austria. We will need to watch the disposition of the U.S. Ninth Army, but our target will most likely be the First Army. We will need to channel their advance towards the Russian advance units."

"And what will our pet Russian Hiwis do?" asked Fegelin somewhat sarcastically.

"They will be inserted between the two forces. If possible, we should also create a unit of English-speaking Germans, dressed in American uniforms, much like Skorzeny's Panzer Brigade 150 in the Ardennes Offensive. Our Russians will attack the Americans, and our Americans will attack the Russians. We will inflict heavy casualties, leave behind our own dead in Russian and American uniforms, and watch as the two real enemy columns come into contact and continue fighting each other."

"And then we come to the aid of the Americans!" Goering exclaimed as if the plan as suddenly just dawned on him.

"Yes," hissed Remke, "and then fight shoulder to shoulder with them to break the siege of Berlin! The New World will come to the aid of the Old World to stand against the Red threat!" Remke surprised himself with his own enthusiasm as he slammed his fist down on the map table, making the scattered colored pencils roll across the map and onto the floor.

Martin Bormann had been quiet during the discussion, his eyes never straying from Hitler's face. He had made a career out of reading the *Führer's* moods and anticipating his needs. He saw the dark eyes flicker across the map and knew he was calculating the rate of advance for the opposing Allied forces.

"Where do you think the Russians and Americans would meet, my *Führer*?" asked Bormann. He felt safe asking this question, since it could be nothing more than a hypothetical map exercise. If Hitler made an angry remark about defeatist thinking, then the plan was dead. If not…

"Here." Hitler picked up a colored pencil and drew a box along the lines of the Mulde and Elbe Rivers. "In the area between these cities…Bitterfeld and Eilenburg on the Mulde, and Wittenburg and Torgau on the Elbe."

Hitler nervously tapped the pencil on the table and ran his hand from Berlin across to the current positions of the U.S. First Army. He looked over to Remke and nearly smiled.

"It is quite a lot of my Reich to gamble with, especially for a Colonel."

"Yes, which is why I have given this plan the codename Operation Gambit. In chess, as in life, one must often sacrifice that which is valuable for that which is necessary." Remke knew that there was nothing left to say. He held his hands behind his back and waited for the decision that would come next. There was total silence for a full minute.

"Burgdorf!"

"Yes, my *Führer*."

"Prepare a *Führer* Directive instructing Colonel Remke to develop a fully detailed contingency plan for Operation Gambit. He is to have access to all necessary resources of the Wehrmacht, Luftwaffe and SS. I expect all agencies to fully cooperate in the planning of this operation. Remke, I will have you report back on your readiness. Then we will decide if we need to proceed."

Hitler was silent as he brooded over the map. "If we need to proceed, then this may be our salvation. Well done, Remke."

Remke swelled with pride, at the same time felt Fegelin's narrow eyes focused on him, simmering with anger and envy.

CHAPTER EIGHT

15 February 1945
OKH Headquarters
Zossen, Germany

Erich Remke stood at attention before the dark walnut desk where General Heinz Guderian sat quietly, holding a single sheet of paper clutched in his hand. Freytag and Boldt stood behind Guderian, one on either side of their general. Remke idly thought they looked like rooks on the chessboard protecting their king.

If that is true, then what am I? he wondered, *a bishop coming at them from a direction they didn't anticipate?* The religious image amused him and he smiled inwardly, while keeping his eyes focused on the wall behind the desk. He knew that whatever the consequences he might suffer from Guderian, he had succeeded in the first step of his plan. The plan that even if it failed, would insure more opportunities to continue killing Russians. For revenge. For Anna.

Remke had been called to attention gruffly by Guderian as soon as he entered the room. That had been a full five minutes ago. Guderian read over the paper in his hand several times, shaking his head in disbelief. Finally he let the sheet headed "Special *Führer* Directive" slip from his hand and fall to the desktop. He looked up at Remke with anger tinged with exasperation, and spoke.

"What exactly is this nonsense?"

"I have not yet seen the *Führer* Directive, Herr General."

"You expected it? Explain yourself immediately."

Remke told Guderian about his invitation to remain after the *Führer* briefing and the conversation that followed, including his proposal for Operation Gambit.

"I had been thinking about this for some time, sir. I had planned on preparing a plan for your consideration. But when the moment presented itself, I chose to act. *Brigadeführer* Fegelin gave me the perfect opening with his half-witted plan."

"Colonel, I should have gone back in there and dragged you out when you did not return with us. I do not expect one of my officers to associate with those lackeys and bootlickers who hang about the Chancellery. Now you have not only brought this directive down upon us, but you have certainly earned yourself an enemy. Fegelin does not like to look bad in front of the *Führer*. He's only tolerated because he married Eva Braun's sister."

"I know Fegelin, sir, and he won't be a problem. And now we have the opportunity to change the course of the war!"

"Do you really think this insane plan has a chance?" Boldt questioned him. "You can't lead a Soviet Army Front around like a dog on a leash-how can you carry out your duties here and lead such an operation?"

Lead the operation? Remke glanced longingly at the *Führer* Directive lying on the edge of the desk. Could it be he had really convinced Hitler? He couldn't afford to let these OKH bureaucrats get in his way. He ignored Boldt and looked straight at Guderian.

"Duties? Is my duty to bring you piles of paper every day telling you the Russians are closer? You already know that! If we don't do something one day soon I'll bring you a final report that the Russians are at the door!"

"That's enough, Remke," warned von Freytag. "We all have to do our duty here and provide a stable chain of command for the Wehrmacht. The alternative is to let those SS idiots run the war and lose it within a month."

"I don't care about your damn squabbles! Something must be done to stop the Russians from overrunning the Fatherland! If it takes the SS, fine. If it takes shooting the Führer, then find some men with backbone and do it. Just wake up and stop hiding behind these useless reports and briefings!"

Boldt's jaw dropped and von Freytag just stared at Remke. The room was silent for a moment as Remke's words hung in the air. Men had been shot for less. Before he could be reprimanded, Remke shifted gears from shouting to quiet persuasion. "We've all been on the Eastern Front and we know what animals the Russians can be to their own. Just think of what they will do to our people after all we've inflicted upon them. Their revenge doesn't bear thinking." His voice trembled slightly as those last words came out. The room was quiet, each man silently acknowledging that ultimate truth.

Guderian finally spoke. "So, Colonel, we are fiddling while Rome burns, in your eyes, of course? Well, there may be some truth in that."

He picked up the orders and wearily handed them to Remke. "I can admire your initiative, Colonel, but I am not pleased at the diminution of military resources to support such a fanciful venture. However, the *Führer* seems to agree with you."

Remke read the order.

Decree of 14 February 1945
By the *Führer* and Reich Chancellor

All means to defend the Reich must be undertaken in the coming months in order to provide the time necessary for the final development and deployment of those secret weapons that will reverse the tide of battle and drive our enemies from the borders of the Greater Reich. All contingencies must be taken into account in the planning of this offensive effort with our secret terror weapons. Therefore I decree that OKH undertake the planning of an operation designed to bring Soviet and Anglo-American forces into conflict with each other, should such forces achieve a break-through in the greater Berlin area. I am entrusting the implementation of this task, code-named Operation Gambit, to Colonel Erich Remke of the OKH staff, who shall act as operational commander with the following stipulations:

1. OKH will provide facilities and support for the creation and training of Special Detachment 200 for the purpose outlined above.
2. *Reichsführer*-SS Heinrich Himmler will provide specialized personnel as required to fill the ranks of Special Detachment 200 with English and Russian speaking soldiers.
3. Special Detachment 200 will be designated under Panzer Brigade Linz, which shall be constituted to protect Special Detachment 200 and to direct enemy forces as necessary to the final operational area.
4. Panzer Brigade Linz will be formed from units at the Lammersdorf test ground, including two prototype Maus Super-Heavy Tanks.

5. 9 Gruppe of Kampfgeschwader 76 will be transferred from Achmer to Dessau to provide Ar-234B jet bomber support for Panzer Brigade Linz. Jagdgeschwader 92 will provide a squadron of Me 262 jet fighter-bombers for air cover. The Luftwaffe component will be designated as Kommando Ritter.
6. All transport commands will provide Operation Gambit and all supporting units with top priority transportation. Units shall be in place for operational deployment no later than 15 March 1945.

Remke finished and looked up with a look of surprise on his face. Guderian was amused. "More than you bargained for, Colonel? Now you have significant resources at your disposal. Twin engine jet bombers, jet fighters, a panzer brigade, and the SS to call upon! I am sure that will make you very popular at Number 8 *Prinz Albrecht Strasse*."

Boldt and Freytag both laughed at the mention of the dreaded SS and Gestapo headquarters, enjoying Remke's discomfort.

"The *Führer* must have taken a special interest in you, Colonel," offered Boldt. "The Panzer Brigade is named after his Austrian hometown, Linz. Don't let it come to grief, since he may not be very happy if his namesake is destroyed."

"If I do not succeed, there will be little left that matters."

"Remke," Guderian cut in, having sufficiently enjoyed his displeasure, "you may have succeeded in getting your plan approved, but it is still only a plan. I hope that the *Führer* will come to his senses and release these units for the battle on the Oder. In the meantime, get to work pulling your forces together." He gestured to Freytag, who consulted a clipboard.

"The general has allocated an office and map room in the reserve barracks for your use. There are half a dozen clerks and a radio operator setting up over there now. The motor pool will assign transport as needed. Submit any requests for other headquarters staff you may have through me. You will certainly need a deputy."

"No need, Freytag. I know who my deputy will be. If he is still alive, that is."

After Remke had left the office, Guderian stood and walked to the window. It was almost completely frosted, leaving only a small clear circle to see through. He watched Remke walk through the cleared snow towards the reserve barracks. He turned and looked at Freytag.

"When Remke first came to us, you told me he was dangerous. That was an understatement."

"Yes, certainly. Now he will have Himmler and the SS angry about stealing Fegelin's idea, and the *Führer* furious if the plan does not go well."

"Oh no, my dear Freytag. That is not what I meant. The greatest danger we face from Remke is if he succeeds. If the Allies are about to join forces, it will mean that the war is lost beyond redemption. If his plan succeeds, it will only mean that the Russians and western powers will fight each other over the corpse of Germany. We will be more thoroughly destroyed than any nation since Carthage. Remke suffers from the same delusion that infects everyone around the *Führer*- that the Anglo-Americans will join us in the struggle against Bolshevism. That will never happen, though they might be tricked into fighting each other. That fight would destroy the little that would be left to us. Yes, Freytag, he is a dangerous man indeed."

Remke turned up his collar against the cold as he walked across the parade ground to his new assignment, the frigid air biting into him as he gathered his thoughts. He had succeeded beyond his wildest dreams, and now he felt both exhilaration and apprehension. He nearly trembled with the power he felt. At this moment of crisis, he held the salvation of the Reich in his hands. His idea had become reality, with men and steel to back it up.

He thought about Anna, just for a fleeting moment. The pain stabbed at his heart, and he sealed off that part of himself, promising that he would bring vengeance down upon those whom had ruined his life. Pushing back the emotions churning under his calm exterior, he continued on. But Anna still flickered at the edges of his mind, and for a brief moment he lost his battle for control. Walking with his head bent, a sound between a moan and a sob burst from his lips, unexpected, terrible, and painful. He held his hand to his face and looked around. There was no one in sight.

Remke stopped and breathed in deeply, exhaling a frosty breath into the brilliant sunlight. *Leave me in peace, Anna. Let me do this.*

He felt his tears freeze in the frigid air. They fell away and he moved on, wondering how long it would take to find Dieter Neukirk and his Hiwis.

CHAPTER NINE

22 February 1945
Elsa Klein's Apartment
Berlin, Germany

White sheets, Dieter Neukirk thought to himself dreamily. *I'm sleeping on white sheets.*

Dieter moved his hand over the sheets, feeling the clean coolness of the crisp laundered bedding. He inhaled deeply and took in Elsa's scent, still lingering from where she had lain beside him. Elsa had risen before dawn to get to work. Dieter had slept through that and felt he could sleep forever. Half asleep now, he could hardly believe he had made it back to Berlin yesterday. As he lay there, thoughts and images from his journey flooded his mind. He knew from bitter experience that there was nothing he could do but let the memories play out and torment him. There were so many of them, and he had seen so many horrible things. The luxury of the clean sheets and warm bed faded, and Dieter shivered with the memory of the freezing winds on the Polish plain.

On the retreat to Breslau last month, Dieter and his men had been constantly fighting, marching or digging in. They had made it to the city of Breslau, by then declared "Fortress Breslau" by the *Führer.* The local Nazi party leader, *Gaulieter* Hanke, put troops and civilians to work digging trenches, tank traps and other fortifications. It was to be a fight to the death, a bulwark against Bolshevism at the border of the Reich. Or so the posters and radio broadcasts said. "Every House a Fortress!" Except for the fanatical SS troops, neither the Wehrmacht soldiers nor the civilians put to work on the fortifications looked ready for a last stand. They were gaunt, worn, and shabby, many wrapped in layers of rags for extra warmth. When the Brandenburg column first entered the Breslau area and passed the line of trenches and pillboxes under construction, they had been greeted by vacant stares from the workers. SS troops stood guard over them, and work continued unabated. They passed women, children and the elderly put to work digging anti-tank trenches out of the frozen earth. Pictures of Hitler adorned the sides of houses and barns, exhorting all Germans to resist to Russian onslaught. Trucks with loudspeakers rumbled by, music blaring out and slogans tumbling word over word into the frozen air. Nazi banners snapped blood red in the winter wind.

This was not what they had expected. The tired men looked at each other, their blank expressions masking their astonishment. Breslau was supposed to be their assembly area, a safe haven behind the lines where German forces were refitting for the upcoming fight. There was nothing here except desperation and resignation. The only fit troops were the well-equipped SS guards. The other soldiers appeared to be remnants of various units that had retreated into the Breslau defenses. The Brandenburg veterans knew that the pitiful defenses and the tired, cold, and ragged soldiers they passed would not last long.

Dieter had been marching next to Hans von Schierke. They stepped out of the line and watched as the men shuffled by. The wounded were in the middle of the column, some walking and the rest carried on litters.

"Hang on, boys," Dieter called out, "just a few kilometers to the railhead. There'll be doctors and warm food there." He watched as they passed by, giving words of encouragement and smiles.

Hans turned sideways and spoke quietly so the men would neither see the expression on his face nor hear his words. "How do you know what we'll find? This was supposed to be a fortress, and all that's in front of the city is a few ditches and spent troops!"

"We have orders," Dieter responded, patting his tunic pocket and feeling those folded, worn orders. "We were to let all German troops through our lines and fall back after them, holding off any Russian pursuit. We are then to pass through the Breslau lines of defense and assemble at the railhead on the south side of the city. We are to be transported to Berlin to be refitted as part of the General Reserve. We've done everything properly, and if there's a train here, by God, we're getting on it!"

The next group was Alois Schmidt and his Hiwis. Dieter fell in with them, saying to Hans, "Get to the end of the line. Make sure everyone makes it to the train. No stragglers, we're getting out of here as fast as we can." Von Schierke jogged down the line of men towards the rear guard at the tail of the column.

An hour later, Dieter could see the rail line they were to follow to the Breslau rail yards. The men grew anxious and excited, shedding their tiredness as the prospect of leaving the eastern front behind drew closer.

"Are we really going to Berlin, sir?" asked Schmidt, as eager faces gathered around him to once again hear and dream about their destination.

"Potsdam barracks, *Feldwebel.* Rest and refit, the orders say."

"Well, I'll be fit enough if I can rest for a month," said Schmidt, smiling at the men around him and winking, "and maybe rest with a nice *Fraulein* for a while!" The men burst out laughing, and Dieter laughed along at the little joke, praying at the same time that there would be a train waiting for them, with enough cars for all his men.

The rail lines soon lead into the main rail yard, which was ringed by anti-aircraft batteries. Work crews were busy repairing the rails from the last Russian air raid. Dieter ran up to the head of the column as it turned a corner around a large warehouse. He stopped in his tracks. There, across the yard alongside a loading dock, was a locomotive with ten freight cars, flanked by two passenger cars at each end.

Dieter directed his men to assemble by companies in the rail yard and moved toward the train. There were black-clad SS soldiers guarding it, grouped around small fires burning in steel drums. They looked suspiciously at Dieter as he passed by them, pointedly not offering a salute to the Wehrmacht officer. As he drew closer, he could see they wore the death head collar tab of concentration camp guards.

"Where is the officer in charge?" demanded Dieter of the nearest guard, who simply pointed towards a small shack at the end of the loading dock. At that point, Hans von Schierke trotted up to Dieter, announcing that everyone was in the assembly area. Together, they went into the shack. As Hans opened the door and they entered the room, a gust of cold wind blew in behind them. Papers flew off a desk next to a coal stove where an SS officer was stooped over, warming his hands.

"Shut the door, you oaf!" he yelled, turning in surprise at the newcomers. His clerk, the only other person in the single-room shack, scurried to pick up the papers. He turned and stood up straight, his black uniform immaculate and boots shining. He was clean-shaven except for a pencil thin mustache over even thinner pursed lips. He smelled of cologne.

Dieter and Hans gaped at him, and then exchanged looks. They hadn't realized how badly they looked, but the officer's remarkable appearance brought it home to them. Their faces were covered with stubble and their uniforms tattered. Hans wore a blanket as a cape over his winter coat, and Dieter wore a once-white camouflage smock over his. They were filthy, and definitely did not smell of cologne.

"Who the hell are you?" the officer challenged, "and shut that damn door!"

Dieter and Hans stood there, neither moving. Finally Dieter turned to Hans and nodded slightly. Hans kicked the door shut with a loud slam. "I am *Hauptmann* Dieter Neukirk, commanding the Brandenburg Division Special Rear-Guard Battlegroup," announced Dieter, giving the name of his force as listed on his orders, which he removed from his tunic.

"These orders from OKH dictate that once we completed our mission and enter the lines at Breslau, we are to have top priority for transport to Berlin. Our mission is complete; there are now no more German units east of Breslau. So, we are ready to depart on that train, immediately."

"What the hell do you think I am, a stationmaster? I don't give a rat's ass for your Wehrmacht orders. Now get out!"

"Who is in charge of this rail yard?" Hans inquired quietly as he looked around the room.

"No one. I am *Hauptsturmführer* Reinhart Egger. I am in command of this train, which carries valuable cargo. I am awaiting transit orders from SS headquarters in Berlin. This is the only train here and the last one, probably. Given the tactical situation, no further trains are expected. All rail personnel have been conscripted for the defense of Fortress Breslau."

"What is the valuable cargo, Egger? And when do you expect your orders?"

Egger did not reply so readily, and seemed uneasy. "It is priority war materials. We are from Auschwitz III. We had to evacuate before the Russians arrived."

"Auschwitz III?" Hans asked.

"Otherwise know as Auschwitz-Birkenau. A slave labor factory complex, actually. Quite large, about 25 square kilometers. We produced large quantities of artificial rubber as our main product."

"Is that what's in the cars?"

"No, our other products. Plus two cars for the guards."

"But when do you expect your orders?" Dieter could tell that Egger was reluctant to answer.

"I do not know. We were ordered here, with instructions to wait for our final destination within the Reich. That was ten days ago. Communications are somewhat difficult, and I expect to hear any time now." Egger grew more agitated, and his voice rose as he attempted to convey confidence that it was evident he did not feel.

Dieter turned to look out the window at the guards by the train.

"Where are the rest of your men?" he asked idly, "I see only about a dozen."

"On detached duty with *Sturmbannführer* Harder. He is in command of all SS combat troops in Fortress Breslau. I am to have them returned if I receive... when I receive my orders. I should not be surprised if you and your men are not also put into the defenses here."

"My orders are direct from OKH, and cannot be overruled by the SS or any *Gaulieter*." Dieter now understood Egger's uneasiness. "How long before you are put into the trenches yourself, *Hauptsturmführer*? I bet that pretty uniform has never seen the bottom of a muddy ditch."

"How dare you speak to a member of the SS like that! I..."

"Just wait a minute, Egger. I only meant to point out that you have a predicament. So do we." Hans took his friend's meaning immediately and asked the clerk who was nervously following the conversation, "Say friend, how about a smoke outside? All I've got are Russian cigarettes, but they're better than nothing!"

Egger nodded his agreement and the two officers were left alone.

"Now look, Egger, we both have a problem. I have transit orders and no train. You have a train but no orders. If things stay that way, we may all end up getting surrounded by the Russians here in Breslau. That means death or capture, and I can tell you one's as bad as the other."

Egger collapsed into his chair and buried his face in his hands. All of his initial officiousness now vanished. "I know, but what can I do? They seem to have forgotten us and I can't get any word through! The Russian bombings are getting worse, and soon we won't be able to repair the tracks anymore."

"Listen to me. I have valid orders. Take your men out on the train with me."

"But I'm responsible for the cargo! I can't leave any of it behind."

"You'll have to leave all of it behind. I have over nine hundred men, with some stretcher cases, which will take additional room. With your men, it will take the entire train."

Egger looked ashen, but Dieter knew he was just looking for a way out. He leaned in and spoke conspiratorially, "Doesn't it make sense to leave your cargo for the valiant defenders of Breslau? I know you would prefer to stay and fight, but you have your orders. At least leave something behind for Harder."

Egger looked up and was about to speak when they heard shouting outside. Dieter rushed out of the shack and saw several men pulling Schmidt and an SS soldier apart. There was a lot of yelling and pushing, and the other SS men, vastly outnumbered, had run towards the fight with their sub-machine guns leveled at the Brandenburgers.

"What is the meaning of this, *Feldwebel*?" Dieter barked.

"Sir," said the SS man quickly, addressing Egger who was several steps behind Dieter, "they have Russian scum in German uniform! I heard them talking to this one. They should be shot!"

"These are our Hiwis," answered Dieter, noting that the crowding Brandenburgers had absorbed the Russian volunteers. "We have over 200 anti-Stalin volunteers, and they're damn good soldiers."

"We will settle the question of these sub-human Slavs later. Attention!" Egger snapped out orders to his men. "You six, assist this officer in the unloading of the train. You other men come with me. We will visit *Sturmbannführer* Harder and see about the release of our men," he paused and looked at Dieter slyly, "now that we have our transit orders".

Egger sent for his staff car. As it pulled up, he told Dieter that the locomotive crew was with his other men. Harder had kept them as insurance that he would not make any unauthorized moves. It would take them some time to get the steam up, but if Dieter's men got the train unloaded quickly, they could be ready to leave before nightfall and the now usual evening bombing raid. As he spoke, Hans strolled up to them.

"Now, *Hauptmann*," Egger concluded, "if you will accompany me to see Harder and show him your, I mean our orders…"

"*Herr Hauptmann*," Hans broke in, much more formally than he ever spoke to Dieter, regardless of their difference in rank, "do you not keep a copy of your orders for safekeeping? Perhaps it would be best to give those to the *Hauptsturmführer* for him to leave in case of any question."

"Yes, excellent idea, Schierke." The orders had been so valuable that Dieter had kept a copy in a waterproof wrapping inside his pack. He withdrew the orders and wrote on them, indicating that these orders included Egger and his men. He had no authority to do so, but he thought it might help.

"Here you go, Egger. It's probably best for you to deal with the SS commander yourself."

"Yes, I suppose so…" Egger answered reluctantly. Slightly bewildered, but now committed, he and his escort drove off.

"Now what was that all about, Hans?"

"Two things. First, my new friend told me that Egger had lost all his men to Harder, and only got those twelve back by delivering a platoon of Luftwaffe ground crew to him. They had orders to report to a new airfield, but Egger struck a deal with Harder and destroyed their papers. He might've turned you over, since you and he probably cooked up something illegal in his office."

Dieter nodded his head. "Smart thinking. Thanks. What's the other reason?"

"Do you know what's on this train?"

"No, just some products from that labor camp."

Hans looked around to see where the other guards were. "Come with me." He guided Dieter up into one of the passenger cars, where there was a small desk and file cabinet. Next to the desk hung a clipboard with sheets of paper, each headed "Manifest". There was one for each car, numbered one through ten. Dieter looked at the first sheet.

"Oh my God."

Car Number One contained 3,000 men's suits and 8,000 women's dresses, bundled and tied in lots of ten, by size.

Car Number Two contained 50 crates of men's eyeglasses and 70 of women's.

Car Number Three contained three tons of human hair.

Dieter stopped at the third sheet, unable, unwilling to know any more of these horrible details. His hands were shaking. He could barely put the clipboard back on its hook.

"These are his 'products', the industrial output of Auschwitz. Mostly Jews, some Russians, Gypsies and assorted political types. Egger's clerk was very detailed."

Dieter had not moved since he placed the clipboard back. He was still staring at the first sheet. "Hans," he finally spoke.

"Yes?"

"Is old Hermann Lenz still with us?"

Hans could not fathom what Dieter meant. "Yes, he's one of the original bunch from the Regiment. I saw him today at the end of the line. Why…"

"And the Lange brothers?"

"Yes, both of them are fine. But what…" Then Hans understood. Lenz had been the locomotive driver on their mission into Holland, so many years ago. The Lange brothers both had worked as boiler tenders on a steamship in the North Sea. Between them, they could operate the locomotive. Without Egger and his men.

"I'll get them." At a glance, understanding flowed between the two men. Hans ran out of the car, and Dieter followed, heading to the remaining six SS men.

"Say, boys," he said, approaching them in a comradely fashion, "you must have your gear somewhere. Why don't you fetch your stuff and then be back here in an hour or so? We'll start the unloading and you can help when you get back. The *Hauptsturmführer* said he wouldn't be back before nightfall."

Dieter watched them glance at each other. He knew what they were thinking – *this officer must be an idiot. We could have our kit together in five minutes, but we'll stretch that out until all the work is done!* Which is just what he wanted them to think. They thanked him and promised to be back quickly. He watched them head out of the yard and then swung into action. He directed men to unload each car, and the wounded to be put aboard the passenger cars.

As he walked to the head of the train, he saw piles of bundles, crates and bales stacked up on the siding. One man lost his grip and a large crate slipped to the ground and split open. Hundreds of dentures spilled out onto the ground. The men stopped their unloading and stared at the dentures littering the ground. "What the hell…" one of them said.

Dieter spun on his heel and screamed at them. "Get back to work, damn you! Get that thing unloaded now or I'll leave the lot of you here!" He felt fury rise up in his throat. His hand was on his holster and he wanted to shoot somebody. The problem was, he didn't know whom. The men resumed the unloading quickly, watching their commander carefully. One of them almost thought he heard him whisper, "I'm sorry" as he left.

In the locomotive cab, the two brothers were starting the coal fire in the tender and Lenz was going over the controls. Dieter climbed up and saw Hans helping to shovel the coal.

"Well, Hermann?"

"No problem, *Herr Hauptmann*. It's an old Polish model, but the basics are quite the same. Once we get a head of steam up, we'll be ready to roll. We've got plenty of water and coal."

"Good, Hermann, very good. I'm going to go back to the last passenger car and see what we have for rail line maps. We've still got to figure out which route to Berlin."

Within the hour, the train slowly pulled out of the yard, with all nine hundred men aboard. The last train from Breslau chugged past the stacked piles of so many lost lives like a thief in the night, quiet and guilty, the promise of life ahead and a crime behind them, unloaded like excess baggage.

I'm lucky to be here, Dieter told himself as he opened his eyes and took in Elsa's bedroom. *I could be fighting Russians in Breslau right now. Instead, Egger certainly is.* He searched himself for any remorse at leaving that man and his troops behind. There was none. *About time they got into a fight with someone who shoots back.*

He finally got up out of bed and looked out the window at the gray Berlin street below. *What next?*

Elsewhere in Berlin at the very moment, another face stared out of another window. The window was at Number 8 *Prinz Albrecht Strasse,*

Gestapo headquarters, and the face was that of Heinrich Himmler. With a sigh, he turned and spoke.

"As you know, your area of responsibility in Amt IV, the Polish General-Government, is no longer in our control, *Sturmbannführer* Hettstedt."

"Yes, *Reichsführer*," Otto Hettstedt replied, carefully listening for any comment or tone of voice that would indicate censure.

"At this date, with our areas of investigation limited to within the borders of the Reich, we find ourselves overstaffed in several offices. We also have been quite successful in eliminating many religious opponents. Therefore, *Sturmbannführer*, I am re-assigning you to a single, critically important operation."

Relief flooded through Hettstedt, quickly followed by fear. He had been hoping for a new assignment that would send him west, away from the approaching Russians. He had no desire to be captured in his SS uniform by the Russians. After his activities in occupied Poland, he was frantic to find a way to surrender to the British or Americans, or to simply disappear in the confusion when the end came. Now he was standing in front of one of the most powerful men in the Reich, awaiting a special assignment. This did not bode well for his plan to quietly disappear. Hettstedt steeled himself and hoped for the best.

"I am at your command, *Reichsführer*."

"Good," Himmler smiled slightly. "Very good." He picked up a folder and handed it to Hettstedt.

"You will serve as my personal liaison with a special OKH operation. Colonel Erich Remke of the OKH staff is in charge of a, shall we say, contingency plan if all else fails in defense of the Reich."

"Is this the Alpine Redoubt?" Hettstedt asked, referring to the rumors of a fortress retreat in the Alps.

"Nothing so fanciful, Hettstedt, although you may be surprised at the concept of this operation. We are obligated to provide certain SS resources in support of this task. Contact Colonel Remke and determine what his needs are. Report to me directly on a regular basis."

As Hettstedt saluted and left with the file, Himmler walked to a door leading to another inner office. He opened it and beckoned General Fegelin to enter.

"I think he will do quite nicely, my dear Fegelin."

"I agree, *Reichsführer*. A mediocre individual, but dutiful."

"Precisely why I chose him. This operation was an SS idea, until that...that upstart Remke stole it from us. Now we will show General Guderian a thing or two!" It was evident to Fegelin that Himmler still smarted from Guderian's comments about his performance as commander of Army Group Vistula. Seeing Himmler's temper was up, Fegelin wisely decided not to point out that the idea had actually been his.

"We will watch this Operation Gambit very carefully. If nothing comes of it, or if it is a disaster, then all we have lost is a single *Sturmbannführer*, and we have plenty of those. If it goes well, then we will step in and take command."

"*Reichsführer*, if this operation is necessary, it will mean the Reich is cut in half…" Fegelin let the words out without thinking. He didn't want to be thought of as defeatist, but he also didn't want Himmler to see how astounded he was at the thought of inter-service bickering when the Allies were about join forces.

"Yes, of course," Himmler said simply. "That's the whole point. Keep me apprised of what the *Führer* is told about the operation. That is all."

Later that afternoon, as a cold rain swept through Berlin, motorcycle couriers sped through the streets, bearing orders for a number of officers and men on leave. One courier pulled up in front of Elsa's apartment house, the address Dieter left when he took his leave. He tramped up the stairs, rainwater dripping from his slicker, and knocked on the apartment door.

"*Herr Hauptmann*? Orders from Zossen. Your are to report for detached duty with OKH immediately. I am to wait for you to gather your belongings and then transport you there."

Dieter was stunned. He was to have a week's leave, and he had spent only one night with Elsa. "What? How?" he stammered.

"I have a sidecar, *Herr Hauptmann*," the courier said, with an apologetic smile. "It's nasty out, but those are my orders."

"Damn! Who issued these orders anyway?" Dieter snapped as he opened the sheet and scanned the orders. His heart sunk when he saw who had issued them. Erich Remke.

Not only do I lose my leave and Elsa, I have to ride in a sidecar in the freezing rain because Remke wants me. How much worse can it get? Dieter knew he didn't want to know the answer to that. He gathered his few things, wrote a note to Elsa, and wearily followed the courier out into the soaking rain, wondering why Erich Remke wanted him.

CHAPTER TEN

4 March 1945
Ramersbach, Germany
Behind German Lines

"Captain Boyle…!" The whisper was insistent in Billy's ear. Frosted breath rose from the man tugging on his sleeve and steamed the lens of the binoculars Billy had been looking through.

"Captain, when can we get the hell outta here?"

"Shut up, Kowalski!" Billy whispered back. He desperately wanted to get out of there himself, but had kept his desire to run in check. He wiped the lens of the binoculars and ignored Kowalksi.

The two men had crawled forward to a small ridge, ahead of the rest of the ten-man patrol. For the last hour Billy had scanned the valley in front of them while Kowalski covered him with his Thompson submachine gun. An hour ago Kowalski had been alert and vigilant. Now he was huddled up against the cold, hugging his Thompson to his chest as if it could warm him.

Billy had taken the patrol out through the American lines after midnight. The men were from the Reconnaissance Platoon attached to First Army HQ, and this was not the first night patrol they had gone out on with the new Captain. Since Billy had arrived over a month ago, he had alternated between long stretches in the field and days at headquarters, analyzing intelligence data and writing his own reports to Colonel Harding in London. As soon as the First Army G2 chief had understood that Billy was not under his direct command, and seemingly not a hindrance to his own activities, he had assigned him a small cramped office and reluctantly allowed him use of the Recce Platoon as long as it did not "interfere with the defense of Headquarters".

The headquarters reconnaissance unit had been built up after the Battle of the Bulge, with fresh troops and veterans from other units. Some of the veterans came from specialized units in Italy that had been disbanded that winter, including a Ranger unit and the 1st Special Service Force, a combined U.S. and Canadian commando unit. These were tough and aggressive troops, who uniformly chafed at the notion of serving as bodyguards to HQ and other rear-area troops. The brass had been badly shaken by German commandos in U.S. uniforms running around behind their lines during the Bulge, and now many generals slept better at night knowing they had a substantial guard of well-armed veteran soldiers guarding them.

Billy had worked them up and down the line, going out on patrol to bring back prisoners and watch enemy night movements. Tonight, they had gone out to see what was happening east of Ramersbach, just a few kilometers from the Rhine River. There had been increased German patrol activity and a series of small, sharp probes against the American line in that sector. There was no such activity in other sectors, and Billy wanted to find out what was behind it. He hated the idea of being out here, but he overcame it when he remembered Eisenhower's heartfelt statement about not being surprised again.

Across from his vantage point, a dirt road ran along a low valley, and two German trucks and a staff car were pulled off to the side under the branches of a stand of tall fir trees. Drivers, a few officers, and guards stood nearby, stamping their feet in the cold, and smoking. When Billy had first seen them, he wondered what they were waiting for. After a few minutes, he heard small arms fire and grenade explosions in the distance, several ridges to their south. The firing alerted the Germans, who began to watch the approach from the direction of the firing. That was when Billy took Kowalski for a closer look. Sergeant Willie Kowalski was now tired, cold and bored, and was also getting on Billy's nerves.

"Listen, Kowalski, we're staying here until I figure out what those Jerries are doing…what's that?" Both men turned as they heard a noise behind them. Kowalski leveled his Thompson directly at the sound.

"Juniper."

"Well-water."

"Come on in," said Kowalski, satisfied at the exchange of passwords. A large form crawled towards the two men. Lt. Jeffrey Rose liked to select passwords that Germans would have a hard time pronouncing, making sure there were always a J or W in each word. It was attention to small details that had kept Rose alive in the Italian Campaign, where he started off as a private in the 1st SSF and ended up as an officer after a battlefield commission.

Rose slithered into the small depression, his six-foot frame and wide shoulders leaving little room left over.

"What's so fuckin' interesting up here, Boyle?" asked Rose. The lieutenant managed to adhere to military protocol back at headquarters, but at the front he acted as if they were all just privates. He often said that if he ever saw a general up at the front, he'd be glad to call him by his rank, but after two years of fighting, the opportunity had not presented itself.

Rose lifted his Springfield M1903A4 sniper rifle to the edge of the ridge and scanned the road opposite them through the telescope mount. Most of his men carried Thompson submachine guns, and as an officer he was expected to carry the light M1 .30 caliber carbine, as did Billy. Rose preferred the accuracy and distance the bolt action sniper rifle gave him, and he was an excellent shot. For "close work", he kept an M3 submachine gun strapped on his back. Known as the grease gun, the M3 was not terrifically accurate, but it was light and fully automatic, with a 30 round clip of .45 caliber ammo.

The Germans in their long greatcoats showed up well against the white snow, even on this cloudy night with only a partial moon. "I can drop the two officers from here, if you want." Rose looked at Billy, and then at the shivering Corporal. "Kowalski, head back to the rest of the squad. Keep a look out."

"OK, Rosie," said a grateful Kowalski, who was gone in a silent moment.

"Why is it OK for him to call you 'Rosie'? You near took my head off when I tried that," asked Billy.

"We don't know each other well enough. Kowalski and me have been in it since the Aleutians."

"I don't plan on being here that long. Did you hear the firing down the line?" Billy asked.

"Yeah, sounds like 5th Battalion got hit." Rose answered, not moving his eyes from the scope.

"I've got a feeling that those Jerries are waiting for their patrol to come in. Why? Why not let them walk all the way back? And why only two trucks and a car? Sounds like there was more men in the attack than that."

"Prisoners?"

"That's what I was thinking."

"We can get closer, over to those stacks of timber." Cut pine logs were stacked along the road, on the side closest to them. They could approach under cover and hide among the logs, barely 40 meters from the closest truck.

Billy nodded, and without a word the two men crawled over the edge of the ridge towards the road. As they drew closer, the sounds of the Germans around the trucks grew clearer. They were obviously not worried about revealing their position this far behind their own lines. Laughter, truck doors slamming, and cigarette smoke carried out to Billy and Lt. Rose. Suddenly, they heard a sharp "*Achtung!*" and froze in place. Billy's heart was pounding. If they had been seen out in the open, he could expect nothing but a hail of bullets within seconds.

"Go!" whispered Rose, "it's the patrol coming back."

Billy looked up and saw the Germans facing off to their right, looking toward the treeline at a line of figures. The staff car headlights flicked twice, signaling their location. The two men sprinted to the woodpile while the waiting Germans were distracted by the incoming patrol.

They caught their breath for a moment, before Rose lifted his head over the top of the woodpile. He tapped Billy's helmet, signaling him to take a look, at the same time slinging the sniper rifle and pulling out the grease gun.

It was a large patrol, almost a full company. They descended a small hill and came out on the road, about 150 meters from the trucks. The first group peeled off in the opposite direction, away from the trucks and towards a small village down the road. Billy and Rose glanced at each other, not expecting this turn of events. Then they saw the line of prisoners. It looked like eight or nine Americans, in single file in the middle of the road, flanked by Germans. This group turned toward the trucks. Following them, there was a rear guard and four Germans, each carrying his own weapon and several others- M1 Garands, carbines, and several Thompsons. Other Germans were carrying American rucksacks and ammo belts. One carried a bazooka.

Billy slumped back under the woodpile, thinking. *OK, prisoners I get. But why weapons? They have plenty, some better than ours. Why a bazooka, when they have the Panzerfaust? Why?*

Rose tapped him again. As Billy peered over the edge, Rose indicated the forward truck with a slight movement of his finger. The drivers and guards were throwing down bundles of something. Blankets? *Why?*

The last of the German troops came out of the woods, and also turned down the road to the village, leaving the prisoners and their escort approaching the trucks. Billy could see that most of these Germans were paratroops, by their distinctive helmets and camouflage smocks. The other troops that had turned down the road were all regular Wehrmacht. *Interesting.*

A tall, young paratroop officer ordered the POWs into a line in front of the trucks. With a quick gesture, he ordered the captured weapons loaded into one of the trucks. Then, in slow and halting English, he ordered the prisoners to remove their clothes and put on the clothes that had been dropped from the truck. This was greeted by confusion, with the Americans looking at each other in disbelief.

"Now!" shouted the officer, in a loud and clear voice. The muttering ceased and the men began taking off their overcoats, shirts and pants. The paratroopers pointed at their boots with their weapons, and the POWs soon got the idea. The clothing and boots were carefully gathered up, and several guards distributed the other clothing. Before handing the bundle to each prisoner, the guard reached over and removed his dogtags. The officer then collected these, as the POWs hurried into their new clothes. These were a variety of old and worn military items. Billy recognized a French greatcoat and saw some blue naval coats of an unidentified nationality. All had "US KG" stenciled on the back. *Kreigsgefangener.* Prisoner of War. These guys were prepared.

The remaining Wehrmacht troops took up guard positions on either side of the prisoners, and the paratroops jumped into the trucks, their officer joining the waiting officers in the staff car. The POWs and their guard marched off down the road, towards the village. The trucks and staff car sped off into the opposite direction.

Within minutes, the scene was empty. The line of marching troops vanished around a corner, and the sound of the vehicles vanished into the distance.

Rose stood up and stretched his legs. "Now what the fuck was that all about?"

"Something bad. Those paratroopers weren't here for prisoners, they only wanted the uniforms and weapons. They even had replacement clothing ready."

"Well, they're gone, but those POWs aren't that far away. With the rest of the squad…"

"No," Billy held his hand up. "We can't. We don't have enough strength to take them and get away. And, we can't let them know we know about this."

"Listen, you bastard, those are our guys being marched off down that road!"

"Don't you think I know that? But if we tangle with those guards, some of our guys are bound to get hit. Our job is to get this information back without the Jerries knowing about it."

"OK, OK. You're right." Rose gazed down the road, hating the thought of leaving those men in captivity. Billy stared at him, hating the idea that he had talked him out of it. They both headed back to the squad. Suddenly, Billy felt the cold deep into his bones.

It was dawn by the time they came back through the American lines. Billy had been silent the whole way back. The squad climbed into waiting trucks for the long ride back to headquarters. The men were tired, damp and cold. Billy pulled himself up into the back of the truck and wearily sat himself down.

Uniforms, weapons, dogtags. Another Bulge? More German commandos behind our lines?

It just didn't add up. Billy had run into a group of those English-speaking Germans during the Bulge. One or two spoke American-style English, but most spoke a formal British-style English or used British idioms.

They must've used up their best men in that operation, so how could they mount another?

Billy felt a gentle kick against the toe of his boot.

"Why so glum, chum?" asked Rose.

"It just doesn't make any sense. They don't have the strength to pull off another Bulge, and we probably wouldn't fall for that trick again anyway. Why go through all that effort, and what were those paratroopers all about?"

"I don't know, buddy. Not our problem right now. Those paras looked like they were getting out of Dodge pronto. They're tough motherfuckers, not like those Volkstrum old men and boys along most of the line."

The trucks finally pulled into the HQ bivouac area and pulled to a skidding halt in front of the mess tent.

"Come on Cap'n, let's get some chow. Some Joe will help."

Billy thought all the coffee in the First Army wouldn't help him figure out this one.

Powdered eggs and hot coffee did help Billy feel halfway human again. He walked over to the chateau that was currently serving as First Army headquarters, having housed a German corps headquarters in previous weeks. Billy was a sharp contrast to the clerks and officers filing into HQ in their clean and pressed uniforms, ready for a full day at the office. His boots were dirty and wet and his field jacket caked with dried mud. Officers carrying briefcases trotted up the main stairs as Billy lugged his fieldpack, weighed down with grenades, at his side.

In his small office, Billy leafed through intelligence estimates from First Army units and information from London. Nothing. He wrote out a memorandum requesting that Army or Corps intelligence officers inform him of any enemy actions in which prisoners or bodies were stripped of uniforms, weapons or dogtags. Half asleep now, he gave the memo to a clerk and told him to distribute it.

Feeling dog tired and dragging himself to his quarters, he told himself to remember to code the memo and transmit it to Colonel Harding at SHAEF in the morning. *Gotta remember*, he told himself as he flopped down on his cot and unlaced his boots. His feet were barely out of them as all thoughts of memos and codes left him and a deep sleep took over.

CHAPTER ELEVEN

10 March 1945
OKH Headquarters
Zossen, Germany

Sturmbannführer Otto Hettstedt drove down the gravel driveway, past the OKH headquarters building, toward the reserve barracks complex and the afternoon meeting. It bothered him greatly that he did not warrant a driver from the SS motor pool. As a representative of Himmler himself, he should be stepping out of full-length staff car, with an aide holding the door open and saluting. Instead, he steered the small sedan towards the barracks buildings and pulled alongside the other vehicles parked there. He looked at his watch and saw he was early, having left sooner than needed out of nervous haste. With a grunt he pulled himself out of the car, dragging his heavy briefcase behind him.

Hettstedt looked at the unfamiliar buildings. Three identical two-story long shapes, each painted a drab gray, stood before him. He chose the one on the right and entered the main door. It opened to a hallway, and noise and laughter spilled out from a door that was marked "Officer's Mess." Hettstedt looked around and decided someone in there might know where Colonel Remke was. He went in.

The room was small, smoke-filled, and crowded with junior officers. Most were eating their mid-day meal, some were drinking, and a tall *Leutnant* wearing the blue field uniform of the Luftwaffe parachute troops was playing a piano in the far corner. Loudly.

He was playing a jazz tune, his long-fingered hands rapidly dancing across the keys. Hettstedt puffed out his chest and weaved between the tables of officers, some of whom were tapping their feet in time to the music.

"How dare you play this degenerate, Negroid music, in a military establishment of all places! Don't you know this form of music has been outlawed?" Hettstedt imagined he cut a terrifying figure in his black boots, SS uniform and black leather trench coat.

The young *Leutnant* looked up with a barely suppressed laugh on his face. "Hey boys, who let the doorman in?" The room erupted in raucous laughter.

"I will put you on report for this!" raged Hettstedt, his voice shaking with fury as he turned to scan the room, "all of you. I'll see you in a penal battalion!"

Leutnant Herbert Benedikt, known as Benny to his friends after Benny Goodman, unfolded his six-foot three-inch frame from the piano bench. He stood very close to Hettstedt and looked down at him.

"Good, go ahead. I don't care. It can't be worse than this farce of an operation. What are you doing here? This area is restricted."

"I am to attend a meeting with Colonel Remke." Hettstedt said officiously, seeing that he was not intimidating this young officer. He tried a different tack. "Take me to him now."

Benedikt glance at his watch, shrugging his shoulders. "It's just about time to go. Follow me." Glancing at his fellow officers lounging around the tables, he smiled at them and said, "Don't drink all the beer, boys. I'll be back with my new friend, and he'll need a drink."

Everyone laughed, and Hettstedt suddenly felt very uneasy.

Leutnant Benedikt strode toward the last barracks building, which housed Colonel Remke and the staff overseeing Operation Gambit. He occasionally glanced to his side to see if the SS officer was keeping up. Hettstedt huffed and half-ran to keep up with the paratroop officer, whose half-smile never seemed to leave his lips.

Herbert Benedikt had joined the elite Luftwaffe parachute troops as soon as he was old enough. His dream had always been to jump into thin air and float to the ground. The idea had fascinated him, as had music in all its forms. He was as likely to play Beethoven or other approved composers as he was jazz or ragtime, but it appealed to his sense of humor that the SS officer and come in as he was in the middle of a jazz riff. His comrades had nicknamed him Benny because he liked big band music and often listened to the outlawed BBC broadcasts.

He had gotten out of the potentially dangerous situation with Hettstedt by bluffing and attacking, throwing his adversary off guard. It had worked today and it had worked in combat many times. He had been in training at the start of the war, but quickly became a combat veteran after drops in Crete and Sicily. He had fought on the ground in Italy and northwestern France, and had gone into the Battle of the Bulge leading a reinforced company of paratroopers riding on the backs of Tiger tanks.

That company was now half the size, but made up of hardened veterans, some of whom had been with Benedikt since the beginning. They had been assigned to Operation Gambit as part of the covering force, in support of the Russian and American uniformed elements. Benedikt thought the plan was crazy, and after surviving four years of combat, he did not relish the thought of ending the war by purposefully placing himself and his men right between the advancing Allied forces. He fervently hoped the plan would never need be put into operation. *Orders are orders,* he thought as he opened the door to the main barracks with a sigh, *but these are insane.* He had obeyed every order given him, but had done so with an open disdain and sarcasm so obvious he was sure Remke would have dismissed him by now. No such luck came his way. Remke cared only about results, not appearances, and Benedikt had delivered. He led Hettstedt through the outer offices, where clerks and a radio operator scurried through their duties.

Dieter Neukirk walked up to the wall map with a radio transcript in his hand. He pulled a red pencil from his pocket and drew arrows surrounding Küstrin and through Sagan in the east. With a blue pencil he marked the Rhine town of Remagen, which the Americans were approaching. He stepped back, trying to see the pattern that Remke saw developing, the pattern that had drawn him here, to work for Erich Remke once again.

Dieter had arrived at Zossen two weeks ago, soaked to the bone in a motorcycle sidecar and demanding an explanation. Remke greeted him warmly and arranged for dry clothes, warm food and drink. In Remke's office, settled in front of a wood stove, warming his chilled body with heat and schnapps, Dieter had listened as Remke spoke of fears for Germany and the coming retribution if the Russians overran the Fatherland. He outlined his plan, and described the meeting in the Reich Chancellery. In Remke's mind, it was divine Providence that had given him this vision, this plan, and placed him in the *Führer's* presence that day in order to secure his blessing.

Remke had flattered and cajoled Dieter. He needed him to head up the Russian uniformed detachment. He had known Dieter since 1939, knew and trusted him. Only Dieter could lead his Russian Hiwis against the Americans. They would follow Dieter into battle against any foe. Would Dieter follow him?

Of course. What else was there to do? Keep falling back as they had since 1943? They were running out of room on all sides. Remke dangled the idea of a sharp, bold move by a small group of men that would alter the course of the war. Dieter took the bait as if he were a starving animal, without thought or consideration.

Dieter found himself swept up in the idealism of the idea. He hadn't felt this way since early in the war, when he believed he was fighting for a Germany surrounded on all sides by enemies, a Germany that had to fight first, expand or die. He had ideals. Since then he had done many things and seen many worse. The war had become an endless retreat, a trail of death, a horror without an imaginable end. Now Remke offered a redemption of sorts, one in which Dieter would play a penultimate role in an audacious plan, reclaim his idealism, save his nation, and...Elsa.

Dieter had thrown himself into operational planning. It had given him a purpose, a sense of warped hope in the midst of defeat. He knew it was just a fantasy, but he dreamt of the Western Allies joining with his comrades to push the Russians back, back over the Oder River, back into the East, away from Germany and all he held dear.

Remke had worked even harder than Dieter these past weeks. The full force of his personality and intellect was focused on Gambit. Nothing else entered his life, nothing else concerned him, only Gambit consumed him. He went out on field exercises with the Hiwis and their German officers and non-coms. They practiced Russian tactics, re-learning the crude movements of their original army. He visited the airfields where his air support units were carefully camouflaged, and stocks of aviation fuel were hoarded. He worked out an extensive radio network for all units to communicate on, and scouted out roads and other approaches to the anticipated battle area.

Remke was now focused on outfitting his Russian and American forces. The Abwehr and the Brandenburgers had stocks of Russian uniforms and weapons from their eastern front operations, using Hiwis and Cossack formations. The openness of the eastern front lent itself to infiltration and raids on enemy rear areas, so there was little trouble in gathering the needed supplies. Men, uniforms and equipment were all in good order. With Dieter's Hiwis and German Russia-speaking Brandenburgers, plus other Hiwis and a group of Cossack volunteers, there were now two full battalions, over seven hundred men.

It was not the same with the American unit, which was the subject of today's meeting.

Hettstedt and Benedikt entered the office and walked to the conference table opposite the wall map. Colonel Remke sat at the head of the table, reading through the latest intelligence reports from the western front. He did not acknowledge them. Dieter turned from the map and sat to the right of the silent Remke. Benedikt nodded to Dieter with a smile as he took his seat. Hettstedt busied himself with his briefcase, removing a file and arranging it neatly in front of him on the table. "Colonel," he began, "I…"

Without looking up, Remke raised the flat of his hand toward Hettstedt, motioning him to be silent. He continued to read. Finishing the last page of the report, he closed the folder and stood. He leaned forward, hands placed on the table. His mouth was set in a grim frown and at his neck the Iron Cross swayed as he angled his body closer to the seated men. The room was silent.

"Gentlemen. The British and Americans are approaching the Rhine in several places. Montgomery is planning a major operation, but knowing him it will be quite some time before he is ready. The U.S. First Army is approaching Remagen as we speak, where the Ludendorf rail bridge has not yet been blown. Patton's Third Army is approaching the Rhine in the Mainz area. When the Rhine is crossed…"

"Never!" interrupted Hettstedt, "The *Führer* has decreed…"

"Shut up, you idiot! The *Führer* decreed that we would hold Stalingrad and that the Allies would be thrown into the sea in Normandy! Now they are all on German soil! Wake up!" Remke screamed these last words, slammed his hand down on the table, his face contorted in fury.

With only a deep breath showing the effort it took him to regain self-control, Remke continued as if nothing had happened.

"We must be operational by 15 March, less than two weeks from now. All units must be ready to move once the Americans cross the Rhine in force, or the Russians force the line at the Neisse River first, then the Spree."

Remke walked around to Dieter's side of the table and clapped his hand on his shoulder, as if anointing him with the familiar gesture. "I have given *Hauptmann* Neukirk the responsibility for outfitting the Russian-uniformed contingent of Special Detachment 200. Report on your readiness, *Hauptmann*."

"Colonel, we have two battalions organized under Russian infantry structure. There are 437 Hiwis, 112 Cossacks, and 104 Russian-speaking German officers, non-coms and enlisted ranks. A total of 753 men. All are outfitted in Russian uniforms and gear. The coats are somewhat of a mix, but that is the case anyway for most Russian infantry, expect for the Guards units which receive the newest and best equipment."

"Arms and ammunition?"

"We have sufficient stocks of Tokarev pistols for officers and non-coms. We have 61 operational DPM light machine guns, about one per squad. There are ample numbers of PPS-43 submachine guns, but we calculate only enough ammunition for a maximum of 500 to be issued. Therefore the two best marksmen in each squad will be issued Mosin-Nagant rifles, both to conserve ammunition and to give us some longer-range accuracy."

"Excellent. Now, *Sturmbannführer* Hettstedt, we have been eagerly awaiting a report on what the SS has to offer for the American side of our operation. To date, we have seen less than fifty English-speaking candidates, half of whom were unfit for various reasons. The equipment sent to us is laughable. Broken down Jeeps, bloodstained uniforms and a handful of weapons."

"Colonel, Panzer Brigade 150 under Colonel Skorzeny utilized all of our resources for operations behind American lines in the Ardennes Offensive. Our stocks of American equipment and personnel proficient in American English are completely exhausted." Hettstedt blurted this out in a rush, having carefully prepared his excuse and practiced it many times. He realized he was sweating as a trickle ran down his right temple.

"Where is Panzer Brigade 150 now?" demanded Remke.

"The formation sustained heavy losses," Hettstedt shrugged, pretending a nonchalance he did not possess, "and the survivors were drafted into Skorzeny's Waffen-SS *Kommando Abteilung*. This unit is currently committed to operations in East Prussia."

"So the SS is unwilling to provide the necessary resources in support of Operation Gambit, as required by the *Führer* Directive of 13 February?" Remke asked, with a raised eyebrow.

"Not unwilling!" Hettstedt stiffened in his seat. "Unable, Colonel."

"Unable does accurately describe your contribution to this effort, *Sturmbannführer*. That is why I detailed *Leutnant* Benedikt and his paratroop company to secure the required equipment."

Hettstedt looked astonished. "But...the Luftwaffe has no such supplies..."

"No, *Sturmbannführer*," Benedikt cut in, "but the *Amis* have plenty. Apparently it never occurred to the SS to go direct to the source. It is a little more difficult than arresting nuns, I'll admit..."

Dieter had to suppress a laugh, and even Remke seemed to be almost smiling behind his grim demeanor.

"This is outrageous!" Hettstedt rose violently from his seat and kicked back his chair. "Do you know who you're dealing with? I report directly to *Reichsführer* Himmler!"

"And I have a *Führer* Directive to carry out. Does Himmler routinely ignore the orders of the *Führer*?"

Hettstedt struggled to regain control, feeling trapped. He knew that the *Führer* Directive gave Remke vast powers, but only in regard to Operation Gambit. He must find a way out of this situation and these intolerable, disrespectful people. Remke's question hung in the air, dangerous, like a sharp blade that had to be grasped. He did so gently, careful not to injure himself.

"Of course not, Colonel. Tell me what you require."

Remke studied the suddenly quiet Hettstedt. He folded his arms and tapped his foot, then rubbed his chin in thought. Could he trust Hettstedt or had he pushed him too far?

"*Leutnant*, report on our current stocks and manpower for the American contingent."

"Colonel, we have 44 M1 Garand semiautomatic rifles, 17 Thompson submachine guns, 23 M1 .30 Carbines, two M1A1 Bazookas with six rockets each. Also two Browning Automatic Rifles. We have only one .30 Machine Gun, but we also have one 60mm M2 Mortar with six White Phosphorous rounds and 24 High Explosive rounds."

Benedikt checked his papers again, adding, "we also have eight .45 Automatic pistols. Sufficient ammunition for pistols and Thompsons; we should probably limit the Garands to 40 and the Carbines to 20 to insure adequate ammunition."

"Uniforms?"

"Over 80 full uniforms of all ranks, although we're a little short of officers. We even have dogtags."

"Current personnel?"

"Twenty-six English speaking enlisted men, although their skills vary, and none of them can be said to speak American style English. We have one *Feldwebel*, very experienced."

"Very well. *Leutnant*, start training this group on the machine gun, BARs, mortars and bazookas. They will be our Heavy Weapons platoon. Put the *Feldwebel* in command, and issue them the Carbines and most of the sidearms."

Remke turned to Hettstedt. "While we are training this group, *Sturmbannführer*, you must find us a minimum of 50 more English speakers. Don't worry about American style English- we only need to fool the Russians, not the Americans. And, get me some officers!"

With that, Remke turned on his heel and walked out of this office to check the latest radio intercepts.

"Gentleman, the meeting is concluded," said Dieter. "We have a final meeting with all staff on 14 March, 1600 hours. The Colonel must report to the *Führer* the next day."

Hettstedt gathered his papers with a frown on his face and walked away without a word. Benedikt was about to ask him if he wanted to have that drink now, but noticed his hands were shaking and thought better of it.

Hettstedt got into his car and slammed the door. He had been working at keeping himself under control since he left the conference table. He was so used to people quaking at the sight of his black SS uniform that he couldn't believe it when these soldiers ridiculed and ordered him about. For the Wehrmacht to treat a representative of Heinrich Himmler like this was unthinkable! Suddenly his frustration bubbled up and he pounded his fists against the steering wheel, a strangled scream hissing out between clenched teeth.

How could this be? How could his power be so useless here? He couldn't understand why these people didn't fear him, not even a lowly *Leutnant.* He had always counted on fear to get his way, and had never before been disappointed. From deep in his gut Hettstedt felt the same trembling rage that he known as a child, when the other boys had taunted him as he failed at all their games.

I'll show them. I'll show them!

It was that damned *Führer* Directive that caused all the problems. Without it, they would be the ones to tremble. He steadied himself and pulled the car out to begin the drive back to Berlin.

The more he thought it through, the more certain he became that Operation Gambit did have a serious chance of success. There was a kind of logic to it, and the forces Remke was putting together could do the trick. Certainly there was nothing to lose, and it had the added appeal of a ticket out of Berlin should...when... it became surrounded. For a variety of reasons, then, he should give Himmler a positive report. He needed Operation Gambit, even if it ultimately failed. In the confusion, he could head west and surrender to the Americans.

So, how to separate Remke and his men from Gambit and the Directive? Apparently he had the trust of the *Führer...*

Then it came to him. How to break that trust with the power of the SS. He would use his power to investigate enemies of the Reich. He would turn his attention to Remke and his officers. All he needed was one bad apple to show up, and it would cast suspicion on the whole bunch. He smiled and relaxed back into the seat as he envisioned Remke and especially that damned Benedikt being led into the cellar prison cells at Number 8 *Prinz Albrecht Strasse.*

Yes, he thought, *that would do quite nicely. And perhaps the command of Operation Gambit for me.*

CHAPTER TWELVE

14 March 1945
St. Ludwig's Hospital
Berlin, Germany

Dieter bounded up the steps of St. Ludwig's, his heart racing at the thought of seeing Elsa, if only for a few moments. He was on his way back to Zossen after meeting with a Signals Officer at the Home Army headquarters on *Bendler Strasse.* Operation Gambit needed to have radio frequency priority in its operational area once things started to happen. There was a string of codes and passwords that would pass between OKH, the Home Army and Special Detachment 200 to alert all participating units. These included the Luftwaffe support units under Operation Ritter and the ground support, Panzer Group Linz. It was all very complicated, but right now all Dieter could think about was stealing a few hours to see Elsa.

It had been three weeks since he had been torn from her side, yet so much had happened it seemed like a lifetime ago. He had arrived exhausted, limping, and hollow-eyed, wearing a laundered but worn field uniform. Today, he was full of manic energy, wearing his best dress uniform, boots shined and peaked cap set at a jaunty angle on his head. He wore his Iron Cross and decorations, having told himself he needed to cut an impressive figure for the Home Army staff officers to take him seriously, a mere *Hauptmann.* But he knew he had planned all along to take this detour, whether there was time or not. His unbuttoned greatcoat billowed in the wind behind him, as he took the steps two at a time.

Inside the hospital, Sister Anneliese was expertly removing a cast from the left arm of Senor Antonio Joaquim Gonsaldes.

"Thank you, dear Sister," Senor Gonsaldes said with a sigh and a shake of his head, "I didn't think I could stand another minute."

"It has healed up nicely, Senor," Sister Anneliese said, holding the frail, white arm in her hands, moving it from the elbow. Senor Gonsaldes looked up at her with a grateful smile.

Antonio Joaquim Gonsaldes had been injured right in front of St. Ludwig's Hospital five weeks ago, in the most prosaic of accidents possible in wartime Berlin. He had slipped on the ice while crossing the street. Brought into the emergency ward, he was treated by Sister Anneliese for a simple fracture of his left tibia. The Sister took an immediate liking to the small, elderly gentleman, who was now the senior Portuguese Consul in Berlin. Senor Gonsaldes was Catholic, and an intensely religious man. He had come in once a week since his accident for a check-up, and to pray with Sister Anneliese.

The Ambassador and most of the embassy staff had already been evacuated to neutral Sweden, following instructions from their government. Gonsaldes had been instructed to remain behind with a few junior and household staff to insure that any Portuguese nationals remaining in the country could contact him for assistance.

"Sister Anneliese, you are a godsend to me, quite literally," Gonsaldes said. "Thank you for your kindness."

"Senor Gonsaldes," Sister Anneliese replied, pulling up a chair and seating herself next to the diplomat, "I have enjoyed our talks a great deal. Hearing about your homeland and your family has provided me with a pleasant rest from this war. The hills of Portugal sound warm and wonderful right now." Sister Anneliese knew by now that Gonsaldes' younger sister was a nun in neutral Portugal, and that he longed to return home after four years in wartime Berlin. She had indeed enjoyed their talks, and she found his religious convictions very deeply held, somewhat surprising for any government diplomat.

"Yes, spring is just coming to Braga," he said, referring to the city where his family came from. "But God has seen fit to place me here, where it seems like the end of the world. Sometimes I wonder why, Sister, and how will it all end?"

Sister Anneliese leaned forward and took his hand in hers. "Senor, it is in God's hands. What matters is how we conduct ourselves. What matters is our soul, not the outcome of battles."

"Yes, yes. But concern for the soul can be difficult when great evil surrounds you. Forgive me, Sister, but Hitler and the Nazis are barbarians, and I fear for your country when the Russians, especially the Russians, are…here." He weakly gestured with his hand, taking in the small room, the hospital, Berlin, everything.

"Whatever happens, Senor, I will know that my faith has sustained me, and the tests that God has placed before me have only given me the opportunity to serve Him more closely. God has tested my countrymen. Some choose to serve the Devil, others turned their heads, and some save their souls by doing what is right."

Senor Gonsaldes began to reply, then stopped. He suddenly understood that he and the Sister were about to move into dangerous territory. They had begun their friendship as a nun and a lonely Catholic man in a foreign city. Now, he saw that there might be more to Sister Anneliese than a simple nursing sister. He considered the situation, and wariness overcame him. He was, after all, a diplomat and duty bound to consider his country's interests above personal beliefs.

Gonsaldes narrowed his eyes and stared at Sister Anneliese. "God and country, Sister. How many oaths link those two entities, yet how often do they contradict each other?"

"I have contemplated that question myself. God and Caesar, yes?" Gonsaldes nodded his head in agreement, fascinated by what he was hearing and the calm thoughtfulness that emanated from the Sister.

"Well, I have learned two things," Sister Anneliese continued. "First, I render my soul only unto God. If any Caesar lays claim to your soul, then he contradicts God and does not deserve loyalty. Second, I have concluded that country is not the same thing as government. I come from Flensburg, a beautiful and small city on the Danish border, by the Baltic Sea. I see no contradiction between God and the country of my birth. How can the soil of Braga that bred you contradict God? How can you serve God and not serve your family and home?"

Gonsaldes bent his head and nodded slightly. He felt a wave of emotion sweep over him, and he thought of his own sister, praying in the convent in the hills above Braga. His first thought was relief that God had not chosen to test her as He had tested Sister Anneliese. Then, with a sudden shudder, he realized God had just tested him, as surely as He made the ice he had slipped on in front of this hospital. In his heart he knew that he was about to be asked a very important question, a question that could change his life. He knew he would not, could not, serve the Devil, but quite possibly he could turn his face and leave St. Ludwig's right now. He could return to his duties with his arm healed, and never need see Sister Anneliese again. No one would ever know- even he would never need know what form the test might take if he got up and walked out the door this very minute. He could thank the Sister for her time and care, and walk out into the street.

"Sister Anneliese," he asked, voice trembling and his eyes brimming with tears on the verge of falling, "how can I help you?"

"Dieter!" Elsa's cry of joy turned heads in the corridor near the main nurse's station. She had been walking down the hall writing on a clipboard, navigating around people and objects without looking up, an unconscious skill learned by anyone in a busy city hospital. Glancing up to see who was on duty, she immediately swiveled her head at the sight of the handsome, well-tailored Wehrmacht officer smiling at her. She ran to him, arms stretched wide.

"Dieter," she repeated, quietly, "you're back, you're back!" They stood in each other's arms for a few moments more, the doctors, nurses and patients flowing around them as if they were a rock in a flowing stream. Dieter almost couldn't bear to tell her.

"Just for an hour or so. I have to get back, Elsa. I have to leave you again. My God, I shouldn't have come at all…" He couldn't believe how wonderful it felt to see her again, and how horrible and wrong it felt to leave her again.

She pulled back just enough to look into his eyes. She could see him struggling with his emotions, and understood. She blinked her eyes and held back tears. *No need to break down now, plenty of time for that later.*

"If it's an hour then, let's make the most of it." She leaned close to whisper in his ear. "I have a little real coffee in my office, and sugar." She winked at him, took his hand and led him down the hall.

They sat holding hands, as the coffee brewed on a hotplate set up on a shelf under the wide window. Her office was small, but had room for two comfortable chairs by the window, with a view looking north over the city from the sixth floor.

"I'm sorry we don't have time to go back to my apartment, Dieter."

"Yes, me too. But I shouldn't even be here right now. Jost will be picking me up in less than an hour. We were supposed to go right back to Zossen with a report on our meetings here, but they ended a little early, so…"

"Zossen! I had no idea you were so close! Can you get away again?"

"I don't really know. No leave has been given to anyone. It's a top secret project."

"What are you doing, Dieter? Is it dangerous?"

"Elsa, right now being a civilian in Berlin is about the most dangerous job in Germany. Between the bombings now and the Russians later, anything could happen to you. Not to mention your other activities."

The last sentence was spoken in a whisper, and with a smile. Dieter was proud of the work Elsa did in helping the hidden Jews of Berlin, but scared for her at the same time. He wanted her safe, and part of him was irritated that she put herself at such risk when the Allies in the air and on the ground seemed dangerous enough without throwing the Gestapo into the mix.

"Dieter," she said, nudging him, "don't change the subject. Tell me what you're up to. If you don't, I'll get it out of Jost when he gets here."

Dieter was bursting with desire to tell her about Operation Gambit. He wanted her to know that finally he was working on a project that would help her, save her, keep her from ruin here in Berlin. He leaned closer. "You mustn't tell anyone about this…"

He told her the whole story, starting from the motorcycle courier right up to his latest round of meetings. He told her all about Remke and his vision for the operation, about the planning and the break-neck speed with which they were organizing all the resources at their command, about how he was beginning to see the outlines of what Remke had predicted and how it all might really come to pass as the Allies crossed into German territory.

He didn't stop as she poured the coffee. He told her about the hopeless defenders of Breslau, the women and old men digging anti-tank ditches in the freezing cold. He told her about the train. He told her about the contents, about removing them from the train to make room for his men, about pulling out of that station and seeing the debris of so many lives left behind.

"Elsa, I can't let the Russians win! Do you know what that will mean after all we've done to them, to the Jews...I won't let it happen! I can't bear the thought of not being able to protect you."

He had begun with enthusiasm and now he felt drained. Even the sweetened coffee didn't revive his spirits.

Elsa looked at him a long time, saying nothing, a blank look on her face. He watched her, waiting for a glimmer of hope in her eyes.

"That is the most monstrous thing I've ever heard. You must stop it."

"What? Elsa, it could save you and our country…"

"Save us? For what? How many more years of Hitler will your Operation Gambit buy us, Dieter? How much time will you add to the Thousand-Year-Reich? How many more of the pitifully few Jews left in Berlin will they round up with the time you'll buy them?"

Dieter just looked at her, open-mouthed. He had thought he was bringing good news, and now it was thrown back in his face.

"Think about what you're saying, Elsa. If the Russians get here before the British or Americans, they will destroy everything."

"Dieter, listen to me. The Nazis have already destroyed everything. Before the first bomb fell on Berlin, everything was already rotten. They've not only destroyed lives, they've ruined the soul of this country. Too many people have let them have their way. There's a reason why there will be retribution, Dieter. Don't delay it. It will come sooner or later. Better that it come sooner, before every innocent person in Germany is killed."

Dieter slumped back into his chair and stared down into the coffee grounds in his cup. All of a sudden he felt worn out and exhausted. Only the thought that he was engaged in some good, instead of in endless fighting and withdrawals, had kept him going the past weeks. Only the thought of saving Elsa had sustained him. Now she rejected his salvation, and accused him of serving only to prolong the suffering. In a tiny place deep in his soul, he knew she was right, but the voice was too small, the denial too great, to say so. Instead, it came out as a powerless, complaining and petulant voice.

"But Elsa, even if I wanted to, how could I stop it? I'm only one man."

Elsa stood and looked out the window. She pointed to a bombed-out building less than a block away from the hospital. "Dieter, do you know what that building is?" Dieter rose morosely and stood beside her.

"No, I don't."

"It's the New Synagogue. Or was. It was built in the mid 1800s and called the New Synagogue because it was the first synagogue that was allowed to be constructed facing the street."

"Fascinating, Elsa, now what…"

"The Prussian government issued a proclamation granting the New Synagogue the right to exist, without harassment, forever."

"Forever?" Dieter grunted with a cynical laugh.

"Yes, forever. It became a symbol of what a cosmopolitan city Berlin was during the last century."

"That's an interesting story, but what does it have to do with me?"

"In 1938, during the Night of Broken Glass, the Nazis destroyed synagogues and Jewish businesses all over Germany. They were about to do the same to the New Synagogue when a single policeman stopped them. He stood in front of that building, holding a copy of the Prussian proclamation, and refused to stand aside. One man, holding a piece of paper, stopped them. One honorable man stopped a crowd of Nazi thugs."

She turned away from the window, unable to look at the bombed-out rubble any more. "The New Synagogue stood unharmed until 1943, when it was hit in an American bombing raid."

Elsa was drained. The stress and strain they were both under showed in the tension between them. At this moment, they didn't have each other. Their own hopes and fears for the future separated them. The room was silent. Dieter stared at the floor, until a single teardrop spattered on Elsa's shoe. He looked up and saw her cheeks covered with tears. He stood, reached for her. They embraced in a silent, desperate hug. They encompassed each other, her moist cheek against his stiff collar. Time seemed to stand still.

Suddenly, the door burst open. Jost Brunner stood in the hall, his large frame heaving and out of breath.

"*Hauptmann!* We have to get back to Zossen now. The Americans have crossed the Rhine!"

Elsa sat her desk, her bent head held in her hands, tears drying on her cheeks. Dieter was gone in a flurry, back to some emergency brought on by the American crossing of the Rhine. Elsa hoped and prayed that he could be dissuaded from this insane plan, this Operation Gambit. She just wanted the war to end. She couldn't envision what it would be like, but she knew it couldn't be worse than this daily walk of the tightrope, with lives in her care. She just wanted the bombing to end, the Gestapo to go away, and Dieter in her arms. What broke her heart was knowing it was not going to be that simple.

There was a short knock on the door, and Sister Anneliese walked in with Senor Gonsaldes in tow. She stopped short as she saw the look on Elsa's face.

"My child! What's happened?"

"Dieter was here. He's gone now." Elsa looked to Sister Anneliese as she noticed the elderly distinguished man holding back behind her. Sister Anneliese gathered herself to the task at hand, meaning to return to Elsa's evident sorrow later. She put her arm around Gonsaldes, pulling him into the room as she shut the door behind them.

"Elsa Klein, this is Senor Antonio Joaquim Gonsaldes, senior Consul of the Portuguese Embassy." Gonsaldes bowed toward Elsa, a conspiratorial smile playing across his face.

"*Senorita* Klein, I have come here in regard to two Portuguese nationals in the employ of the hospital. It is time to evacuate them to Portugal before Berlin becomes surrounded. I will return tomorrow morning with the exit visas, and escort them personally to the airport."

"Who…?" Elsa was confused and surprised.

"Carlita and Consuela DiGama," Sister Anneliese said proudly, "our Portuguese twins!"

"Leah and Sarah?" whispered Elsa. The two young girls had been hidden within St. Ludwig's for weeks as Elsa searched for a way to get them out of Berlin. This was unbelievable luck. She rose from her desk and walked up to Gonsaldes.

"Senor Gonsaldes, I don't know where you came from, but God bless you."

Senor Gonsaldes smiled, and blushed. “God indeed has blessed me today, ladies. I shall return as soon as I have the documents prepared.”

CHAPTER THIRTEEN

17 March 1945
First Army Forward POW Camp
Mayen, Germany

Captain Billy Boyle walked along the barbed wire enclosure, mud sucking at his combat boots, with Lt. Jeff Rose beside him. Trailing them was a wiry, dark-haired corporal cradling a shotgun in his arms. German POWs looked at them from behind the enclosure, a mixture of defeat and bravado showing on their faces. In most cases, especially with the younger ones, defeat won out. Except for the occasional tough veteran, they looked played out and forlorn in their uniforms stripped of belts, helmets, and weapons. Soldiers in captivity looked different, Billy thought. There was something pathetic about the clothing when you took away the equipment and military hardware that hung off a combat soldier. All that was left, especially in winter, was a bundled scarecrow with wide, hollow eyes staring out from under a cap or rags wrapped around head and face.

Billy scanned the crowded enclosure, feeling pity and fear. He couldn't imagine himself caged like that. Rose looked indifferent, both towards the POWs and the biting cold wind that blew around them and was beginning to freeze the muddy track they walked on. Corporal Levi Mandelbaum looked out over the German prisoners with undisguised hatred and contempt. First Army division G-2 had informed Billy that a senior SS officer that had been taken prisoner and was being forwarded to this main POW clearinghouse. He hoped that the man would have some new information about the existence of the elusive Alpine Redoubt SHAEF was still bugging him about.

"There's that SS fucker," Mandelbaum growled, pointing out an officer with the barrel of his Winchester Model 97 Trench Gun. The POWs nearest the fence dove for the ground as he did so, revealing the leather-coated form of an SS *Brigadeführer.* He stood out in sharp contrast to the gray-green and muddy uniforms around him. His black trench coat and uniform looked as if he were about to go on parade. Mandelbaum uttered a sharp laugh.

Billy signaled to one of the MPs at the main gate. The SS officer was released into his custody for interrogation. As he was brought out, Billy could see that his appearance was not as immaculate as it first appeared. He looked like he had lived in his uniform for several days and there was mud splattered over his boots and the back of his coat. His eyes were nervous, darting about and wide with terror as the MP grabbed him by the collar and threw him towards Billy and his group. He slipped and fell sideways in the mud, falling at their feet, his right arm nearly buried in thick cold mud. Corporal Mandelbaum stepped forward, and with a casual smile, lowered the barrel of the pump-action shotgun to the SS officer's nose.

"Guten Tag, Schwienhund. Ich bin ein Jüde."

Rose gave the officer a sharp kick in the side to get him up. With the shotgun prodding him in the back, the group led him away from the other POWs. Billy could see that his face was white, and sweat ran down his temples even as his frosted breath played out in rapid, shallow breaths. He was now half covered in mud, any arrogance remaining after his capture gone and replaced by primal fear.

Perfect, thought Billy, *just perfect.* Billy was a skilled interrogator, and he liked his subjects off-balance, their defenses down.

They led the *Brigadeführer* away from the POW enclosure, to a large stone and timber barn that was currently serving as Billy's forward post and the billet for the First Army's HQ Recce platoon. Jeeps with mounted .30 caliber machine guns and halftracks were pulled up in front of the barn. Several men were repairing the engine of one halftrack, and others were grouped around a small fire.

"Lookee here boys, real live SS brass!"

Catcalls and open scorn were heaped upon the *Brigadeführer* as they marched him through the group of men, and into the barn. It was dark inside, and Billy halted as they took a moment to allow their eyes to get used to the relative darkness.

"Down here," motioned Billy. They turned into a large stall that had been turned into an interrogation room. The barn was built into the side of a hill, so there was no window except for a small rectangle of light six feet up on the wall facing the door. The walls were stone and the floor hardpacked dirt. Billy walked over to a small table and sat on a wooden chair. A rough stool faced the table. Corporal Mandelbaum pushed the officer toward it with the barrel of his shotgun.

"*Setzt dich.*"

"I speak English." The *Brigadeführer* sat down, looking straight at Billy, taking in his Captain's bars. "I prefer to speak directly to the highest ranking officer present."

"What you prefer, *Brigadeführer*, is of no consequence here. I also speak German, as does the Corporal here. For the sake of Lt. Rose, we will proceed in English. I happen to be the highest ranking officer present. Now, what is your name?"

"Manfred Dichter, SS *Brigadeführer*, Stuttgart."

"Well, Manfred, we don't often see SS bureaucrats up on the front lines with the average *Landsers*. Very commendable. What were you doing on the road south of Remagen?"

"I have given you my name, rank, and duty station. Nothing else is required."

Corporal Mandelbaum had stepped forward as if to join Billy. As he passed Dichter, he pulled back and slammed the butt of his shotgun sharply against Dichter's cheekbone. Dichter's head snapped and he howled in pain. Mandelbaum moved on as if nothing happened. Billy took no notice.

"It is against the Geneva Convention…" Dichter moaned, cupping his hand around the blood dripping from the skin split over his cheekbone, his left eye blackening already.

"Geneva's in Switzerland, Manfred. You're in here with us." Billy went quiet, holding eye contact with Dichter and letting the meaning of both the sudden violence and his words sink in.

"Please, I have never harmed anyone…" Dichter's voice wavered and he looked as if he were about to cry. "I am not really a soldier…"

He stopped and his eyes widened in terror as he watched Mandelbaum sling his shotgun and pull a switchblade knife from his field jacket pocket. He pressed the handle and a bright gleaming blade snapped out, the *snick* sound loud and sharp in the small room. Mandelbaum ran his finger down the blade, checking its sharpness. Dichter pulled his face back, as if a fraction of an inch distance from the threatening blade would make a difference.

"Manfred," Billy said calmly, leaning back and locking his fingers behind his neck, "one of the many virtues I lack is patience. I can't stand a long drawn out interrogation. So here is the only deal you'll get from us. Let's have a nice little chat, here, just us. You tell us what we want to know, and we won't hurt you anymore. When we're done, we'll bring you back to the POW cage and tell the guards in earshot of your buddies that we couldn't get anything out of you. You'll have that cut to show how we beat on you, and you can tell them what a hero you were. Everyone wins."

"What if I decline?"

"Manfred, that would be very unwise. In that case, the Lieutenant and I would have to leave the room for a while. Corporal Mandelbaum would stay in here alone with you, for about half an hour, while we smoke some cigarettes and decide what to do next. By the way, Manfred, did you know the Corporal's family is Jewish, from Hannover? That's why he speaks such good German. He's wondering how many of his aunts and uncles he'll find alive when we get to Hannover. He'll probably want to talk to you about that in private if we have to leave the room."

Dichter was shaking. He looked at his bloody, trembling hand, then up at Corporal Mandelbaum, who was grinning widely as he pulled a whetstone from his pocket and began sharpening the switchblade.

"Yes, yes...I'll talk with you. Ask me anything. Just don't kill me, please."

They began the interrogation. Billy shook a cigarette from the green Lucky Strike pack and offered it to Dichter.

"Smoke?"

Dichter took it, the shaking in his hand still evident but not as dramatic, since Mandelbaum had closed up the switchblade. Billy lit both cigarettes.

"Now, Manfred, tell me why a high-ranking SS officer such as yourself was so near the front line."

"I was instructed to interview the commander of the Wehrmacht formations on the heights above Remagen as to the reason the bridge was not blown up in time. Orders direct from Berlin, from Himmler or perhaps the *Führer* himself. There was all hell to pay when the *Amis*...you, crossed the Rhine. Normally I would have sent a subordinate, but this was top priority, so I went myself. My driver became lost, since we had tried to take only back roads because of the *Jabos* – fighter planes. We had stopped to ask directions at a farmhouse when a single *Jabo* strafed our vehicle. The driver was killed and the car burned. I started to walk back, but evidently went the wrong way. An American patrol found me in the woods and took me prisoner."

"Did you want to be taken prisoner?"

"No! I...it didn't enter my mind at first. Then, in the woods, I began to wonder what would happen if I failed in my mission. The Wehrmacht commander at the Remagen bridge will certainly be shot. I didn't know what would happen to me. When the patrol found me, I was somewhat relieved."

"A real hero, huh?" Rose spoke up for the first time.

"I am only an office manager in Stuttgart. I have never been in the army. What good would I do at the front?" Dichter was beginning to whine, justifying himself to his captors.

"What other duties are you responsible for?"

"Mostly morale. We read letters from the soldiers at the front to their families, to be sure that no defeatist attitudes are communicated. We have a legal department that institutes field court martials in conjunction with the military police."

"Meaning you execute troops who aren't energetic enough in the defense of the Reich," said Billy, unable to hide his distaste even for purposes of the interrogation.

"Everything is done according to military law."

"How many soldiers have you found innocent?"

Dichter was quiet and simply stared at the ground. Billy leaned forward intently.

"Manfred, if a common *Landser* got separated from his unit and was found by you hiding in the woods, waiting to be captured, what would you do to him?"

"Well, the military police would…"

"I don't care about the *Kettenhunde!* What would happen to that soldier?" The German military police wore a metal identity tag around their neck, hung by a short chain. They were commonly known as Chain Dogs by the *Landser.*

"He…I don't know…" Dichter buried his face in his hands as a contained sob burst out of his throat.

"You'd have hung him from the nearest tree or telegraph pole, with a sign on his chest saying he was a traitor to the Reich. We've seen your work."

The room was quiet. Each of them looked at Dichter with a disdain he could feel, thick with disgust, filling him with shame. Not only was he the hated SS, he was also the enemy of the common soldier of every army, the rear area brass who sentenced youngsters to death. Rose spat on the ground, and said to Billy, "Time to slit this fucker's throat. He's not telling us anything."

"No!" Dichter raised his hands in protest. "No, please…" he blubbered, tears streaming down his face.

"Seems like you're holding back on us, Manfred," Billy said with a snarl. "I think you're more than an office manager or paperpusher."

"Paperpusher?" Dichter looked at him quizzically.

"Bureaucrat, clerk, whatever. I think you're probably more important than that. Who do you report to?"

Billy could see that Dichter was struggling with himself. At this point in the interrogation a stronger man would have called his bluff. He could sense Dichter weakening and making the calculation in his head. *If I tell them everything they won't hurt me anymore.*

"I worked in the Occupied Territories office, Amt IV-D, in Belgium in Counterintelligence. Since…our departure, I have been assigned to organize SS military police in this area to instill discipline in the forward troops. The *Führer* himself established my office of Flying Special Tribunal West as a mobile court to stiffen resistance. We have problems with deserters and shirkers…"

"So you dispense military justice? Personally?"

"Yes. I must report each week to Berlin how many enemies of the Reich we have found and dealt with."

Rose moved directly behind Dichter and spoke quietly, as if were controlling an intense anger.

"Two days ago, on patrol behind your lines, trying to scout a route around the Erpeler Ley above Remagen, we found three kids strung up." Rose glared at Dichter as he remembered the young German boys whose uniform sleeves were longer than their arms. "They had those signs in German on their chests. What'd they do?"

"They were Hitler Youth who were assigned to the bridge defense. The signs said 'I am a coward who deserted the *Führer*'. They ran off when the *Amis* came across the bridge."

"So you hung them?"

"Yes," answered Dichter indignantly. "As a warning to others. It is all quite legal."

Rose glared down at Dichter. Nobody said anything. Rose pulled the grease gun forward from where he had it slung around his back. He pulled the bolt forward with a metallic snap that caused Dichter to jump in his seat.

"No, please, I didn't do anything wrong…"

"How many times have you heard that yourself, you bastard?"

"Hold on!" Billy spoke out loudly with his hand raised up to halt Rose. He looked at Dichter carefully. Now the man was fully broken, shamed not only in front of his enemy, but also in his own eyes. He looked at the soft hands that signed so many death warrants, and felt his bile rise. Time to move onto the real agenda.

"Let's all calm down. It's not like Manfred was killing our boys, after all. Now, Manfred, if I like your answers from here on out, we won't return to this topic. OK, boys?"

Rose and Mandelbaum grunted their assent. Billy waited a few seconds.

"What do you know about the Alpine Redoubt?"

Billy could see the anguish on Dichter's face. At this point in the interrogation, he wanted to please his questioners more than anything, to give them what they wanted so they'd leave him alone. Billy could see he had nothing to give.

"*Ach*," Dichter said, frowning and wiping his tear-streaked face, "that is nothing more than propaganda from *Herr* Goebbels. We are working night and day to make sure enough men stay fighting on the eastern and western fronts. We couldn't possibly build such a Redoubt anywhere except in Goebbel's imagination."

Billy sighed inwardly, frustrated again in the quest for the Redoubt. He came up with a quick idea to try to rattle Dichter.

"Nice try, Manfred, but I happen to know that special operations have been conducted to obtain American uniforms and weapons in support of the Redoubt project. Probably for special units to steer us away from sensitive areas as we advance. Or to pull us into a trap?"

"Nonsense! Where do you get your intelligence? I've never heard of such a ludicrous idea."

Neither have I, thought Billy. *Oh well, worth a try.*

"You must be talking about that special OKH operation," Dichter said, searching his mind for something of value to tell the Americans.

Billy froze, trying to not show his excitement. He tossed the pack of Luckies to Dichter and used all his self-control to respond as if he couldn't care less.

"OKH operation?" he said, lighting his own cigarette and squinting through the smoke rising into his eyes. He leaned forward with his Zippo and lit Dichter's Lucky.

"Yes, something big from the Wehrmacht. A special operation run from HQ at Zossen. We were told to forward any American equipment or uniforms to an SS contact in Berlin. Of course, we had nothing, why would we? They never pressed the matter, so I just forgot about it, until you asked just now."

Billy thought long and hard, pulling on his Lucky Strike as if it might contain all the secrets of the world, if only he could inhale them deeply enough. *Berlin? SS? Wehrmacht?*

"Who was the Berlin contact?"

"Ah…let me think," Dichter replied, now feeling himself on firmer ground, giving the *Amis* what they wanted. "Hettstedt, Otto Hettstedt, a *Sturmbannführer*, I believe. Yes, Otto Hettstedt."

Dichter was quite pleased with himself, smiling up at Rose and Mandelbaum, nodding his head in agreement with himself.

"So Hettstedt never came looking for his equipment?"

"No, but just a few days ago he did send a request for any English-speaking soldiers we might have in our area. The memorandum was quite specific. American-style English was preferred, but British English was also desired. The troops were needed for a special operation, code-named...ah...no, it eludes me. I gave the orders for our military police teams to be on the lookout for any such soldiers, then left for Remagen yesterday."

"You can't remember the code name? Think, man!"

Dichter agonized, fear showing through. "No, I hardly paid any attention to it. No, sorry."

Billy sighed. "How did the request come through? By radio?"

"No, it was unusual in that it came by special courier."

Billy paced back and forth across the same room. He asked about other SS operations, about military defenses behind the Rhine, about civilian morale and anything else he could think of. It was useless. Except for this one enticing nugget of information, Dichter was worthless. Finally, he ended the interrogation.

"OK, Manfred," Billy sighed, feeling exhausted by the interrogation and the despicable Nazi officer, "we'll keep our bargain. You go back bruised and battered, but triumphant."

"I have kept my bargain. I request, Captain, that I be escorted back by an Aryan soldier." Dichter looked only at Billy, fearful of the menacing Corporal Mandelbaum at his side.

"Fuck you, Heinie," Rose said as he kicked out the stool from under Dichter, who fell on his rear with a thump. Rose then opened the stall door and yelled out, "Kowalski, up here on the double! Help Mandy take this Kraut back to the cage."

"Captain, you promised...," begged Dichter from the floor.

"Yep, and I keep my promises. These two men will escort you back to the POW cage. There will be no need to harm you unless you try to escape, and I doubt you've got the guts for that."

Kowalski entered the doorway, Thompson at the ready.

"Let's go, *Brigadeführer*," Mandelbaum said, kicking Dichter roughly until he got up. "The Captain says to bring you back to the cage alive and that's what I'm gonna do. If you wanna try anything though, just remember there's a Polack and a Jew with guns pointed at your back." Smiling and winking at Billy, Mandelbaum shoved Dichter out of the room. As they got to the door, Dichter held on to the doorframe and turned back to Billy.

"I just remembered, Captain! The code name, it has something to do with chess! Yes, chess, I'm certain." He smiled pathetically, hoping for some small measure of response. He got nothing more than a shove in the ribs.

Billy and Lt. Rose followed them out and watched them march Dichter back to the POW cage. The sun was just beginning to set and the muddy tracks were starting to freeze over, ice crystals showing in the ruts.

"Let's have a drink," Billy said, and went back into the barn. Their radio room, headquarters and living areas were all on the second floor of the barn in a single room, heated by an ancient wood stove. They walked over to a table near the stove, and Billy stared down at a map of the front along the Rhine. Rose bent down and pulled up a bottle of liberated Moselle wine, and filled up two mess tins.

"To the good cop," he offered in toast.

"To the bad cop, and to the really bad cop when he returns," responded Billy with a grin as they clanked mess tins. Both men drained their wine. Billy poured himself another.

"Damn, what a useless bastard," said Rose, wearily.

"I dunno, he almost came up with the code name at the last minute, but I don't think he really knew anything. Chess!"

"Could be a million things. But why do they want American gear? And English speakers? Can't be to fool us if they're gonna use Limey-accented guys."

"No, but maybe it's not for up close work like in the Bulge. I just don't get it. What good would a small unit in American uniforms do at this point anyway?" They drank and smoked in silence. Finally Mandelbaum returned.

"Well, Captain, he made it back safe and sound, just like you promised."

"Good work in there, Corporal. Didn't take him long to drop his drawers for us."

"Nope," said Mandelbaum with a satisfied grin as he grabbed the bottle of wine and took a long drink.

"You look like the cat that ate the canary," Billy said, "what are you up to? You got him back alright didn't you?"

"Yeah, Captain, I did. I know you want to keep your word to these bastards so when the others see you comin' they won't shit their pants. So I got him back fine, played up what a tough bastard he was and all that. Did just like you said."

"So?" Rose asked expectantly.

"Well, then I walked along the cage until I saw a six foot *Feldwebel* talking with his buddies. Gave them a few smokes and told them Dichter was one of those SS bastards that went out with the Chain Dogs and strung up their *Kameraden*. Never promised not to do that."

In the morning, the frozen body of SS *Brigadeführer* Manfred Dichter was found outside the POW barracks, his neck broken and a look of surprise and terror on his lifeless face.

CHAPTER FOURTEEN

24 March 1945
OKH Headquarters
Zossen, Germany

Erich Remke sat at his desk and rubbed his eyes. They were irritated and felt gritty from lack of sleep. Since the crossing of the Rhine at Remagen by the Americans, he had worked nearly non-stop. The surprise advance had caught the German high command unprepared, and Remke had gone into high gear to insure that Operation Gambit would be ready in case this was the first move in a major Allied offensive.

Two weeks later, Operation Gambit was ready to take to the field. It was now apparent that while the American seizure of the bridge at Remagen was a disaster, it was not the herald of a major campaign. It seemed more like an accident, an opportunistic plunge across a bridge no one had ever thought would be left standing. The Americans were pushing troops and tanks across, but they were not breaking out over open country. Their bridgehead was strong, but still a bridgehead, contained by German formations brought up quickly and the formidable obstacle of the Erpeler Ley, the heights above the city known by the Americans as Flak Hill.

Hitler's directive had ordered Remke to have Operation Gambit ready by 15 March. He was four days ahead of schedule, and about to walk into the conference room and conduct the final pre-operational briefing. He held his head in his hands and let out a tired sigh. Things had been happening at a rapid, even dizzying pace since he had joined Guderian's staff in January. Even then, he had seen that something drastic would need to be done to forestall the inevitable defeat that everyone around him refused to see or acknowledge. Working for Guderian had provided him access to Hitler, and his own audacity had won him command of the very operation he had conceived of to save the Reich, and give Erich Remke what he desired more than anything on earth.

Finally! Finally he held the power in his hands he had dreamt of! He would do it. He would wreck havoc on the Russians, using the Americans as his pawns. It was so perfect. They would pay for Anna, pay in blood and killing that would continue for as long as he could keep the war alive. He would have his revenge…images of Anna came into focus in his mind, happier days…

Remke balled his right hand into a fist and slammed it down on the desk, sending papers and pens flying. No! He could not think of those things now! Control! Control. He waited until his breathing returned to normal, and wiped a sliver of sweat from his brow. He could not let down his defenses, not until the last bullet was fired.

They were all waiting for him. He sat until he was certain he was calm and in control. Several minutes passed.

Remke stood up and smoothed the barely perceptible creases in his uniform. He checked the polish on his boots, gleaming black. His medals were in order, and he glanced down with pride at the DAK cuffband on his right arm. Afrika Korps survivors were a rare sight these days, and the cuffband was like a talisman to Remke. *If I made it this far, I can make it to the end,* he thought as he moved towards his office door and the officers waiting for the briefing.

"Attention!"

Feldwebel Jost Brunner was the first to catch sight of Remke entering the room. The officers surrounding the table had been talking in small groups, and instantly snapped to attention. The room went immediately quiet.

"At ease, gentlemen. Please be seated."

Officers settled into their chairs and junior aides and a few non-commissioned officers like Brunner stood against the wall behind their officers. Remke stood at the end of the table, taking in the group of men that made up Operation Gambit.

"We have not trained together as I would have liked. The current situation does not permit us the luxury of time to get to know each other. Units are more cohesive when they have trained together and built up camaraderie based on common experiences. Our mission must be our common experience."

Remke walked around the table and clapped Jost Brunner on the shoulder, and gestured toward Dieter. "I have served with these two Brandenburgers before, and I can assure you they and their men are the best." Remke smiled his best commanding officer's smile, letting the others know he was in a good mood, building up their spirits.

"The rest of you are also excellent officers, and each of you is responsible for a key part of Operation Gambit. I am confident you will all do your duty, and what we lack in familiarity we will make up for in experience. Right, *Hauptmann* Benedikt?" Remke set his smile directly upon the newly promoted Benedikt. Remke had secured the appointment just yesterday so Benedikt's rank would be appropriate to his mission. He couldn't afford for a mere *Leutnant* to be entrusted with a critical role in his plan.

"Yes, Colonel! We will all do our duty, even this brand-new *Hauptmann*." The men laughed and Remke knew they were in good spirits and well prepared.

"Very good! Now, report by section."

Dieter stiffened in his seat and began his report, "Section 1, *Herr* Colonel. Special Detachment 200, Russian-uniformed section. Two battalions, a total of 768 officers and men with the recent addition of several Russian-speaking Luftwaffe ground troops. We have sufficient Russian transport for the 8th Battalion, and Russian-marked German vehicles for the 9th. The 8th Battalion will be our lead formation, and the 9th will dismount once contact is made. We are ready to depart as soon as the order is given."

"Excellent! How are the Hiwis doing?"

"They are eager to fight, Colonel. They know they have little future with their former Soviet comrades."

"Your attack plans are finalized?"

"Yes sir. We will send out our scouts to make contact with the Americans. At first we will hold our fire, and wait for the *Amis* to report back that they've made contact. At the same time, we'll bring up the rest of our troops, move forward and attack. Normal procedures would be for the enemy to radio for senior officers to come forward. The men have been told to let any radio-equipped vehicles escape."

"Good, very good. We need senior officers to observe the attack so they will be believed. You must press the attack aggressively, but keep your forces together on a narrow front. The Americans must be convinced that this is a deliberate attack, not just a mistaken meeting engagement."

"Understood, Colonel. In the 1939 Polish campaign, we did have casualties when we met up with the Russian forces occupying eastern Poland at the Curzon line. We can be certain the Allies are concerned about something similar, so we know our attack must be ferocious in order not to appear to be just a mistake."

"Of course. Review your withdrawal plans."

"We will push forward until we either hit a main line of resistance, a headquarters area, or a counterattack. We will fall back slowly, making sure to maintain contact with the American forces. Our route will lead towards the Russian lines, where we will attempt to link up with Panzer Group Linz. Obviously, our dead will be left in place for the Americans to find."

Remke slowly nodded his head. Everything seemed ready and well planned with Dieter's group.

"Section 2, *Obersturmführer*?"

Obersturmführer Felix Strauch was in command of the American-uniformed section. His SS rank was just below Dieter and Benedikt's, equivalent to a First Lieutenant. After initially dragging his feet, *Sturmbannführer* Otto Hettstedt had come up with an excellent commander for the American group. Strauch had been with SS Kommando Otto Skorzeny during the Ardennes Offensive, wearing the uniform of an American MP, misdirecting traffic and spreading rumors behind the lines. His American-accented English was perfect, as a result of working in the Texas oilfields during the 1930s. Strauch was wounded in the retreat from the Ardennes and had just been released from the hospital a week earlier, then sent directly to Zossen.

"Colonel, we are in good shape with the Heavy Weapons Platoon. They are familiar with their weapons and *Feldwebel* Heinrichsohn has trained them well, including work on their English phrases. We have one American half-track that we're using as a command and radio vehicle."

"And the other platoon?"

"The Infantry Platoon is questionable. I wouldn't recommend using them to fool the *Amis*, but Russians shouldn't be a problem. We have 22 enlisted men and one officer. Plenty of standard infantry weapons and uniforms. No American vehicles except one Jeep. We've painted our trucks with the Allied white star for both platoons. Some of the men have only been with us a few days. I can bring them into the field, but their combat quality is not what it should be."

Remke walked along the table with his hands held tightly behind his back. Only the constant flexing of his clasped fingers betrayed the struggle he tried to hide from his men.

"We all know the purpose of our mission," Remke began, looking only at the floor as he walked up and down the length of the conference table. He stopped and turned to the large situation map tacked to an easel, running his hand along the current line of the front facing the Russians.

"With the resources at our disposal, we must bring the American and Russian forces into conflict. That conflict must spread rapidly, before either side realizes the other did not start it. We have gone to great trouble to outfit our American and Russian sections to fool the enemy when we attack them." He stood quietly for a moment, studying the map. Then he turned and looked Strauch straight in the eye.

"You force is small, *Obersturmführer.* Two platoons cannot hope to successfully attack the advancing Russians."

"Of course, Colonel. As you know, we plan to ambush their forward column, pull back, and hit them again when they move up."

"Your men are not ready for even such a simple fire and movement maneuver. They could become easily separated and the Russians wouldn't even notice a few scattered Americans."

Strauch began to reply, but Remke's grim face told him the matter was not up for discussion. He knew Remke was basically right. With a small and unready force, he could not hope to pull off a series of hit and run attacks. He looked up at Remke, understanding what was coming.

"*Obersturmführer*, once we deploy, you will place your infantry platoon in position astride the Russian advance. Dig in the Heavy Weapons Platoon behind them. There will be no pulling back. If they run, shoot them down. We need dead American bodies for the Russians to find." Remke waited for his words to sink in.

"No one is to be captured. We cannot afford a live German in American uniform to be held by the Russians. You must be certain every man from the Infantry Platoon you leave behind is dead, and that the Heavy Weapons Platoon is fully engaged. Use the machine gun, bazookas, and mortars to full effect. When you have exhausted that ammunition, you may pull back your remaining force before you are surrounded. Leave those weapons in place as further evidence of the American attack."

Benedikt looked at Strauch and Remke in surprise. "Are you saying that if the Russians don't kill our men, we do?"

"I am saying, *Hauptmann*, that our mission must succeed. If a man falls in battle and his sacrifice helps to save the Reich, what does it matter where the bullet came from? If you do not understand that, perhaps you are not ready for the responsibility that your promotion requires of you!"

Benedikt was confused and stung by the words. He could only stammer out, "I...I understand, Colonel."

"Good. Strauch, the last part of your order remains the same. If feasible, you will link up with Panzer Brigade Linz and attack the Russians jointly. It is only a slight chance that they will notice, but if they do, the news of German-American attack on Russian forces will be very useful. Do you understand your orders, *Obersturmführer*?"

"Precisely, Colonel."

"Excellent. Section 3?"

"Panzer Brigade Linz, Section 3 reporting, sir," said Benedikt, attempting to recover his composure. "I have a reinforced company of paratroopers, 127 enlisted men and officers. We received excellent reinforcements from other Luftwaffe formations, and we are armed with the latest version of the StuG 43 Assault Rifle. We also have an ample supply of the new *Panzerfaust* 150 model anti-tank weapon."

"And the Panzers from Lammersdorf?"

"Two of the biggest tanks I've ever seen, Colonel. There are two prototype models of the *Maus* super-heavy tank, 188 tons! They mount two guns, a 125mm and a 75mm, with front armor plate 240mm thick! They are unbelievable, monstrous. The Lammersdorf proving ground also has six *Jagdtiger* tank destroyers with the 128mm gun that they will let us have, along with about 50 *Panzergrenadiers*. We are also bringing along mechanics, spare parts, and recovery vehicles. We have excellent firepower, but these armored vehicles are slow and not very maneuverable. Once they are in position though, these eight armored vehicles will decimate anything in front of them. They have an effective range of 4,000 meters!"

"You were not able to secure any Tiger or King Tiger Panzers?" Remke questioned.

"No sir. I was told that the two *Maus* were worth a dozen Tigers, and to be thankful we got those and the *Jagdtigers*. Every other Panzer they had has been ordered up to the line in any case. I think Lammersdorf gave us the *Panzergrenadiers* just to be sure we took care of their last vehicles."

Remke smiled ruefully. He was glad Benedikt made even a half-hearted attempt at humor, given the decision he had just announced to sacrifice a platoon of men.

"How will your men be transported?"

"The *Panzergrenadiers* will ride on the Panzers, and they have two command halftracks, *Schwerer Panzerspähwagen* 231s with radios. I have trucks for my men, one Puma armored scout car, and four FLAK Panzer IV *Wirbelwinds* with quad 20mm anti-aircraft guns."

"Make sure the *Wirbelwinds* have as much ammunition as possible. You will need it against Allied aircraft, and they are also effective anti-personnel weapons. Section 4, report." Remke addressed a Luftwaffe officer, the newest addition to their group.

Flugkapitän Karl Wendel had been notified only days ago that he had been given command of Kommando Ritter, the air cover component of Operation Gambit. He had just scored his fifth aerial victory in his new jet-powered Me 262 against the endless Allied parade of Flying Fortress bombers. Wendel had commanded a flight of six Me 262s, the *Schwalbe*, or Swallow as the pilots called the new jet fighter. They had cut into the formations of American bombers, outrunning the fighter escort and ripping apart the Fortresses with their four 30mm cannon. The Me 262 was an elegant and formidable combat aircraft, and Wendel had initially been irate at being transferred to a ground support operation. During the last two days he had learned everything about Operation Gambit and his role in it. He was to command a flight of twelve *Schwalbe*, in addition to ten of the fast Arado AR 234B jet bombers. Wendel was astonished at the top secret nature of the operation, its potential implications, and the ruthless nature of Erich Remke. All he could do now was report.

"Ten Ar-234B jet bombers of *Kampfgeschwader* 76 have been transferred from Achmer to Dessau, effective 0900 today. *Jagdgeschwader* 92 with twelve Me 262 jet fighters will arrive at Dessau by 1400 today. We also have three JU-88C radar-equipped night fighters. Ground crews are already in place, in addition to new anti-aircraft positions around the Dessau airfield."

"Do you fully understand your role in the operation, *Flugkapitän*?"

"Absolutely. The fighters have a dual role. First, to provide air cover for the ground units of Panzer Brigade Linz, including the American and Russian-uniformed elements. Second, to protect the Arados if they are brought in to support *Hauptmann* Benedikt and his force. The night fighters will patrol the operational area and provide escort in case we mount a night bombing raid."

"It is critical that your pilots all understand what they must do. No matter what the opposition, the bombers must complete their mission if they are called in." Remke walked to the head of the table and sat down. Dieter watched him carefully and knew he was on the point of exhaustion. Instead of sitting ramrod straight as he normally did, Remke slouched back in the chair, rubbing his temples as he spoke.

"The most difficult part of this operation will be to channel the Americans and the Russians to where we want them. They must both come upon Sections 1 and 2 almost simultaneously. I have been given significant firepower on the ground and in the air to make sure that happens. The latest in Panzer and jet aircraft developments have been given to me to carry out this plan." Remke gathered himself together and shook off the fatigue. He leaned forward and looked at the men listening to him. He wanted them to feel as deeply as he did, to be as committed as he was.

"The Führer himself gave these orders, and directed these resources to us. The Reich is under terrible attack from the air and on the ground, yet he personally directed that Operation Gambit be given these powerful weapons. Our force is small yet potent. When we engage the enemy, we do not need to defeat him. We need only force his movements into a particular area, attack and deceive him, then vanish. Remember that. Now, for the most important Section. Section 5, Communications, report. "

Leutnant Gustav Stieff was the most junior officer present, and probably the oldest. He was overweight, graying at the temples, and unkempt in comparison with the other well-groomed officers. A thirty-year veteran of the German Army, he had fought in the trenches during the First World War, and then served in the Signals Section at Zossen after the war. He had risen to the senior non-commissioned rank of *Hauptfeldwebel*, or sergeant major in charge of maintaining all radio equipment at the OKH headquarters. Stieff had been very comfortable with his rank and position, happy to be senior to all other enlisted men at headquarters. He knew how to keep officers off his back so he could run his shop the way he wanted to.

When Remke was organizing his headquarters, the first thing he did was to interview Signals officers for his staff. He quickly found that the junior officers there relied on their *Hauptfeldwebel* for the operations of the Signals section. Within days, Gustav Stieff found himself promoted and transferred to Operation Gambit. He was not at all happy about this. Suddenly he was snatched from his comfortable billet where he had been senior to every other enlisted man, to a top-secret operation where he was junior to every other officer.

Whatever he felt about the change, he knew everything there was to know about radio operations, and knew most radio operators in the OKH command network. Remke put up with his grumbling because he knew he was invaluable to the operation. Stieff shuffled through the papers in front of him, clearly nervous in his first officer's briefing.

"*Leutnant* Stieff?"

"Ah, yes sir…mobile communications teams are in place with Sections 1, 2, and 3 as reported. We are linked into the Luftwaffe radio network thanks to the *Flugkapitän* here. Your field headquarters radio team is ready to deploy. We have two armored command vehicles, *KL Panzerbefelswagens*, with duplicate radio systems. We have sufficient trucks and fuel for the rest of the field staff, including those rejects we have for an HQ guard, along with one *Ostwind* 37mm anti-aircraft vehicle."

Remke had kept about 20 of the men rejected for service with the Russian or American contingents as his headquarters guard. They were not the best, but he knew he needed a few men to act as sentries and perhaps a rear guard. They would be very close to the fronts coming together, and he wished he had a reserve force at his disposal.

"I know you don't have much regard for my elite palace guard, *Leutnant*," Remke joked, "but I'm glad to hear you have everything in place. We will all be depending on you. Each section will need to communicate with each other, and with headquarters. That includes my mobile HQ, and our main HQ here at Zossen if we are out of action."

"Yes," Stieff replied as if he were explaining things to a slow child, which is how he viewed most officers. "We have frequencies assigned to each section, and they can communicate with each other and both headquarters units. If the field HQ is knocked out, the radio team here can coordinate and report to OKH and Berlin. We are linked in from our headquarters in this building to Exchange 500. We will have priority access to communicate anywhere within the Reich." Exchange 500 was the central nervous system of the German high command. Buried seventy feet below ground, it housed a vast radio, telephone and teleprinter network that connected military units with all government departments. In the early years of the war, it was said a U-Boat commander off New York City could talk to Luftwaffe pilot over Moscow by connecting through Exchange 500. With the diminishing borders of the Reich, the boast was no longer quite so impressive.

"Good work, Stieff. My apologies for making you an officer, but you've done well anyway!" Stieff grunted at the compliment, and looked around the table, glad his part was done.

One man remained silent at the conference table. At the very end, *Sturmbannführer* Otto Hettstedt sat quietly, taking notes as the meeting progressed. He had offered no comment and remained passive as the details of the plan were discussed.

"*Sturmbannführer* Hettstedt," Remke addressed the SS officer, "you have done well at least in supplying us with *Obersturmführer* Strauch and some of his men. Now I have one last duty for you to perform. You are to remain here at Zossen after we depart and oversee the radio team. We need a senior officer here to report to OKH and the Führer on the outcome if the field HQ is not operational."

Hettstedt looked up at Remke, showing no trace of the hatred he felt for him.

"Of course, Colonel. I would be honored. I have some duties in Berlin to complete, but I will be here at a moment's notice as soon as you depart." He even smiled.

"We leave here for Wittenberg on the Elbe River no later than 10 April, unless the tactical situation changes dramatically before then. Stay in touch with this headquarters." He turned to the rest of the officers.

"Prepare your men. Draw all the supplies you can carry. Once we reach Wittenberg, we will wait to deploy the Sections as the tactical situation develops."

"Colonel," Dieter asked, "what other German forces will be in the area?"

"As part of this plan, Twelfth Army is drawing its formations north, away from the American line. They will attack towards Berlin, serving to block Russian forces to our north, which will protect our flank. They are leaving light screening forces and some FLAK units in place. They do not know of Operation Gambit and will not be told. The security risk is too great."

"What shall we do it we meet up with them?" Dieter asked, hoping the answer would not be what he expected.

"If you can talk with them, fine. Have them pull out of the immediate area. If not, if they fire upon you, eliminate them. Do not be squeamish. We cannot let a few *Volkstrum* or Hitler Youth interfere with the success of this operation."

"Old men and boys?" Dieter said, startled at his own frank response.

"Yes, a few old men and boys now to save many more later. Dismissed."

Otto Hettstedt left immediately and headed for Berlin. Dieter and Benedikt walked out with Jost Brunner towards their barracks.

Once outside, the three men stopped to breathe in the cold air. They stood in silence as the feeble warmth of the sun fell on their faces. Icicles dripped from the roof of the concrete building behind them. They looked at one another, each knowing what the other was feeling and reluctant to voice it out loud. As if the question had been spoken, Benedikt asked, "What choice do we have?"

"Yes," replied Dieter thoughtfully, "what could one man do anyway? What difference can just one man make in this insane world?" Jost looked at him, surprised and hopeful at this hint of resistance.

Back in his office, Erich Remke fell onto the ancient leather couch and watched the flames dance in the fireplace. Remke felt glad for the warmth and relaxed, feeling there was nothing else that he could do, for the moment at least. His eyelids were heavy with sleep, and as he drifted off he saw faces, happy faces that would always be with him only in the twilight of sleep. His mother and father, great-aunt Zilla, and…Anna. Anna smiled wistfully, and in his dream they walked through the gardens of her family's neighboring estate in East Prussia. He saw himself, younger and idealistic, before the war and the killing. Anna telling him she would wait for him until the war was over. Anna smiling and weeping at the same time, telling him to keep himself safe for her. The letters between them, at first full of love and dreams. Slowly, her letters hinting at fear and danger. News of Russian bombers over East Prussia. Her parents sick and unable to be moved. His letters to her, pleading with her to leave before it was too late.

Then the dream turned dark, and Anna was no longer with him. He could see the Russians pouring over the estate. They had broadcast to the world their victorious crossing of the easternmost German border, land that including his family estate and Anna's. In his dream he searched for her amidst the Russian soldiers pouring through the house yelling "*Komm, Frau*". He could not stop them as they swarmed around him. He could not find Anna. He could only hear her screams, hear her calling his name as the Russians took turns with her. As they always did, her screams finally grew loud enough to wake him.

Remke awoke with a shudder and buried his head in his hands and wept.

CHAPTER FIFTEEN

30 March 1945
SS Headquarters
Berlin, Germany

Brigadeführer Hermann Fegelin let out a breath as he looked over the list of names on the single sheet of paper lying on top of his immaculately neat desk. He moved the paper slightly so it was aligned exactly in the center of his desk blotter. He shook his head slightly, as if amused, and looked up at *Sturmbannführer* Otto Hettstedt. Hettstedt squirmed in his seat, nervous at being called into the presence of the SS personal liaison to the *Führer.*

"My dear Hettstedt," Fegelin began, "what can you have been thinking?"

"I am only thinking about doing my duty…"

"Duty? These names that you are investigating, they are all part of a special operation ordered by the *Führer,* an operation you yourself are part of! I don't understand why you are investigating your own comrades…"

Fegelin picked up the sheet and read down the list. "Erich Remke, Dieter Neukirk, Herbert Benedikt, Hans Schierke, Jost Brunner, and several others."

"*Brigadeführer* Fegelin, these men are not proper National Socialist comrades. They disparage the SS constantly, and I've heard them make countless defeatist remarks. Colonel Remke has convinced the *Führer* of his plan, but I am not sure of his loyalty, or that of all his men."

"First, Hettstedt, you must understand that you do not possess the authority to have ordered this investigation. This is a highly sensitive and delicate matter. What if you do find one of these men to be disloyal, or to have a questionable racial background? What then?"

"Why arrest them, of course!"

"And you will tell the *Führer* that his personal operation will never be carried out? The last ditch effort to save the Reich?"

"I would think the *Führer* would be glad that the SS uncovered a plot against his plan, and would reward us with the command of the operation." With this said, Hettstedt leaned back in his chair, more at ease than he had been since he came into the office.

"Well, well, *Sturmbannführer*. Perhaps I have underestimated you. Indeed." Fegelin considered the situation carefully, weighing the benefit to his own position. He really had nothing to lose. "Continue the investigation, but take no action against any of these men. Report anything you find to me…and to *Reichsführer* Himmler, of course."

"Yes, *Brigadeführer!*"

"Be sure to keep this investigation quiet, Hettstedt. We can't afford to incur the wrath of the *Führer* before we have solid evidence. Now, you say Remke has actually put together a decent operation. Is he really ready, and is it feasible?"

"Yes, everything is in place. They plan on leaving Zossen for Wittenberg near the Elbe River in two days. As to feasibility, there is a chance, a slight chance, that it could all work. Remke has ordered me to remain at the communications center at Zossen after they take to the field."

"Very well. Proceed, and report back here with any results before they depart Zossen. If nothing develops, then go to Zossen and keep us updated from there. Dismissed."

Hettstedt walked out of Fegelin's office, feeling exhilarated at the turn of events and having been taken in the confidence of an intimate of the *Führer*. He also felt intense relief at the thought of getting out of Berlin. Remke's order posting him to Zossen was now confirmed by the SS command. It was only twenty kilometers south of the city, but it was well away from his own superiors. If things went badly, it would be easy to slip out under the pretext of bringing a message to Remke, or Neukirk, who would be closer to the American lines.

Hettstedt returned to his own office, flushed with self-importance and a vision of his own survival. He looked at the aides and clerks scurrying around the outer office, frantic with activity. Telephones, teletypes, and radios all emitted their own noises, the ringing, clacking, and static rising above the hum of voices engaged in the daily bureaucratic business of the SS. Hettstedt laughed inwardly. *Soon you all will be dead men, and I will be gone from here.*

"Heinz," Hettstedt barked at one of the clerks, "where are the Gestapo reports I asked for!"

"They are being typed up now, *Sturmbannführer.* The agents went through all Gestapo, SS and Wehrmacht files and pulled together everything we could find. That initial report is being prepared now, and there are two Gestapo agents conducting field interviews now."

"I want that report as soon as it's done, and I want a dozen Gestapo men out tracking down anyone connected with these men! Now!"

"But *Sturmbannführer...*"

"Do not contradict me!" By now all eyes in the office were on Hettstedt. The SS staff went about their business, but conversations stopped and glances were exchanged, everyone intrigued by the outburst. Otto Hettstedt had never been known as one to work long hours or demand reports ahead of time. "Obey this order instantly! If you or anyone else has any questions, they may be addressed to *Brigadeführer* Fegelin. By his order, this is a top priority investigation!"

"Yes sir!" The clerk jumped to his feet and stood at attention.

Better, thought Hettstedt, *much better.*

Not far from SS headquarters, across the Spree River, which ran through the city, a bored Gestapo agent ground out one of a countless number of cigarettes on the wet pavement. He was watching a building across the street from where he stood, in the doorway of a recently bombed out building. Behind him, wisps of smoke curled upwards from charred timbers. Rubble spilled out onto the street almost shoulder high, hiding him even further from pedestrians. He silently cursed the Allied bomber that dropped its load on this side of the street instead of the other. If only that building had been destroyed, he wouldn't be standing here now freezing and watching who went in and out.

On the ground floor of the building, there were several small shops, all closed now, repairing bomb damage to their fronts. In the center of the structure, a stairway led to the upper floors where there were offices and a few apartments. The top floors housed the offices of some of the few remaining neutral diplomatic staff left in Berlin. The Gestapo regularly watched these offices, noting German citizens who went in and investigating their backgrounds. The Gestapo knew the diplomatic staff by sight, and noted their movements as well, reporting any suspicious contacts outside of their offices.

Senor Antonio Joaquim Gonsaldes, Portuguese Consul, walked out of the building and stood for a moment, looking at the damage across the street as he pulled on his gloves. He adjusted his scarf against the cold, and walked off. The agent noted his time of departure, sighed wearily, and lit another cigarette. He waved his hand forward, signaling another agent who had been seated in the hallway behind him.

"The old Portuguese man, probably going to that hospital again by the direction he took. Follow him and see if that's where he goes." The second agent left without a word, thankful to be moving in the damp cold.

Senor Gonsaldes walked directly to St. Ludwig's Hospital. He smiled when he saw Sister Anneliese at the nurse's station, his grin a message that everything was ready. She led him by the arm down a corridor and to Elsa's office. Neither of them noticed the man who entered just seconds later, and without taking his eyes off them, sat in a waiting room chair and pulled out a newspaper.

"Senor Gonsaldes, it is good to see you again," Elsa said, rising from her desk and kissing him on the cheek. "How is your arm?"

"Better, and getting stronger. But that is not why I am here, Senorita. Everything is prepared." Gonsaldes withdrew a packet from his inside coat pocket and laid it down on her desk. He opened it and shook out papers and two Portuguese passports.

"The DiGama sisters, Carlita and Consuela, were actually the daughters of our embassy gardener and his wife, another domestic. They were killed along with their mother in an unfortunate traffic accident in 1941. They were twelve and thirteen years old. I handled the return of the bodies to Portugal, but their passports remained in our files here."

"So these are not forgeries?" Elsa asked.

"No, except that I took the photos you gave me and replaced the originals with them. The passports clearly show that these children entered Germany with their parents in 1939, when they were ten and eleven years old. The ages match well with your two girls."

"God took those two unfortunate girls so he could save two others," Sister Anneliese whispered sadly.

"They are safe in heaven, Sister," Senor Gonsaldes replied, "now let us bring Leah and Sarah safely into Portugal."

"Are you leaving, Senor?"

"No, not quite yet. I will send my housekeeper and secretary home with the two girls. There are letters here showing that they were employed by the embassy as domestics after their mother was killed in an air raid in 1943."

"When will they leave?"

"Tonight. There is a Portuguese freighter docked in Hamburg. They will take a train out of Berlin this evening and reach Hamburg in the morning. The freighter leaves as soon as they get there. It will only wait until noon, so it must be now. It is supposed to snow tonight all across northern Germany, so hopefully the bombings will not be a problem." Gonsaldes felt excited and scared, but not nervous. He felt the danger, but he also felt more alive than he had in years.

"You've thought of everything, Senor!" Elsa said with feeling.

"Everything but yourself," Sister Anneliese said, "how will you get out?"

"My government has just ordered me to close down the consulate and return home. The staff departing is a natural first step. I am sending them out via the freighter because it will be less dangerous to board a train in Berlin for a destination within Germany. And once they are on board the ship, they are on neutral territory and cannot be touched. I will fly to Switzerland once I know they have boarded, and then onto Portugal, where I will await them."

"Forgive me asking, Senor Gonsaldes, but do you trust your staff?"

"I don't blame you for asking, but do not worry yourselves. My housekeeper is a family servant, as well as my personal secretary. They both live on my family estate and are trusted employees, almost part of the family."

"What will happen to the girls once they arrive in Portugal?" asked Elsa.

"I know several prominent Jewish families in Braga. There is a small community of Jews there, and I am sure one family will take them in. If not, my family will care for them until they are old enough themselves."

Sister Anneliese's eyes brimmed with tears as she folded her hands in prayer. "Bless you, Father, for sending this man to deliver your children." She looked up and saw Senor Gonsaldes beaming with pleasure and excitement and a tear trickling down Elsa's cheek. "Now enough of this bawling," she announced in her best head nurse tone, "we have work to do. Let's get those children ready!"

"My secretary and housekeeper will be here in the embassy car at 1700. We have just enough petrol left for a drive to the train station. The car has diplomatic license plates, so there should be no problem getting through. Now, I must go."

Gonsaldes looked at both of them sadly.

"I will not return here again. There is no reason to draw any suspicion to either of you should anything go wrong. After this war is over, if you are ever in need of any assistance, come to Barga and ask for the Gonsaldes family. You will not be turned away. God bless you."

Senor Gonsaldes left the hospital feeling an odd mixture of sadness and joy. He hated leaving those courageous women behind, but he also was uplifted at the thought of seeing his warm, beautiful homeland again. When the Foreign Office found out about the passports, he would certainly be fired. A minor disgrace, the loss of a pension, these were a small price to pay for the honor of doing God's work. Deep in thought, he never noticed the Gestapo agent trailing along behind him.

Later that afternoon, Senor Gonsaldes escorted his housekeeper down the stairs to the waiting embassy car. He shook hands with his secretary, a tall dark haired and mustachioed man in his late thirties.

"Take care of them, Pablo," Gonsaldes whispered as they held each other's grip. Pablo bowed his head, obedient and sad to be leaving the Senor behind. He gathered up the housekeeper's bags and stowed them in the trunk of the car. Gonsaldes embraced the stout woman and smiled at her. "Soon you will be home!"

He waved as the car pulled away from the curb, then turned and walked upstairs to his office, to await word on their safe arrival. It would be a long night.

Across the street, a new set of eyes had taken over the second shift. He noted the departure of the secretary and housekeeper. Nothing unexpected, many diplomatic personnel were leaving Berlin. It would all go into his report, as usual.

Senor Gonsaldes worked at his desk, going through his files. Most would be left in place, unimportant bureaucratic paperwork. He made two piles, one of sensitive documents that he would take down to the building's furnace room and burn. A smaller pile of documents, reports he had recently written on the state of the Reich government, morale, and military reports, he would take with him in the diplomatic pouch. The work consumed him, taking his mind off the time as he waited for the phone call.

The phone rang, surprising him as he sorted through a file on German industrial output. He lifted the heavy black receiver as it rang a second time.

"Hallo. Portuguese Consulate here."

"Excuse me, I am calling for *Herr* Fischer?"

"You must have the wrong number. This is Senor Gonsaldes, the Portuguese Consul."

"I am sorry…Goodbye." The line went dead. Gonsaldes put the receiver down with a smile. Pablo had asked for *Herr* Fischer, which meant that all was well, they were boarding the train with the girls. *Herr* Fuchs would have meant there was a problem and they were returning, *Herr* Hoffmann a more serious problem and they were leaving without the girls. No call at all would have meant disaster.

Gonsaldes continued to work, finishing near midnight. He lifted the box of files to be burned and carried it down to the basement. The coal fire was low, but hot. He opened the door and threw in the cardboard box. It blazed in the oven, and Gonsaldes felt warm at last. *In a few days at most, the sun over Braga will be warming me!*

Very tired now that his work was done, he pulled himself slowly up the stairs. He walked through his office to the small apartment he lived in. He walked to the window and watched the snow starting to fall. There was not a star visible in the sky. *Good, a safe journey and no death from the sky tonight.* He was glad for the fliers and the civilians. There had been enough death and destruction. The war was winding down, and somehow he found death even more offensive now that the end was almost here. He also admitted to himself, perhaps selfishly, that he would be glad to get an uninterrupted night's sleep. He left the connecting door to his office open, so he could hear the telephone or the door. He fell asleep within minutes.

Gonsaldes awoke at dawn, feeling very nervous. His heart was pounding. What if they didn't make it? The relief he had felt last night at their boarding the train was now gone, replaced by a fear that they wouldn't make it to the ship. So many things could go wrong. He went through the motions of washing and dressing, and ate a meager breakfast of bread and cheese. And waited.

The morning passed slowly, and Gonsaldes realized that he felt very lonely. He was the last of his countrymen in Germany. He bowed his head in prayer, begging for strength. And waited some more.

An hour later, there was a sharp knock at the door. It startled him, and as he got up he felt dizzy and sweat broke out on his forehead. He steadied himself for a moment, and the rapping on the door continued, while at the same time the person outside tried to open the door, which was locked.

"*Herr* Gonsaldes?"

"Yes, yes, I am coming." He shuffled to the door, unlocked and opened it. A young boy, in a messenger's uniform from the telegraph office, stood outside his door.

"Telegraph for *Herr* Gonsaldes, sign here."

He signed, and gave the boy a Mark as a tip. "Thank you, sir!" he said, smiling, as he raced off on his next delivery.

"No, young man, thank you!" Senor Gonsaldes said, "and thank God!" He read the telegram again to be sure.

TO: ANTONIO JOAQUIM GONSALDES, PORTUGUESE CONSUL, BERLIN
FROM: CAPTAIN MARTINO ALVEREZ, PORTUGUESE FREIGHTER LISBOA

FULL CARGO RECEIVED INTACT AND ON BOARD THIS MORNING. DEPARTING IMMEDIATELY.

ALVEREZ, 0930
14 MARCH 1945.

CHAPTER SIXTEEN

6 April 1945
First Army Headquarters
Spa, Belgium

There are some pleasures to Army life, thought Billy Boyle as he relaxed in the solarium of the chateau that served as General Hodge's headquarters for First Army. *But not for the GIs out there.* He shook his head ruefully as he looked out the window at the wet, cold, and gray landscape. He shivered as if he were still out there.

"More coffee, sir?"

Billy jumped in his seat, startled by the voice. He laid his hand palm down on the table to steady himself. He took a deep breath and answered, wishing the time would come when the slightest sound didn't send his heart racing.

"Yes, please."

The orderly poured a hot stream of delicious-smelling coffee from a silver serving pot into a fine china cup at Billy's table. The chateau's solarium served as the breakfast mess for senior First Army staff. Normally, a Captain would not be invited, but as a SHAEF officer and a known relative of Ike's, Billy was granted certain privileges. Class A uniform was required, but today Billy didn't mind. After a week at the front crawling through mud, spending nights on patrol, and days interrogating sullen POWs, he was glad to be back at HQ, with its comfortable beds and hot food. He had looked forward to wearing clean socks, polished dress shoes, and his London-tailored short Eisenhower jacket. He sipped his third cup of coffee, having just finished a fine breakfast of real eggs, bacon, and warm bread. There had been a time when he would have reveled in the luxury, as would any sane man who had been at the front. Today, he felt empty and guilty.

He had brought back the Recce Platoon with him for a rest of their own. They were billeted in a large farmhouse about a mile forward of HQ. They didn't have these comforts, but they were away from the front, dry, and had ample food. Drink, he was sure, they would find themselves.

Billy watched the sky clearing. It had rained all morning, but the clouds were breaking up now, and patches of sunlight were trying to break through. *Could be a beautiful spring day*, Billy thought. *Be nice for those poor slobs out on the line.* He sighed, drank some more coffee, and picked up a copy of Stars and Stripes from the table and leafed through it. The bridge at Remagen was big news, but Billy knew the engineers were racing against time to keep it from collapsing. He also knew something that the Stars and Stripes would never print, that Ike himself had ordered the Remagen bridgehead to be expanded no more than 10 miles, in order to save resources to support Montgomery's drive in the north. *Can't afford to upset Monty's big battle plans, just because we got across the Rhine before him!*

Billy read a while longer, glanced at his watch, and then reluctantly left his elegant surroundings, knowing he had a lot of work ahead of him. He was here to attend a meeting of all the First Army divisional G-2 officers at 1400 hours. Billy had to spend the morning going over the intelligence reports that had accumulated on his desk since he had been at the front. At the meeting, he would listen to each division's intelligence officer summarize his perception of the enemy's strength and intentions along his section of the front. For all the self-importance of the senior officers here and their self-assured air, Billy reminded himself that these were the same guys who missed the German build-up before the Bulge, right under their own noses. He doubted they would have anything new, but he would ask them again about Germans taking GI uniforms and weapons, and code names that had to do with chess. *Tough day at the office,* he thought.

Two hours later, Billy finished reading the last of the intelligence reports and SHAEF summaries. Nothing jumped out at him. No German commandos in GI uniforms reported anywhere, no special code names for operations of any sort. The Germans were fighting a down and dirty defensive battle along the Rhine, with little apparent resources for special operations. They contested every village and crossroads, sometimes with just a few troops with *Panzerfaust*, sometimes with a brutal counterattack. But nowhere could he find any evidence of even a hint of a subtler stratagem. Either no special commando operations were planned for this section of the front, or they were missing something completely.

Billy tossed the folder he was holding onto his desk, leaned back in his chair, and swung his legs up, stretching back and linking his hands behind his head. It was his favorite position for thinking. He stared at the situation map on the wall above him. To the north, Montgomery and his Commonwealth forces were planning a major offensive to cross the Rhine within a few days. In typical Montgomery fashion, it was an overblown affair with a huge artillery bombardment and parachute drops planned. Billy thought how the Germans could disrupt such an offensive. Knowing Montgomery as they did, the enemy could easily surmise he would conduct a major set-piece battle to cross the Rhine, whether he needed to or not. But there were few Americans participating, beyond the airborne units and Simpson's Ninth Army, which of course was limited to a minor supporting role. No, it didn't make sense.

Maybe a raid behind Allied lines? Germans in American uniforms were more likely to fool a bunch of Brits than Yanks. Even though Skorzeny's commandos dressed in American uniforms had caused a major panic during the Bulge, there were actually very few of them who could speak English like an American. Maybe the Jerries learned from that, and would use them next time against Montgomery himself? *Hhmmm.* Billy continued to stare at the map, lost in thought. He didn't hear someone enter the room behind him.

"Hard at work, Captain?"

Billy swiveled around in his seat and almost lost his balance as one of his boots caught a pile of files and sent the papers flying in every direction. He struggled to his feet and stood up in the midst of papers scattered on the floor. He groaned inwardly and tried to reply cheerfully, "Colonel Harding, sir, what a pleasant surprise!"

Colonel Samuel Harding dropped his briefcase on the floor, tossed his wet trench coat over Billy's chair and sat down on the only other chair in the room. "A surprise, I'm sure," Harding said with a half grin, "did I disturb your beauty sleep, Billy?"

"No sir," Billy chuckled, trying to show Harding he took it as a joke, although there had been a time when Harding would have kicked the chair out from under him if he found him like that at SHAEF. "I've been going over these reports before the G-2 meeting this afternoon, and just got to thinking about something I've been trying to figure out. What are you doing here, anyway?"

Harding pulled out a cigar from his tunic pocket, lit it slowly, and puffed a few times to get a good glow going. Only then did he look up at Billy. He seemed to be thinking how much to reveal.

"I've been up with Monty going over his Rhine crossing operation. You know how he is, lots of little details." He turned his attention back to his cigar.

"And you just happened to be in the neighborhood…"

"Well, any excuse to get out of the office. Nothing but rain and paperwork waiting for me back in London."

Billy relaxed and leaned against the desk, waiting for Harding to get to the point. He eyed his chair, now holding Harding's coat and a puddle of rainwater dripping off the waterproof material.

"It's raining here, too, Colonel."

"Knew I couldn't fool a trained detective, Billy." Harding leaned forward and hesitated before he lowered his voice. "Your reports have been great, you've done good work. We've gotten a good feel for the actual situation on the front lines, combining what you've sent us with other sources."

"Thanks, Colonel, but you didn't come all the way down here just to pay me a compliment."

"No." Harding tapped the ash off his cigar. "We know we can expect some hard fighting ahead, especially when we come up against the SS and other hard-core units. Even the old men and boys they're putting into the line can knock out a tank with a *Panzerfaust* before they take off."

"Colonel, did you know that the men at the front are starting to talk about not being the last guy to get it? Nobody wants the last bullet on the last day."

"The GIs aren't the only ones getting nervous. Ike's capped the Remagen bridgehead at four divisions."

"So we can supply Monty's 'big push' over the Rhine instead of the crossing we beat him to!" Billy did not try to hide his frustration.

"Captain, may I remind you we are here to beat the German army, not the British? And…" Harding hesitated, and then checked himself. "Never mind. You've heard the standard SHAEF argument before. Anyway, it's like Churchill said, the only thing worse than having allies is not having them."

Harding pulled his briefcase closer to him and opened it. "In addition to Monty and your Remagen bridgehead, Simpson and the Ninth Army are pushing for a direct attack on Berlin. Being between Monty and First Army, he's in a good position."

Billy watched Harding's eyes and listened to his tone. He heard sympathy and a trace of regret.

"We're not going to take Berlin, are we?"

Harding knew exactly whom Billy meant by "we". He meant the Americans, or even the British. The closer the Anglo-American armies came to the Soviet armies, the clearer the divisions between them became. Harding felt obliged to utter the standard SHAEF line again, and was upset with Billy at putting him in the position of a mouthpiece. "Yes, *we* are, dammit, *we* meaning the Allied forces!"

"OK, OK," Billy put his hands palms up, "I get it. The Russians take Berlin. Fine with me. I don't mind missing out on the house-to-house fighting."

"I didn't say that, and what I didn't say doesn't leave this room."

"Jesus, Colonel, I've been in this job too long. I actually understand what you just said." Billy laughed, and Harding did too, appreciating Billy's talent for defusing tense situations. He got back to his main point.

"So we're watching the military situation very carefully. We don't want any more surprises. Ike is very concerned about the Alpine Redoubt, or the National Redoubt, as the Germans are calling it. Since the British are heading north, we would be the ones to deal with it, along with the British and American armies coming up from Italy."

"Goebbels has been all over the radio broadcasts about it."

"Personally, I don't believe a word of it. Aside from the propaganda, there is no hard evidence of any actual buildup in the Alps or defensive preparations." Billy could tell from the fervor with which Harding delivered this speech that he had made it many times before, but without success. "The biggest clincher of all is that they haven't even named a top commander for this famous Alpine fortress. If this was the real deal, they'd be crowing about Guderian or Manstein or some other top general preparing the defenses."

"Sounds logical. But you're the minority opinion?"

"Yep, even though we have good intelligence that Ernst Kaltenbrunner, head of the SS in Austria, is going to Berlin next week in order to persuade Hitler to name him head of the National Redoubt and start construction! Which means they have nothing in place yet!"

Now Harding was up and pacing, pointing with his cigar at Billy to make his point. "It also means that while we're chasing ghosts in the Alps, the Germans could be organizing something else entirely that we could miss. That's what really worries me. That's why I'm here."

"Colonel, that's just the kind of thing that I was thinking about when you came in…"

There was a knock at the door. Lt. Jeffrey Rose rapped twice and opened the office door. "Briefing is starting up, Billy…oh, sorry…"

"Colonel Harding, this is Lt. Rose, CO of the Headquarters Reconnaissance Platoon and my guide to the other side."

"Sir." Rose came to attention.

"Relax, son. I've heard good things about you. Forceman?"

"Yessir, 1st Special Services Force, until they split us up and I ended up here with some of my boys. Wasn't much to do until Captain Boyle showed up," Rose answered with a ready smile.

"He's certainly kept you busy. Meeting starting up?"

"In five, sir."

"OK, let's go. Billy, we'll continue this discussion afterwards."

He stood up and stopped both men. He spoke to Billy in a whisper. "I'm here to observe only- just a courtesy call. Do not refer to anything we've spoken about. Understood?" Harding waited for his answer, blocking the doorway.

"Understood, sir."

Harding smiled. "Alright, let's go. So, Lieutenant, I'm glad to hear someone still appreciates the Springfield rifle. I carried an '03 back in the last war…" Billy followed behind as the Colonel and the Lieutenant chatted about their favorite rifle, as if they were old pals.

Predictably, the meeting of G-2 Intelligence staffers took longer than planned. With the appearance of Colonel Harding, everyone took their time with their own reports, trying to impress the SHAEF Intelligence Deputy. Harding began by taking copious notes, and then stopped when he realized he was only encouraging each officer to drone on. For a while he listened carefully, then grew bored and irritated. No one had anything new to say. Each report was just a longer version of the written intelligence summaries he had reviewed two days earlier in London.

Billy watched Harding, and knew he was quietly losing his temper, drumming his fingers on the table and looking vaguely disinterested. As the last G-2 officer summed up, Billy thought about not asking again about American uniforms, weapons, and chess code names. At the last second he decided to give it one more try, even if Harding was about to get up and walk out. As he did, he could see Harding's expression change suddenly. By the look on his face, he was obviously no longer bored.

Billy's questions were greeted by a collective groan. He had asked them so many times before that someone responded, "Give it a rest, Boyle!" Nobody had anything. The meeting broke up. Harding remained in his seat.

"Boyle and Rose, stay here," Harding growled. The others halted, curious about Harding's demeanor. "The rest of you, dismissed!"

"First, Captain Boyle," said Harding, visibly attempting to control his temper, "tell me why you never reported this matter to me, and then tell me everything about it. Everything!"

"Colonel, I did report it! Right after Rose and me went behind the lines and saw those paratroopers."

"German paratroopers?"

"Yeah. They had taken a group of Americans prisoner. They stripped them of uniforms, weapons and dogtags. We both saw it, then we came back here, drove most of the night. I sent out a coded message to the Division G-2s asking if they heard about anything like that. Then I had a copy sent off to you at SHAEF…" Billy sat back, stunned at his own stupidity, remembering thinking about the message and collapsing into sleep instead. "Oh no!"

"What, Captain?"

"I didn't send it, Colonel, I'm sorry. I was about to, and then I fell dead asleep. When I woke up, I must've thought I had sent it with the others."

"Colonel," Rose broke in, "we had been up more than 30 hours, and had a long patrol behind the Kraut lines. I was dead tired when we got back here and hit the sack. Captain Boyle went into HQ and worked at his desk after I couldn't even keep my eyes open."

Rose's words seemed to calm Harding down somewhat. Billy looked as down in the dumps as anyone could. "I screwed up, sir."

"Damn right, Captain. But I'll kick your ass later. Now, let's deal with the situation. What about the reference to chess code names?"

"That was going in this week's report to you, Colonel. I have it mostly typed already. We just learned about it four days ago."

"Cut the excuses, Boyle, and tell me about it!"

Between them, Billy and Rose got out the full story of their patrol and the interrogation of the SS officer, ending with his remembering the operational code name had something to do with chess.

"Lieutenant, everything I am about to tell you is covered by the Official Secrets Act, which means imprisonment or worse if you talk about anything I'm about to say." He waited for Rose to acknowledge this, and then continued.

"I told Captain Boyle earlier that I was here because I'm concerned we might be missing another German surprise. Everyone is worried about Berlin or the Alpine Redoubt, or they're overconfident and think the war is going to be over tomorrow."

"And this has something to do with chess?"

"I'll get to that. One reason the Jerries suckered us in the Bulge was that they maintained almost total radio security. All our radio intercepts and traffic analysis showed very little activity. They must've kept to landlines or transmitted orders verbally or by courier."

Harding had to leave out the real reason, although this version was close enough to the truth. The Germans did not rely on radio transmissions during the planning for their Ardennes Offensive, thereby depriving the Allies of access to any orders they could decode using ULTRA. They thought there was a high-level spy somewhere in OKH, and hoped to circumvent that agent by not using the usual radio communications network that included Exchange 500 and Engima-encoded radio transmissions. They were wrong about the spy, but right about not using the radio network.

"What I've been doing for the last month is going over all our intelligence sources, including your reports, for hints of anything similar."

"How could you pick out anything from all that information?" asked Rose.

"By looking for anything that referred to an operation tangentially. If that operation was blacked out everywhere else, then it means something. Something top secret, maybe a last ditch effort."

"You found something." It was a statement, not a question. Billy had worked for Harding too long to not pick up on the signs that he was closing in on a long-sought-for quarry. He could feel the tension and excitement in Harding. Rose looked back and forth between them, understanding that he had walked into the kind of secret world that only existed among officers at the highest levels. He wished he were back on the line, where you knew who was who and which way to aim your rifle.

"Yes, but it meant very little until today. Two weeks ago, we intercepted, through one of our agents, a Luftwaffe order concerning tactical air coordination with something called Operation Gambit." Harding looked at the two men to see if they recognized the term. The agent was in fact ULTRA, and only a BIGOT could be trusted with that information. For anyone else, Harding attributed any ULTRA information as coming from a "top agent". It was how most people expected things worked in the intelligence game.

"Is gambit the chess term we've been looking for?"

"A gambit is a chess strategy where you give up a smaller piece in order to gain a larger advantage."

"So what the hell does that mean?" asked Rose.

"Maybe nothing," said Billy, answering for Harding. "But the Germans are more likely to name their operations after something that actually refers to the tactical situation. Like Sealion for the invasion of England, or Watch on the Rhine for their Ardennes Offensive."

"It's not that you could figure it out, but they often have a hint of the operation in the name," explained Harding. "We take the opposite approach, and pick neutral names from a pre-selected list. If a name even comes close, we go onto the next one."

"OK, so what are they giving up?" Billy walked over to a situation map on the table. "Looks like they're fighting hard everywhere they can. I don't think they control the situation on the ground enough to decide where to give up a pawn. And what would a pawn be, a city, a river, what?"

"Good questions. For now, we have to assume Gambit is a neutral term. There's one other important thing, though. The Luftwaffe order defined the operational area for Gambit." Harding walked over to the map and tapped four cities. "Between Wittenberg and Torgau on the Elbe, and Bitterfeld and Eilenburg on the Mulde River. The order was for any aircraft not assigned to Operation Gambit to avoid that box once the activation order was received."

The three men stared at the map. They were silent, each doing their own thinking and calculating. Finally Rose spoke up.

"So, we've got Operation Gambit, which will happen something like 300 miles behind enemy lines between two rivers. It involves GI uniforms and equipment, but probably not in large quantities, since we have only our own report of POWs being stripped of uniforms. We know the SS couldn't provide any. Also that the SS and Luftwaffe are both involved. Anything else?"

"Only that no other reference to or orders concerning Operation Gambit have been intercepted," Harding stated. "The Luftwaffe radio message was a mistake. Whoever sent it is probably carrying a *Panzerfaust* on the eastern front right now."

"So Operation Gambit is very, very top secret," Rose concluded. Harding nodded and pulled another cigar out of his tunic pocket. He lit it and puffed, deep in thought for minutes. He stared at the map and frowned for a while. Then the frown eased. Harding gestured with his cigar, bits of ash floating down over the Mulde and Elbe rivers.

"That's pretty flat country out there, isn't it?"

Oh noooo, no, no, no… thought Billy.

"Yeah," answered Rose. "It's lowland country. Lots of cleared farmland, some forest areas." Rose caught Billy's glance at him and thought he was questioning his knowledge of the area. "What? I have a 1935 Michelin guide to Germany!"

Billy just rolled his eyes and waited for it to come.

"You know," said Harding, as if he just thought of the idea, "that would be pretty good terrain for a team to parachute into, don't you think, Billy?"

Oh crap!

"Piece of cake, Colonel," Rose answered, looking at Billy. "Right, Captain?"

Right, you fucking boy scout.

"Right," Billy answered with a total lack of enthusiasm. "How are we gonna get back?"

Harding and Rose looked at him as if he were from another world.

"We haven't even got you there yet, Billy, give me a chance. Maybe a Lysander landing at night, or maybe the cavalry comes to your rescue."

Harding and Rose exchanged amused glances, and then turned their attention to the map.

"Lieutenant, Forcemen are all jump-qualified, aren't they?"

"Yes, sir. I've got six of my boys from the Force with me. They're all qualified radio operators too."

"Excellent. Put a plan together. As soon as we force the Rhine and break out, we'll drop your group into the area. Make sure you have sufficient radio equipment and can give Captain Boyle a thorough tour of that box." Harding tapped the map and turned to Billy, about to speak, when Billy stood up and stopped him.

"So this is the easy last assignment you promised me, after dragging me out of that hospital? Parachute a few hundred miles behind enemy lines and look for some Nazi plot that we don't know a damn thing about?"

"Whoa, Billy, I know this is a little more that you banked on, but don't worry. This is just a reconnaissance, all you need to do is see what's going on there and report back. We'll either fly you out or you can hunker down in the woods and wait for us. Once we cross the Rhine at all points, it'll be a horserace."

Billy fell back down in his seat and rested his head in his hands. He couldn't believe it. He had a very bad feeling about this job. He looked up at the map on the table in front of him. The Elbe River seemed a long, long way from here. Boston seemed a million miles away.

"Colonel, do you remember when you told me the war was going to be over by Christmas? Last Christmas? And that the Germans had nothing left to throw at us?"

"I was wrong then, Billy. I don't want another goddamn surprise. That's why you've got to go on that mission. You've already helped me put some pieces of this puzzle together. Now you've got to finish the job. That's an order." Harding's face showed determination, and his intense desire not to be caught napping at this point in the war.

"Don't worry, Captain," said Rose, who was clearly charged up at the prospect of a secret mission, "it'll be a piece of cake. We'll take good care of you." He smiled. Billy didn't.

CHAPTER SEVENTEEN

11 April 1945
SS Headquarters
Berlin, Germany

Sturmbannführer Otto Hettstedt clung to the side of the overcrowded horse-drawn trolley car. Electric trolleys had long ago stopped running, due to damage the constant bombing caused. Normally, Hettstedt reported to work a bit later in the morning and avoided the crowds at this early hour. This morning, he was unusually eager to get to his desk. The night staff had pulled together the last bits of information for his final report on the individuals involved in Operation Gambit. Hettstedt was so excited at the prospect that he hardly minded the press of flesh on the crowded trolley that forced him to hang onto the side in such an undignified position. Every other morning, he would sit and silently curse the other riders and dream of the day when a brightly polished staff car would arrive at his door to take him to work. The dream and desire were so real that he allowed himself to think about it now, oblivious to the destruction all around him. He saw himself emerging from an elegant apartment building, the doorman bowing slightly as he walked swiftly by, pulling on his leather gloves. Just outside, his driver opened his door and clicked his heels as he came to attention. Inside the car, he could feel the soft leather…

Abruptly the trolley halted, and Hettstedt swung forward, holding on for dear life as he steadied himself. The dream was gone, and he saw the trolley had stopped at the intersection of *Prinz Albrecht Strasse* and *Wilhelm Strasse*. He stepped down, and waited for the trolley to pull ahead. Looking down the road to No. 8, he thought about how wonderful it would be to have all those who had disdained him in the cellar prison there. He would show them, and it would start today! He walked briskly around the rubble in the street, anticipating coming events.

Just two weeks ago, Hettstedt had reviewed the files on Remke, Neukirk, and others that had been collected from Wehrmacht, SS, and Gestapo files. Initially, there had been nothing to incriminate any of them. He had been surprised at the number of special assignments that both Erich Remke and Dieter Neukirk had been on. From raids on Allied oil lines in Iran to French Morocco in North Africa, they had ranged beyond the borders of the Reich at its greatest extent. Neukirk was a natural leader, commanding his dwindling band of Brandenburgers in every theater of operations. Remke's name appeared in more varied situations, from his last posting with General Gehlen on the Russian front to von Rundstedt's Paris headquarters before the Normandy invasion, and as a special liaison with the Vichy French before that. The files showed nothing but praise for both of them.

Hettstedt had been disappointed, but he kept on digging. He knew that sooner or later he would find a small detail, something unusual, something that would be not quite right. He would know when he saw it, as you would know a thread might unravel as soon as you pulled on it.

He didn't notice the thread immediately when he first saw it in Dieter's service file. Something nagged at him, though, a notion in his naturally suspicious mind that told him to go back through the Wehrmacht file. He had leafed through the forms and documents until he came to it. A simple, standard form required of any officer on active duty who planned to get married, to be submitted to his commanding officer. There, on the line indicating the name of the future bride was the name Elsa Klein. He had remembered her immediately. She was a thread to be pulled. He now felt a superior smug satisfaction at the thought of the fear Dieter Neukirk would feel when he heard his precious fiancée was in Gestapo custody.

Hettstedt had instantly ordered a thorough background check on Elsa. He then reviewed his file on St. Ludwig's Hospital. Staff there had been checked when the Wehrmacht had taken over the hospital. Several had been taken into custody simply to see if time in the basement of Number 8 *Prinz Albrecht Strasse* would cause them to reveal anything about their co-workers. Nothing had come of that, except that the return of those prisoners had demonstrated the power of the Gestapo. There were some reports, however, of certain irregularities in paperwork. Identity papers of civilians killed in the bombings had not been returned to the Gestapo as required. That in and of itself was not uncommon, given that papers were often destroyed or scattered in the explosions and fires that came with the bombing raids. What drew Hettstedt's attention was the fact that it had been noted at all, indicating a greater volume of missing papers than was usual. The notation was over two years old and had never been followed up on, a tiny detail in a mountain of paperwork, hidden away, waiting to be uncovered. To Hettstedt, it shone like a beacon, announcing itself and begging to be noticed. He took notice, with a vengeance.

He had ordered tabulations on the number of bombing victims who had died at three Berlin hospitals, including St. Ludwig's. He then had them compared with the identity papers returned to the Gestapo by those hospitals. This information indeed existed, but it was scattered in bits and pieces throughout files in several government offices in Berlin. It had finally been collected just two days ago. When he put the figures together, it was clear to see. The information had been there all along, he had just never looked at the problem this way. The other two hospitals returned between 70% and 80% of identity papers from deceased patients. St. Ludwig's returned fewer than 40%. His investigators had been very precise, even breaking down the data into counts of male and female and age groups. The papers returned by St. Ludwig's were mostly from older patients. The lowest category of return was for young girls.

Hettstedt had immediately suspected the papers were being supplied to Jews hiding in Berlin. He himself was from Essen and had never liked the Berliners and the city's left-wing workers. They had called the working class section "Red Berlin" when he had been posted here. He and his comrades had certainly dealt with that threat, but the number of Berliners willing to hide enemies of the state continued to frustrate him. Luckily, there were enough loyal citizens in the city and the Gestapo was still finding hidden Jews in attics and other hiding places throughout Berlin.

Then the enormity of it hit him. The transfer of over one hundred recuperating patients when the Wehrmacht had taken over the hospital! One hundred nurses' aides had accompanied them to safety in Bavaria. One hundred Jews! Openly smuggled out of the city under his nose, and on government transport at that! There were various letters and memorandum on file from the hospital making the proposal to the Wehrmacht and arranging the transfer. *Herr* Doktor Kappelen, whom Hettstedt remembered from his hospital visit, signed them all. In one, Elsa Klein was designated to provide the nurses' aides for the transferred patients. Elsa Klein, fiancée of *Hauptmann* Neukirk!

He had her. And that meant he had Dieter Neukirk, which meant he had Operation Gambit within his grasp.

The next day, Hettstedt discovered that an enlisted man carried on the ranks of the Brandenburg Division, as Hans Schierke was actually Hans von Schierke. Von Schierke was a distant cousin of Fabian von Schlabrendorff, one of the chief conspirators in the 20 July 1944 plot against Hitler's life.

Von Schierke had been observed meeting with his cousin several times prior to 20 July. After the failure of the coup, he had dropped out of sight. Transcripts of von Schlabrendorff's interrogation showed that he denied that his cousin had any part in the plot, and that the meetings had simply been family get-togethers. No matter. Von Schierke had not been found after 20 July, and now Hettstedt had found him, hidden in plain sight under Dieter Neukirk's command in the Brandenburg Division. The missing "von" was clever, but Hettstedt's investigation had turned up the fact that the Hans Schierke on the Brandenburg payroll did not match up with any service records in the Wehrmacht files. It was another loose thread that Hettstedt pulled until it came apart. His joy knew no bounds. With a traitor in the ranks of Operation Gambit, he had even more evidence than he needed.

The evidence against Neukirk and Operation Gambit ran through his head as Hettstedt walked through the main office to his desk. He called out to his clerk as he passed by. "Heinz, is the final report ready?"

"Yes, sir. The typist brought it up early this morning. It is on your desk. And *Meister* Paul Popitz is waiting to see you."

Meister was a Gestapo police rank equivalent to a *Feldwebel.* Popitz was assigned to foreign diplomat surveillance in *Amt* IVF, and had been detached to Hettstedt's special investigation.

"I must see *Brigadeführer* Fegelin immediately. Tell him to wait."

Hettstedt strode to his desk and threw off his coat. He picked up the thick report and signed the cover sheet. Popitz was just a lowly policeman. He would have to wait while Hettstedt dealt with the highest Reich security matters. Hettstedt tried to control his mounting excitement as he headed up the stairs to present his findings to Fegelin.

Brigadeführer Hermann Fegelin leaned back in his chair and crossed his booted feet on the corner of his desk. He lit a cigarette with a gold lighter and exhaled languidly. He flipped through the report while Hettstedt stood quietly at attention in front of his desk.

"*Brigadeführer...*"

Fegelin held up the flat of his hand without looking at Hettstedt, silencing him as surely as a verbal command. He detested Hettstedt and his pretensions to higher rank and influential circles. That was Fegelin's territory, and he made sure that no star shown brighter than his in the *Führer's* eyes. Except Himmler's, of course.

He could tell Hettstedt was in an excited state and expected to be rewarded or commended for his work. He was pathetically eager. Fegelin decided to deflate him for a moment, and looked up at Hettstedt while he flicked his cigarette ash. "Only one traitor in the whole bunch? Disappointing, *Sturmbannführer.*"

"But sir, we have the Klein woman who is Neukirk's fiancée. She is clearly involved with providing Jewish criminals with false papers. And Neukirk had to know about von Schierke changing his name..." Hettstedt was on the verge of pleading when Fegelin interrupted him.

"So how do you plan to proceed?"

"We pick up Fräulien Klein and interrogate her to learn who else at St. Ludwig's is involved with hiding fugitive Jews, and if Neukirk had knowledge of it. I will then pick up von Schierke. With both of them in custody, we are certain to get one to break and sign a confession against Neukirk. With that, the Wehrmacht command of Operation Gambit will be discredited, and you and the *Reichsführer* will be able to take control."

"And the operation is ready?"

"Gambit is fully operational. The thrust of the Russian advance actually is as Colonel Remke predicted. His forces are in the right place to take advantage of that. They are small, but very powerful. It indeed could work."

"Wait outside, Hettstedt." Fegelin indicated the door. A puzzled Hettstedt left to wait in the anteroom. As soon as the door shut behind him, Fegelin swiveled his legs off his desk and dropped his mask of indifference. He picked up the telephone and dialed *Reichsführer* Himmler's direct line.

"*Reichsführer!* I have Hettstedt's report. It is everything we need." Fegelin reviewed the evidence Hettstedt had found.

"We should have confessions within the week. I can then present our findings to the *Führer*...yes, sir, I am sure it would be more appropriate for you to make the report. Yes, *Reichsführer,* I will tell him to proceed...yes, cautiously. Heil Hitler!"

Fegelin rested the telephone in its cradle and smiled. He had wanted to see if Himmler was fully behind the plan for the SS to take over Operation Gambit. If Himmler had allowed him to make the report to Hitler, he knew he could not count on the *Reichsführer's* support. If anything went wrong, he would be left out in the cold, without any written authorization. But Himmler had jumped at the chance, meaning he trusted the information about Gambit and its chances for success.

But Fegelin had his own precautions to take. He opened his door and called Hettstedt in.

"*Sturmbannführer,* I have told *Reichsführer* Himmler about your work and recommended you to lead the special squads to take the traitors named in your report into custody." He watched a mix of confusion and pride play across Hettstedt's face. Of course he had expected he would take the lead in arresting Klein and von Schierke, but he was also flattered that Himmler himself knew of his work.

Fegelin had thrown him off balance and clearly showed Hettstedt that he was dependent on his largess in this affair.

"Why…thank you, sir."

"Not at all, my dear Hettstedt. In my opinion, you deserve it. Now, the confessions are a foregone conclusion. Simply decide if Klein or von Schierke or both will provide what we need. But do not harm them too severely. We may want to bargain with Neukirk for a confession about Remke."

Hettstedt understood immediately. They had nothing specific on Neukirk, but to save his fiancée and friend, perhaps they could get him to incriminate Remke and make Gambit a totally SS operation. He nodded, eagerly, in agreement.

"And remember, Hettstedt," Fegelin leaned in and lowered his voice conspiratorially, "Remke is still a favorite of the *Führer*. We must be certain of all our information before moving against him."

"Very well, *Brigadeführer*, I understand."

"Good," Fegelin went over to Hettstedt and casually put his arm on his shoulder as he walked him out of the office, "remember that you are now working on a matter of the highest Reich security. Your orders come through me from *Reichsführer* Himmler himself. You must proceed with lightning force, but remember not to eliminate any of these suspects. We may need them for a greater gain."

"Yes, sir. Will you approve the report and issue the orders for this action?"

Fegelin put on a stern face and looked Hettstedt straight in the eyes. "*Sturmbannführer*, at this level we do not issue written orders. You have the full authority of this office to conduct this action. Draw what security troops you need. Paperwork is for the lower levels, Hettstedt. Do well in this action and we can skip a grade and promote you to *Oberführer* when it is concluded."

Hettstedt's eyes widened. He felt that he had been accepted into an elite circle of the SS. He snapped to attention and stuck out his arm in the Nazi salute. "Heil Hitler!"

"Heil Hitler!"

Fegelin smiled encouragingly as Hettstedt left.

Idiot, he thought.

Hettstedt trotted down the stairway, bursting with energy. He strode into his office, eyes darting about the room. He felt taller, more powerful, almost godlike. He was acting on behalf of the *Reichsführer* and his personal representative to Adolf Hitler! He had spent the entire war rooting out nuns and priests in foreign lands, far from the seat of power, a virtual unknown in Berlin. Now he was close to the throne, and he bathed in the reflected power. He almost giggled out loud when he thought about his escape plans, too.

I will either be a hero and save the Reich, or if that fails, be across the American lines before these poor fools know what hit them. Perhaps…perhaps I can tell the Americans about Operation Gambit…too late to help, but it ought to be worth something to them.

Hettstedt tucked that thought safely away. He could not let it interfere with what he had to do now, but just knowing it was there was comforting.

"Popitz!" he bellowed, "come in here now!"

Meister Popitz sat back in the upholstered chair opposite Hettstedt's desk and breathed a deep sigh as he dug out a notebook from his raincoat pocket. Popitz was a police officer, and had been one for ten years before the Gestapo took over the criminal police force. He had been following suspects and standing in shadows for years, and he didn't mind a bit to sit in this warm office and wait for Hettstedt to get to him.

"Yes, what is so important?" snapped Hettstedt.

"Well sir, I had been on diplomatic surveillance duty before you pulled me in for this investigation." He paused as he flipped through his small tattered notebook.

"And…?"

"And I ended up watching a…an Elsa Klein," he said as he found the name in his book, "I had evenings, from the hospital, to her apartment, and so on. Nothing much ever to report." Popitz stopped speaking and seemed to be lost in thought. Hettstedt was irritated and about to demand that he get to the point.

"That's what bothered me."

Hettstedt froze as he realized Popitz did have information that might be important. "Go on," he said solicitously, "what bothered you?"

"Well," Popitz replied as he wetted his finger to turn the page in his notebook, "I had been watching a Senor Antonio Joaquim Gonsaldes, last senior Portuguese diplomat in Berlin. Right up to 13 March, after which I was pulled into this detail. He had broken his arm in a fall in the street, and was treated at St. Ludwig's Hospital. He kept going back there, more times than necessary, but I thought, he's an old man, maybe it bothers him. Anyway, walking is a damn sight better than standing still in the cold, I'll tell you that."

"You have a very difficult job," Hettstedt said flatteringly.

Popitz just shrugged a policeman's shrug. "So I followed him to the hospital that last day. It was very strange. He left with two young girls. Now I tell you, I've seen a lot of old men take a fancy to little girls…"

"What girls?" Hettstedt demanded.

"Well, I don't know. I was pulled off the detail. He had seen a nursing Sister, Sister Anneliese, at the hospital each time he went. And, he also saw Elsa Klein a few times." Popitz smiled slyly. He was enjoying drawing this out and teasing Hettstedt.

"Why didn't you put this in your report?"

"Well, I was ordered to record everything Elsa Klein did and everyone she saw during my shift. And so I did."

Hettstedt fumed with impatience, but forced himself to be calm. "Are you telling me he never returned to the hospital?"

"Not once. The day I saw him bring back the two girls was the last time he set foot in the place. I figured he got what he wanted and didn't need to go back." Popitz raised his eyebrows and smiled knowingly at Hettstedt.

"So why are you bothering me with a dirty old man?"

"Well, I went back on diplomatic surveillance just yesterday. Went back to watching Senor Gonsaldes. I expected to see those two girls. I didn't. They're gone. I checked with the other fellows on duty, and they said the girls left that same day. Went to the railroad station with his housekeeper and assistant. So I asked myself, why would an old man bring two girls home from the hospital and then not even spend the night with them?"

"Yes, why?"

"Well, I checked their destination. Hamburg. Boarded a Portuguese freighter out of Hamburg harbor. Girls had valid Portuguese passports, all in order."

"So, it's odd, but…"

"Well, the only problem is, I ran a check on those girls. Just got the files out of storage this morning. The names on those passports were of two Portuguese female nationals who died in 1941."

"Heinz!" Hettstedt bellowed at the top of his lungs for his clerk. Popitz was startled at the loudness and ferocity behind the cry.

Heinz ran from his desk to the doorway of the office. "Yes, sir!"

"Get a car and two security men. Have it up front immediately. Then have a company of security troops ready in trucks within the hour. Popitz, come with me. You're going to take me to that Jew-smuggling Portuguese bastard, and then we search the hospital!"

"Well, *Sturmbannführer*, you don't have the authority to take a neutral diplomat into custody…"

"I have the highest authority! I am acting on behalf of the *Reichsführer* himself. Now come with me or I will have you shot for disobeying a direct order." Hettstedt growled out these last words. Popitz could see he had played out his little teasing game too far. He could see in his face that Hettstedt would actually prefer to show his power by having him shot, right now.

"Well, sir, let's go then. Just as long as you have the authority, I'm your man."

"Good." Hettstedt pulled his Walther pistol from his holster, checked the clip, and chambered a round. "Let's pick him up."

Heinz had called for the car. It was waiting out front with a driver and another SS guard as they walked down the steps. Hettstedt stepped in as the guard held the door for him. He felt excited and a little nervous. His power swirled around inside his head, dizzying him with its lethalness. He never even thought about the fact that *Brigadeführer* Fegelin had approved everything he was about to do, except for the arrest of a neutral diplomat.

In his small office, Senor Gonsaldes poured three glasses of sherry and turned to hand them to his two guests. Senors Juan DeCarlos and Hernando Ferreia of the Spanish Embassy had come to bid farewell to their neutral colleague. All three men were about to depart Berlin for their respective capitals, and had gathered for a final toast.

"Gentlemen," Gonsaldes began, "to our departure from death and ruin."

"And safe return to our homelands," replied Ferreia. The three men touched glasses and drank. As the men drained their sherry, they heard the sounds of heavy footsteps drumming up the stairs. They each froze, holding the empty glasses to their lips, eyes turning to the door and the sound of pounding feet beyond.

The footsteps halted abruptly at the landing outside the office. There was a moment of silence. DeCarlos and Ferreria exchanged nervous glances. Gonsaldes' hand began to tremble and his heart pounded in his chest. His glass slipped through his fingers and shattered on the floor. Suddenly the door crashed open and slammed against the wall. Gonsaldes saw two soldiers crash into the room, followed by another man in plainclothes. His knees felt weak and there was a throbbing pain in his chest. He could hear his heart beating more rapidly. Then he saw a figure in black storm into the room, push aside the others and yell out his name. He tried to reply, but couldn't. Suddenly, there was a final grasping pain, then oblivion.

Otto Hettstedt marched into the room, pistol drawn and snarling out Senor Gonsaldes' name. Power was surging through him, the power he always felt when his victims were cornered and at his mercy. Whenever his men crashed down a door and forced their way into a room, he felt the blood surging in his veins and the strength pulsating from his body. To go wherever you wanted, to have no door or room sacred, no limit to your power, was the ultimate stimulant for Hettstedt. He always savored the final moment, when he would confront his quarry and watch him be carried away, screaming his innocence to indifferent ears.

As he called out this victim's name, he watched him slip slowly from his grasp, eluding him in these final moments. The man turned white, his hands shook and Hettstedt could see his legs wobble and begin to give way. The old man fell to the floor, and quietly escaped the SS through death's door, his good heart giving out as if the presence of Hettstedt and his men was simply too much to bear.

DeCarlos bent over the body while Ferreria turned on Hettstedt. Everything had happened so quickly it took a moment for him to form any words. He waved his fist in Hettstedt's face as DeCarlos looked up and shook a sad "no" with his head.

"How dare you! How dare you force your way onto neutral ground like this! My god, you've killed him!"

Hettstedt felt the sweat break out on his brow. He saw Popitz and the two SS soldiers staring at him. This is not how it was supposed to go. He tried to regain control of the situation. "Who are you two?"

"We are Spanish neutral diplomats, damn you!" DeCarlos rose from Gonsaldes' body and confronted Hettstedt. "Your government will hear of this, you little toad! This office is Portuguese territory, and you have entered in violation of every known international law, and caused the death of a fine old man, a colleague, and a friend. And a good friend of the Spanish government. Now give me your name and commanding officer!"

DeCarlos punctuated this last sentence with a finger stabbing at Hettstedt's chest, advancing on him in blind anger, unafraid of the drawn pistol in his hand. Hettstedt felt everything crashing down around him, confusion swirled through his head where seconds before there was decision and power. He jammed the pistol back in his holster and turned around and walked out of the room without a word. The two soldiers followed immediately.

Meister Popitz stood to one side, observing everything. He stood without saying a word, so quietly that it was almost as if the two Spaniards didn't notice him. They both knelt to straighten out the crumpled body of their friend, gently placing his hands folded upon his chest. Popitz walked two paces and knelt beside them.

"Well, his name's Otto Hettstedt, *Sturmbannführer* out of Number 8 *Prinz Albrecht Strasse.* And damned if I know who his commanding officer is!"

CHAPTER EIGHTEEN

11 April 1945
St. Ludwig's Hospital
Berlin, Germany

It was a warm day. There had been no bombing raid that night. For Berlin in the spring of 1945, those two things were cause for celebration. Dieter Neukirk walked down the street leading to St. Ludwig's, noticing buds bursting out on the trees and shrubs blooming green amid the rubble. *Even in a ruined city, surrounded by death, life goes on,* he thought. He felt unaccountably happy. Some of that was due to the warmth of the early spring sun, but most of it was because he had been able to spend the night with Elsa. Remke had given him permission to spend the night in Berlin, in advance of another morning meeting at the *Bendler Strasse* headquarters. Elsa had worked late, and came home to find Dieter waiting with a sumptuous meal. He had brought rare delicacies from the OKH kitchens- ham, sausages, fresh white bread, cheeses, a bottle of French cognac, and real coffee. He smiled as he remembered her smile of delight when she saw the table laid out. She had devoured the food, smacking her lips, and talking non-stop with Dieter between mouthfuls. They ate, laughed, drank, and talked, thankful of the quiet, warm night without explosions and fire. He joked with her that she was happier to see the sausages than him, and she said of course, sausages were rarer than soldiers these days. She thought it was hilarious and Dieter pretended to be indignant. His smile widened again as he thought of it, and as he thought of their lovemaking. It had been too long since their last time. It seemed everything conspired to keep them from one another's bodies- the war, Remke, her work, her mission, and Dieter's duty. Last night though, it was as if nothing else existed. Nothing but their passion, touch, and warmth.

Now Dieter was on his way with the remnants of last night's feast, for a mid-day meal with Elsa before returning to Zossen. It was only minutes ago that he had made up his mind about what he would do when the time came. He looked forward to telling Elsa and hoped she would be proud of him. Tomorrow he left Zossen for Wittenberg, to await the inevitable meeting of the Russian and American forces, to launch Operation Gambit and to do what he must do. He knew he might never see her again.

As he walked towards the entrance of St. Ludwig's, he saw Elsa sitting at a bench in a little grassy area to the right of the main entrance. She waved happily. "Dieter, here! Let's have a picnic!"

Dieter walked over, leaned down and kissed her on the mouth, lingering over the taste of her lips. She pulled back, laughing, "Dieter, what will the sisters think?"

"I don't care, unless it's Sister Anneliese. She puts the fear of God in me." He sat and unwrapped the food, spreading it out on the bench between them.

Elsa smiled bravely, then suddenly held her hand to her mouth. A tear ran down her cheek. "Oh Dieter! It's almost too painful to see you and then have you go away again. To have you, good food, sunshine, and no bombing, it's almost too much to bear."

"Aren't those all good things, *liebchen*?

"Yes," she said, "but it just means that I won't have you tomorrow, the bombers will be back, and when will it all end? How will it end? When will I see you again? Will we live through this and be together again, Dieter?"

"I don't know...I can't really believe it will end, but it has to. And we have to survive. You must survive. You've done so much good, saved so many lives, and I...I've been nothing but a soldier, doing what I'm told."

She wiped tears away and held his hand in hers. "Dieter, you have been very brave, on the battlefield and off. You didn't have to take in Hans when the Gestapo was looking for him. You told me how you forged the paperwork for him. And I know from Jost how well you care for your men, German and Russian boys alike. You've kept many of them alive through the worst of it."

"Elsa, I don't know if we've seen the worst of it yet." It was time to tell her. "Our mission is on. We leave tomorrow."

"No." Her hands tightened on his, as if to keep him from leaving. Her face was anguished. "No, please, don't go."

"Elsa, it isn't so much the going. It's what we have to do."

He had always been secretive about his missions. He often told her about little things, special things about foreign lands, funny things that happened, or the loss of a special comrade. But he had never told her about the awful terrible things that happened. He never really told her the truth.

"What is it, Dieter?"

He didn't answer her directly. "You know, I've been thinking about that policeman you told me about. The one outside the New Synagogue. In a way he was really lucky. He had a chance to make a difference. How often does that really happen, that one man can decide to do his duty as he sees it, not as everyone else does? And really make a difference?"

She knew he wasn't really asking her, and just watched him, silently.

"You decided what your duty was, and made a difference the first time you took in one of those hidden Jews." He lowered his voice and glanced around the little park. "You've saved hundreds, Elsa, while I've been off fighting for the Nazis, doing their bidding, burying my men from France to the Caspian Sea, you've been here rescuing the innocent."

"Dieter, I know you've never done anything terrible like the SS. You have to fight, but at least you do so with honor."

"Honor. That policeman understood honor. And duty. It's not about obeying your superiors and doing what they tell you to do."

"What is it to you then?"

"Soldiers often mistake obedience for honor. Honor and duty are about doing what's right in your heart, to make a difference. My body wears this uniform, but my soul is where my honor lies, and that ultimately will decide how I act, and how I am remembered, in this world."

"Is it…Gambit?" she whispered. He nodded slightly.

"Yes."

"Oh, Dieter, I just want you to come back to me!" She flung her arms around him and sobbed. Tears soaked into his uniform. They stayed like that for a long time.

Finally they pulled apart so they could see each other's eyes.

"Dieter, do what you have to do. Do what is in your heart, and then make sure you come back to me."

"I will. I want to come back and marry you, have children with you. I want our children to be as proud of their father as they will be of their mother."

She didn't contradict him. She knew exactly what he meant, and no amount of denial could change that. He had reached a decision. He would not allow the killing to be continued because of his actions. She didn't know exactly what he was going to do, but she knew he could not play the role assigned him in this last barbaric act of the war. She kissed him, a long full sensual kiss, her tear-stained soft cheek brushing against his as they held each other. He drank her in.

It seemed like only minutes had passed, but it was time to go.

"I have to leave now, Elsa."

"But you haven't even eaten anything."

"Take the food with you, maybe you have some kids stashed away who could use it." He tried to smile, to sound nonchalant.

"I can't bear to say good-bye to you, Dieter."

"Don't. Just remember I'll come back for you, no matter what happens. Don't forget that. No matter what." He kissed her quickly, afraid to lose himself in her touch once again. He stood up, looked at her one last time, burning the image in his mind. Then he turned without a word and left.

Elsa sat and watched Dieter until he turned a corner and vanished. She then packed up the food and walked sadly back into St. Ludwig's. There were no hidden Jews in the hospital right now, but she planned on sharing the food with Sister Anneliese. They would both be working late tonight. She put the food away in her office and went out to the main desk to check on the morning admissions. The flow of casualties had been steadily increasing the last few days, as Russian pressure on the Oder River defense line built up. Thinking about it Elsa realized that had a lot to do with Dieter's departure. *They must be about to break through,* she thought to herself glumly. *We should get ready for more casualties…*

The screech of tires reached inside the hospital and startled Elsa. She heard muffled sounds of car doors slamming and boots hitting the ground. SS security troops entered through the main doors in a rush. Shouts came from other directions as additional troops came through the side entrances. Elsa looked around, not understanding what was happening. Patients in wheelchairs were shoved aside as the torrent of troops continued to pour in. Several nurses and a doctor rushed out to see what was happening and were roughly pushed to the side and held.

Several SS officers entered. Elsa felt frozen in place, frightened and alone in a swirling sea of black uniforms. One of the faces approaching her seemed familiar. She recognized Hettstedt and felt a sick stab of fear. It was finally happening, what she had dreaded for years, so close to the end. They were coming for her.

"Search the building! Look everywhere for hiding places and any civilians!" Troops scurried off in every direction. Hettstedt turned to the officer commanding the SS detail. "Bring me *Herr* Doktor Kappelen and Sister Anneliese immediately." He then turned with a deathly smile and bowed mockingly to Elsa.

"I see Fraulein Klein has been kind enough to greet us here. Take her!"

Two men grabbed her from behind, each roughly taking an arm.

"Don't worry my dear, your boyfriend will be joining you soon. At Number 8 *Prinz Albrecht Strasse*. We'll all have a little party there."

As she was led outside, Elsa turned to see Hettstedt laughing at her. Even in her frightened and confused state, she could sense desperation and madness in the sound. She gave a little prayer of thanks that Dieter had left just before the raid, and then let herself get very, very scared.

They tied her hands very tightly behind her back and put her in a truck. Two guards stayed with her. From the open-topped truck, she could see the hospital and hear the search as it proceeded floor to floor. There were shouts, screams and loud noises. Several windows were broken as chairs and other objects were thrown out in the searcher's frenzy. Elsa watched in terror, thankful only in the knowledge that would find no hidden Jews today. Soon she could watch no more and hung her head and wept.

Boots stomped down the main steps and Elsa turned her head to look. What she saw made her gasp. Two SS men were dragging Doktor Kappelen by his arms down the steps, his limp feet bouncing behind him. Blood dripped from his face. When they got to the truck, they tied his hands and heaved his unconscious body up onto the floor at Elsa's feet.

"You should be glad you came quietly, missy!" The two guards laughed and turned away from her. Two more guards came from the hospital with Sister Anneliese in tow. She held her head high, as if she came down the steps of her own accord. The guards were quiet this time, and actually helped her up onto the truck. One came up with her to tie her hands. She immediately knelt to examine Kappelen, when the guard restrained her.

"I'm sorry, Sister, it is not allowed. I must tie your hands."

"Then do what you must, young man. Only you will have to live with your shame." The guard tied her and sat her down next to Elsa. He avoided their eyes as they drove away from the hospital, towards Number 8 *Prinz Albrecht Strasse* and the Gestapo cells in the basement.

The truck pulled into the back of the SS headquarters building. The two women were taken down from the truck and led inside. Kappelen was still unconscious as he was carried in. Elsa had a last glance at Sister Anneliese just before they were put into separate, small, cold, dark cells. Before Elsa could turn around, the heavy door slammed behind her and she was alone. More alone than she had ever been in her life. Dieter's last words now seemed to mock her. How could he ever come back for her, to this place?

She had found the mattress and curled up on it. Perhaps she slept, but there was no way to know. Suddenly the darkness was broken as a key turned in the lock and the door swung open. Elsa squinted her eyes against the sudden light.

"Hello, my dear, so glad you accepted our invitation." Otto Hettstedt felt triumphant with his three captives safely ensconced in the Gestapo cells. He stood in the doorway, feasting his eyes on Elsa. He enjoyed seeing her fear as she sat on the bed, looking up at him.

"What do you want?" she asked.

"I have what I want, the question is, how difficult will it be for you?"

"Please, I don't know what you mean…"

"Shut up!" Hettstedt advanced on her and slapped her face, hard. "Do not lie to me, you Jew-loving bitch! You are a traitor to your race, and you are totally under my power now." He stepped back, folded his hands behind his back, and allowed her to recover for a moment. He eased his tone a bit, to show his confidence.

"I know everything about your activities. I know about you and the Herr Doktor and the Sister. I know about the identity papers that you did not turn in. I know about the Jews you sent to Bavaria, and about all those you've probably given documents to since then." He paused to let his words sink in, and to watch their effect.

"I'm surprised it took you so long." Elsa tried to remain calm, but she could hear her voice waver.

"Oh, there will be many things here that will surprise such a young, delicate woman as yourself," Hettstedt laughed. "Would it surprise you if I told you I also know about von Schierke and how Neukirk sheltered him after he tried to kill the Führer? I know enough about you and your boyfriend to put both your necks in the hangman's noose."

"Why are you telling me this? Why don't you kill me and be done with it?"

Hettstedt leaned down and snarled in her face. "Because it's not going to be that easy, my dear. I want more than just Neukirk. I want his commander, Colonel Remke. And you are going to help me get him."

"How? I hardly know the man- Dieter tells me nothing of his work…"

"How?" Hettstedt laughed hysterically again. "Let me show you how. Come with me." He grabbed her arm and dragged her out into the corridor, down three cells to the right. There were dull thudding sounds coming from inside. Hettstedt gestured to a guard to open the door.

"I saw the guards treating the Sister kindly at the hospital. Many of these men have no experience dealing with traitors to the State from within the church. My men have much experience, and no such qualms about applying National Socialist justice to enemies of the State. See what awaits you, my dear, if you do not cooperate with me." He led her by the arm to the open door.

Sister Anneliese was on the floor, a pool of blood around her face. Two plainclothes Gestapo agents stood over her. They had halted their activities when the door opened. At a nod from Hettstedt, they resumed. Vigorous kicks began to hit Sister Anneliese in the back and head. She curled up more, protecting herself instinctively and crying out in pain at each cruel kick.

"NO! STOP! I'll do whatever you want…don't hurt her anymore, please." Elsa ran towards the crumpled figure on the floor, only to have one of the agents push her back roughly into the corridor. Hettstedt took her arm again and brought her back to her cell.

"I will be picking up Neukirk tomorrow. Once he is in custody, you will both sign confessions naming Erich Remke as your accomplice in assisting fugitive Jews and other enemies of the State."

"Will you stop torturing Sister Anneliese?"

"It has already stopped. She will have medical assistance, and nothing else will happen to her, unless you fail to cooperate."

Elsa felt miserable. She had often wondered how she would stand up to Gestapo beatings. She never thought it would be someone else's misery that would thoroughly and totally destroy her resistance. She couldn't bear to think of what more they would do to the Sister and what they would do to Dieter if she didn't cooperate.

"I will do whatever you ask."

Hettstedt smiled back at her. "Yes, you will. You certainly will, my dear. He turned and closed the door behind him. Elsa sat on the mattress and held her head in her hands. She could not even cry. She was stunned by the violence she had seen and by the destruction of everything she held dear. In the darkness she felt as if she were in a black abyss at the end of her life, and even if she were to walk out of the cell the darkness would never end.

Hettstedt walked down the corridor, highly agitated. He knew he had made a critical mistake with the old Portuguese diplomat. He had only a short amount of time to rectify that error. If he gave Himmler and Fegelin everything they wanted, they would surely overlook one old man's death. Everything included Erich Remke, and he intended to have him.

He passed Sister Anneliese's cell. The Gestapo men stepped out and one asked him, "What about her?" He pointed with his thumb at the form inside the cell. She was moaning softly on the floor, trying to lift herself up.

"Leave her. I no longer need her."

CHAPTER NINETEEN

12 April 1945
Foreign Ministry
Berlin, Germany

Foreign Minister Joachim von Ribbentrop stood at the full-length window overlooking the *Wilhelm Strasse* and surveyed the destruction of the Reich's capital city. He was dressed, as usual, in a formal diplomat's frock coat and old-fashioned starched collar. This was his usual mode of dress, unless he donned the theatrical Nazi uniforms he had designed for the Foreign Service which were regarded as ludicrous by the career civil servants in that department. Von Ribbentrop looked every part the distinguished aristocrat and played the role to the hilt. He was actually nothing of the sort. A former champagne salesman before the rise of the Nazi party, he had added the "von" to his name to disguise his humble origins.

A favorite of Hitler, von Ribbentrop's position in the Nazi government had nevertheless declined during the war years. The short-lived Russian-German pact of 1939 had been his high-water mark. After the invasion of the Soviet Union, there was little need for diplomatic initiatives and his role became more one of a functionary. This caused von Ribbentrop to guard his remaining prerogatives very carefully, and was why he had called SS *Brigadeführer* Hermann Fegelin to his office today. He gazed out the window and caught sight of his own reflection, sighing at the sight of large dark bags under his eyes. He shook his head disapprovingly at his own image.

He turned away from the window, escaping from the ruined city and reflection. He sat at his desk and pressed the intercom button. "Send him in now." He picked up a pen and began writing furiously in a file of papers.

"The Foreign Minister can see you now," the secretary announced to Fegelin, as if she was doing him a great favor. He got up from where he had been waiting impatiently and entered von Ribbentrop's office. He did not know the nature of the meeting, only that it was an urgent matter relating to the SS, which was his concern, and foreign relations, which was von Ribbentrop's.

"Ah, Fegelin, one moment please." Von Ribbentrop continued to write, without looking up or offering a chair. Fegelin, vaguely irritated but curious about the purpose of the meeting, simply sat in the chair opposite von Ribbentrop and waited. He crossed his legs casually and tried to appear bored.

Finally, von Ribbentrop laid down his pen and closed the file. He clasped his hands in front of him looked sternly at Fegelin, who asked, "What exactly is the purpose of this meeting?"

Von Ribbentrop ignored the direct question and replied in a lecturing tone, as if Fegelin were a rather dim-witted student.

"I am sure you realize the importance of our relations with neutral powers in these critical days for the Reich, Fegelin. I am working day and night to insure that we have the good offices of several neutral powers available to us for potential negotiations. The Japanese ambassador has been assisting us in working with the Swedes on an approach to the Soviet Union to discuss an armistice."

Fegelin had heard of this futile attempt to contact the Russians and arrange a separate peace that would allow the Germans to hold off the Americans and British in the west. He also knew that just days ago Hitler had absolutely forbidden von Ribbentrop to go any further with his plan.

"Yes, yes," he replied hurriedly, "I know all about it. Do you wish me to bring it up again to the Führer for you?"

Von Ribbentrop stood up suddenly, anger clouding his face. "We will be talking to the Führer, yes, but not about that! We shall talk about how your men, acting on your direct orders, have assaulted and murdered a neutral diplomat! Now when we need good relations with neutrals the most, you have destroyed my work!"

"What are you talking about?" Fegelin was shaken. The displeasure of the Führer was intensely frightening to all those in his inner circle, who routinely maneuvered to gain greater favor at the expense of anyone else who showed weakness.

"Do you know that in just two days I must issue an order to all remaining neutral diplomats to leave Berlin? I was going to say that we could no longer guarantee their safety due to the terror bombing and Soviet attacks. Now it will seem as if they are not safe from the SS!" Von Ribbentrop had worked himself up into a rage, bellowing out his accusation and looking down at Fegelin.

"My God, man! Tell me what you are talking about!"

Von Ribbentrop visibly calmed himself and walked back to his desk, seated himself and opened a file. He adjusted his reading glasses, alternately looking down at the papers and over the top of the glasses, peering at Fegelin.

"Yesterday, the Portuguese envoy Antonio Joaquim Gonsaldes was enjoying a visit from two Spanish neutral diplomatic colleagues, as he prepared to leave Berlin and return to Portugal. In his office, which by international law is neutral territory, I may add. Disregarding this, one of your men, a *Sturmbannführer* Otto Hettstedt, burst in on the group, seeking to arrest Gonsaldes. As this Hettstedt was threatening him, the elderly Gonsaldes suffered a heart attack and died. In the presence of the Spaniards."

Fegelin stiffened as the implications of Hettstedt's act hit him. The Führer would be furious, and von Ribbentrop was likely to tell the tale to his greatest advantage, placing blame squarely on Fegelin. It would give von Ribbentrop the perfect excuse for the failure of any of his latest diplomatic initiatives.

"Early this morning the Spanish government lodged an official diplomatic protest with our ambassador in Madrid. The Portuguese government followed suit and has demanded an investigation. An investigation! What have you done, Fegelin?"

"*Sturmbannführer* Hettstedt had no orders or authorization from my office for this action. If indeed this actually happened at all. How can you be sure? Perhaps the Spaniards killed him and are blaming the SS."

"Don't be an idiot, Fegelin! One of your own SS police officers identified Hettstedt as in charge of the action. The man told the Spaniards his name after he left."

That's two heads I'll take, Fegelin thought to himself, frantic to get back to Number 8 *Prinz Albrecht Strasse* and deal with this crisis.

"Can you tell me if you know why Hettstedt tried to arrest this Gonsaldes?" Fegelin hated even asking the question, revealing that he knew little about his subordinate's activities.

"Something connected with arrests he was also making at St. Ludwig's Hospital. Apparently Gonsaldes got involved with smuggling Jews out of the country in connection with staff at the hospital."

Fegelin suddenly understood. Hettstedt had gotten too ambitious in following up leads in his investigation of Elsa Klein.

"You may inform the Spanish and Portuguese governments that this was an unauthorized action taken by a low level officer acting without written orders. There will be an immediate investigation and a prompt response to this violation of neutral territory. The SS will not tolerate rogue officers acting illegally." Fegelin drew a deep breath, congratulating himself on not having given Hettstedt anything in writing. He was confident that he could distance himself from his actions easily.

Fegelin's seeming capitulation took von Ribbentrop by surprise. He would have preferred an open conflict, which he could have brought to Hitler for his ultimate decision, surely in von Ribbentrop's favor. This was quite something else. He decided to give the issue a little time to develop, to see what would happen.

"I can do that for you, Fegelin, if you promise a prompt response. Can you lay your hands on this Hettstedt?"

"*Herr* Minister, that is exactly what I mean to do." Fegelin got up and walked out without another word. He had to act immediately, and that meant seeing Heinrich Himmler about this before anyone else did.

Fegelin entered the SS headquarters and made for Himmler's first-floor office. Himmler was in, and seemed to be expecting him.

"Are you conducting foreign policy now, *Brigadeführer*?" Himmler let a small grin appear briefly on his thin lips.

Damn, the man has eyes everywhere! "Our plan to take over Operation Gambit is almost ready to implement. However, we do have one small problem to overcome."

Himmler said nothing, but simply raised an eyebrow that seemed to severely question Fegelin's use of "we". Fegelin told him about receiving Hettstedt's report yesterday, his orders to him concerning the arrests, and the Gonsaldes incident. Himmler thought for a while.

"So we have the Klein woman in custody? What about Neukirk?"

"I believe Hettstedt is on his way to Zossen now to take him into custody. That was his plan, in any case. He was going to take several squads of security troops in case of any trouble with the Brandenburgers."

Himmler tapped his fingers nervously on his desktop. He thought out the potential problems, advantages and disadvantages. Everything was calculated around how the Führer would react. Himmler feared his wrath more than all the Allied bombs that could fall on Berlin. Finally he spoke.

"You can still salvage the situation if you act quickly. You must establish for the record that Hettstedt's actions in regard to Gonslades were unauthorized. He needs to be apprehended and dealt with immediately.

Once we have him, and Neukirk, we can move on Remke and go to the Führer for overall command of Gambit."

Himmler paused, and Fegelin noted that Himmler had not used "we" until he spoke of having Hettstedt in custody, which of course meant eliminated. Fegelin understood fully. He would have done exactly the same.

"Send a coded radio message to Zossen," Himmler continued, "for the officer in charge of Hettstedt's security force. Once Neukirk has been taken, he is to arrest Hettstedt as well and bring them both back here. Then we go to see the Führer. Only then. And make sure the order is coded. I don't want it going out in the clear."

"Yes, *Reichsführer!*"

"Be sure you deal with this promptly, *Brigadeführer.* The Russians are building up on the Oder for an offensive. It could come within days or a week at most. The Americans are about to take Nordhausen and the V-2 facility there. There is not much time left before Operation Gambit begins, with or without us. I prefer it to be the SS which saves the Reich for the Führer."

"I will issue the order at once, and go to Zossen myself to oversee the operation."

"No, you are needed here. Issue the orders, monitor the situation, and report to me this afternoon."

"As you wish, *Reichsführer.*"

Fegelin went back to his office, determined to gain control over the situation quickly. Himmler planned to keep him close by, in case Hettstedt eluded them. He knew where the blame would fall if he failed to produce Hettstedt. He barked an order for his aide to come into his office and take down a radio signal.

"Find out who commands the security detail *Sturmbannführer* Hettstedt took with him this morning..."

"It was *Untersturmführer* Wertholz, sir. I saw them leave less than an hour ago."

"Good. Send him a coded message to the OKH communications center at Zossen. It is to be delivered to Wertholz only." Fegelin began to dictate.

"Proceed with your action to arrest Dieter Neukirk and Hans von Schierke. Once Neukirk is in custody, you are to disarm and arrest *Sturmbannführer* Otto Hettstedt and return him and the other prisoners to Berlin. Do not interfere with other Operation Gambit personnel. Inform Colonel Erich Remke of your orders from the undersigned when all prisoners are in your custody."

"Is that all, sir?"

"For that message, yes. Send it out under my name as an Enigma code. Now, tell me, which of our police officers accompanied *Sturmbannführer* Hettstedt yesterday?"

"*Meister* Popitz was looking for him yesterday, with some information about a foreign diplomat..."

"Enough. Type out the following transfer order..."

Within an hour, a stunned *Meister* Popitz was confronted by two SS guards, stripped of his Gestapo identity badge and informed that he had been included in the call-up of a *Volkssturm*, or People's Guard, anti-tank battalion. He was allowed to keep his pistol, given a helmet, a *Volkssturm* armband, and two *Panzerfaust* anti-tank rockets. He was put on a truck with other office workers called up from various government buildings. They were all middle-aged and as much in shock as Popitz. He sat down on the bench as the truck drove through the eastern suburbs towards the Oder. The man opposite him asked, "Where do you think we're going?"

"Well, I'd say we're going to hell, my friend."

At just about the same time, the Enigma coded message was being decoded at the OKH Exchange 500 Zossen communications center. The radio operator decoding the message had used the Enigma machines hundreds of times, and was quick with it. Behind him, *Leutnant* Gustav Stieff was making a final inspection before departing with the rest of the Operation Gambit staff. He glanced over the shoulder of the young radio operator as he worked on the message.

"Well, Karl, keep up the good work..." He stopped in mid-sentence as he saw the decoded words on the communications form.

"Yes, *Feldwebel*...I mean *Leutnant*." Karl turned and smiled up at Stieff.

"I'll take that message out for you, son."

"Well, I guess that's alright. It's for some SS officer on his way here."

"Yes, I see. I'll take care of it. *Auf Wiedersehen*, Karl. Stay out of trouble."

"You too, *Leutnant*.

A little too late for that, my boy. Stieff went out to find Dieter Neukirk, fast.

Outside of London, at Bletchley Park, the Allied center for intercepting and decoding German signals traffic, the message had been decoded and sent onto SHAEF headquarters before it was in Stieff's hands. Colonel Harding's staff read it and had a summary written and coded for transmission to him at First Army HQ within ten minutes. He had given them a number of key words to look for in any Enigma messages. With this one, they had hit the jackpot. Remke had been scrupulous about avoiding any kind of radio transmissions, handling all communications by land lines or direct transmission of written orders. Fegelin, unaware of this, had sent the first and only radio communication referring to both Operation Gambit and Colonel Erich Remke.

CHAPTER TWENTY

12 April 1945
352nd Fighter Group Airbase
Asche, Belgium

Even with the sun out, trying its best to warm the cool early April air, it was freezing inside the hangar. The concrete floor was cold and damp, and Billy wore his gloves constantly. He and Lt. Rose had set up plywood between two smaller tables to make one large map table. They were standing over it now, pouring over detailed maps and aerial photos of the area between the Mulde and Elbe rivers where they were to drop.

Behind them and extending the length of the hangar were even longer tables with white parachutes hanging above them. They silently swayed on their hooks as stray breezes gusted in under doors and around windows, looking like ghosts staring over their shoulders. Billy was irritated by the image as he constantly caught the movement out of the corner of his eye. Sergeant Kowalski and Corporal Mandelbaum were re-packing their parachutes for the thousandth time, as they all impatiently waited for the order to begin their mission. Six other enlisted men sat and sprawled on stacked cases of supplies and gear pushed up against the hangar wall. Most were cleaning their Thompson submachine guns. Corporal Luther Willard was intently testing all the components on the team's new SSTR-5 OSS radio. This newest version of the radio unit designed for behind the lines use had just been delivered to the front, and Luther was enthralled with it. A southern boy with a drawl and slow, plodding exterior, he was Rose's best radioman and electronics expert. They had been together in the 1st Special Services Force, as had all the handpicked soldiers that made up the ten-man team. Except for Billy, who felt like a helpless passenger on a runaway train.

"Rosie, this here receiver weighs only two and three-quarters pounds. The transmitter has two tubes runnin' in tandem, so if one of 'em busts, we can still get on the air," Luther said excitedly. "Damn! This here's one fine radio. Thousand mile range, too."

"Did we get two of them?"

"Yep. We're gonna to wrap 'em in blankets and pack one in my sack and one in the supply canister."

"Take good care of them, Luther. We may have to holler for the cavalry. You got the call signs for First Army forward units?"

"Got 'em. HQ, artillery support, tactical air support, we're all set. We could order up a hot meal with this baby."

Rose smiled, lit a cigar and puffed contentedly. "Good job, Luther. Looks like this might be our last job, let's do her right."

Luther's smile lessened just a touch. His young face looked up at Rose and a flicker of shared pain and memory played across it. The smile came back in a second.

"Sounds good to me, Rosie. One more time."

Billy leaned back on the map table and shook his head. He couldn't understand if Rose and his men were glad to be going behind the lines one more time or not. He knew he was scared shitless at the thought of parachuting into the inferno of retreating and advancing armies, neither of which even spoke his language.

The hangar door opened and two Army Air Corps pilots sauntered in. Billy and Rose had been waiting for them to go over the final selection of the drop zone.

Rose looked up and squinted through his cigar smoke. With the cigar clamped tightly in the corner of his mouth, he called out to the two pilots.

"You're late! Have a hard time finding the place?"

The older of the two pilots nudged the younger man and pointed his thumb at Rose and laughed. "Not with you puffing on that stogie. We just followed the stink, and here you are." Rose and the pilot shook hands as Rose turned to Billy and introduced them.

"Captain Billy Boyle, this is Captain Henry Malcolm and Flight Lieutenant Trevor Dinsdale. Our transportation, courtesy of the Office of Strategic Services."

"Pleased to meet you." Billy shook hands and observed the two pilots. They were as unmatched a pair as he had ever seen. The Captain was American, short and stocky, and dressed in khakis that looked like he had slept in them. He wore a leather flight jacket and an Air Corps cap with the wire brim removed. Everything about him was slightly disheveled, and he looked as if he hadn't shaved in a day or so. The Englishman was younger, taller, and trimmer. He wore an impeccably tailored RAF dress blue uniform, and had a neatly trimmed thin black moustache.

"Call me Mac," said Captain Malcolm. "Rosie here never passes up a chance to rib us about getting lost. Back in Sicily…"

"Now Mac," Dinsdale interrupted, "let us not let Captain Boyle think we can't find our own arses when we need to. Rosie, lead on to the maps and show us where you need to go, won't you?"

"C'mon." Rose walked over to the map table and said to Billy, "Trevor here is royalty or something like that. For a snotty Englishman, he's OK."

"Only a minor baronet, old chap. No need to get down on bended knee."

"How long have you guys been flying together?" Billy asked.

"Since North Africa," Mac answered. "I got hooked up with the Special Air Service to learn how they inserted agents behind enemy lines. When I went to the OSS, Trevor came with me."

"Mac and Trev are the best," Rose stated. "They'll get us there, don't worry."

It's not getting there I'm worried about, it's getting back, thought Billy as he nodded silently to Rose. They all gathered around the map table.

"Here's where we're headed," Rose began. "Between the Elbe and the Mulde rivers, south of a line between Wittenberg and Bitterfeld and north of a line between Eilenburg and Torgau. A box about 50 by 35 kilometers."

"What's your objective, old boy?" asked Trevor.

"Purely reconnaissance," answered Billy. "We need to observe enemy activity in that area and report anything suspicious."

Mac leaned closer and studied the map. "Good area for a drop. Pretty flat, lots of meadows and farmland out there. Lots of streams and ponds, gotta watch out for 'em."

"What Mac is describing is called the *Dübener Heide*, or Heath. Pretty country. I spent some time there before the war, visiting my cousin at Leipzig University." Trevor looked up from the map and saw Billy looking at him quizzically. "Don't look so surprised, old bean. Remember the Royal House of Windsor originated in Germany. Lots of rellies over there. Cousin Wolfgang and I had a great time tearing around the heath on our motorbikes. Terribly glad he's a POW in Canada. He's a Luftwaffe fighter pilot and a damn good one too. I rest easier knowing Wolfie's not up there looking to bring me down for another visit!"

"So you've been on the ground here," Rose stated, bringing them back to the task at hand.

"Most of it, yes. Right here, on the east side of the Mulde River, the roads connect at Bad Düben. Just northeast of there, right between the two rivers, there's the only hill in the area. Here." he stabbed a finger in the middle of the drop zone.

"From that point you're no more than ten or fifteen kilometers from the three main roads that run in a triangle along the Elbe and then back to the Mulde from Torgau and Wittenberg."

"Not a bad location," Rose said thoughtfully. "That hill is 182 meters high. If everything else is as flat as you say, we should be able to observe those roads and maybe even each river."

"It's really the only location," Billy said. "If everything else is flat ground or villages, then we'll stick out like a sore thumb and not be able to see much anyway. There's just one problem."

"What's that?" asked Mac.

Billy looked at Rose, who was already nodding his head in agreement. It was Luther who spoke up from the crate where he was sitting and listening to the conversation.

"Well, shit, Captain, if it's such a good observation post, then there's bound to be Jerries already there!"

As Luther spoke those ominous words, a jeep pulled up outside the hanger, skidding to a halt no more than five feet from the door. Billy looked out at the mud-splattered jeep and saw Colonel Sam Harding step out. By the look on his face and the manner of his arrival, Billy knew he had some news, and it was bound to be bad. He left the table and walked toward the door as Colonel Harding slammed it open.

"Billy, I need to talk to you. In private." Harding did not even acknowledge the other men in the room.

"Yes, sir. This way, sir." Billy led Harding down the length of the long tables, past the hanging parachutes. They were out of sight and hearing of the group at the other end of the hangar.

"We've found something out about Operation Gambit. Specifically, the commander." Harding paused a moment and put his hand on Billy's shoulder.

"It's Erich Remke. Colonel Erich Remke."

The name hit Billy like a sledgehammer. All he could think to say was, "He's still alive?"

"It's got to be the same man. Something as mysterious as this is right up Remke's alley. But that's not all." Harding pulled a small slip of paper from his pocket.

"First, don't even bother asking me where this information comes from. It's very top secret." He looked at Billy and waited for acknowledgement.

"OK, no questions."

"Alright. It appears that the SS are out for Remke, or at least two of his men. They are hunting for them right now at OKH headquarters in Zossen."

"And we know that Gambit is an OKH operation!" Billy cut in.

"That's not the half of it. There's an SS officer leading the detail to arrest one of Remke's officers and an enlisted man. His name is Otto Hettstedt."

Billy thought for a second before he nearly shouted, "The same SS guy looking for American uniforms that Dichter told us about…"

"Wait, there's even more," said Harding, with a grin, "and it gets harder and harder to swallow. But, the junior office in charge of the guard detail has orders to arrest Hettstedt also, as soon as he has the others in custody."

"How can you know that…never mind." Billy caught himself before going any farther. "What the hell does it all mean?"

"That's what you're going to find out. We know the name of the operation and where it will take place. We know who the commander is and that he is a very capable officer. We know that several of his men are in big trouble with the SS, and that there's some kind of plotting within the SS also."

"I knew you didn't pull up here with good news, sir." Billy said ruefully.

"I hopped in a jeep as soon as I got the message. I wanted to tell you in person."

"Thanks, Colonel. How much can I tell the other guys?"

"Just tell them we know Remke's name. No need to confuse them with everything else."

"I'm confused enough for everyone right now." Harding laughed and clapped him on the back as they walked back, past the ghostly shrouds hanging all around them. Billy didn't feel like laughing. He suddenly felt a desire to get on with the mission and find Erich Remke.

"Nothing much new to report, boys." Billy said, trying to act nonchalant. "Intelligence has learned the name of the commanding officer of Operation Gambit. It's a Colonel Erich Remke. I've run into him before. He's a very resourceful and determined officer."

Rose studied Billy as he spoke and then looked at Harding, standing back, away from the group. He could tell there was more to the story than a simple identification of an enemy officer. SHAEF Intelligence deputies didn't race around Belgium in a jeep to tell junior officers than kind of detail.

"OK, Billy, thanks for the information. While you were gone we were talking over the problem of Hill 182." In military parlance, hills and elevations that were unnamed were called by their height in meters. "Mac, would you fill Billy in?"

"We don't want to reconnoiter that area before we go in since that might tip our hand. Instead, when we go out, there will be a small raid by medium bombers, A-20 Havocs, on Wittenberg. Their flight path will take them directly over Hill 182. Four of the Havocs will make a low-level bombing run on Hill 182, then return to base."

"So the Germans might think they jettisoned their loads before hitting Wittenberg?"

"Quite," answered Trevor, "although I doubt Jerry's in good enough shape right now to put two and two together. Just in case, though, the Wittenberg raid gives us a good cover."

"Are we going to have a fighter escort?" asked Billy.

"We hardly need to worry about the *Luftwaffe* these days, but yes, we're going to have two P-61 Black Widow night fighters with us. There will be two others flying with the Havocs, and they'll drop flares to light up the hill for the bombers."

"Sounds like you guys thought of everything," Billy said admiringly.

"Well," Trevor said with a smile, "when you've got operational priority and the whole damn Air Corps is sitting on its rump because there's nothing left to bomb, it's not too bloody hard!"

"When do we go?" Rose asked, looking at Harding.

"It'd be tonight if it wasn't for the cloud cover moving in. If it clears, tomorrow night."

"We'd better contact the Bomber Group and the night fighter squadron," Mac said to Trevor. The unlikely duo trotted out to the communications hut.

Billy looked down at the map, wondering where Remke was now and where he was headed.

I hope you're headed straight for Hill 182, you bastard.

CHAPTER TWENTY-ONE

12 April 1945
OKH Headquarters
Zossen, Germany

Leutnant Gustav Stieff found Dieter Neukirk supervising the loading of his unit's radio equipment. It was being loaded on the only German half-track that was part of Section 1, Special Detachment 200. All other transport was made up of either Russian trucks or Russian-marked German trucks. The armored half-track was necessary to protect the precious radio, which would enable Dieter's unit to coordinate with the other sections and call in air support if necessary. The *Schwerer Panzerspähwagen* 231 had been painted in camouflage colors, with all numbers and markings removed.

"*Herr Hauptmann! Herr Hauptmann!*"

Dieter looked up at Stieff, clearly distraught. *Feldwebel* Jost Brunner stuck his head out of the halftrack rear entrance and climbed out.

"Gustav, what's wrong?" asked Dieter.

"The SS are coming for you! For you and Hans, too!"

Jost and Dieter exchanged glances, both of them instantly thinking of Elsa. Jost put his hand on Dieter's arm.

"They can't have her, she would never betray you," said Jost instantly, his disbelief contradicted instantly by his reassurance to Dieter.

Dieter tried to clear his head and think clearly. He could see Stieff was still frustrated and trying to get his attention.

"It's unbelievable! It's just lucky I was there when the message came in…I didn't know what to do…"

"Slow down, Gustav," Jost said soothingly. The two had been good friends before Stieff's promotion, and he preferred to still be treated as another non-com. "Tell us about the message."

"It was an Enigma message that came into Exchange 500 for an *Untersturmführer* Wertholz- he's in charge of the security detail Hettstedt is bringing here."

"Hettstedt?"

"Yes, he's coming to arrest you and Hans. But once he does, Wertholz is to take him into custody also."

"What?" Dieter could not comprehend what was happening or why.

"How much time do we have?" Jost asked, not bothering to try to understand why this was happening, but rather focusing on how to stop it.

"The message didn't say. I'd guess that it was sent after they left Berlin, otherwise they could have told Wertholz in person. An hour at most, or any minute now."

"Who sent the message?" Dieter asked, still trying to fathom the purpose behind the affair.

"*Brigadeführer* Hermann Fegelin."

"My God," exclaimed Jost. "He's near the top of the heap. Why is he interested in you?" Jost and Dieter had both thought the arrests had something to do with Elsa and the hospital, and Hans' involvement in the plot against Hitler. Fegelin's involvement meant something else entirely. Himmler's personal liaison to Adolf Hitler would not be sending such a message unless it had a major significance to his boss.

"We have to tell the Colonel. Jost, get Hans and meet us in Remke's office. Gustav, take your communications unit and get out of here now. We'll meet you at the Wittenberg field headquarters. For the record, I am accepting this radio message from you for delivery to *Untersturmführer* Wertholz."

"You're a good man, *Herr Hauptmann*. Good luck."

Dieter walked quickly across the courtyard towards the main building and Remke. All around him troops were loading equipment and weapons on trucks for the 90-kilometer trip to Wittenberg. They had commandeered a large farm on the outskirts of the city, across the Elbe River and nestled in a small wooded valley near the village of Eutzsch. It provided excellent cover from the air and access to the main operational area, with a high ridge to the south that gave them a clear view along the Elbe River valley. About 12 kilometers to the south a small rise was visible that marked the center of the *Dübener Heide*.

Dieter's mind raced furiously as he approached the main building. He knew he had to find out if Elsa was in danger, and warn her if she had not already been arrested. If she had…he stopped that thought. The possibility was unbearable. The rest of it was a mystery to him. Why would someone like Fegelin or even Himmler care about him, or Hans? Someone no higher in rank than Hettstedt could deal with them, even a junior *Untersturmführer* like Wertholz. It must be…the sudden realization hit him like a thunderbolt and literally stopped him in his tracks. The SS was after Operation Gambit! They were going to use charges against him and Hans to force an SS takeover of the operation. They had probably used Hettstedt to investigate them right from the beginning to find just such an excuse. And since Hettstedt had also been part of Gambit from the start, they were probably going to throw him to the wolves just to show it wasn't inter-service rivalry. It was the only thing that made sense.

Dieter stopped in mid-stride as he mounted to steps to open the door. He had made up his mind that he would do whatever it took to stop Gambit before it succeeded. He had told Elsa about it just yesterday, as much to make the decision real to him as to tell her. He had to admit he had really told her to convince himself, to give himself the backbone he needed when the time came. He couldn't bear the thought of disappointing her once she knew.

Dieter turned from the door, not quite ready to enter. He took a breath and looked up at the sky for a moment. The sun was low and it lit the sides of the whitewashed buildings. It was a beautiful, sideways light that he always enjoyed. Strange, he thought, how beauty shines through in even the worst of times. He thought of Elsa and their future. Of the next generation of German children. Would they grow up in a never-ending war, or in peace? Would they be little Hitler Youth, taught to march in step, or free to speak their minds?

He hadn't thought exactly how he would stop Gambit. He hoped it would simply fail in some obvious manner, and he would not have to endanger his men in some attempt at sabotage. But he would stop it, because the cost would be too great if he didn't. It would be far greater than a few hundred veteran soldiers with the mark of Cain already upon them. But first, there was the SS to deal with. If they took over, there would be no chance to stop Gambit. He turned and opened the door.

Dieter wanted Benedikt with him. He looked in the briefing room first, and then found the newly promoted *Hauptmann* in the mess hall with his two junior officers. He signaled him to come with him. By the time they arrived at Remke's office, Jost and Hans were right behind them. Dieter knocked and entered.

Remke stood before the fireplace, a roaring fire burning as he fed documents into it. He wanted no trace, written or otherwise, to survive at Zossen once they departed. The OKH headquarters was essentially indefensible. It was situated on open terrain, and all defensive forces were located north, in the main line of defense in the Berlin suburbs. Once the Russians broke across the Oder River, they would be here in a matter of days.

"Gentlemen, are you ready to depart?" Remke asked as he tossed the last of a handful of papers into the fire. Turning to face the small group, he saw the looks on their faces and immediately knew there was a serious problem.

"What has happened?" Benedikt and von Schierke also both stared at Dieter with questioning looks on their faces. Dieter steeled himself and tried to be concise.

"Colonel, we have intercepted a radio message which informs us that an SS detachment commanded by *Sturmbannführer* Hettstedt is on its way here to take myself and von Schierke into custody."

Remke allowed himself the slightest hesitation as he took in this information. "What are the charges, and why do you refer to this enlisted man as *von* Schierke? His name on the rolls is Hans Schierke."

"Colonel, permission to speak?" Hans asked, standing to attention. Remke nodded stiffly.

"My name is von Schierke. Count Hans von Schierke, actually. I transferred into the Brandenburg Division under an abbreviated version of my name in order to avoid reprisals from the Gestapo because of family connections to some of the individuals involved in the 20 July coup attempt. *Hauptmann* Neukirk had no knowledge…"

"Enough." Remke cut him off. "I doubt such a name change on transfer papers could escape the notice of an officer as capable as *Hauptmann* Neukirk." Remke fixed Neukirk with a withering glare.

"However, Count," Remke mockingly bowed to von Schierke, "you are an excellent soldier. The men look up to you and follow your lead. I wondered why you had not been made an officer. Now I understand you were lying low amongst the Hiwis of the Brandenburg Division. I have no inclination to hand you over to the SS, and certainly not a key officer such as the *Hauptmann.*"

"Thank you, sir."

"Neukirk, tell me about this message. How did it come into your hands? Do you have any idea why Hettstedt has turned on you? I thought he had actually grown more cooperative recently."

Dieter could tell that Remke assumed he was involved due to his falsifying the transfer papers. He hoped that was true, and saw no reason to complicate matters further by telling him about Elsa.

"Sir, there's actually more to it than that." Dieter related the details about the radio message and the order for Hettstedt's arrest. He told them all about his suspicions, including the implications of Fegelin's name on the radio message.

"Fegelin! Damn him!" Remke shouted as he paced back and forth in front of the fireplace, thinking rapidly. "Fegelin originally came up at the *Führer* briefing with an insane idea about recruiting British POWs to fight the Russians, reasoning that it would draw the Anglo-Americans into the fight with us. It was ridiculous, but it gave me the opening to propose Gambit. Fegelin took it as a slight in front of the *Führer*. Plus there's bad blood between us over an incident in Paris."

"Then Dieter's right," Benedikt offered. "Himmler wants to take us over."

"Which means two things," Remke agreed. "He thinks we have an excellent chance of success, and the Russians must finally be ready to move on Berlin. Do you know how many men there are in the SS detail?"

"Not exactly, but there's only an *Untersturmführer* in charge- no more than a platoon."

The telephone rang on Remke's desk, startling them all. He picked it up and identified himself, spoke a few quick words, and then hung up.

"They're at the front gate. I told the watch officer to take his time reviewing their orders and letting them in. We have perhaps ten minutes."

"Colonel, my parachute company is at your disposal!" Benedikt offered.

"Good. Has *Obersturmführer* Strauch left yet?"

"Yes, Colonel," Jost answered. He left an hour ago with his men and the HQ staff and guard."

"Excellent. We won't have to worry about testing his loyalties. Now here is the plan…"

Erich Remke stood outside on the circular gravel driveway in front of his headquarters building. An early evening chill was setting in, but he wore no jacket. He hadn't wanted to cover any of his medals, knowing that in a potential confrontation with the SS, a look at his impressive array of medals, including the Close Combat badge, Iron Cross with Diamonds, and the *Afrika Korps* cuffband might give him a moment's edge. He stood with arms behind his back, feet slightly spread apart, willing himself to be calm.

Nothing must stop me now. We are so close to victory.

Two trucks pulled into the circle, and Remke could see Hettstedt in the front seat of the first truck. They braked to a halt and Hettstedt got out and walked toward him. Remke watched the SS guards line up outside their trucks, counting them as they drew up in formation. Twenty men and one officer. Wertholz followed Hettstedt once his men were in order.

"I have been expecting you, *Sturmbannführer,* but I didn't think you'd bring us reinforcements."

"Colonel Remke, I must inform you that I am here on a mission authorized by SS *Brigadeführer* Fegelin and also with the knowledge of *Reichsführer* Himmler himself." Hettstedt puffed himself up with this pronouncement, meant to intimidate Remke. Instead, Remke calmly looked at Hettstedt, taking in the nervous twitch and darting eyes. He could tell the man was wound up very tightly.

"I am honored. The nature of this mission...?"

This was not going the way Hettstedt wanted it to. He wanted Remke scared and obedient in the face of his newfound power. Instead, the man was infuriatingly polite.

"You must deliver Dieter Neukirk and Hans Schierke into my custody. They are wanted for interrogation as enemies of the State."

"That is a very serious charge. May I see your orders?"

"I am acting on behalf of *Reichsführer* Himmler! Call him if you wish, but tell me where Neukirk and Schierke are now!"

"Far be it from me to interfere with State security, *Sturmbannführer*. I will deliver them into your custody as soon as they return."

"From where?" Hettstedt was pleased at this turn of events, certain that Remke had finally recognized him as an important person within the SS hierarchy.

"Neukirk took a small detail to the motor pool to draw another vehicle and some spare parts. You're very lucky, actually. Most of the unit has departed already. One of the command vehicles chose to blow out its transmission at the moment of departure. Neukirk took Schierke and two other enlisted men with him to get another half-track and additional parts in case we run into further problems. They won't be back for another hour or so."

"We will wait here," announced Hettstedt, looking around the courtyard. "Once they enter this area, there will be no escape."

"Excellent idea. Would you and the *Untersturmführer* join me in my office for some coffee while we wait?" Remke watched Wertholz look expectantly at Hettstedt. It had been a long ride, and the thought of coffee was tempting.

"Certainly, Colonel. Wertholz, tell your men to watch for anyone entering the courtyard and detain them. You may join us." Hettstedt enjoyed demonstrating to the junior officer how easily he managed such an impressive-looking *Wehrmacht* officer. Wertholz gave his men instructions and followed them inside, hoping for real coffee and perhaps some schnapps.

The office was warm from the fire, and Hettstedt sat in the chair next to it while Wertholz stood near him, as befitted a junior officer. Remke lifted the telephone receiver and called the mess for some coffee.

"You must forgive the lack of office staff today. We are moving everyone to our field headquarters. You will take your place at Exchange 500 as planned, *Sturmbannführer?*"

"Definitely, Colonel, as soon as this business is resolved." Hettstedt certainly planned to be part of Operation Gambit, but not as Remke planned it. Not as a glorified messenger boy, but something much more impressive. They chatted for a few minutes, and then the office door opened. Jost Brunner entered, dressed in a white orderly's jacket and carrying a tray with a coffeepot and cups. He set the tray down on the desk and poured the coffee. After everyone was served he stepped back respectfully and folded his arms behind his back at parade rest.

Remke took a sip and set his cup down on his desk. He removed a slip of paper from his tunic pocket and handed it to Hettstedt, a thin smile creeping up at the corners of his mouth.

"*Sturmbannführer,* I almost forgot. This message came for *Untersturmführer* Franz Wertholz just before you arrived. I'm sure it was meant for you as the senior officer in charge of this detail."

Hettstedt had to hold his coffee cup in one hand and unfold the message with the other. There was no table or other surface near the chair or where Wertholz stood to set down a cup. Hearing the message was addressed to him, Wertholz stepped closer, reading over Hettstedt's shoulder while sipping his coffee.

Outside, the twenty SS guards broke out cigarettes and began to smoke and talk among themselves. They kept a loose formation, in case their officers stepped outside and they needed to form up in a hurry. There was no sign of anyone else in the courtyard and they relaxed, glad to be out of the trucks after the long drive.

Suddenly there was movement everywhere. Soldiers in paratroop smocks and their distinctive helmets ran at them from around the back of the three buildings. From the rooftops three stories above them, on each side, other paratroopers rose up and leveled their StuG 43 Assault Rifles at the crowded group of guards. They were caught milling about, lighting cigarettes and with their Schmeisser submachine guns slung carelessly over their shoulders.

"Hands up! Hands up!" Benedikt yelled. The SS men stood dumbly by, not moving, not understanding what was happening. "Hands up, damn you!"

Finally one of the SS men reached for his Schmeisser and brought it up towards Benedikt. Before he could aim, a burst of fire from a trooper on the roof caught him full in the chest and drove him down. The other guards froze. The sight of one of their comrades in a shattered bloody heap on the ground was enough for them. These were not combat troops. They were used to beating down doors and hauling off defenseless enemies of the State. They looked at each other, and back at the determined men surrounding them. They dropped their guns and held up their hands immediately.

Remke glanced at Jost as Hettstedt and Wertholz read the message together. The look on Hettstedt's face was blank, except that his mouth was wide open. Wertholz was a few seconds behind him, and then he came to the order to arrest Hettstedt. He looked up at Remke and the orderly at the opposite end of the room. Realization dawned on him that he had been neatly separated from his troops. At that moment the sound of shouting and gunfire was heard outside. Wertholz, grasping what was happening, threw his cup to the floor and reached for his holster, drawing out his Walther pistol.

Jost pulled the Russian Tokarev automatic from behind his back and in one fluid motion brought his arm around and fired a single shot. The sound was explosive in the small room. Wertholz' head snapped back and exploded as the round went in right between his eyes and burst out the back, splattering the wall with blood and brains. Wertholz slammed against the wall and slid to the floor, blood pooling all around him.

The office door burst open and Dieter knelt in the doorway, pistol in hand, looking for a threat. He quickly saw Jost with the smoking pistol and Wertholz on the floor. Hettstedt was half up from his chair, frozen in fear, his mouth trying to work but no sound coming out. Benedikt ran in from the courtyard, von Schierke just behind him.

"Everything is under control. We had to shoot one of them, but the rest gave up easily. They're being disarmed now."

"Lock them in the basement cells," Remke ordered. "Leave them food and water and tell them they'll be released within a few days. Tell them their officer was a traitor and that they must remain here for questioning. That ought to keep them wondering for a while." Before the war, these barracks were part of the *Wehrmacht* penal system, where soldiers under sentence performed heavy labor duties around the post and were locked up when not working. Since the war, all penal sentences were served in special battalions on the eastern front, and the cells had not been used in years.

Jost went over quickly to Hettstedt and removed his pistol from its holster. Hettstedt looked terrified and pleaded, "Please don't shoot me..." as he looked down at Wertholz. He then went pale and vomited over the corpse.

Jost dragged the shocked Hettstedt out of the room, into the outer office. He shut the door behind him, closing off the room that now stank of blood, vomit and cordite. He shoved Hettstedt down into a chair and stood behind him as Remke and the others gathered in front of him.

"Well, Otto," Remke began, "you certainly have gotten yourself in a lot of trouble. First you turn on us, then your SS bosses turn on you. Tell me why."

"You shot him." Hettstedt could not believe what had just happened. He almost had done it, then that message and the terrible explosion…he looked back at Jost and said again in a quiet voice, "You shot him."

Remke stepped forward and slapped Hettstedt savagely on the face, the sound almost sounding like a whip. "Snap out of it, man. Tell me what Fegelin wants with you and what he's going to do. Now!"

Hettstedt looked at them and comprehension slowly dawned on him. *Gonsaldes.* He tried to form his thoughts and speak. He was alone now, these men were his only hope. They had killed Wertholz, but Wertholz would have followed his orders and brought him back as a prisoner.

"*Brigadeführer* Fegelin had me report to him on Operation Gambit. He…he and Himmler wanted it for the SS if it looked like it was going to work. They wanted me to find some pretext that would allow them to go to the *Führer* and get him to take control away from the *Wehrmacht.*"

"What exactly did you find out?" Benedikt asked, glancing up at Jost with a slight nod. Jost dug the barrel of his Tokarev into Hettstedt's neck.

"I'll tell you, I'll tell you! I found out about von Schierke changing his name, probably with the connivance of someone in the Brandenburg Division. He was suspected of involvement in the 20 July plot, but the Gestapo lost track of him. That was the first thing."

"And?" Jost demanded with another shove.

"Then I found out *Hauptmann* Neukirk was engaged to Elsa Klein of St. Ludwig's. I had met her once before, and had some suspicions about that hospital. I had nothing else to go on, so I began to investigate her."

Jost, Hans and Dieter exchanged nervous glances. Hettstedt failed to notice Dieter gripping his pistol tighter, and continued, bragging about his investigation.

"I figured it out, you see. The papers, everything. St. Ludwig's had the lowest return rate of identity papers…"

"What the hell are you talking about?" demanded Remke.

"Why Jews, Colonel, Jews. Hundreds of them. His girlfriend has hidden and smuggled hundreds of them out of the city. She gave them identity papers from people killed in the bombing raids."

Dieter lunged forward, grabbing Hettstedt by the collar with one hand and shoving the barrel of his pistol into his throat with the other. "What did you do with her? If you've hurt her, I swear…"

Remke stepped in calmly and pulled Dieter back. "Holster your weapon, *Hauptmann*, now is not the time to get hysterical." He looked down at Hettstedt, feeling revulsion at the sight of the soft, fleshy man in the black uniform. Vomit was drying on his chin and on the tips of his boots. He exuded fear and self-pity. This was the face of those who make war on helpless women, who hunt down the defenseless, and quiver at the thought of an honest fight. Memories began to stir within Remke, but he was well practiced at stilling them. He willed himself to go on.

"Tell me everything, Otto. The whole truth, and then we'll see if we can help you. You really have no one else in the whole world, no one but us, and we're all ready to put a bullet in you if you don't tell us everything."

He did tell them everything, how he found out about Gonsaldes and his attempt to arrest him, and the heart attack. About Fegelin's refusal to give him written orders and his now apparent flattery. About the raid on the hospital. About the order to use Elsa to implicate others. Everything, except Sister Anneliese's condition when he left her. When he was done, Remke was amazed at his vanity and stupidity.

"Fegelin played you for a fool. There are no direct orders connecting your actions to him. You alone are responsible for the death of a neutral diplomat. He even used you to come here, into our stronghold, to take Neukirk and von Schierke. If you succeeded, he would have them and you. Remember that you're a part of Gambit also. He could show Himmler and Hitler that the whole Operation was rotten, even down to a renegade SS officer. He would have had the whole lot of you shot, unless there was a chance to get something further on me. He hates me. Either way, he would have ended up in command of Gambit."

Everything made sense now to Hettstedt. "Yes, he wanted to use Neukirk and his girlfriend for that. Threaten each of them with the death of the other until he got what he wanted. I am a dead man."

"Elsa is in *Prinz Albrecht Strasse*." It was not a question from Dieter, only a helpless, forlorn statement. Remke looked at him and saw the agony in his eyes. Something stirred deep within him. He had seen that look many times, the look of a man imagining the worst terrors inflicted upon the woman he loves. The look of a man who knows that the unimaginable has happened and who was powerless to prevent it. He had seen that face many times, in every reflection he passed. As he looked at Hettstedt, he thought of the rage he had felt against the Nazi leaders as they abandoned the ancient German lands of East Prussia to the Russians, leaving Anna and her family defenseless. He looked again at Dieter, wondering if Elsa Klein called her lover's name out in the night when they came for her.

Remke walked away from Hettstedt and went to the nearest window, opening it up and letting fresh cool evening air flow in. He closed his eyes and breathed deeply. For the first time since Anna's death, he felt something in his heart besides a desire to kill that eased the pain just a little. He had met Elsa briefly, and passed by her picture on Dieter's desk many times. She was a pretty woman, not as beautiful or delicate as Anna with her long blonde hair, but stunning in her own plainer fashion. And brave, too. Anna had stayed to care for her parents when she could have run away. Elsa sounded like a woman who didn't run either. Could he leave her to the likes of the Gestapo, just as Anna had been left for the Russians? Could he condemn Dieter, his loyal protégé, to a fate that had nearly driven him mad? Suddenly it felt as if Anna was nearby, trying to speak to him.

It's all right, Erich. I know you couldn't save me. You would have if you could, but you were far, far away. But you can save her. Save her for Dieter. Save her for me. Save her for yourself.

Tears rolled down his cheeks, the first tears of real sadness he had cried for her. Not the tears of fear or the sobs of a broken man, just a deep, inconsolable sadness. He felt his men's eyes on his back and he struggled for control. When he was sure his voice wouldn't break, he wiped the tears away and tried to sound confident and in command.

"Otto, you were actually very convincing when you arrived here. Have you really gotten so far without any written orders or authorization?"

Hettstedt looked up, surprised at the turn in the conversation.

"Well…yes. I really thought I had the backing of Fegelin. And Himmler did receive me once and encouraged me in my investigation."

"So your own belief in your superiors, plus your rank and uniform, did the job for you." Remke sounded like he was thinking something through. He straightened his shoulders and turned towards the group.

"*Sturmbannführer* Hettstedt, how would you like to end the war safely in an American POW cage, delivered to them in a Wehrmacht officer's uniform, courtesy of the Brandenburgers?"

"Colonel," Dieter said angrily, "I'm not…"

"Quiet down, boy," Jost said as he gently laid a hand on Dieter's shoulder. "I think the Colonel has a fine idea. Count me in."

"Me too," echoed Hans, looking at Remke.

Dieter and Benedikt asked at the same time, "What…"

"I can't believe my officers are so thick," said Remke with a smile. "Now Otto, tell me. Long life or an SS noose?"

Hettstedt did not hesitate for a moment. "What do you want me to do?"

CHAPTER TWENTY-TWO

13 April 1945
Kurfürstendamm
Berlin, Germany

The staff car sped along on the *Kurfürstendamm* through the *Grünewald*, the forested park on the southwestern edge of Berlin. The headlights were taped over except for a small slit on each, allowing a narrow spot of light to shine on the rain-soaked pavement. It was two o'clock in the morning, and there was no other traffic on the road. The *Kurfürstendamm*, or Ku-Dam as it was known to Berliners, was a main artery into the city from the south. The road wound through the forest before entering the suburbs and then into the once-elegant final stretch of the famed Ku-Dam with its smart shops and cafes, now blasted into heaps of rubble. A truck followed closely behind the large car.

Dieter gazed out the window, thinking wistfully of the long hikes he and Elsa had taken through these woods. It seemed ages ago and so unreal now. Then he looked around at the occupants of the vehicle, and he realized this was as unreal as he ever imagined anything could be.

Jost Brunner was driving, and sitting next to him in the front seat was Hans von Schierke, dressed in a black SS uniform taken from one of their prisoners. It matched the uniform Dieter wore, also taken from an SS guard. Colonel Remke lounged in the seat opposite him in the rear passenger compartment of the staff car, resplendent and aristocratic as always in his own *Wehrmacht* uniform. Next to Dieter sat a very nervous Otto Hettstedt, wringing his hands worriedly, plagued by second thoughts.

"Colonel Remke," Hettstedt said in a whining voice, "are you certain you want to go through with this? Not only is it dangerous, but also why should you risk your life for this woman? She is clearly guilty of harboring Jews…"

"I don't give a damn about the Jews. I need Neukirk here focused on Operation Gambit," Remke snapped back at him. He softened his tone, regretting the outburst. He wanted Hettstedt to be a confident, willing partner in what they were about to do. "He plays a critical role that can be filled by no one else. I don't want him worried about his fiancée in a Gestapo cell when the future of the Reich hangs in the balance."

Hettstedt did not reply, and continued to wring his hands even more rapidly.

Remke removed Hettstedt's pistol from his coat pocket. He removed the bullets from the clip and one from the chamber, replaced the empty clip and handed the Walther to Hettstedt.

"Here. Take your pistol."

"Unloaded? What if I need it?"

"Don't worry about a thing. Neukirk and von Schierke will be with you at all times. Think of them as your personal bodyguard. I will be with you also."

"Hans," Dieter said, "do you have your silencer?"

Hans reached inside his greatcoat and pulled out a Walther P-38 with a silencer attached to the barrel. He held it up for Hettstedt to see.

"The Count will protect you," Remke said smiling, "and he will also quietly kill you if you betray us. But there should be no reason for that, right Otto?" Hettstedt nervously nodded in agreement. The car slowed a bit as they left the *Grünewald* and entered the city proper. "Coming up on the Tiergarten, Colonel," Jost announced. "We should be there in ten minutes, barring any roadblocks."

"Very well." Remke looked straight at Hettstedt. "Remember Otto, once we're done here, you are safe with us. We keep our bargains. You can get rid of that SS uniform and we'll put you in a Major's uniform of the Wehrmacht. Once we're in the field we'll lead you to the American lines and you can give yourself up. You won't be the only one. You'll finish out the war safe in an officer's POW camp, with no embarrassing questions about your SS duties. And no Russians."

"Yes, yes," Hettstedt stammered. "You will keep your bargain?"

"The Colonel already told you," Dieter said grimly. "You need not doubt anything he told you. Anything." Hettstedt took his meaning, and kept quiet.

"All right, one more time," Remke said, and gave his briefing again. "We pull up to Number 8 in front and Jost waits with the staff car outside.

The truck pulls in to the courtyard entrance just before that, on the south side of the building. This puts them opposite the side entrance of the south wing. It also gives us vehicles at two exit points in case something goes wrong. *Sturmbannführer*, you lead the way inside. Hans directly beside you. Dieter and I behind. We go through the front entrance, up the staircase to the main hall. We pass the auditorium on our right, then take the next staircase down. That connects us with the south wing of the building and the Gestapo prison. You've told us there are guards inside and at the prison entrance, but you have freedom of movement within the building." Remke waited for Hettstedt to acknowledge this. He agreed with a quick nod. Remke thought he looked a little more confident. He hoped so.

"Good. Then a quick trip to the basement cells. Have Elsa, Doktor Kappelen, and Sister Anneliese released into your custody. You are going to use them as bait in a special action at the hospital, in case anyone asks."

"That should not be a problem. I doubt anyone of my rank or higher will be in the building at this hour, unless Himmler has called one of his emergency meetings. We will avoid that corridor in any case."

"Absolutely," Remke agreed. "We then take the prisoners up one flight and out the side of the building to the truck. There are two of our men in the back of the truck and two in the cab. They will load the prisoners into the rear of the truck. Dieter, you stay with them. The three of us walk out to the front and get in the staff car, then we all drive straight to Wittenberg. It's about 100 kilometers, so we should arrive by dawn. Any questions?"

"Ah…the Sister…" Hettstedt was nervous again, his eyes flitting back and forth between Neukirk and Remke. "She may need some assistance. Some of the guards were much too rough with her."

"My God," muttered Dieter, "what kind of animal are you?"

Remke watched Hettstedt's face crumble into fear. He realized it had been a mistake to bring Neukirk along. He was too emotional and failed to see the need for Hettstedt to feel safe and secure with them so he would have the self-assurance and arrogance to carry this plan out. Remke stared at Neukirk, trying to will the younger man to get his passions under control.

"*Herr Hauptmann!* " Remke said sharply. Dieter turned his face to Remke. "I am sure the *Sturmbannführer* regrets any overzealous actions on the part of the lower ranks. He is obviously not to blame for such an unfortunate incident. Correct, *Hauptmann* Neukirk?"

"Yes sir." The two men locked stares until Dieter repeated, "Yes sir, I understand."

"Very well. In any case one of the men in the truck is a medical orderly. He can care for the Sister until we get to Wittenberg. Get ready, everyone, we're almost there."

Hettstedt tried to stop wringing his hands and overcome his fear. He knew this was his only chance to survive. Everyone had betrayed him, after all he had done. His only chance was with two men he had planned to arrest as enemies of the State and an insane Colonel on a mission to avoid defeat and keep the war going. He almost felt like laughing at the idiocy of it all. Instead, he focused on hoping that Sister Anneliese was still alive. He wondered what these men would do if they knew he had ordered the Sister beaten. Would they keep their bargain? The staff car pulled to a halt at the curb, the truck going a little further beyond to pull over at the gated entrance to the dark, looming building. Number 8 *Prinz Albrecht Strasse.*

The four men exited the car and walked to the main entrance. Rain pelted them as they walked the few steps from curb to the three short curved steps that ascended between two ornate columns. Due to the weather there were no guards posted outside, but two SS men snapped to attention when Hettstedt burst through the door. He gave them a gruff "Heil Hitler!" and then shook off his wet leather greatcoat before leading the group through the narrow foyer to the large staircase leading up to the main hall. There was no challenge. They ascended the staircase and entered the main hall. Swastika banners hung along the walls and a marble bust of Hitler gazed at them as they walked by. Dieter shivered involuntarily and his heart began to race as he thought of Elsa just one floor below. Remke caught his eye and nodded encouragingly. Everything seemed to be going smoothly.

The second staircase was just a few meters away. It led either down to the *Hausgefängnis*, or Gestapo prison, or to the main floor of the south wing. The *click-clack* sound of their bootheels as they walked across the marble floor echoed off the walls. The sound grew louder and Hans glanced back at Remke, putting this left arm on Hettstedt and pushing him faster to the staircase. There was another group of men walking down the corridor from the south wing, their sounds mixing with the echoes in the hallway.

Dieter could see Hans had his right hand resting inside the front of his opened greatcoat. The staircase came closer, but Dieter could not tell if the other group of men would continue across the hallway that arched over the stairway, or turn left and come down the stairs, heading either to the basement or the main hall. Voices began to emerge from the corridor. Just inches from the steps, Dieter caught a glance of a short man with a receding chin and prince-nez glasses emerging from the hallway one level above. Heinrich Himmler, *Reichsführer* of the SS himself, was only meters away from them.

Himmler was reading from a clipboard which he was handing to an aide. Dieter ducked his head down, even though he was sure Himmler could not possibly know him. Hettstedt and Hans were now several steps down and Dieter and Remke were right behind them as the other group passed above them, crossing over the stairway as they descended.

"Have von Schlabrendorff transferred to Dachau immediately, I don't want him here any longer," said Himmler to his aide. "If he dies, let him die there."

The sound of boots and the obsequious voices of his aides followed Himmler down the hall. Dieter relaxed as they descended the stairs, thankful of their narrow escape. If Himmler had seen Hettstedt.... Then Dieter noticed Hans looking at him beseechingly. Of course! Von Schlabrendorff was his cousin, his link to the 20 July plotters. He was still alive, and right here, although his future seemed limited.

Within moments they were in the main guardroom in the *Hausgefängnis*. To their left was a short hallway with various rooms for the guards, including a small kitchen. To their right was the entrance to the cellblock. A guard seated at a small table stood to attention.

"*Sturmman*," Hettstedt said, addressing the private by his SS rank, "I am here to take into my custody three prisoners." He studied the arrest list posted on the wall, which showed prisoner's names and cells, as well as arresting officer. He knew this was a dangerous moment. If for any reason this guard knew of his own arrest order, they would never get out of here. He indicated the three prisoners on the list.

The guard looked at Hettstedt and the tall Wehrmacht officer standing quietly behind the two other SS guards. He squinted at the list and asked, "Are you *Sturmbannführer* O. Hettstedt?"

"Of course I am, you idiot!" Hettstedt raised his voice and slapped his hand irritably on the table. "I brought those three in and now I need them out for a special action at dawn."

"Excuse me, *Sturmbannführer*. I must follow procedures."

Hettstedt couldn't reply. Dieter felt his heart sink. If this fellow demanded written orders, they would have no choice but to leave, or shoot it out. Neither appealed to him. He noticed Hans unbuttoning his coat, slowly. The guard turned to a small desk with a telephone and a stack of papers. Hans' hand began to come out from the folds of his coat.

"Would you sign the release form, *Sturmbannführer?*"

The sound of the four men releasing their breath at once sounded thunderous to Dieter. He was amazed the guard didn't notice and sound the alarm.

"Of course, *Sturmman*. Very proper, I like that." Hettstedt scrawled his name on the forms and the guard dutifully wrote out each prisoner's name, the date and time.

"This way, sir." The guard picked up a set of keys and unlocked the cellblock door. The door opened to a long, wide corridor that was divided by a guardroom that ran up the middle of the corridor and separated the rows of cells along each wall. Hettstedt had explained that guards on the night shift would take turns sleeping in the guardroom if there was not much activity. This seemed to be a quiet night.

"Prisoner Kappelen is right over here. Cell 16." The guard led them to a cell along the left wall. He unlocked and opened the door. The bright lights in the hall seemed to flood the tiny dark cell. An old man, huddled on a mattress on the floor, held his hand over his eyes.

"No, please, let me sleep…"

"Stop your blubbering, old man," the guard said roughly, "you're going on a little trip. Get up!" He kicked Kappelen and Dieter forced himself to not go to his aid.

"Pick him up. We don't have all night." Remke's stern voice cut through the moans of Doktor Kappelen as the guard pulled back his foot for another blow. The guard was confused for a moment by the *Wehrmacht* officer giving orders. The only *Wehrmacht* officers he had seen down here were usually on the other side of cell door. An officer was an officer, though. He pulled up the old man by his arms and shoved him out into the corridor.

Hans held the Doktor by his arm and guided him. Dieter stayed in front, not letting Kappelen see his face, fearing he might blurt out his name and inadvertently give them up.

"Cell 28 next, Prisoner Klein." The guard led them around the end of the guardroom, to the row of cells in the opposite wall. He selected a key from his chain and worked the lock.

"Get up," he announced in a bored tone, "you're being transferred." He smiled at Hettstedt, guessing that a "special action" at dawn would mean these prisoners would not be coming back.

Elsa had heard the footsteps in the hall and had gotten up to be ready in case they were coming for her. When she heard the word "transfer" she didn't know what to think. Then the door opened with a clank and the light blinded her. The guard reached in and grabbed her by the arm, pulling her out into the hall.

"Come on, these men don't have all night!"

Dieter stepped back so he was behind the guard. He tilted his helmet back so Elsa could see his face, at the same moment putting his finger to his lips and shaking his head.

Elsa saw him immediately. Out of the corner of her eye she had glanced at one of the guards in the hallway and instantly knew it was Dieter. She had been thinking of him constantly and his image was burned into her mind. At first she thought she was hallucinating. She looked straight at him, and he cautioned her to silence. It was really Dieter! She almost fainted, putting her hand out to the wall to steady herself.

"Next, Cell 39, Prisoner Anneliese, no last name." The guard moved down the line of cells.

"Move!" A rough voice yelled and Elsa felt hands push her towards Sister Anneliese's cell. Dieter's hands. Tears welled in her eyes and her lower lip began to tremble.

We're not out of here yet, she thought to herself. *Hold on.*

Elsa looked around her to see whom Dieter was with. She saw Hans, and knew that Jost must be somewhere nearby. With a shock she saw it was Hettstedt next to Hans! And Colonel Remke with Dieter.

Am I dreaming? Have I gone insane?

Her thoughts were interrupted as the door to Cell 39 opened and she heard the guard speak to Hettstedt.

"Too late for this one. She's dead."

Dieter held Elsa back and looked into the cell. Sister Anneliese was on the floor, her face caked with blood. A bucket of water and a few bloody rags were the only evidence of medical care.

"I heard they beat up her pretty good when they brought her in," the guard said conversationally. "Well, you'd know that sir, wouldn't you. I hope these two will be enough for you." The guard walked past them to the guard station by the door that led to the stairs to the side door in the courtyard.

Dieter let go of Elsa and walked into the cell. Sister Anneliese's hands were still clasped together, as if she had been praying when so died. They had taken her rosary from her, but twined around her hands was the delicate gold chain and small cross she had worn around her neck. She had obviously used that as a comfort in her last prayers. He heard Elsa sob as Remke took her by the arm and led her away. Dieter knelt and kissed the Sister on her forehead, took the cross and chain from her hand, and walked out the door, too saddened to even feel anger.

Dieter joined the group at the door. Remke barked at him, "You! Take this prisoner! That's what we brought you for!" He shoved Elsa toward him. He took her by the arm and she had to fight the urge to collapse in his arms.

"Two prisoners, released to *Sturmbannführer* Hettstedt." Their guard showed the release forms to the final guard at the door to the exit staircase. This guard was a *Rottenführer*, roughly equivalent to a corporal. He was a little older and looked perhaps a little smarter that the first guard. He read the release forms and slowly began to fill in his name, date and time.

"Yes, *Sturmbannführer*, I remember these two. I was on the hospital raid with you. You boys new here?" He glanced up at Hans and Dieter.

"We've only been in Berlin a week," said Dieter quickly. "Transferred in from the Nordhausen camp."

"So the new boys get to go out in the rain at night, eh?"

"*Rottenführer*," Hettstedt broke in, "We are in a hurry. Save the enlisted men's talk for the mess."

"Yes, sir. Everything's in order. Do you need any assistance with these prisoners?"

"No. We have a truck and men waiting in the courtyard."

The *Rottenführer* opened the stairwell door and walked up one flight with them. The courtyard door was also locked and he opened that for them, holding the door for the officers as they passed. He glanced at the waiting truck. Nothing out of the ordinary. He stood in the doorway for a moment and watched them put the prisoners in the truck. The rain began to blow into the open door and he closed it and walked back down to the cellblock.

Something nagged at the *Rottenführer*. Something was out of place. He sat down at his table and lit a cigarette. He couldn't figure it out. *Sturmbannführer* Hettstedt was definitely a pompous ass, but he did his job. That Colonel was a little unusual in the *Hausgefängnis*, but he had been with Hettstedt and must've been part of an SS operation. He couldn't put his finger on what could be wrong.

Must be my imagination, he thought.

He went back to leafing through the latest copy of the *Volkischer Beobachter* newspaper. There was an item about the Luftwaffe 9th Parachute Division deploying on the northeastern side of Berlin for the defense of the city. There were pictures of the paratroopers in their distinctive smocks and helmets, preparing defenses.

Wait a minute! Those were paratroopers waiting in that truck, not SS men!

At that moment a *Kübelwagen* with two military policemen pulled up beside the staff car waiting by the front entrance. One of the two *Kettenhunde* climbed out, the driving rain drenching him as he stood by the driver's window and signaled Jost to roll it down.

"No vehicles are to park here!" He pointed to the lamppost on the curb directly in front of the staff car. There was a sign prominently posted with a large P in a circle with a red line through it.

"Tell it to the *Sturmbannführer*. He's inside with my Colonel. Some meeting with the SS bigwigs." Jost shrugged his shoulders in his best non-com fashion at the ways of officers. It didn't work.

"No vehicles are to park here!" he repeated. "Papers!"

Jost withdrew his identity papers and handed them to the Chain Dog. He looked them over in the beam of his flashlight and tossed them back to Jost, apparently satisfied.

"*Fedelwebel*, you cannot remain here. We must enforce the parking ban in order to keep the roadway clear for emergency vehicles in case of a bombing raid." Jost began to protest, but the military policeman cut him off. "I know, this isn't bombing weather, but my *Fedelwebel* will have my head if there are any unauthorized vehicles on the street. Use the car park in the courtyard back there if you want, but you must move out."

Jost knew he couldn't argue very well about another non-com's orders to his enlisted men, so he wearily agreed and put the staff car into reverse, and backed up to the drive leading to the courtyard. He could park the car right in the entrance and still keep an eye on the front door.

The *Rottenführer* strode past the guardroom door and banged on it, signaling the men inside to their posts. As he went to the telephone six men spilled out, hooking up their belts and putting on helmets. The looked to their *Rottenführer* for guidance, not knowing if there was an inspection or problems with the prisoners. He was busy on the telephone.

"Give me the Watch Officer!" There was always an officer on duty in the building through the night, in the communications center. He was supposed to supervise all activities during the night and report to senior staff officers in the morning. Usually he just slept and left the routine matters to the non-commissioned officers. Tonight was no different as the *Rottenführer* could tell from the groggy voice at the other end of the line.

"*Hauptsturmführer* Schaffenburg here."

"*Rottenführer* Hanke here. Sir, was *Sturmbannführer* Otto Hettstedt scheduled to come in tonight?"

"Hettstedt, Hettstedt..." Hanke could hear papers shuffling. "Yes, Hettstedt. He was supposed to arrive earlier today, actually. *Untersturmführer* Wertholz was supposed to bring him in with several others. They're overdue now." Schaffenburg was looking at a copy of the radio message sent by Fegelin. He had been waiting for Wertholz to report in all night.

"Overdue?" Hanke didn't understand. "Do you mean he was supposed to pick up the prisoners earlier?" Now it was Schaffenburg's turn to be confused.

"What are you talking about? Hettstedt is in custody by now. He is to be brought into the *Hausgefängnis* with two other prisoners by Wertholz any moment now." Hanke suddenly got very nervous.

"Sir, I must report that no one in the guardroom was informed of this." He swallowed nervously before continuing. "And that *Sturmbannführer* Hettstedt just left here after taking two prisoners with him." There was a stunned silence on the other end of the telephone, followed by a yell that made Hanke pull the receiver away from his ear.

"STOP HIM!"

Hanke pointed to the men now milling around him.

"You four follow me. You others secure the exits. Let no one else enter or leave!"

He unlocked the staircase door and bounded up the steps, drawing his pistol. The other men had their rifles with them. He fumbled excitedly with the keys at the exit door and unlocked it, swung it open and stepped out into the courtyard.

"Halt! Halt or we shoot!"

When they had emerged from the building, Doktor Kappelen was still unaware who had taken him out. He recognized only Hettstedt, and was certain he had come to kill him. He was very weak and nearly delirious. The walk up from the cellar had taxed him severely after his beating and more than two days in a cramped cell. His legs gave out and he collapsed, Hans still holding him up by one arm. Remke moved to help him, and called out to the two paratroopers in the rear of the truck to help.

Elsa felt in shock, looking up at Dieter in disbelief and to Kappelen with concern. Dieter cautioned her, still gripping her arm tightly.

"Not yet, someone may still be looking." He had seen the guard close the door after watching them walk across the courtyard, and he didn't yet know if any other curious eyes were upon them. They walked slowly to the back of the truck. Hettstedt stood by while the others lifted Doktor Kappelen's limp body up into the truck. He looked around nervously, his eyes darting back to the door and to the lighted windows on the top floor.

"Hurry up!"

"Don't lose your grip now, Otto. We're almost out of danger," said Remke confidently.

"I can't believe Fabian is in one of those cells," Hans said. "I probably walked right by him." He was up on the truck bed, having handed Kappelen off to the medic who had laid him out on a pile of blankets on the floor and was covering him. He reached out a hand to Elsa to help her up when he saw the staff car pull into the head of the driveway and brake there.

"What is Jost doing?" he asked to no one in particular. Suddenly the side door they had just come out burst open, light from the staircase spilling out into the courtyard and reflecting off the wet cobblestones. They heard a shouted command and saw a pistol pointed at them and men with rifles crowding behind the *Rottenführer* as he stood just outside the doorway.

Jost had been looking back at the activity in the courtyard, wondering if he should back up further and pick up Remke and the others. He couldn't see them all clearly in the rain, and decided to wait here in case one of them was exiting via the front entrance for some reason. He then saw the door fly open and the guards gathered around it. He jammed the car into reverse and sped backward into the courtyard.

The sudden movement from the staff car racing backward toward them startled Hanke. He glanced at it and back at the group around the truck. No one had moved. He hesitated, unsure of what to do next and hoping that idiot *Hauptsturmführer* had alerted the guards at the front entrance.

Dieter saw Hans reach into his coat. He threw Elsa down under the rear gate of the truck and knelt in front of her, pulling his Schmeisser up as he did so. Remke drew his pistol and also went into a crouch.

Hans focused on nothing but the target, bringing his silenced Walther out with his right hand and cupping it in the palm of his left to steady his aim. It was hardly necessary at this distance. As he was bringing the weapon up he had the split second thought that the SS men were fools to be standing in a lighted doorway like that, bunched up and back-lit.

The moment Hanke hesitated was his last. There were two muffled sounds from the truck and Hanke fell back, as two bullets thumped into his chest. The other guards literally didn't know what hit him. Hans methodically shot two others before the last two reacted. Two rifle shots rang out in the courtyard, echoing off the walls. This was followed by a burst from Dieter's Schmeisser that flung one guard back. The last guard pulled the door closed as he retreated inside, firing one last shot from his rifle before he withdrew and locked the door behind him, grateful to be alive.

Dieter swiveled around on his heels and saw Elsa was unharmed. He pulled her up and handed her up to Hans. Remke got up and looked around to check for casualties.

"We've got to get out of here, is everyone alright?"

"He's not." Dieter pointed to Hettstedt, stretched out on the ground, rain pelting his lifeless face. One of the Mauser shots had torn through his throat and the blood drained out from him, running in red rivulets between the cobblestones. They all glanced at him for a moment. His eyes were frantic, darting back and forth, seeking to understand what had happened. Then they rolled up in his head.

"Hans, in the car with me," Remke ordered. "Dieter, up in the truck. Hurry!"

Remke ran to the car and jumped in the back. It sped down the drive and into the street, turning left so as to not cross in front of the main entrance. The truck rumbled out behind them. Two guards were running down the sidewalk towards them and others were spilling out the front door. Lights were turned on all over the building. Dieter aimed his Schmeisser and loosed a spray of bullets that caused the closest guards to dive for cover. He looked back at the rest of them in the truck.

The medic was tending to the *Doktor*, and the other paratrooper was putting a blanket over Elsa's shoulders. She was shivering, but her eyes focused on Dieter. He moved towards her and she embraced him.

"Dieter, you said you'd come back for me, no matter what," she looked up at him, tears in her eyes and her teeth chattering from the cold, "and you did."

She buried her face in his chest and held him tightly as they leaned against the back of the truck. The paratrooper draped another blanket over both of them and smiled gently, then turned away to give them what privacy they could find with each other on this cold night of death and redemption.

CHAPTER TWENTY-THREE

13 April 1945
SS Headquarters
Berlin, Germany

SS *Reichsführer* Heinrich Himmler glared at his assembled staff. He was tired and very angry. He had been up all night, since the gunfire in the courtyard had thrown everyone into a panic. There were rumors of Russian paratroopers, assassination attempts, and other plots. It had taken the rest of the night to sort things out.

"Gentlemen," Himmler began icily, "yesterday I entrusted *Brigadeführer* Fegelin with the task of securing three arrests, one of these being one of our own, this Hettstedt. Fegelin sent out an officer and two squads of security troops to do so. Today, we find those troops incarcerated in cells in a deserted, remote building at OKH headquarters in Zossen. No one remaining there has any idea how they got there. Their officer is found with his brains blown out. The very man that was to be arrested returns here with unnamed accomplices and releases two of our political prisoners. I am in the building, and armed enemies of the State are roaming our hallways! A battle breaks out in the courtyard and four of our men are killed, but not before they shoot and kill Hettstedt, who could have told us what happened."

Himmler fixed his glare on Fegelin, who stood in back of the others, hoping to escape notice. Fegelin prepared himself for the verbal onslaught, but Himmler targeted someone else, preferring to keep Fegelin off balance.

"Kaltenbrunner, is not the Reich Security Main Office responsible for security in this building? Should I have my personal escort battalion surround the place?"

Ernst Kaltenbrunner, head of the RSMO since the assassination of Reinhard Heydrich, was a totally dedicated Nazi and rumored to be even more cold-hearted than Himmler. He was ruthlessly efficient and was able to adroitly avoid blame when things went badly. He had no problem shifting the responsibility for the entire matter to anyone else.

"*Reichsführer,* if my office had been notified of the unusual nature of *Brigadeführer* Fegelin's instructions concerning the arrest of Hettstedt, he would have been apprehended as soon as he entered the building. As it was, there was absolutely nothing out of the ordinary for anyone to take notice of. If not for the prompt action of one of my men, they would have all gotten away."

"Not quite prompt enough," countered Himmler, ignoring the fact that the man had been killed for his troubles. "But your point is well taken."

Kaltenbrunner understood that he had been cleverly used by Himmler to focus the blame on Fegelin. It did not concern him in the least, nor did the loss of his men. His prestige was intact, which is all that mattered.

"Fegelin, as Kaltenbrunner so ably points out, your handling of the Hettstedt matter was sloppy. We will discuss this further in private. For the rest of you, make sure those in your departments know that this is a sealed matter of the highest State security. No mention of it is to be made, and no reference is to appear in any official documents."

"*Reichsführer*, may I suggest that the personnel records of the men lost last night show they volunteered for duty at the front, and that they were killed defending the Reich at the Oder River?" Kaltenbrunner offered.

"Very good. Please see to it." Himmler appreciated this touch. It cleaned up the loose ends. "Fegelin and Jüttner, remain. The rest of you are dismissed."

Obergruppenführer Hans Jüttner was head of the *Waffen*-SS, the combat troops in the field under SS command. He had little to do with the Hettstedt matter and calmly waited to see what Himmler wanted with him. Fegelin was very nervous. What happened last night had greatly unnerved Himmler, who initially thought it was an assassination attempt aimed at him, and then appeared disappointed to learn it wasn't.

Himmler offered neither of them a seat. He came to the point quickly.

"Jüttner, what combat troops do we have in Berlin, available for immediate assignment? We need some combat-experienced troops to clean up this matter. Our internal security troops are obviously out-classed."

"The only combat unit, besides your escort battalion, which does not have an assignment on the line is the SS Frundberg Division. It's refitting after evacuating from the Courland Peninsula in Latvia."

Himmler ignored the comment about his escort battalion, which was his own personal bodyguard. He certainly had no plans to allow it to be used up as a common infantry unit before he needed it.

"You will provide up to a battalion of motorized troops for Fegelin's use in a matter I will discuss with him now. Dismissed."

Jüttner gave Himmler the stiff arm Hitler salute and left, glad to be out of this with only the loss of a battalion. As soon as the door shut behind him, Himmler began to rage.

"You incompetent buffoon! If you weren't married to Eva Braun's sister I'd transfer you to a penal battalion immediately! How dare you allow this to happen here! What if Hitler were to find out we allowed the *Wehrmacht* to waltz in here and release whomever they liked?"

"My apologies sir, I didn't know..."

"You don't know anything! You don't even know where they are now! I want Neukirk and this other man, von Schierke. I want to go to the *Führer* as we originally planned and take over Operation Gambit! If this man Remke can walk in and out of here, then he's the man to carry it off, and I want him to do so under the SS banner. If he succeeds, Fegelin, he'll be the most powerful man in Germany after the *Führer*. And do you know what will happen when he tells the *Führer* that you tried to stop Gambit by sending Hettstedt after him? Think about it, dear boy. Eva and her sister won't be able to save you then."

A knock on the door interrupted them as Fegelin considered the implication of Himmler's statement. Even now, at the eleventh hour, Himmler was plotting to gain his master's favor in case the fantastic plan worked. He knew he would be sacrificed in a moment if it suited his needs.

The knocking continued.

"I am not to be disturbed!"

"But *Herr Reichsführer*, it is most urgent!" The aide opened the door a crack without permission, risking Himmler's wrath. It must be very terrible or very good news, thought Fegelin. The aide stepped into the room and stood at attention.

"*Reichsführer*, Roosevelt is dead!"

"What? Are you certain?"

"Yes sir, it's been confirmed in several news reports. Roosevelt is dead and the American presidency has been taken over the vice-president, Truman."

"That is wonderful! This is the sign we've been waiting for!" Others who had heard the news gathered outside Himmler's office or, depending upon rank, came in once they saw he was in an ebullient mood. They congratulated each other and celebrated the good news, which seemed like an omen of relief after the months of retreat and defeat.

"This is the first sign of a split between the Communists and the West," announced Himmler. "They will not be able to sustain this unnatural alliance without Roosevelt!" The small group cheered and applauded. Himmler moved towards Fegelin and put his arm around his shoulder. His attitude had totally changed.

"Fegelin, you must succeed this time," Himmler said quietly. "This is our chance, and it will not come again. Get Operation Gambit for me. With it we will exploit this gift and rip the Allies apart!"

Fegelin felt dizzy with the possibilities. He knew what Himmler said was true. It was a miracle that Roosevelt would die now, just when the confusion of a new, unknown American leader would benefit Gambit the most.

"As you command, *Reichsführer!*"

CHAPTER TWENTY-FOUR

13 April 1945
Aboard a Douglas C-53 Skytrooper
10,000 feet over Germany

Captain Billy Boyle crossed his legs in front of him and tried to get comfortable in the cold, hard metal seat. With only eleven men in the Skytrooper transport, there was room among the twenty-eight seats for arms and legs to stretch out. Comfort, though, was hardly a possibility, with each man encumbered by parachute, pack, and weapons in the unheated cabin. The plane vibrated constantly as the twin Pratt and Whitney engines roared into the night.

Billy fidgeted in his seat. He couldn't get comfortable and couldn't settle himself down. He was anxious about the drop, and felt a nervous twitter in his gut as his mind rebelled against the thought of leaping out of an aircraft into the darkness above enemy territory. He had parachuted at night before, and the waiting before the jump had always been the worst for him. More than that, he ached to get into action and come to grips with Remke. Until he learned about Colonel Erich Remke's involvement in Gambit, he had only reluctantly obeyed the order to go on this mission. Suddenly it had become personal, and he knew that nothing could keep him from stopping Gambit. And stopping Remke. Killing him. He thought back to Paris, and the last time he had seen Erich Remke. The German had bested him and left his mission in ruins, and a beautifully brave French girl in the hands of the Gestapo. The only mistake Remke had made was not to kill Billy when he had the chance.

Now I'm coming back for you. Won't you be surprised?

Lt. Jeff Rose sat across from Billy, relaxed and seeming to sleep. He opened his eyes and looked down the cabin at the nine other men, each silently wrapped in his own thoughts. He leaned forward to Billy.

"I still can't believe he's dead," he half-shouted over the din of the engines. Billy was staring at the opposite wall of the cabin, but his thoughts were still in Paris. He heard Rose but it took a second for him to come back to the present.

"Who?" he asked confusedly.

"Roosevelt, you asshole. Who else?"

"Oh, yeah. Me, too. I guess I thought he'd always be the President."

The news of Roosevelt's death had stunned everyone. It seemed inconceivable not only that he was gone, but that he died just short of the victory he had worked so hard to achieve. The men had boarded the Skytrooper quietly, without the usual banter. The mission had assumed a more serious demeanor, as if FDR's death had given each man a personal reason to make this last jump. No one could explain it or had spoken about it, but they were all now totally dedicated to the success of the mission, to stopping Gambit. To give anything less than all they could now seemed almost sacrilegious.

It had hardly mattered to Billy. He was shocked, certainly. His extended family were all heavily involved in Democratic politics back in Boston, and a picture of FDR hung in his parent's living room. But as the other men spoke quietly with each other about the President's death, Billy had focused on the mission with a deadly intent, pouring over maps of the area and the latest intelligence reports.

The last report brought in by Colonel Harding was almost too fantastic to believe. The German Twelfth Army, responsible for holding the line of the Mulde River against the Americans, seemed to be pulling back towards Berlin, leaving only scattered units to man the line. Harding thought it logical that the Germans would think the defense of their capital city against the Russians more important than an extended river line which the Americans would breech quickly in any case. Billy thought it odd, since it would only hasten the meeting of American and Russian forces southwest of Berlin. It meant that they would encounter fewer German forces in Gambit's operational area, which should have pleased him. But something was not quite right about it, and Billy couldn't figure it out, which bothered him greatly. When he wasn't thinking about Remke, he was thinking about what the Twelfth Army pullout could mean.

"Rosie, old chap, get your boys ready," Flight Lieutenant Trevor Dinsdale said, poking his head out from the pilot's compartment, "we're beginning our descent to the drop zone."

"Gear up!" Rose shouted to the men, who quickly began adjusting helmets, packs, and weapons.

"How come everyone else can call you Rosie, but you jump all over me when I do?" asked Billy as he tightened his helmet strap.

"Haven't known you long enough," answered Rose, as he always did. Dinsdale chuckled and smiled at Rose.

Leutnant Josef Falkenberg lifted off his Ju-88C-6 night fighter from the Dessau airfield, moments after being ordered into the air by *Flügkapitan* Karl Wendel. Flakenberg and two other Ju-88 night fighters had recently been assigned to *Kommando Ritter*, the special air unit assigned to protect a top-secret ground operation. Falkenberg and his crews knew no more about it than the fact that they had to protect a specific area between the Elbe and Mulde rivers. German radar had just picked up a group of Allied bombers headed for that territory, and Flakenberg was leading his flight to intercept.

The two squadrons of A-20 Havoc medium bombers had flown southeast over Germany, taking a dog-leg route that would turn them sharply north just east of Leipzig, in order to avoid that city's anti-aircraft defenses. The northerly leg of their route would allow them the fly directly over Hill 182, where two of the escorting P61 Black Widows would drop their flares, and four of the Havocs would drop their 4,000 pound bombloads on the hill. The Skytrooper transport and its two night fighter escorts were about ten minutes behind, and the plan was to drop the paratroopers on level ground on the west side of Hill 182, about 5 kilometers away. There would be fires from the bombing run, and they hoped Hill 182 would be clearly visible.

"The Havocs have overtaken us," announced Dinsdale. "Everything is on schedule." Flying at a top speed of 185 miles per hour, the slower transport had left the airfield hours before the bombers. All flight elements were now in place.

"The four Havocs that will hit Hill 182 are dropping back," Dinsdale explained to Billy. "They'll make the return flight with us until we're…"

"Get up here!" Mac shouted from the cockpit. Dinsdale turned instantly and jumped back into the co-pilot's seat.

Leutnant Falkenberg received a radio transmission from *Flügkapitan* Wendel as the three night fighters flew on an intercept course towards Leipzig.

"They've turned north. Bitterfeld radar shows medium bombers heading directly for Wittenberg. Change course to 95 degrees. The bomber stream is thinning, there are slower elements in the rear. Attack them first and then pick up the others on their return."

"Acknowledged."

Flakenberg banked his Ju-88 and the two other aircraft followed. The night fighter's radar was limited, and they had to be vectored toward their target before they could pick them up. Falkenberg pushed the fighter to its maximum speed of just over 300 miles per hour to catch up with the bombers, wondering why some of them were slowing down. Most medium bombers, like the Havoc or Marauder, could fly faster than the Ju-88C with its ungainly radar antenna protruding from the nose of the aircraft. Pursuit from behind was usually useless. He flashed on his radar to see if he could pick up the rear elements of the flight yet.

"Our little friends have picked up fighters closing on us," growled Mac as Dinsdale put his headphones on. "Didn't expect to see anymore of those gwad-damn things." Billy and Rose had followed him forward, sticking their heads in through the narrow door.

"Night fighters?" questioned Rose.

"Oh, yes, definitely night fighters," said Dinsdale almost cheerfully. "Jerry doesn't send his regular blokes up in the dark, they're as likely to run into each other as us." Dinsdale stopped and listened to another radio transmission from the escorting fighters. He and Mac exchanged grim glances. Dinsdale then changed to a smile and turned to Rose.

"Rosie, please do get your boys ready. Just in case. There're three of them closing on us at 300 miles per hour. With us at a top speed of 185, it's only a matter of time." He looked at them and winked. "Not to worry though, we've got two escorts and your Black Widows are ten times better than anything Jerry has. Simply wizard, those aircraft."

"C'mon Billy, let these guys fly the plane. They know what they're doing." Rose clapped Billy on the shoulder and led him back to his seat.

"Listen up!" Rose announced, "We may have to jump a little early. There's a few night fighters coming up on us. We won't stand a chance if this crate has to keep flying on the straight and narrow, so we may have to jump early and let these guys fly evasive maneuvers back to our lines. OK?" Everyone nodded.

"OK. Just means a longer walk."

"They have to drop us at Hill 182," Billy said with conviction.

"The aircraft won't make it there on a drop approach," Rose said, as if Billy were thick-headed. "They have to fly low and straight for that. One night fighter could chew us up in ten seconds."

"We can't waste time getting lost out there," Billy yelled. "They have to get us there!"

Leutnant Falkenberg's radar operator leaned toward him in the cramped cockpit and yelled excitedly, "Three targets, dead ahead!"

"Be specific, man!"

The radar operator turned back to his radar indicator and watched the luminous screen. "Three targets, sir, ten kilometers ahead. Lead aircraft dropping to 1400, now 1300 meters. Two other aircraft slightly above."

Two escorts and a crippled bomber, thought Falkenberg. He keyed the radio to his two wingmen. "Follow me in towards the lead aircraft."

In a small grove of pine trees on the top of the rise known on Allied maps as Hill 182, Major Klaus Branau listened to the roar of bombers coming from the south. He leaned against the sandbags surrounding the 20mm anti-aircraft gun and stared up at the sky. He was in command of the 401st Flak Brigade, a composite group of anti-aircraft units left in this area after the pullout of Twelfth Army. He had placed an 88mm anti-aircraft gun and three 20mm guns on this hill, figuring he could defend against ground attack from here as well. He had both dug-in and mobile anti-aircraft units between Wittenberg and Eilenberg. With many Luftwaffe fields being overrun in the east and the west, there were plenty of anti-aircraft crews available for air and ground defense. While he had sufficient anti-aircraft units, there were just two companies of regular ground troops to patrol this large area. Because of that, he was a little nervous about the withdrawal of Twelfth Army from all around him, especially the Panzers. Still, the *Amis* and the Russians were not breathing down his neck, yet.

Branau scanned the night sky for the bombers. He had no searchlights, and didn't plan on wasting ammunition firing blindly into the dark. The dull roar of aircraft engines grew louder, and he thought he could see dark shapes momentarily flit across the stars. Then the sounds began to fade towards the north. Heading to Wittenberg, or even Berlin, perhaps.

But not quite. As the loud engine noise faded, he could hear a fainter noise still in the sky above and to the south of him. Then, definitely, a different sound, one or two aircraft circling…

"*Alarm! Alarm!*" shouted Branau, suddenly aware that this was not just a raid passing over their heads. His crews ran to their guns, the 20mm next to him swiveling up into the sky, hunting for the source of the sound.

The brightest light he had ever seen burst above him, followed by other flares burning in the sky, descending slowly to earth. Everything was bright white, brighter than daylight. The 20mm began to fire at the lights, blindly, frustrated and seeking out the planes they could clearly hear above them.

Through the pounding of the gun and the drone of the planes, Branau heard another sound. It was only a slight whistling noise, growing louder. Branau knew exactly what it was, he just didn't know why. The gunner next to him heard it too.

"*Ach, Scheisse!*" It was the last thing either of them heard. The ground erupted as 500-pound bombs from four Havocs tore into the hill. The bomb run was over in less than a minute. Fires raged, guns and equipment lay broken and scattered on the hilltop, and the earth was blackened as large shell holes smoked from the explosions. Ammunition exploded, continuing the inferno. Before the two Black Widows joined up with the departing Havocs, they flew in low over the burning hill and made a strafing pass, shells from their four 20mm nose cannon chewing up the landscape. It mattered little. No one was left alive, and fires lit up the sky in every direction.

"B Flight reports they hit the hill," Dinsdale yelled back to the cabin. "They took some triple-A but hit the target dead on. Fires and secondary explosions as they left."

"Glad we hit it," said Billy. "Now let's get there in once piece."

Mac flew on, ignoring Billy's comment and listening to the reports from the Black Widow pilots about the German planes, now about to catch up to them.

Falkenberg led the flight in a vee formation, expecting that the two escorts would peel off to either side and come around on his flanks. This way his wingmen could engage the fighters and allow him to hit the bomber ahead. The extra aircraft gave him an advantage, but only in the initial attack. If these were American Black Widow fighters, he knew they would be out-classed within minutes. He had one opportunity to hit and run, and he planned to make the best use of it.

Ahead, the Black Widows did split off, one banking to the right and one to the left, coming around for a side or rear attack on the German planes. Falkenberg's radar operator yelled, "fighters coming in four o'clock and eight o'clock low!" The *Ami* were trying to hit them from under, a favorite night fighter tactic. Falkenberg then did the unexpected, increasing the throttle on his two Junkers Jumo engines and climbing, increasing the distance between his planes and their pursuers. Then suddenly he thrust the throttle down, going into a steep dive towards his quarry, the bomber dead ahead.

He could hear gunfire, not the heavy sound of cannon fire, but probably the Ju-88's defensive armament, the single rear firing 13mm machine gun operated by the radar man. He closed on the aircraft ahead, not near enough for a clean shot yet.

The air around him came alive with tracer bullets as the Black Widow's multiple 20mm cannon sought out their targets. Just one quick burst from that much firepower could rip a Ju88 to shreds. Falkenberg knew now his opponents were Black Widows. He should start flying defensively, weaving left, right, up and down as he knew his wingmen were now doing. He kept flying straight ahead.

One of the other Ju88s rolled and tried to evade the fire aimed at it. The pilot vainly attempted to corkscrew around and avoid the hail of bullets, as his rear gunner fired back at the muzzle flashes, closer than he had expected. The Black Widow kept with him, and finally closed the circle just a fraction tighter than the German plane. The American pilot lowered his flaps, not wanting to overshoot his target, at this same time pressing the fire button. Dozens of 20mm shells chewed up the fuselage of the Ju88, ripping through the cockpit and sending the aircraft into a steep and sudden dive, trailing smoke and flames.

The other Ju88 wingman had swung around, in the opposite direction his pursuer expected, as he went to the aid of his partner. Too late to save him, he did catch he Black Widow with one deflection shot, emptying a burst from his four forward machine guns and one 20mm cannon at the target. The bullets stitched along the wing root, leaving a wispy trail of smoke behind. Knowing he could not outlast two Black Widows, even though he had hit one, the Ju88 pilot dove steeply and turned in the opposite direction from his flight leader, hoping at least to draw them away from Falkenberg.

Falkenberg closed on the plane ahead, following his radar operator's intercept directions. He could tell he had a few seconds grace before the *Ami* night fighters returned for him. He dove again, picking up speed for the final approach from below and behind, where he could avoid the worst of the bomber's defensive fire. Then suddenly he could make out the shape ahead and above him. A transport! No defensive fire at all. This was going to be easy. He maintained his approach and brought the plane clearly into his sights and squeezed the trigger, just as his radar operator opened up with his machine gun.

The Black Widows had not taken the bait. The lead *Amis* plane was just above and behind them, giving the radar operator a moment to open fire. The Black Widow returned the fire of the single machine gun with its four 20mm cannon, hitting the JU88 square in the rear fuselage and literally sawing the plane in half, but not before the Falkenberg had fired a single, sustained burst directly at the Skytrooper.

Inside the Skytrooper, the bullets from the Ju88 erupted through the floorboards and exited out the ceiling, working their way from mid-fuselage to the cockpit. As soon as Mac heard the fighter open fire, he had yawed the plane to the left, trying to turn inside the arc of fire to escape it. He avoided most of the 20mm shells as he moved the plane away from the stream of fire, but those shells that did hit the plane caught it on the right side.

Within seconds it was over, the bright explosion signaling that the escorts had done their job. Billy looked out the transport window and could see the shattered aircraft falling to the ground in burning pieces. He looked around quickly. Rose was across from him, on the right side of the plane. The man seated next to him was dead. A shell had come up through the wooden floorboards and hit him under the chin. It had lost some velocity coming through the flooring, and had not exited the man's head. Except for the blood seeping out the entry wound, he looked fine, still sitting upright in his seat.

Rose's leg was bleeding. He looked up at Billy. "Miller's dead. I just got some splinters in my leg from the floorboards. Check the other men." He took out Miller's first aid kit from his pack and began to bandage his leg.

Sergeant Kowalski spoke up from the rear of the plane. "Everybody's OK back here. What about up front?" He pointed toward the cockpit and Billy could clearly see how the line of bullets had arced towards the co-pilots seat. He rushed forward as quickly as his pack and parachute would allow. He looked inside. The co-pilot's window was shattered and blood had splattered the instruments in front of him.

Dinsdale looked up at him and smiled weakly. He was very pale. Mac was fighting to keep the plane on an even course, and trying to assess the damage.

"I think it's actually looks worse than it is, old bean," Dinsdale said, trying to sound confident. "Mac did a splendid job evading that Jerry, but he managed to send a few rounds my way. The arm's cut up a bit and I'm bleeding like a stuck pig from this scalp wound, but it could be worse, eh what?" Dinsdale grimaced in pain and Billy knew it was worse than he was letting on. He decided there was no reason to tell them about the dead man in the cabin.

"Is the plane OK?" Billy asked.

"Some cables must've been cut. I don't know how long I can hold her up," Mac answered, not taking his eyes off the controls except for quick glances at his co-pilot. "If Treve can manage it, we may have to jump with you. This crate might not make it back."

Rose limped forward and saw Dinsdale, covered in blood.

"What the hell happened?"

"Not to worry, Rosie. Just a few scratches," Dinsdale answered as he poured powder from a sulfa pack onto his right arm. He looked faint, and perspiration broke out on his brow.

"Mac," he began, "something's wrong with the right rudder. I'm not getting any response, I can push it all the way to the floor."

Rose pushed Billy aside and stepped forward. He looked down at Dinsdale's right leg, which he was pushing down on the rudder. Below the calf, the leg was cleanly severed. Rose pulled a morphine syringe from his pack and jabbed it into Dinsdale's left thigh. Startled, he looked up at him with surprise and a hint of fear in his eyes.

"Take it easy, buddy. We'll take care of you." Rose began to bandage Dinsdale's head wound. "Don't worry about a thing, you'll be home in no time." Dinsdale looked startled and confused. Finally he looked down at his right leg.

"Oh dear me. Mac, never mind about the right rudder." He tried to smile, but fainted instead. Rose applied a tourniquet below his knee and covered Dinsdale with a blanket.

"Mac, you gotta drop us now," he said, looking at the Englishman with concern.

"No!" Billy announced firmly, "and that's an order."

Rose turned to Billy in a fury. "Are you nuts? He can't jump with us, not with that leg. He could bleed to death before Mac gets him back. If he turns back now, there's a chance!"

"The mission is more important than any one man."

"Now I know you're nuts," Rose said, his voice getting louder as he got angrier. "You didn't give a rat's ass about this mission until you heard about this Remke guy. Now you're gung ho and ready to sacrifice Treve and probably anybody else. Well, Captain, it don't wash with me. We're not here to settle your personal score with this Nazi."

"If Remke is involved, then it's big, and important."

"Yeah, next you'll tell me it could affect the outcome of the war. Guess how many times I heard that one from the brass sending us out on their pet projects."

Billy didn't know what to say. Rose sounded like him talking about Harding. He couldn't believe it had come to this. He couldn't believe who he was becoming. But it was too late to turn back now.

"This time, Lieutenant, you just may have a ringside seat to the outcome of the war." He looked at Mac. "How much farther?"

"See that tiny patch of light on the horizon? That should be Hill 182. About a half hour out." Mac looked over at Trevor. He looked sick at heart. He had also been in the business too long to question his orders.

"I'll get you there." He stopped and exhaled deeply. "I just really thought we'd both make it, after all these years. Hang on, you little English twit!" Tears welled in his eyes as he grimly flew on. Suddenly the radio squawked. Mac listened and turned to Rose and Billy.

"You might want to decide now. One Ju-88 got away and they think he's patrolling out ahead of us. One of the Black Widows got hit in the dogfight and is loosing altitude and airspeed. We effectively have only one escort."

"Can't you evade again and let our escort hit him?"

"Not with the hits we've taken. I think I can keep her steady, but that's it. We can't maneuver or climb."

"Why doesn't the Black Widow go after him?" Billy was getting frantic now.

"Because if he does, and misses him, then we're sitting ducks. One pass is all it takes."

Billy looked down at the ground. There were no lights, nothing to mark where they were. He looked at the map Mac had been marking to show their progress. "Can you get us over the Mulde?" he asked Mac.

"Sure! There's a partial moon, rivers and lakes show up fine."

"OK, drop us across the Mulde, then get out of here. We avoid the night fighter and you get Trevor back as quick as possible."

"Glad to oblige, Captain."

Rose picked up the flight map and studied it for a minute. "Adjust your course 20 degrees west. We want to come down in the *Dübener Heide*, outside of *Bad Düben*, not in it."

Mac caught a sliver of light reflected off water in the distance.

"Coming about 20 degrees. That's it. Get ready. I'll punch out the canisters and then hit the jump light." The Skytrooper carried external pods for equipment canisters, which the pilot dropped from the cockpit. The red jump light was the signal for the paratroopers to go.

Rose looked at Mac. "I'll buy you guys a beer when we get back, after the docs patch Treve up, OK?"

"Sure, Rosie. Catch you later. Get the hell outta here now."

"Good luck, Mac," Billy offered, feeling like a heel.

"Yeah, sure. You too."

As Billy left to take his place at the end of the line, he saw Mac lay a hand gently on Dinsdale's arm, then take it back quickly to regain control of the plane. Rose brushed past him to take his place at the front. He was the jumpmaster, and would give the signal to go and be the last to jump. He stopped and looked at Billy with grim determination. "You're very lucky, Boyle. Damn lucky." He moved up.

"Ready!" Rose shouted to the men. There were ten in all in line. Miller still sat in his seat, his equipment keeping him upright, mute testimony to the uncertainty of what lay ahead. No one looked at him. Rose watched the green jump light. He heard the clunk of the canisters being detached from the undercarriage, then the green light turned red.

"Go!" Rose slapped Corporal Mandelbaum on the shoulder as he turned to leap out into the night. Kowalski followed and then the rest of the men. Willard and Billy brought up the end of the line, since the radio man and the officer in charge were deemed the most important. Rose watched Billy go and followed him out.

In an instant the cabin was empty. A dead man sat lifelessly as wind whipped through from the open door, blowing chewing gum wrappers, wood splinters from the bullet holes, and other debris around his feet. There was no sound other than the roar of engines as Mac put the Skytrooper into a 180-degree turn, flying full throttle and straining the aircraft to get his friend back to the nearest airbase, alive. He put his hand gently again on Trevor's arm, taking it away when the yoke in his left hand began to shake. He swore to himself, then prayed. He didn't even glance down to watch the parachutes behind him float gently to earth, landing on the dark, rolling meadowland, deep in enemy territory, between three powerful armies.

CHAPTER TWENTY-FIVE

15 April 1945
Operation Gambit Field Headquarters
Eutzsch, Germany

The three-story farmhouse and attached barns stood at the end of a narrow valley, the final destination on a dirt road winding its way several kilometers from the main thoroughfare to Wittenberg. To the rear of the farm buildings, the hills rose steeply on both sides, and patches of green worked their way up the slopes, blending into thick stands of pine reaching to the sky. It was a wet morning, the dew thick on clumps of green grass growing wildly everywhere. A stream gushed down the hillside in back of the house, fresh clear water bubbling over moss-encrusted rocks. The cows plodded along the hillside, lazily inspecting the two people trudging up the hill on the narrow packed earth path that followed the stream. Elsa held tightly onto Dieter's arm, allowing him to pull her along as the path grew steeper.

"Oh, Dieter," she panted, "I didn't realize how weak I was." They both stopped and turned to look at the farm and valley below them. Dieter stood quietly next to Elsa, holding her arm as she took in deep gasping breaths.

"Are you alright?" he asked.

"Yes, just a minute." She patted his hand reassuringly. "Isn't it beautiful, even with all this?" She gestured with her hand to the sight below them, then rested it on her chest as if to calm her breathlessness.

Camouflage netting was strung from the barn and other buildings to trees on both slopes. Trucks, halftracks, armored cars and anti-aircraft vehicles were parked tightly together underneath. The buildings housed over a hundred men, the remainder spread out in farmhouses along the farm road that stretched the length of the valley. Remke had hidden his force very carefully. Allied aircraft flying overhead would see nothing more than a quiet dead-end valley with farms and houses dotting a road that led nowhere.

A squad of Benedikt's paratroopers was stationed near the intersection with the main road, hidden in a small glade of trees. Their lookouts could spot any trouble headed their way. If any SS troops turned down the dirt road, they would be cut off and surrounded in minutes. As a further precaution, Remke had stationed other men outside the Wittenberg *Schloss*, the castle complex where he was supposed to have quartered his men. If the SS were going to hunt them down, they would probably head there first.

These were not the thoughts in Dieter's mind right now. He drank in the green beauty before him, the rich fertile smells of the farm merging into the clean pine-scented air. He held Elsa's hand even tighter.

"I can't even believe we're together, much less here taking a walk on a spring day," he said with a smile. In the two days since they arrived here from Berlin, Dieter had hardly left Elsa's side. She was tired, weak and for a while in shock after experiencing a Gestapo cell and the sudden violence of her rescue and escape. He was overjoyed to have her back, and incredibly frightened at the prospect of losing her again, either to the SS or to the unknown but looming future of Operation Gambit.

"This seems so far from Berlin and the war," Elsa answered wistfully. "Even with all the soldiers, it seems a different world. Quiet."

"That's because we're hiding, remember?"

"That sounds wonderful to me. Can we hide here from everyone until the war is over?"

Dieter thought how she sounded like the young girl he had first met, full of questions, hopes, and joy. He avoided this question, even though he knew she didn't expect a real answer. It was a question of the moment, unreal, just as this peaceful walk was unreal.

"Let's go. It's just a little further." He took her by the arm and they climbed up the path to the crest of the hill. At the top, it leveled out in a thin stand of pines amid slabs of granite. A rough-hewn bench perched near the edge of an overlook. The sun was up high in the sky, warming the early spring air. They sat on the bench and Elsa rested her head on Dieter's shoulder. Silence passed between them, the sights, smells, and sounds of the forest filling the space around them.

"What's going to happen now?" she asked, finally.

"If the SS doesn't find us, if the Allies don't bomb us, then we wait. Wait for the Americans and the Russians. It could be any day now, or it might never happen. If Berlin falls quickly, it could be all over before we could do anything."

"Is that what you hope?"

"I have no hope other than to spend the rest of my life with you. Perhaps right here, a nice farm."

"Dieter, the world is going to come crashing down around us at any moment. What are you going to do? What are we going to do, you and I?"

Even on top of this hill, alone above the valley, Dieter looked furtively around and lowered his voice, leaning in closer to Elsa. "We must warn the Americans when they get closer. They must know that this attack is not real. At just the right moment, I will give the order to my men to move west, and surrender to the Americans. I will go out ahead of them and warn the Americans."

"What if they shoot you as spies, for being in Russian uniforms?"

"We will keep our *Wehrmacht* tunics with us, and put them on just before we reach their lines."

"And where will I be? With you?"

"No, it will be too dangerous. I will try to take you with us when we take the field. Jost will look after you, and bring you across the lines with the rest of the men."

"It sounds so simple."

"I wish it were. Finding the right moment will not be easy. We have to worry about getting away from Remke and then surviving getting through to the American lines. And I can't just leave my Hiwis behind. There has to be way out for them. If the Russians catch up with them, they'll kill them all."

"What about the other group, the men in American uniforms?"

Dieter shook his head ruefully. "I think they're on a fool's errand. There are too few of them to make a difference, and half of those aren't even ready. I think the Russians will roll right over them and not even notice the color of the uniforms."

"Dieter?"

"Yes, *liebchen*?"

"Don't leave me behind. No matter how dangerous it is, I want to be with you." There were no more words left to speak. They sat wrapped in each other's arms, letting the sunlight play across their faces, dreaming dreams of peace and solitude.

Less than fifteen minutes later, Dieter heard someone coming up the trail. He turned to see Hans von Schierke, wiping sweat from his brow and walking towards them. He looked worried. Dieter jumped to his feet. "What is it?"

"Remke wants you. It's started. The Russians are pouring across the Oder."

Colonel Erich Remke watched von Schierke scramble up the hillside after Dieter Neukirk. The man had been useless since they had brought Elsa back from Berlin. It was understandable, but it was also about to change. Remke paced the room, once a pleasant sitting room but now his headquarters office. Maps were pinned to the walls and rolled out on a large table. A radio was set up in the corner, but they did not broadcast, only listened for signs of the SS closing in on them. So far, nothing.

Remke stopped and picked up a delicate porcelain figure from a shelf. It was hand-painted and quite beautiful. He hated it. Its domesticity and femininity offended him, here in the midst of his plans to continue and even enlarge the war. He wished he could have been within the castle walls where his headquarters were supposed to have been. There he would have walked on hard, cold stone floors among ancient arms and armor that had seen centuries of warfare. It would have sustained him, nurtured his hatred, kept him focused. Instead, here he had to bear with the comforts of a country home and a small but prosperous farm holding. Half of his men had come from farms, and had taken to milking cows and walking through the barns as if this were a holiday. This morning he had heard several of them talking about getting back to their own farms and families soon. It was not the kind of talk a combat commander wanted to hear from troops he would force to face almost certain death within days. Any sign of softness in his men had to be eliminated, just as he had to root out and crush any softness within himself.

Although, he comforted himself, *many of these boys don't even know if their families are still alive, especially if they're from east of the Oder River. As am I. It's all just talk, pure fantasy.*

Yet, the fantasy tugged at him, too. His hand curled around the figurine, wanting to crush it, smash it down to the floor and erase its image, eliminate this softness. He couldn't. His hand shook as he carefully placed it back on the shelf.

Anna. She had loved such pretty, useless little things. Everything he saw or touched made him think of her. For the past year he had hardened himself, killed for the joy of killing and the momentary release it gave him from anguish, guilt, loneliness, and longing. Now he had to watch another man walk hand in hand with his true love, rescued from almost certain death. It was pure agony, and unexpected. He had helped Dieter, sheltered Elsa here within his headquarters, drawn down the wrath of the SS, but worst of all, opened up a great wound in his heart. He could not ever have Anna again, but neither could he summon the mantle of death that had comforted him and contained his sorrows. Dieter and Elsa's joy mocked him and all his plans. Softness. Softness crept up on him and was ruining the killing machine, as sure as rust would ruin the best blade. The rage came up within him like bitter bile and he turned, smashing his fist down on the shelf, the porcelain figurines dancing in air and cascading to the floor. They lay in a chipped and broken heap at his feet, taunting him no more with their beauty and perfection. He looked at them and willed himself to feel nothing.

Perfect. He waited for the others to arrive. There was much to do.

Hauptmann Herbert Benedikt leaned into the corner as he downshifted his BMW motorcycle and then opened up the throttle as he sped down the back road leading out of Wittenberg. On the straight stretch of country road, he felt the exhilaration of speed as everything but the pavement in front of him became a green blur. Not quite like free falling from an airplane, he thought, but it would do. For a moment he let himself enjoy the wind whipping around him and power of the machine, then began to think about what he had just seen.

Earlier in the day he had set out to visit his men in the Wittenberg observation post. He had only been there for ten minutes when they saw the convoy coming in on the main road from Berlin. It looked like a battalion of troops. They had surrounded the castle, coming in from three directions and dismounting from the trucks some distance off. Benedikt had seen they were not the sort of SS guard or security troops they had dealt with before. These were Waffen-SS, hardened combat troops from the eastern front. They had approached every castle entrance under cover, sealing it off before the first squads burst through the main entrance. These were not men who would be easily ambushed. He watched the fruitless search for another minute, instructed his men to bring back word of where the SS went next, then left to return to headquarters. Benedikt felt his blood up, ready for action, as he had always felt before a battle. He also felt a weariness he had never experienced before, and a growing concern about what he would soon call upon his men to do. He had brought them into battle before, and watched many of them die. The men who had been with him the longest were a tight-knit group, united by pure survival. Now they were battling the SS as well as the Allies, and trying to pull off the most amazing strategy he had ever heard of. Would they be heroes or villains if they pulled it off? Heroes in whose eyes? That, Benedikt decided, was the real question. Who would judge their actions, now and in the future? He had never been a religious man, but he did feel the weight of a difficult decision beginning to bear upon his shoulders.

Maybe I need to be the judge of what's right and wrong.

For a soldier, especially a German soldier in the sixth year of this war, it was not a question with a simple answer. He had been taking orders all his life, and had sworn an oath to obey the *Führer*, and Hitler had ordered this operation. But didn't the *Führer* owe his people something, too? Didn't any leader have a responsibility not to destroy his own people and nation? With the war obviously lost, wasn't it the responsibility of the government to end the suffering as soon as possible, not prolong it? Hadn't they all killed enough?

Myself included.

With the veteran's ability to deal with the immediate situation, he carefully put those thoughts away and slowed, making a left turn onto the dirt road that led to the farmhouse. He pulled over to the side of the road, stopped and stood with the BMW idling powerfully beneath him. He lifted up his goggles and shouted towards the trees.

"Christian, Erik!" Two camouflaged soldiers rose up from the treeline and waved back to him. "The SS were at the castle- about a battalion, Waffen-SS. Keep a good lookout!"

"We'll radio in their strength if they come by." Benedikt nodded and took off down the road, alerting the men stationed at each house and farm as he went.

Remke stood silently as his staff entered. He stood with his hands behind his back, erect and formal. It was the first time they had seen him out of his dress uniform. He wore the gray-green *Wehrmacht* field uniform with a dappled camouflage *Panzergrenadier* tunic. His Iron Cross showed at the collar, and the brown and black DAK cuffband stood out over the camouflage pattern. Remke looked calm, professional, and dangerous. One by one they came in, Dieter first, then *Obersturmführer* Felix Strauch, in charge of the American-uniformed section. *Leutnant* Gustav Stieff and *Flugkapitän* Karl Wendel followed him in. Remke looked at them and waited a moment, then asked, "Where is Benedikt?"

The roar of a motorcycle speeding down the road answered the question for him. They waited as Benedikt pulled up and scrambled up the steps into the farmhouse. Removing his goggles and helmet, he told them about the Waffen-SS in Wittenberg.

Strauch knew the least about what had gone on previously, and looked anxiously at the others. "What in God's name is going on here?"

"What is going on here, *Obersturmführer*, is that you are following the orders given to you by your commanding officer, as authorized by the *Führer's* special order. Do you understand that?" Remke questioned harshly.

"Yes, sir, but I..."

"There is no need to concern yourself, Strauch," Remke cut in, speaking in more soothing tones. "I will tell you that the SS political leadership has attempted to take over this operation, now that it stands some chance of success. Are you familiar with Himmler's record as commander of Army Group Vistula?"

Strauch knew that Himmler had failed miserably and had quietly been relieved of command by Hitler. He could not argue that Himmler should be given another chance as a military leader. "I understand, sir."

"You simply need to carry out your orders as given to you. I have been ordered by the *Führer* to carry out Operation Gambit, and I have ordered you to do your part. If you are not prepared to do so, tell me now!"

"I am yours to command, Colonel." Strauch believed in Operation Gambit, and knew enough of SS political infighting to not trust command to them. Satisfied, Remke spoke to them all.

"You all have overcome many obstacles in this war. This is just another, perhaps one of the final obstacles you must overcome. We all have our orders. Any other unit, which tries to stop you, is in direct violation of the *Führer's* Special Decree. Do not forget that." The other men all nodded their understanding. If they trembled at the thought of fighting the Russians, Americans, and the SS, they did not let their Colonel see it.

"Now, as to why I called you together. It has begun. Artillery bombardments opened up along the Oder and Neisse rivers last night and early this morning the Russians attacked along the entire front. They are hitting the Seelow Heights directly east of Berlin very hard, and they crossed the Neisse just south of Forst."

"That's only 130 kilometers east of here!" said Stieff, looking at the map laid out on the table.

"Indeed," said Remke casually. "And there is nothing between the Russians and us but a very worn-out Fourth Panzer Army. They are falling back to the Spree River now, but will not be able to hold it long."

"Then it is a matter of days," Dieter said.

"Yes," Remke answered. "You must all steel yourselves for what we must do. There can be no thoughts other than success, to continue the battle against the Bolsheviks with the Anglo-Americans. It is up to you men in this room, at this time, to save the Reich. No other thoughts," he repeated, looking directly at Dieter.

"All units will leave tonight, starting at midnight," Remke continued, shifting his eyes away from Dieter but leaving his meaning clear. "Strauch, you and your men leave first. Proceed to Dommitzsch, 30 kilometers southeast of here. It is one of two crossings over the Elbe between here and Torgau. Given the axis of the Russian attacks, I think this a likely crossing for them, and a good ambush point. Scout the area and prepare your ambush as instructed."

"Yes, sir."

"Benedikt," Remke said, "send two platoons with Strauch to cover his flanks. Once they engage the Russians, your men should withdraw from the area. Have the Heavy Panzers and the *Panzergrenadiers* move out to Pretzsch, here, on the Elbe."

"Another crossing point," said Benedikt, studying the map.

"Yes. They will either oppose the Russians there to force them down to Dommitzsch, or come to the aid of our forces if necessary. Pretzsch puts them between Strauch and Neukirk."

"And the rest of my company?" Benedikt asked.

"You and the remainder of your men will provide flank protection to *Hauptmann* Neukirk and his Hiwis. They are the priority unit in this operation."

"Where do I go?" asked Dieter.

"Here," Remke pointed. "Bad Schmiedeberg, on the road to Bad Düben. That's the natural crossing point on the Mulde River, and will allow you to observe where the Americans go once they cross the river. There is a castle in Bad Schmiedeberg where you can establish your headquarters. Several kilometers down the road there is an overlook which will make a perfect observation post. Set one up there immediately." Dieter leaned down to look at the area. The road net branched out from to Bad Düben, and the high ground Remke had selected was a perfect observation point, giving a clear view of all the main roads leading out of to Bad Düben. If the Americans crossed there, he could easily hit them on any of those roads. The observation post was almost a guarantee.

"Will you be here at headquarters, sir?" asked Dieter, hoping Remke would stay behind.

"Of course not. *Leutnant* Stieff will remain here in charge of communications, with one of the armored radio cars and half a dozen men. Civilians temporarily in our care will remain here with him." Remke paused, again drilling Dieter with his stare. "I will have a mobile field headquarters with the rest of the headquarters guard, the other armored command vehicle and the Ostwind anti-aircraft vehicle. I will travel between you and Strauch as we watch for the enemy's advance."

Dieter knew that Remke would spend most of his time with him, since his larger unit had a better chance of success. He also noticed that the Heavy Panzer unit was quite closer to him than to Strauch. Almost as if they were watching over him, just in case. Did Remke suspect anything?

"Wendel, note these dispositions, and be sure to give us good air cover. We can't afford to get caught in an air raid, like the one that hit Wittenberg."

"Yes, sir. We lost two night fighters in that raid, but that shouldn't affect our daytime air cover."

"Stieff," Remke asked, "do all units have the codes for calling on air cover and air strikes?"

"They do, sir. We have set up special codes and targets within the operational area. It should take only minutes for our *Luftwaffe* friends to arrive."

"Excellent. You all have your orders. Neukirk and Strauch, have your men start wearing their American and Russian uniforms under their *Wehrmacht* tunics tomorrow. We must be ready for anything, including enemy parachute landings."

"What other German units are in the area?" Benedikt asked.

"Twelfth Army began their pullout two days ago, as part of the overall plan. They are moving north towards Berlin. The pullout was done in stages, mostly at night. It should be completed this evening, before midnight. There will be only a few static FLAK units left in the area. Essentially, we have the Elbe-Mulde operational area all to ourselves."

Suddenly the door slammed open and one of Benedikt's men from the Wittenberg observation post entered. "Sir, sorry to interrupt, but I thought you'd want to know. The SS battalion is heading out of Wittenberg, along the southeast road, the one that runs on the west side of the Elbe."

"Through Pretzsch and onto Dommitzsch," Benedikt said. His meaning was clear.

"Wait until they clear Pretzsch, then bring in the Heavy Panzers as planned," Remke ordered. "That will cut them off. Benedikt, you'd better take your full company to escort Strauch to Dommitzsch. Take care of this problem fast."

Dieter opened the door to the room he and Elsa shared, on the upper floor of the farmhouse. Elsa sat in the single chair in the room, looking out the only window. It was a gabled window, and she had it open, letting the clean, warm air breeze in over her. The view was up the valley as it rose behind the farm, and the greens against the blue sky were beautiful.

"You're going, aren't you?"

"Yes," he said, feeling guilty while at the same time knowing everything was running at a pace beyond his control. "Elsa, he's ordered me to leave you here, with Stieff and a few men."

"No! I won't stay behind again!"

"Listen, Elsa. We can't just disobey an order. I have a feeling Remke is keeping a close watch on me. I don't want to give him a reason to watch any more closely. And the SS are searching for us. It could be very dangerous to be traveling around out there."

"Dieter, it's very dangerous everywhere right now. What are we going to do? How can we stay together?"

"Tomorrow morning, go for a walk again. If you continue on the path we took today, it goes down the other side of the valley and along another ridge. On top of that ridge there's a hut for hikers. It probably hasn't been used since 1940. Find it. Come back here and pack up your kit, and sleep in your clothes. If the SS come down that road, head out to the hut. In any case, go there after dark in two nights. Slip out of here, don't let anyone see you. I'll come to the hut to get you." Elsa smiled, in spite of her fear and concern.

"I guess I have to believe you when you say you'll come for me."

"Yes, you do."

She looked up at him, and asked when he was leaving.

"Tonight. Midnight."

She stood up and went to the mirror, brushing her dark hair. She put down the brush and began unbuttoning the army issue shirt they had given her to replace her ruined clothes. She finished the last button, then unbuttoned her slacks and let them drop to the floor. Dieter went to her, put his hands around her waist and felt her warm skin, felt her slight shiver at his touch. They kissed, and Dieter tried to remember everything, every caress, every feeling and desire, every teardrop he kissed away, every pleasure. He wanted to be with her forever, and he knew he might never see her again. He tried to remember everything.

CHAPTER TWENTY-SIX

16 April 1945
Outside Kossau, Germany

Corporal Mandelbaum slithered out of the line of trees, crawled down the sloping hillside and then up another. Billy watched him raise his binoculars and scan the village below, then scan across the horizon. Mandelbaum turned back to Billy, gave a slight shrug, then crawled off over the crest, out of his vision.

Lt. Jeff Rose turned to Sergeant Kowalski. "Kowalski, take one man and go two kilometers south, towards Aufhausen. Keep your heads down and get back here on the double!"

"OK, Rosie." Kowalski and another man were gone in an instant, vanishing amongst the low trees and shrubs in the meadows of the *Dübener Heide*. Rose crawled backwards into the trees, back to where Billy and the other men were hiding.

"It's real quiet. I sent Kowalski and Mandelbaum out in opposite directions along the road, for two kilometers. We'll know more when they get back."

"OK, maybe we can make some sense out of this and get the hell out of here," Billy replied.

Two nights ago, they had come down in a deserted portion of the wild *Dübener Heide.* They had landed reasonably close together, but there were twin disasters waiting for them on the ground. PFC Rowley, the most experienced radio operator after Corporal Luther Willard, landed in a jumble of large boulders atop a small rise of land. They found him upside down in a crevase between two jagged boulders, his neck broken.

Now two men of the ten-man detachment were already dead before the mission on the ground started. It was not a good omen, and the bad luck didn't stop there. When they retrieved the two equipment canisters, they found them pockmarked with bullet holes from the night fighter attack. A bazooka they had brought was totally ruined, and the rockets for it useless. Far worse was the SSTR-5 radio packed in the container. It had taken a 20mm cannon shell straight through. It was thoroughly destroyed.

The second radio, carried by Luther and wrapped in blankets in his pack, fared only slightly better. The wind had drifted Luther onto the edge of the boulder field, and he came down on top of one of the largest boulders. His parachute dragged him off, and he fell backwards off the boulder. He landed on another rock, broke two ribs, and heard a crack that he knew wasn't a rib. The second SSTR-5 was badly damaged, perhaps beyond repair.

They had buried their chutes, and Rowley, before setting out north-north-west to Hill 182. The eight men proceeded slowly, allowing Luther to keep up with them. He was wincing with every step, but he would not allow anyone else to carry the damaged radio. They skirted the village of Aufhausen, keeping off the roads and to the low ground as they walked through meadows, stands of trees and shrubs, and across streams. The sound of engine noises drifted over the *Heide* from the road, and they could hear trucks in the village.

They came upon the outskirts of the next village, Kossau, which lay below them now. It was nestled between three rolling hills, with roads leading into the village between each. There was a church, several larger buildings in a town square, and a few homes clustered close together. They crossed the first road, one man at a time, scurrying across the pavement low and quiet. As the last man crossed, a low humming sound grew louder as a column of trucks, their lights blacked out, came down the road from Aufhausen. There was no cover, except for a stand of trees atop the low hill behind them. The hill was between two of the roads that fanned out from Kossau, and gave them an excellent view of the village and roads.

Unfortunately, it also boxed them in. Unknown to Billy, they were now right in the middle of the withdrawing Twelfth Army. All units south of Bad Düben had been ordered to withdraw in stages, using the country roads that led through Kossau, in order to avoid observation or getting caught in an air raid on one of the larger towns.

For two days, they waited in the trees. By night, the roads were full of German vehicles. By day, the village was crawling with Germans, and soldiers on foot marched down the roads, taking cover at the sound of any aircraft overhead.

Billy had been frustrated beyond belief. He had already lost two men and two radios, and now he was in the middle of a significant movement of German troops. Perhaps this was part of Operation Gambit, but that knowledge was useless without a way to communicate it. With no radio contact possible and surrounded by Germans, Billy's mission was a bust. And Remke was out there somewhere, eluding his grasp with every passing hour.

During the two days, Luther had worked with the radio constantly. He was determined to find the problem. The tubes were both working, and he checked and re-checked the electrical circuits.

"Thing is, Captain," he had explained to Billy, "this here radio oughta work. Everything looks OK, but something got banged up when I fell. Problem is, I never worked with this model before. I'll get it, though, don't'cha worry!"

The men were quiet, waiting for the patrols to return. The only sound was from Luther, flipping the pages of the technical manual as he traced the wiring diagrams with his finger.

Billy edged over to Rose, who was watching the village through his binoculars. There was still an edge of tension between them, unresolved since their near-confrontation on the plane. Billy knew that Rose viewed his sudden enthusiasm for the mission with suspicion. The death of his two men had not made it any easier for Rose. He was still dedicated to carrying through the mission, but was watching Billy's every move to make sure his men didn't get dragged into a private war. The regular war was bad enough.

With their forced confinement, they had managed to be civil to each other. There was an unspoken agreement between them to carry on as best they could, knowing that there was nothing to fight about while they were trapped here.

"This is where they say 'It's quiet out there, too quiet' in the movies."

Rose looked over at Billy and allowed a half smile as he lowered the binoculars. "Yeah, and usually right after that a hundred Indians jump up and attack the wagon train."

"What do you think it means?" Billy asked the same question they had been asking themselves all morning. During the night, the traffic on the roads began to thin out. By early light, there had been no traffic for the last hour. No sounds came from the village. Every other morning, they had heard engines and the shouts of officers directing their men. This morning, complete quiet.

"I dunno. They all headed away from the Mulde River. Maybe the Russians are attacking and they need them to defend Berlin?"

"But that leaves this front wide open for us. Why give up the Mulde line of defense?"

"Well," Rose considered, "that don't make sense. But all we know is what we see in front of us. Maybe it isn't along the entire river."

"No, but we counted more than a full division going through here. That's a lot for Jerry to pull out, given the shape they're in."

"Yeah, well, whatever the reason, now maybe we can leave…" He stopped and quickly lifted the binoculars up again. He watched for a second. "Mandelbaum's coming in."

Kowalski was sighted moments later, coming in from the other direction. They jogged bent down across the low ground and crawled up the hill. They were careful to shield themselves from the view of the village, but Rose could tell by the way they carried themselves that the danger was gone.

"Not a soul, Rosie." Mandelbaum said. "There's some old folks and kids in the village, but not a single soldier. The locals are all in the square, looks like they're as surprised as we are."

"Same thing towards Aufhausen," chimed in Kowalski. "No one on the roads, just civilians in the village. Real quiet."

"Damn it!" Billy exploded. "The front's wide open and the goddamn radio's busted! Luther, can you get that thing to work?"

Luther had been sitting with the radio headphones on, working the dial. His eyes were closed and his fingers worked the frequency dial very, very slowly. He didn't hear Billy. He opened his eyes and was startled to see seven sets of eyes watching him.

"Whoa! Didn't know you fellas were watching. Might have some good news, Captain, and some bad."

"What is it?" Billy barked at him.

"Well, I think I just heard a transmission. Can't pick it up again, though. Somethin's messed up with the frequencies."

"What's the good news?"

"Hell, Captain, that was the good news. If I heard 'em once, it means I can get this receiver to work. Bad news is I still can't transmit a damned thing."

"Alright, Luther, keep trying. Good work."

"Pack it up, Luther," Rose ordered. "We're getting out of here now while we can cross that road. Gear up!" The men pulled on their packs and policed the area for any trace of their stay. They buried C-Ration containers and other refuse. With Mandelbaum taking point, they silently crept out of the stand of trees and made their way to the road. It was highly dangerous to cross open country in the middle of the day, but Rose was determined to get them out of the trap they were in, between two roads and the village. Keeping the hill between them and the village, they crossed a field to a drainage ditch along the road that had blocked their way north. Using hand signals, Rose told Kowalski to cross over and Mandelbaum to watch the route from the village. When each gave the all-clear sign, he tapped the men one at a time to cross over. There were low trees and shrubs on the other side that gave some cover. Beyond that, gently sloping hills rose up slightly on their route north. The hillside was covered in short grass. Suddenly Mandelbaum signaled them to stop crossing, and a second later Rose heard the sound of cowbells coming up from the village. He cursed himself as he understood. In his haste to leave, he had picked a crossing point that led right into a grazing pasture. With miles of meadows and forest, he had chosen the closest crossing point without thinking. Damn! He slammed his fist down into the side of the ditch. Four men across, four on this side. Even if they all got across, they'd be seen before they could reach cover. If they stayed here, they'd been seen too.

"What are you going to do?" asked Billy. Luther had just made it across and he didn't want to be separated from that radio, now that there was a chance it could work. "Get across, fast," answered Rose, as he took out his .45 automatic and began to affix the silencer. He hated the thought of killing the farmer, since it would tip off the Germans, and also because the poor bastard just happened to be in the wrong place at the wrong time.

In that instant they all froze. The sound of a heavy vehicle came from the opposite direction. Rose motioned everyone to get down. From around the curve to their right came an open truck, towing a 40mm Bofors Anti-aircraft weapon. The crew in the truck wore *Luftwaffe* blue uniforms and were talking and laughing among themselves. The truck passed by and turned the corner leading to the village. Then they heard the sound of brakes screeching and cows scattering, their bells and mooing creating a cacophony of sound that was nearly drowned out by the shouts of the farmer and driver, each yelling at the other to clear the road.

"Now!" said Rose in a loud whisper, as they jumped out of the ditch and ran to the other side. "Woodis," he pointed to one man, "take Luther's weapon, I know he won't give up that radio."

"OK, Rosie," Woodis answered, taking Luther's Carbine. "You need any help, Luther?"

"No, I can make it." Rose signaled Mandelbaum to take point again. They ran along to treeline at the bottom of the pasture until they reached a stonewall that marked off this pasture from the next. They ran straight up the hill, Rose bringing up the rear, the sounds of the near-accident fading behind him. They scurried down the opposite slope and vanished into another line of trees. They stopped for a moment to let Luther catch his breath. He was bent over, breathing deeply.

"It's OK, fellas," he said as he looked up with a smile. "It only hurts when I breathe." Woodis handed him his Carbine and they headed out, single file. Billy fell in next to Rose.

"Now we know not every Jerry pulled out."

"Yeah, but those were *Luftwaffe* troops, probably part of an AA unit. Why would they pull out all ground support and leave those guys behind?"

"I don't know, Rose," Billy answered. "But I do know something's up, and like it or not, I can smell who's behind it." Rose didn't answer him. He pulled out his compass and checked the heading. They were going due north, towards Hill 182.

CHAPTER TWENTY-SEVEN

16 April 1945
Pretzsch, Germany

Benedikt surveyed the ground around him from the turret of his Puma armored car. It had taken them longer than they expected to get the two slow *Maus* heavy panzers into place, but they now had a perfect firing position. The small town of Pretzsch spread itself out on the west bank of the Elbe, on the downward slope of a ridge that ran across the river. From the top of the ridge, there was a clear line of sight across the river, and along both roads leading to Dommitzsch and Bad Schmiedeberg. If the SS came back up the road from the south, they would be annihilated. If Dieter needed support to the west, the guns of the two *Maus* panzers and the four *Jagdtigers* could easily be brought to bear. They could also hold off the Russians here, for a while anyway, forcing them downriver to Dommitzsch and Strauch's ambush.

Benedikt directed the placement of the *Panzergrenadiers*, their half-tracks and two of the *Wirbelwind* anti-aircraft vehicles. Satisfied at last that these troops could hold this vital crossroads, he drove off in the armored car with another *Wirbelwind* in escort behind him. The quad 20mm anti-aircraft guns swiveled and searched the skies as they sped down the open road, always a dangerous activity for German forces. This time though, the *Luftwaffe* was in evidence. They saw two Me 262 jets screech by, their graceful swept wings tracing an arc across the sky as the jet engines thundered.

Benedikt tapped the driver on the shoulder and pointed to a road on their right. They pulled in and parked next to another Puma armored car.

Hans von Schierke stepped out and greeted Benedikt. Hans was acting as liaison with Benedikt's forces, reporting back to Dieter on a regular basis.

"They've vanished." Hans shrugged. For the past twenty-four hours they have been searching for the SS troops last seen heading towards Dommitzsch. "We've been up and down this road a dozen times. No one has seen them in Dommitzsch- there is a *Luftwaffe* anti-aircraft unit there and they've seen no other units since Twelfth Army pulled out."

"Is Strauch all set?" asked Benedikt.

"Yes, he found some good ground just half a kilometer from the bridge. He's digging in now. Here, I marked it on the map for you." Hans handed Benedikt his map of the area.

Hauptsturmführer Hugo Raalte eased back in the chair in the comfortable *Gasthaus* in the tiny village of Dahlenburg, hidden in the middle of the *Dübener Heide*, just off the main road to Dommitzsch. He raised a glass of schnapps in toast to himself and drank. "A stroke of genius, Karl, a stroke of genius!" His aide, *Untersturmführer* Karl Goche, bowed and answered, "I congratulate you, sir."

"Those bastards at headquarters would have let us die out on the Courland Peninsula if they didn't need us to die for them in Berlin! Well, the hell with that!"

The SS Frundsberg Division had retreated to Latvia with ten other divisions after the recent Russian offensives. They held a diminishing line against the Russian onslaught, and were pushed almost into the sea. They waited weeks, expecting evacuation by sea. Hitler continually refused, exhorting them to "fight to the last man and the last bullet." Thousands died uselessly, until the transports finally came to take off the survivors. Hitler had ordered that all equipment, tanks and vehicles be loaded first, and only then the men. There were no tanks or any other equipment left, and word of this order told the survivors that their leader was not only indifferent to their fate, he was ill-informed as well.

As the remnants of the Frundsberg Division rested and refitted outside of Berlin, Raalte and the officers and men of his company were of little mind to die in the final and inevitable battle for Berlin. The assignment to search for Remke's unit, in charge of a full battalion, was a godsend to him. It got him out of Berlin, and when they found Remke was not at the Wittenberg castle, he had realized they had free reign to roam the countryside, and time to avoid a return to Berlin. It was indeed a stroke of genius, to send the other two companies off on a wild goose chase, leaving him and his loyal men alone, close to the American lines.

Raalte had already drunk too much schnapps, but he hardly cared. "Have the other companies reported in yet?"

"No sir," replied Goche, "they are well to the east of the Elbe."

"Ha! Good!" He lifted his glass again. "Too bad boys, say hello to Ivan for me!" He downed the schnapps and looked at his aide, swaying slightly in his seat.

"Karl, I vowed that if we ever got out of Courland, I would not let them chew us up again. I've commanded this company since '43, and by God I'll see you boys home safe at the end when it comes. Which is any day now."

"Sir, the men, and I, respect you. We will follow you, as ordered."

"Are you certain, Karl?"

"Remember when Himmler came by and showered us with medals?"

"Yes, that spineless bastard!"

"Each platoon's non-com collected them in a chamber pot, and wanted to send them back to Himmler, full of their piss and shit. I of course put a halt to that, but thought you would want to know."

Raalte sputtered as he tried to take another drink, and laughed hysterically. When he calmed down, he stood up and slapped Goche on the back. "Come on then. Such men deserve to be surrendered to the Americans. And if we run into this Remke and his men we're supposed to be after, then tough luck for them if they stand in our way."

He grabbed the half-empty bottle of schnapps and walked out of the *Gasthaus*, barking orders to his men.

Remke's staff car sped down the road with his personal anti-aircraft vehicle behind him. The *Ostwind* armored car mounted a rapid-fire 37mm cannon, and searched the skies for enemy planes, protecting the staff car like a nervous mother hen.

The car pulled into the Bad Schmiedeberg castle courtyard and halted near the tower entrance. It was a small castle, a single tower rising from twenty-foot high walls which encompassed several small structures built into the sides of the interior walls. It had been a garrison castle, not built for living or luxury, but simply to house soldiers collecting the tolls on the road. Remke asked *Feldwebel* Schmidt, on duty in the courtyard, where Dieter was.

"Up in the tower, sir," Schmidt answered. "Quite a view from up there." Remke bounded up the steps to the top, where he found Dieter and Jost Brunner scanning the horizon with binoculars. They turned and saluted. He dismissed them with an impatient wave of his hand.

"Do you have an observation post set up on that hill yet?" Remke demanded. The hill was visible down the road, off to the right, about two kilometers distant.

"Yes sir, I just came back. There's a squad over there now and we're in radio contact. We ran into some *Luftwaffe* men burying their dead."

"What?" Remke lowered his glasses and frowned. "Tell me everything."

"There was an 88 stationed on that hill. It was an excellent spot for it. It seems that during that raid on Wittenberg a few nights ago, some bombers targeted the hill and destroyed the gun emplacement."

"You mean that the Allies deliberately bombed that hill?"

"It seems so."

"Did any other anti-aircraft emplacements get hit?"

"No sir," Jost interjected, "the *Luftwaffe* non-com said the others were all operational, but they didn't know what to do next because they lost their officers in that raid."

"It's clearly one of two things," Remke stated flatly.

"What, sir?" Jost asked. Dieter already understood.

"Either the Americans are planning on crossing the Mulde, right in front of us, and wanted to take out that emplacement before they came up that road," he said, pointing to the road that passed the hill and the castle, "or…"

"Or they know about us," Dieter finished for him.

"Either one means an interesting next few days," Remke said with a smile. "I doubt they could know much, if anything about Operation Gambit. But we can't underestimate the possibility. Be on alert here." Remke scanned the horizon again in all directions. "Where are your men?"

"The 9th Battalion, with the German Russian-marked vehicles, is based here and in the woods behind the castle. The 8th, with Russian trucks, is in the woods along the road between here at the hill." Dieter pointed along the road. To the right was cleared farmland, dominated by the hill beyond it. To the left of the main road was a pine forest, which rose gradually up from the road to a low ridge that paralleled the road.

"We can either attack them here, from this position, or move out towards Bad Düben when they cross the Mulde."

"Very good. Are there *Luftwaffe* units to your front?"

"Yes, there are 20mm batteries at Bad Düben and Söllichau, a little village at the end of this ridge. Should we bring them in? They have no one in command and will probably be overrun once the Americans get here."

Remke considered for a moment. "No. You will either see them running down this road or hear them firing. That will alert you that the Americans are close." With that, Remke consigned the men to their deaths, for the slight advantage of a warning that would come soon enough in any case. Dieter was not surprised.

"What is the latest report from Benedikt?" Remke asked as he moved onto the next subject.

"The SS have vanished without a trace. There were reports of them crossing the Elbe at Pretzsch, before we got there, but it apparently was not all of them."

"Strange. Not that I mind one less headache. Contact Benedikt and tell him to meet me at Dommitzsch. If we don't find anything today, I'll send him up here to you as planned."

"Yes, sir." Jost left them alone as he climbed down the tower staircase to the radio room.

The two men said nothing as they looked down the road. The sun was low in the sky now, the brightness from the west causing them to shade their eyes. Dieter wanted to speak but felt awkward and tense with Remke now. He had known him since the beginning of the war, and had learned much from him about surviving. He now owed him everything for allowing the rescue of Elsa. He had not had a chance to thank him properly since the return from Berlin. It seemed that Remke had avoided him since then, and was overly formal and stern, beyond even his usual strict military bearing. Dieter turned to Remke and extended his hand.

"Colonel, I have not thanked you…"

Remke looked at Dieter at first with surprise and then disgust. He turned on Dieter, raising his hand and slapping him across the face. Dieter fell back against the tower wall, stunned beyond belief. Remke came right up to him, inches away from his face, towering over him in a sudden rage.

"Do not even think of it! You are a dead man now, don't even think of a life after this, do you understand! You have nothing but this mission!" Remke's face was contorted and spittle jumped from his lips as he spoke.

Dieter was completely at a loss and could only stammer, "I only meant to thank you for saving Elsa…"

Remke drew his Walther automatic pistol and aimed it Dieter's forehead. His arm was shaking and Dieter could clearly see the safety catch was off. Dieter's eyes widened in fear. Remke spoke to him in controlled, clipped tones.

"Do not ever speak of Anna again to me. Follow your orders precisely and I will not kill you. Those are the only two things I require of you. Do anything else and you die. Is everything clear?"

"Yes." Dieter could barely manage to croak out that last word. Remke holstered his pistol and spun around, and descended the staircase. Dieter sat down on the hard stone floor, listening to Remke's vehicles roar out of the courtyard, trying to make sense out of what just happened.

Anna? Who is Anna?

Jost climbed back up the stairs wearily. "He'll be gone all night. This would be a good time for you…" Jost stopped in mid-sentence as he saw Dieter slumped on the floor with a stunned look on his face. "What happened?"

"Jost, my old friend, I think our Colonel has gone insane."

Jost extended his hand to help Dieter up. "God help us if our officers all take so long to see the obvious. I could have told you he was crazy the first time I saw him riding that train into Holland!"

Dieter smiled sadly as he got up. "You've really spoken the truth this time, Jost, about more than Remke. I knew Hitler was insane the first time I heard him speak, but I did nothing. Nothing but fight for him like Remke wants me to fight for him. I've done my duty, and look where it's gotten our country."

"Well," said Jost in his broad Bavarian drawl, "there's duty to the army and the government, then there's duty to God, and to yourself. They're not always the same, young man."

"I wish I had understood that before now." Dieter folded his arms against the parapet, and looked out at the setting sun. Jost put his arm around his shoulder.

"Now, if you had, would you be here in a position to end this insanity? No, you'd be in a penal battalion or dead, and no help to us at all. So, stop your bellyaching and go get Elsa while the Colonel is out roaming the countryside. We'll figure out what to do when she's safely here. Get some sleep, I'll wake you before midnight. Benedikt's motorcycle is in the courtyard, you can make good cross-country time with it."

Dieter felt Jost's wisdom and friendship wash over him. He looked at the older man who had been through so much with him. "Do you talk to all *Hauptmanns* like that?"

"Only the ones who need it, boy. Go."

CHAPTER TWENTY-EIGHT

16 April 1945
Wolfen, Germany

Lt. Colonel Howard Sadler braked the jeep in front of his headquarters tent, switched off the ignition, and got out cursing. "Goddamn sonuvabitch!" Captain Barney Canfield, his Intelligence Officer, got out of the passenger seat slowly, unwrapping his white knuckled hands from the door and seat. He followed Sadler into the tent as the sentry on duty snapped to attention. Seconds later, the escort jeep with its mounted .50 caliber machine gun pulled in behind the Colonel's jeep, other officers spilling out and filing into the tent like chicks trailing after a mother hen. Sadler didn't wait for the rest of his entourage to enter the tent as he began to rant.

"There's not a single damn German out there!" he yelled, pointing towards the Mulde River, "and we're ordered to stay on this side of the fucking river!"

Orders had come down from First Army HQ the week before. All units were to approach the Mulde River line, hold and go no further. Headquarters didn't want any American units running into Russians before the link-up had been properly planned. This made eminent sense to most veteran GIs, who were glad of a break and a chance to rest up. It definitely did not make sense to Lt. Colonel Howard Sadler, the newly appointed commanding officer of the 537th Regimental Combat Team.

Colonel Sadler paced back and forth within the narrow confines of the tent. He stroked his moustache nervously as he waited for the rest of his officers to file in, thinking about what to do next. Everything depended upon his getting into action. Sadler had spent the last two years in various rear-area supply posts, and had never requested a combat command before. He was a loud, brash and self-aggrandizing officer, very aggressive with subordinates in his rear-area commands. He had risen quickly in rank, due as much to his ability to claim credit for other's work as his own. He had been very comfortable behind the front and sure of seeing the end of the war without ever encountering any danger. The only problem was that Sadler had political ambitions. There was very little he was actually suited to do, and he planned to use his rank and wartime service to gain political office. With the war finally winding down, Sadler had requested a combat command, hoping to participate in one final battle that would secure his reputation. With one glorious moment, his political future would be certain. His rear-area service need not be mentioned - the voters could surely assume that he had been in combat since the Normandy invasion.

Sadler had known it would not be easy to take over command of the 537th RCT. His junior officers had known he had no combat experience, so he tried to look and act the part. He lived in a tent in the field, saying he wouldn't take up residence in anything better than his men had. He drove his own jeep and led reconnaissance patrols like the one today. He wanted the support of all his officers when he made his big move.

All his planning had come to nothing. For the last week, the 537th RCT had been waiting outside of Wolfen, on the west bank of the Mulde River. It seemed certain to Sadler that the war would end with him sitting in this damn tent without a single battle to his credit. Today it had been too much. He had jumped in his jeep, taking his Intelligence Officer along and trailing another jeep with aides and guards. They crossed the river and drove in every direction for an hour. They didn't see a single German soldier. Sadler was certain this was his moment.

"The front is wide open, and we're supposed to sit here and wait until the Germans reinforce this area. We could lose hundreds of lives trying to cross this river later!"

"But sir," Captain Canfield protested, "Corps Intelligence hasn't heard about any German withdrawal, and our orders haven't changed. We could get chewed out for crossing over today."

"Hell, Canfield, that was just a little patrol, no one's going to say anything about it." Sadler looked at the map, stroking his moustache again. He made a decision. To hell with Corps.

"We're crossing over. Canfield, inform 1st and 2nd Battalions, my Headquarters Platoon and the Reconnaissance Platoon. We leave in one hour. The 3rd stays here on reserve and to keep up appearances. We'll inform Corps HQ once we've made it to the Elbe."

There was silence in the room as his staff exchanged uncertain looks. "Well?" snapped Sadler.

"Yes, sir," answered each officer.

"Then get going. We move out in one hour." He turned to his second in command. "Major Thomas, you are in charge here. Hold Easy and Fox Companies in readiness and keep Corps off my back."

"What if they order you to return, sir?"

"The radio vehicles will cross over with us, but I'll keep them well to the rear. That way any order to return would, ah, take some time to get to me. Now get moving!"

Sixty minutes later, the column pulled out and crossed the river. The Recce Platoon led the way in their halftracks, followed by the Headquarters Platoon in jeeps with mounted .50 caliber machine guns, and two battalions in deuce-and-a-half trucks. Once out of sight of the river, Sadler ordered the two radio vehicles and an infantry squad to drop back.

"Wait one hour, then follow us, slowly. Send a jeep up with any communications," Sadler ordered the technical sergeant in charge of the radios, "except with an order to return. Do you understand me?"

"I get it, sir. Which way are you headed?"

"Due west, through this area, to a town called Pretzsch on the Elbe River."

His planned route took him directly by Hill 182 and Dieter's Hiwis at Bad Schmiedeberg.

CHAPTER TWENTY-NINE

17 April 1945
On the road to Eutzsch, Germany

It was after midnight, and Dieter opened up the BMW full throttle down the deserted country road. Only a narrow beam of light shown through the taped headlight, but even this was unnecessary. The dirt and gravel road was almost white in the moonlit night, and he could easily see the twists and turns it took. His mind was racing, hoping Elsa would be waiting at the hut in the woods, and trying to plan out his next moves. How could he make contact with the Americans? What about the SS and Remke? What about his own men? He knew he could count on Jost and Hans, possibly Benedikt. Would the others follow him, or were some so dedicated to the mission there would be a fight? Where could he hide Elsa where Remke wouldn't find her, but where she would be close to him when he made the break for the American lines?

One problem at a time, he told himself. He slowed the motorcycle and turned into a field, crossing it until he came to a farm track. He followed the rutted path past several fields, until it finally became a path in the woods. He shut down the BMW and pulled it off the path. Making his way up the wooded slope in the dark was more difficult than he had imagined, and he tripped over roots and rocks, falling repeatedly. Light from the partial moon did not penetrate the canopy of pine branches above him. He had to stop several times to get his bearings and catch his breath, until he emerged on the ridge near the hut, somewhere off to his left. He walked slowly and cautiously down the dark path, waiting to quiet his breathing and listening for any movement ahead. Soon he could make out the hut a few yards ahead. It was dark and quiet. He stood by a tree and observed the area for ten minutes. There was always the chance that Elsa had been followed, that some of Remke's personal headquarter guard were waiting for him, inside or outside the hut. He heard nothing but the wind swooshing through the pines. He drew his pistol.

Slowly, picking each step deliberately, he walked in a low crouch to the door of the hut. Standing to the side, he lifted the latch and held it. Waiting until another gust of wind blew loudly into the pine trees, he opened the door slightly and stepped inside. He immediately felt the muzzle of a gun pressed to the side of his head. He could feel the tremble in the hand that held the gun as it quivered slightly against his skull.

"Who is it? Speak or I'll shoot!"

"Elsa, it's me!" The gun fell away immediately and she hugged him fiercely.

"Dieter, I'm so glad to see you! Do you know what's happened?"

"What? First, tell me what you're doing with that pistol, then tell me what's happened." They sat down on the bed and he holstered his pistol and took hers from her, snapping on the safety. She snatched the Luger pistol back from him with a flash of anger.

"Don't treat me like a helpless girl! My father had one of these from the Great War and taught me how to shoot when I was a child." She snapped the safety off again and put the Luger in her jacket pocket.

"Alright, I'm sorry. Now tell me everything."

"After you left I thought a pistol might come in handy if the SS came. I have no intention of letting them take me back there. I asked Stieff if I could have one. I told him I was afraid of the Russians. He gave me this the morning after you left. He had me out in back of the barn doing some shooting practice when they came."

"Who?"

"The SS. Those Waffen-SS that were looking for you at the castle, only not a battalion. Less than a company, I think. Stieff went out to talk to them while I hid in the woods. I heard them questioning Stieff about where Remke was. Stieff said he was out patroling west of the Mulde River and was due back in two days."

"Did they believe him?"

"Yes, I think so. They said they had been sent off by their battalion commander to search east of the Elbe, and when they found nothing they decided to search the area around Wittenberg again."

"Smart move. It puts the river between them and the Russians."

"Yes, and they don't seem too eager to move."

"They're still there?"

"Yes, they've taken over, but Stieff and the other men are moving freely about. They must be waiting for further orders."

"Damned odd. So that's why you greeted me with a gun to the head."

"Dieter, there's only one way this is going to end, and that's with you and I, together and alive and the war ended. Anything else is unacceptable." She looked at him with simple, sincere determination. He knew that if it wasn't him, she would have fought and died rather than be taken prisoner. He had always envied her ability to make a decision about what she wanted, and follow through with determination. While he was plagued by moral dilemmas, Elsa acted. It was one of the things he loved about her. He looked at her, her eyes alive in the darkness.

"Alive, together, in peace. Who would have ever thought such a simple thing would be so hard? Come, let's go. We need to be back before dawn." She squeezed his hand, and he waited for her to thank him for coming to her rescue once again.

"Good. Do you have any food? I haven't eaten since yesterday."

Dieter smiled, and pulled a wrapped package from his pocket. "Here's some bread and cheese. I told Jost to have some hot soup waiting. Now eat as we walk, we've got to get you back and hidden before Remke gets back." They got up and walked down the path, Elsa munching hungrily on the black bread and cheese. She finally stopped eating long enough to ask, "Why should Remke give a damn where I go anyway, after he helped get me out of that prison?"

Dieter told her about the incident in the tower, and about the name Anna.

"He's crazy," she said with a shrug.

"Yes, that does seem to be the prevailing opinion."

It was almost dawn when they got back to the small castle at Bad Schmiedeberg. Hans von Schierke was waiting outside, pacing in the courtyard, wrapped in a greatcoat against the night chill. Dieter switched off the engine and Hans walked up to them, smiling.

"Elsa, it's good to see you safe, or at least with us."

"That's safe enough for me, Hans. Now where is that hot soup? I'm hungry and chilled to the bone." Hans led them inside to the kitchen, where a large pot of soup sat simmering on top of an ancient wood-burning kitchen stove. The room warm and the smell of food wafted up to them. Jost was in a chair by the kitchen table, asleep and snoring.

"The picture of domesticity!" Dieter joked. They all laughed as Jost awoke with a start. He jumped up, immediately awake, and engulfed her in a hug.

"Sit, sit, my child. You need some soup to warm you up."

The four friends sat around the table, enjoying the warmth of the room and each other. Elsa told them about the SS at Eutzsch and her escape to the hut. It felt to Dieter like a stolen hour, with the rest of the world asleep, Remke, the SS and their other enemies all far away. Elsa looked at him and smiled, as if to say, see, this is what it will be like when it's over. He smiled back, and tried not to think of what the morning might bring.

When they were done, Jost took Elsa to a room at the far end of the castle. He brought her blankets and extra clothes, water to wash in, and told her not to venture out of the room unless it was an emergency. He bade her goodnight and left. She put the Luger under her pillow and was asleep in seconds.

The sun was beginning to dawn in the east. Dieter and Hans walked up to the tower to scan the western horizon at first light.

"How are the men doing?" Dieter asked as they climbed the staircase.

"As well as can be expected. They're keyed up about the operation, but there are a thousand rumors flying about. Hitler's flown to South America, the Swedes are going to negotiate a truce, America is going to withdraw from the war- that one has been popular since Roosevelt died. Foolishness." They reached the top of the stairs and walked out onto the tower, over to the stone parapet facing the rising sun.

"Hans, as soon as the Americans get close enough, I'm going to cross over to them and warn them about Gambit. Then I want you and Jost to bring the men over to surrender. All of them."

"Right out from under Remke's nose?"

"Yes. The order will come from me. The men will obey me, I'm certain. But if Remke interferes…"

"By tomorrow the paratroopers will be on our flanks, providing 'protection', and the panzers will be in our rear. Do you think Remke is suspicious?"

"I think he is insane, and perhaps suspicious of me. What do you think Benedikt will do?"

"He's certainly not afraid of a fight, and he took on those SS troops in Zossen," Hans answered.

"Yes, but that was to keep Operation Gambit intact, to prevent its failure at the hands of the SS. Getting Elsa away from the Gestapo was a romantic gesture. Asking him to go against a *Führer* directive and betray his immediate superior officer is quite another."

"I agree. I think he's a good man, but we may be asking too much of him. He hasn't been with us long enough to go along without a good reason, but he might." Hans thought for a moment, then asked, "When will you go to the Americans?"

"When they cross the Mulde. If we wander off now looking for them, anything could happen. I need to speak directly to someone in command of the American units that will be in front of us, to make sure they understand about Gambit, and don't fire on us when we surrender. The two battalions can't stay in place and wait for the Americans, in case Remke realizes what we're doing and tries to take direct command. We have to move towards them, and that could easily be seen as an attack."

"It's not going to be easy..." Hans was cut off by a distant explosion, from the west. It echoed off the ridge in front of them. Men camped in the woods along the road ran out, weapons in hand, looking for a threat.

"Call the observation post and bring back a report, fast!" Dieter ordered. Hans was gone in an instant to the radio room.

~

The eight men trudged through the low underbrush in the scrub pine forest. Not all of the *Dübener Heide* was open meadow. They had slogged through a marsh and then up and down a series of low hills covered with boulders. Rose explained to Billy it was the remains of rock left by glaciers in the last Ice Age. Billy didn't care. It was almost dawn and they had covered little ground.

"We've got to find a better way," said Billy disgustedly.

"OK, take ten!" Rose ordered. The men flopped down where they were. Most were asleep in seconds. Rose pulled out his map and studied the area under the beam of a red-lensed flashlight.

"We're somewhere in here," Rose said, pointing his finger to open space on the map. "The heart of the *Heide*, rough country. The village of Söllichau is probably just over that hill or the next. It straddles the road and rail line to Bad Schmiedeberg, both of which pass within less than a kilometer of Hill 182."

"If the railroad track gives any cover, why don't we follow that up once it's daylight? The Germans haven't been running many trains during the day, and we'd hear it coming anyway."

"That's an option, but not for a while. We still need to head up that way." Rose pointed in the opposite direction from the village.

"Why?" said Billy excitedly. "Why not get into Söllichau now, while it's still dark, find the rail line, and hustle out on it? Why go through more of this shit?"

"Because, Captain," Rose said angrily, with the sarcastic tone he always used to explain the obvious to higher-ranking officers, "it's an inhabited enemy village. I plan on getting us to Hill 182 alive, then it's your show."

"We have to take a chance now, Lieutenant," Billy answered in the same tone. "If we take the rail track from Söllichau, we can make it to within sight of Hill 182 today. We can observe, rest up, and then get up the hill during the night. If we keep going through this crap, we'll be another day late and dog-tired when we get there. It could be too little too late."

Rose didn't like going through the village or even close to it. But he had to acknowledge Billy was right. It would mean the difference of a full day. He needed more time to think. "Luther! Wake up! Try that damned radio one more time."

"Sure Rosie. Pretty good spot up here for reception, if she'll work." Luther set up the radio and fiddled with the dials. He got a blast of static. "Yowie! That works." He twisted the dial to their frequency and heard the clear sound of an American voice. He held up his earphones so the others, leaning in, could hear.

"Archer, this is Longbow, Archer, this is Longbow. Come in Archer." It was repeated several times, followed by "Archer, are you there?" There was a moment's silence, and another, different voice came on and began the same plaintive message.

"That's our call sign!"

"Good work, Luther. Now get them on the horn and tell them to stand by." Outgoing messages had to be brief, otherwise the Germans could triangulate their position if they were listening to the right frequency.

Luther's face dropped as he tried to send. "No can do, Rosie. She's only receiving. Still can't get her to send."

"God damn it! That thing's just dead weight."

Luther looked hurt, as if Rose was talking about him. "Rosie, I'll git her to work, just wait and see. Gimme some time, that's all."

"Alright, you and Boyle both want time? Then get your lazy asses up, we're gonna haul ass outta here." Rose set off at a trot, heading in the direction of Söllichau, Billy a close second.

The village was just over the next hill.

Rose cast a concerned eye towards the eastern horizon on his right. It was already false dawn. Reflected light from the sun still beyond the horizon had increased visibility, easing the affect of the darkness. They were just at the edge of the woods looking out on cleared land that sloped down to the houses at the edge of the village. To their rear, the hills they had just come out of continued, stretching in a ridge all the way to Bad Schmiedeberg. The main road out of the village was about a kilometer away. Even closer than that, they could make out a small railway station. The tracks led out of town, paralleling the road. Rose had sent Kowalski out for a closer look. He came back, flowing invisibly in from the shadows.

"We got about three hundred yards of level track on open ground. Then it goes into the trees, far as I can see. Good cover."

"OK. Kowalski, you go first with Woodis, Santiago and Burke. Mandelbaum, you follow with Luther and the Captain when I give the signal. I'll cover you all from that stonewall by the station. When you're all into the woods, I follow. Got it?"

Heads nodded. "Kowalski, give me two minutes to get into position. Then you go." Rose patted Kowalski's helmet as he got up and ran down to the station. There was a stucco-covered stonewall that ran in front of and around the side of the station. Rose leapt over it and looked around. He could see down the road into the village and up to where the men waited, as well as down the track. Everything looked OK. He leaned his Springfield rifle against the wall and pulled the burp gun from around his pack. He watched Kowalski lead the first three men down from the trees. They came down the hill and halted at the track while Kowalski stuck his head out and peered around. He looked over at Rose and gave the thumbs up. Rose signaled him to move forward.

Thompson at the ready, Kowalski led the men out. They were about fifty yards down the track when the first sliver of light beamed out from the horizon. Rose looked back up at the group in the trees. They were now clearly visible as their faces looked out, watching Rose for any signal. Irritated, he motioned for them to keep their heads down. He looked back at the other group, now farther along the track. The sun was further over the horizon now, light illuminating the pine trees along the track. Things began to take shape and focus. Suddenly Rose saw movement in the trees, something large, something that didn't belong…

"HIT THE DIRT!" He stood up and bellowed out again, "Hit the dirt!"

The snout of a 20mm anti-aircraft gun stuck out of the trees and swiveled towards the group on the track. It was a camouflaged gun emplacement in the trees, up the slope from the track as it curved slightly to the left, before it vanished into the woods. With the camouflage netting draped over it, it had been invisible in the dark. The same rays of light that betrayed its presence to Rose also highlighted the four men walking along the track.

The gunner had seen them, but first assumed they were workers from the village. As the rays of light lengthened, his loader dropped his jaw and whispered, "*Amis, Amis!*" The gunner swiveled the gun around and down at the moment Rose yelled his warning. He looked up at the source of the yell and fired his first rounds off high.

Kowalski heard Rose and looked around quickly and caught sight of the gun's movement before diving to the side of the tracks. Twenty-millimeter tracer rounds flew over his shoulder as he dived for cover. Woodis, Santiago and Burke were a fraction of a second slower and took the force of the burst as the gunner kept firing. The burning shells ripped through them as they stood in a row, throwing them back with chests burst open. They fell like rag dolls over the tracks, blood gushing down onto the rails and smoke and fire flowing from their clothes and flesh as the phosphorous from the tracers burned off.

As quickly as it had begun, the firing stopped. The gunner looked down the track, smoke curling out the barrel of the 20mm gun, the only sound a slight hydraulic whine as he traversed the weapon. He was sure he had seen four men, but he only counted three bodies. He swung the gun back and forth, depressing the barrel as much as possible, searching for another target. Two other crewmembers sprang out of the covered bunker in back of the sandbag emplacement, rifles at the ready. Kowalski lay under some bushes at the side of the track, slowly and carefully pulling himself into the woods. Slowly and smoothly enough for the movement not to attract attention. His Thompson was in the dirt at the bottom of the ditch. No going back for it now. He was going to have to get close enough for grenades.

Rose swore to himself, kicking himself mentally for not remembering the *Luftwaffe* anti-aircraft unit they had seen earlier. If there was one in the vicinity, there was bound to be another. And these bastards had picked themselves a perfect spot, good camouflage in the woods, covering the road and the railroad station against air attack. He thought all this in an instant while removing the lens covers from his telescopic sight. He didn't know if Kowalski had made it. If not, this was their only chance.

The anti-aircraft gun fired again, chewing up the edge of the woods, searching for the fourth American. Rose looked behind him, wondering if there were other German soldiers in the village, and if he were going to get caught in the middle. Nothing moved behind him. Satisfied, he gripped the Springfield and brought it up to rest on the top of the wall. He sighted through the scope, knowing he had just seconds if the gunner had spotted him.

One of the other crew saw him first. He raised his Mauser and got off a wild shot, hitting the side of the station above Rose. But it pointed him out to the gunner, who began to turn his gun toward the station and the low wall.

Rose found the gun emplacement through the scope and fought to center his sight on the gunner. He saw a blur and knew it was the gun swiveling in his direction. He fought to stay focused. The gun lowered and then he saw the gunner's head clearly, his mouth open in what must have been a yell as he fired. Rounds slammed into the wall to Rose's left, and he steadied himself, waiting for the right moment. In the back of his brain something flashed that one of his Force instructors had told him. There is an illusion of safety behind a telescopic sight. You have to remember that you are vulnerable when you're shooting. The sight makes you feel powerful, but it doesn't hide you.

He pulled the trigger. The firing stopped. He worked the bolt and found the target again. The loader was shaking the gunner, who was sitting upright, his helmet askew. As he shook him, a rivulet of blood ran down from his forehead as he fell over. The loader stepped into his seat, and Rose pulled the trigger again. The second man fell, a bullet in the heart. More rifle fire peppered the building. The other two crewmen stayed away from the deadly seat on the 20mm gun. Rose dropped his head below the wall as masonry chips rained down from the side of the station. When they saw him drop down, one of the crewmen jumped into the seat and began to fire at him with the 20mm gun. Shells hit the wall he was hiding behind and chunks of rocks began to fly off. His cover was not going to last long, and there was nowhere else to go. He curled up in a ball as rounds slammed into the stone wall and the building behind him, showering him in debris.

Kowalski crawled closer. The trees were thick, giving him good cover, but it also meant he had to get close for a clean throw. He could hear excited, frantic yells in German and could tell the crew had their hands full. He got up and ran between the last few trees. He could see the two remaining crewmen working the anti-aircraft gun, peppering the wall where Rose was with constant fire. He took a grenade from his jacket, pulled the pin and tossed it into the emplacement, followed by one more. He turned and ran into the woods, diving behind the biggest pine tree he could find.

The loader heard a clunk as something rolled against the ammunition cases stacked up behind the gun. He turned and saw the grenade rolling lazily toward him. Then another clunk, a blinding flash, then nothingness.

Rose heard the two grenade explosions and knew Kowalski was alive. He looked up over the wall in time to see the secondary explosions as the packed ammunition blew up, destroying the gun emplacement. The explosion blew the gun out and it rolled down the slope, coming to rest in the ditch. Rose stood up, coughing out cement and rock dust, and looked around again. He saw a few doors open and shut quickly in the village.

He signaled Mandelbaum, Luther and Billy to come down. He walked over to the ruined bodies of Burke, Santiago and Woodis, removed their dogtags, and dropped them in his pocket along with Rowley's. Kowalski slid down out of the woods and joined him. He stood by his side.

"You saved my life, Rosie. Again."

Rose looked at Kowalski, thankful that he had made it, and for reminding him one life saved was better than none.

"I owed you one. OK, let's move out. Take the point."

"Sure, Rosie." Kowalski ambled agreeably down the track. Billy and the others stood around, looking at the dead bodies.

"Come on, there's nothing to do here. Let's go." Rose motioned them to move ahead of him. Mandelbaum and Luther started off. Billy wanted to ask what had happened, but thought better of it. He jogged off after the others, Rose bringing up the rear. As he entered the woods, he looked back one more time, and could see the villagers anxiously peering out of their houses. And the dead bodies.

CHAPTER THIRTY

17 April 1945
Dübener Heide, Germany

Remke's armored command car sped down the dusty dirt road as his *Ostwind* anti-aircraft vehicle and halftrack escort raced to keep up with him. He had left Strauch's position just at dawn as Dieter radioed the news of a distant explosion in the direction of the Mulde River.

Remke stood in the turret as the wind and dust whipped around his head, beating his gloved hand in excitement and frustration on the rim of the turret. It was all about to happen. He could hardly believe that all his maneuvering and planning was about to actually bear fruit. As the car roared down the road, he saw himself being carried closer to that perfect state, a future of killing and revenge that would keep his pain and agony at bay. He had no home, no family, no hope left other than the war. He had spent every day of the last five years in one uniform or the other. What would he do in civilian clothes? The thought disgusted him. He felt strong and inviolate in his uniform and the feel of his pistol at his side reassured him. He knew that the day the war ended, the wall of death he had built around him would simply fall away and the loss of Anna and everything else he held dear would consume him. It was a possibility he could not allow.

"Get *Hauptmann* Neukirk on the wireless!" he shouted at the radio operator. A minute later Remke was demanding, "Neukirk, any sign of the Americans yet?"

"No, sir," came the reply through the radio's static and the noise of the fast-moving vehicle. "Nothing since the explosion. I've sent some patrols out but they've seen nothing."

"You see I was right about that FLAK unit, it was an excellent tripwire. We wouldn't have known they were this close if it wasn't for them."

"Yes sir," Dieter could only agree. The Luftwaffe crew were nothing but pawns, sacrificed in Remke's game.

"Do not engage the Americans until I get there. Watch them closely. I am less than an hour away. Out." Remke switched off the receiver without waiting for a reply from Dieter. There was nothing more to be said. Everything was in place, and it would only take his firm hand to guide them into their final, deadly positions.

"Get me Benedikt now," he ordered the operator. He snapped orders to Benedikt, telling him to move two *Maus* super-heavy Panzers up to Bad Schmeideburg, along with two of the *Jagdpanthers* for support. At a top speed of 20 kilometers per hour, it would take them some time to get in position.

Remke heard a noise off to his left, a faint rumble of vehicles over the noise of his own small convoy. His eyes darted about until he saw they were coming upon a road on the left that merged with the one he was on. It came out of the woods, at an angle, so he couldn't see anything but where it emptied out onto the main road. He was almost paralleling it now, and he tried to see between the thick pine trees as he got closer to the intersection.

Suddenly a column of halftracks and trucks spilled from the forest road in front of him, turning left just in front of his vehicle. The driver slammed on the brakes, the armored vehicle sliding to the right and almost off the road to avoid a collision. The stream of vehicles continued for a moment, until one braked to a halt and soldiers began to spill out amid shouts and commands. Several heavy machine guns mounted on halftracks swiveled in his direction. Waffen-SS troops surrounded his vehicle.

Remke knew he was severely outnumbered. He looked back to make sure that the *Ostwind*, with its powerful 37mm anti-aircraft gun, was leveled at the vehicles ahead. It was. He looked back down at the men surrounding him, suddenly aware that something was not quite right. Then he saw it. They were drunk. Many were unsteady on their feet, and some were laughing with each other.

Standing in the turret, Remke assumed his most authoritative tone and barked down at them. "Who is in command here?"

His question was not answered, but it did have the effect of quieting the soldiers closest to him. They looked stupidly at each other, then in the direction of the convoy. The sound of raucous laughter drifted down the road, and a band of officers turned the corner, lead by *Hauptsturmführer* Hugo Raalte, carrying a bottle of brandy. They would have looked comical if Raalte hadn't been waving a pistol in the other hand.

"Well, well, well," Raalte said, smiling at his officers, "look what we have here…a *Wehrmacht* Colonel! Could this be the famous Erich Remke? Do I have the pleasure?" Raalte bowed mockingly and almost lost his balance, laughing loudly as his grinning aide righted him. Remke realized there was no point in denying his identity.

"I am Colonel Erich Remke. I am engaged in a special mission by order of the *Führer*," he stated empathetically, holding up his papers, "and no unauthorized units are allowed in this operational area. Get out of my way at once!"

"Karl," Raalte nudged his aide, "look, a *Führer* Order! We've seen those before, haven't we? 'Defend the Courland Peninsula to the last bullet and the last man!' Remember that one, boys?" The men laughed, a dark menacing undertone murmuring through it. Remke realized not only were they drunk, but that all order had broken down. Was it like this everywhere?

"Courland? What unit is this and who are you?" Remke demanded.

"Colonel Remke, allow me to introduce myself. I am *Hauptsturmführer* Hugo Raalte, of the SS Frundsberg Division, late of the Courland Peninsula."

"I thought Frundsberg was destroyed in the Courland?"

"All but, my dear Remke, all but. These men are the survivors of a unit I have commanded since 1943. We were brought out to once again fight to the last man in the final battle of Berlin. We have you to thank for this wonderful trip in the country." Raalte took a long pull on the brandy bottle and handed it to the man next to him. He lifted his pistol and the soldiers surrounding Remke's vehicle lifted their weapons, pointing straight at his head. They may have been drunk, but their aim was true. Remke did not move.

Raalte jumped up on the runner and aimed his pistol through the opening. "Get out of the way!" he ordered impatiently to the radio operator, then fired four shots into the radio, as the terrified operator scurried back in the enclosed space, holding his hands over his ears as the shots echoed fiercely inside the vehicle.

"Karl, the *Ostwind*." Raalte smiled up at Remke as several soldiers rousted out the occupants of the anti-aircraft vehicle, then slide a grenade down the barrel of the 37mm gun. It and the shell inside exploded, bursting the barrel and rendering the gun useless.

"Now, Remke, you will not be tempted to radio our whereabouts or fire on us."

"What exactly are you doing?" asked Remke, more puzzled than concerned at the moment. Raalte was evidently not going to take him into custody.

"Living, Colonel Remke." Raalte hissed at him, leaning close enough for his alcohol-fouled breath to cause Remke to pull his face back. "We are through with dying. We've died for the *Führer* long enough. We left more comrades in the Courland than we took out, and all for nothing!" He spat viciously and lifted the pistol to Remke's chin.

"I don't know why Himmler wants you so bad, and I don't give a fuck. He's hiding outside of Berlin already anyway. So don't get in our way!"

It was all clear to Remke now. He looked at Raalte with disgust. "You're going to surrender. To the Americans."

"Damn right we are, aren't we boys!" Raalte turned to his men who cheered wildly. He jumped down and grabbed his brandy bottle back. "So, Remke, live a little! We are! It's all over except for anyone fool enough to take the last bullet of the war in the gut. We plan to drink every drop of liquor in this province on our way to the *Amis*. Enjoy yourself now! We'll all be in POW camps for quite some time."

Raalte stumbled back with his men as they boarded their vehicles and took off in a cloud of dust. Remke waited a few minutes and then told his driver to move on. He slumped back in the seat, now seriously worried about how far this defeatist attitude could spread. He had to act fast. Then he thought about Raalte's words.

Live. Enjoy. He shrugged mentally. They were as alien to him as the thought of surrender.

~

Billy crawled through the underbrush that grew down to the edge of a small gurgling stream. He halted at the bank, next to Rose who had been steadily watching the fields beyond the stream through his binoculars. Two hours earlier they had left the railroad track as it approached a town marked Bad Schmiedeberg on their maps. They had worked their way across the open meadows, seeking cover in the folds of ground as best they could. Now they were resting in small copse of trees atop a small rise. Behind them was farmland, criss-crossed by dirt roads and tracks. Ahead of them were rolling meadows bordered by a wooded ridge that overlooked a major roadway. To their left, dominating this landscape only a few kilometers away, was Hill 182. Billy and Rose had crawled forward to get a better view of their objective.

"Finally," said Rose, "there it is. Hope it's worth it." He handed the binoculars to Billy, who took them without comment and focused on the large hill. He set them down, took off his helmet and reached his hands down into the cold running water, splashing his face and wetting the back of his neck. It was warm enough for a summer's day, and the water refreshed him.

"Listen, Rosie, I know you think I'm on a wild goose chase, or just after Remke for personal reasons. But something is going on here, with this Operation Gambit. Why do you think the Germans withdrew from this area?"

"I told you, don't call me Rosie! It could be as simple as they pulled out to defend Berlin. Or, they all ran away. Who knows? We sure haven't seen any Germans in GI uniforms." Billy knew that Rose had a good point, but didn't want to give in. After the loss of half the men, the mission had to have some meaning.

"No, but I'm telling you that Erich Remke would not be put in charge of a small-time operation. If he's involved, it's dangerous. Guaranteed."

"Well, whatever," Rose said with a frown, "we gotta grab some shuteye. Let's get back to those trees and hole up until dark. Then we'll check out that hill." Rose grabbed the binoculars and backed out on his belly, leaving Billy alone. He put his helmet on and looked out over the landscape. He knew the answer was out there. He knew Remke was out there, waiting for him. He knew one of them would die here. Or both of them.

Rose returned to the grove of trees, mostly small birches growing in clumps amongst the meadow grasses, sprinkled with wildflowers. A path wound through it, coming from the tilled farmlands behind them and descending down to a weathered plank bridge that crossed the stream. Billy followed him up cautiously, both of them avoiding the path and keeping low.

They found Luther working on the field radio. He hadn't given up on it, and they found it at least useful to listen to Allied transmissions. Sergeant Kowalski was lying prone on the other side of the grove, keeping watch on their rear. Corporal Mandelbaum was curled up in a small depression, already asleep.

"OK, Luther, wrap it up and get some sleep. Kowalski and I will take first watch. Billy, hunker down there with Mandelbaum." No one needed any prodding. They were all dead tired, and Billy was thankful he didn't have to stand the first watch. He found a spot just off the path near the edge of the treeline, secluded by bushes and a small hummock of long grass. He looked around and saw Rose across the path, hidden and vigilant. He closed his eyes.

Rose made himself comfortable and settled into silence. He had a good view of the surrounding terrain, but not as much cover as he would have liked. The trees were thin and tall, none of them large enough to hide a man. It was the best they could do out on the open meadow, and unless someone came looking, it would do just fine.

Five minutes passed, and Rose listened to the sounds of the countryside. There were no planes, no distant vehicles, and no talk to invade the sounds of a country meadow. The wind rustled the trees and grasses; swift-running water jumped and bubbled in the stream below. An occasional bird shrieked, and Rose counted three hawks circling lazily overhead. Five minutes later, he heard another sound intruding on the sounds of nature. From behind him, filtering in through the trees on the wind, he caught the sound of a voice. He listened intently, shutting his eyes to concentrate on the sound.

There! Again an indecipherable voice leapt out of the surrounding noise. Gradually, the voices became clearer, and closer. He tilted his head toward the sound, knowing something was not quite right and trying to figure it out. He knew he heard German voices, but what was that other sound? Russian? That couldn't be right. The voices were talking and now laughing freely among themselves. Not the sound of Germans with Russian prisoners. Rose slowly turned himself within his hiding place to face the source of the sound. They were coming up from the plowed land behind them. They were probably on the path and would walk straight into the grove in minutes. Through the thin stand of birches he caught a glimpse of four helmeted heads casually walking along the path before it turned into the grove.

The voices awoke Billy and he inched his head up slowly, trying to see which way they were coming without revealing himself. He could see a vague shape across the path that he knew was Rose. Then he saw the four Germans. Billy forced himself to lie perfectly still, knowing that the slightest movement would be noticed in this thin cover. Just in case, he withdrew his M3 trench knife from the sheath tied around his boot and held it close to his body, careful not to let the shiny surface show. He knew that a single shot would certainly alert other patrols in the area, and if they were seen, this four-man patrol would have to be taken out silently. With five of them, it shouldn't be a problem, except that Rose and Kowalski were at different ends of the grove, only one of them within striking range. Four of them, then, with Rose's silenced pistol, should be plenty. Billy was sure that the approaching noise had awakened Luther and Mandelbaum, but he was suddenly thrown into a fearful doubt as he thought he heard a sharp intake of breath, almost a snore, from where Mandelbaum lay.

Rose had already screwed the silencer onto his automatic pistol, and calculated the same odds Billy did about taking the patrol. Excellent, assuming Luther and Mandelbaum were alert. Poor if they weren't. Poorer if the patrol spotted Kowalski, too far down the path for them to strike quickly enough.

Rose winced as he heard Mandelbaum, cursing him for the heavy sleeper that he was. He knew if Luther tried to wake him, he might make even a louder noise. The lead man in the patrol entered the grove, passing by the spot where Kowalski was hidden. He looked tired, as if at the end of a long patrol, probably not as attentive as when they started out. The man behind him carried his rifle over his shoulders, both hands draped over the stock and barrel. They were definitely close to home, their guard relaxed. Rose prayed they would just walk on by. They came closer, booted feet shuffling, an indistinct question answered by a weary "*Ja, ja.*" The first man passed Rose, ahead of the others, almost out into the open. The second man came abreast of him. Suddenly, the routine sounds of four armed men walking were interrupted by a loud snoring snort, as Mandelbaum, still deeply asleep, drew in a heavy breath.

Rose could see the face of the second man just across from him, turning, still in surprise, to seek out the source of the sound. He stood and in one fluid motion stepped out from the bushes, extended his arm and there was a small *pumpf!* from the silencer and the soldier's head snapped sideways, a crimson spray bursting out from under his helmet. Dealing with the next immediate threat, Rose spun to his left, sunk down on one knee to make himself a smaller target, and sent two rounds slamming into the third man's chest. He staggered back, falling against the fourth German. Rose turned around, just as the lead man was turning to react. He brought the pistol up, squeezed the trigger, and…nothing. The pistol was jammed, and for a fraction of a second, both men were frozen. The German lifted his rifle to fire directly at Rose, not ten feet away. Rose tried to work the slide to release the jammed cartridge, as he watched the rifle barrel swing around towards his chest.

Suddenly a figure burst from the bushes on the other side of the path, throwing himself at the German's legs and knocking him down as the rifle dropped from his grasp and clattered down to the path. Billy got up on his knees threw himself on the German, and his knife, propelled by his weight, drove through ribs up to the heart. Billy pushed his hand up on the German's chin, shutting his mouth against any last sound as he held the knife, buried up to the hilt in his chest.

The last man in line had thrown off the dead man pinning him down, and picked up his rifle, aiming it at Rose, who had finally ejected the jammed cartridge and worked the slide, chambering another round. Rose looked up to fire at the German, who had his rifle leveled, and saw a surprised look dawn on his face. His eyes widened, he dropped the rifle, and fell flat forward, the hilt of a V-42 Special Services Force stiletto buried between his shoulder blades.

Kowalski walked up from a dozen or so paces behind the dead German. Everything had happened in less than fifteen seconds. The four Germans were all dead, sprawled along the path, and the silence had been unbroken, except for the scuffling of feet and the light clatter of rifles dropped to the ground. Billy stood up, feeling slightly sick and dazed as he always had when he killed a man in hand to hand combat. Rose quickly checked the bodies to make sure they were all dead, then went over to where Luther and Mandelbaum had laid down to sleep. He parted some low bushes and looked down into the small depression. They both were still asleep, Mandelbaum on his back, mouth wide open, breathing slowly and loudly, on the edge of another snore.

"Wake up, you bums!" Rose growled. He turned away, checking on Billy and Kowalski. Luther and Mandelbaum stumbled out from their hiding place, astounded at the scene before them.

"Shit, Rosie, did we sleep through all this?"

"Goddamn right you did, Corporal. Now you guys pull these bodies off the path and hide them. Check them for papers." While Luther stood wiping the sleep from his eyes, Mandelbaum went over to where Kowalski was wiping the blood from his knife on the tunic of the German he had killed.

Rose walked over to Billy, laid his hand on his shoulder, and asked, "Are you OK?"

"Yeah," Billy answered distractedly. With obvious self-discipline, he pulled himself together. "I'm fine. Thanks."

"No, thank you. You saved my life. I owe ya. By the way, feel free to call me Rosie now. Welcome to the club." He smiled at Billy's look of surprise.

"Hey, Rosie, lookit this!" Kowalski called out. "These guys are wearing brown pants. I never saw the Jerries with that kind of uniform." Billy dimly heard Kowalski and his mind was catching up with him. It reminded him of something else that he had noticed as he jumped the German soldier. His rifle. It wasn't a German Mauser. What was it?

Rose and Billy knelt down to look at the German on the path that Rose had shot in the head. Rose picked up his rifle. "This is Russian. A Mosin-Nagant, standard Soviet infantry rifle. They all have them."

"Holy shit!" Luther stepped back from the body he was checking for papers. He had opened up the tunic to look for an inside pocket. Under the German tunic was distinctive collarless Russian infantry blouse, with shoulderboards and medals, just as they had seen in countless pictures and newsreels.

"Holy shit," Luther repeated, "are these guys Russians?"

"Rosie," Kowalksi asked, fearful of the answer, "did we just kill our own Allies? They coulda been wearing German uniforms over theirs to sneak through to meet up with us!"

Billy sat back on the ground, trying to focus, trying to make sense of what had just happened. He noticed he still held the bloody knife in his hand and tossed it aside. He closed his eyes and held his head in his hands. He tried to put together everything he knew, to see how the Russian uniforms fit in.

Operation Gambit is headed by Erich Remke, professional soldier, intelligence operative, fluent in many languages, and a man with few scruples. Operation Gambit is after American uniforms and gear. Operation Gambit has a specific operational area, which we're now in. No American uniforms in sight. German units withdraw from this area, except for AA defenses. Now we find four men in Russian uniforms, wearing German army tunics, with Russian weapons. No papers. Wait...if Remke had been after American uniforms, then would it stand to reason he'd also be after Russian uniforms? Maybe, but why?

Billy lifted up his head and looked at the dead body next to him, wishing that they had kept one of them alive to interrogate. Then he saw it, as clear as day on the dead man's uniform. Then he knew. It all made sense, everything fell into place. And he knew that Erich Remke could pull it off, if anyone could. He stood resolutely.

"These are Germans. They're dressed in Russian uniforms to fool us. And I bet there's another bunch of them to the east in American uniforms, waiting for the Russians."

"How do you know that?" asked Rosie. "Even if it's true, how could they fool us with these German outfits and helmets on?"

"Because they're still waiting for our guys to get closer. Remember, they don't know we're here yet in force, so they're still wearing their German uniforms."

"But how can you be so sure they're Germans?" Rose demanded. "I think Kowalski might be onto something about Russians infiltrating through German lines to contact us."

"Look at this." Billy lifted up the left arm of the dead German. The cuffband read *Brandenburg.* "These guys are Brandenburgers, a special *Abwehr* unit. Commandos, experts in operations deep behind enemy lines. They know languages, weapons, everything about Allied forces. They were even speaking some Russian as well as German when they came up on us. The Russians wouldn't just happen to have Brandenburg Division uniforms lying around. They wouldn't use them anyway, they'd attract too much notice."

"OK, makes sense," said Rose, thinking it through. "What's the part about fooling us?"

"It's my bet that there are a lot more of them around here, waiting for American forces to get close. Then they take off the German tunics, and attack us. We think it's the Russians coming after us. At the same time, there's another Brandenburg unit dressed in American uniforms, attacking the Russians heading west."

"That's why the big pullout!" Rose exclaimed. It now made sense to him also. "They wouldn't want any regular forces getting in the way of what would have to be a top secret operation!"

"Yeah," said Kowalski, now dropping his Russian patrol theory. "They'll probably each pull back, and lead us and the Russians smack into each other. But what good does it do the Germans?"

"It might not really help them at all," Rose answered, "but they might think so. Get the Allies fighting with each other, maybe one or the other will ask them to help. I could see Goebbels preaching about a holy war against the Commies."

"All I know is that we don't need another war on top of the one we have," Mandelbaum said. "A lot of our guys will get killed."

"And I know something about the Russians," Billy added. "I've dealt with them before. They're totally paranoid. It wouldn't surprise them to hear the Americans are trying to push them back to their own borders. They'd believe it. We would have another war on our hands, and maybe the Nazis could survive by playing each side against the other."

"And we're sitting here with a busted radio," Rose said disgustedly. "OK, let's get these bodies hidden."

~

Elsa found Dieter changing into a fresh uniform and filling a pack. "What's happening?" she asked.

"Remke's on his way. You had better get back to your room."

Elsa looked at his gear and weapons laid out. There was food, a medical pack, and plenty of ammunition. She looked up at him with a great sadness in her eyes.

"You're going to the Americans, aren't you? It's about to happen."

"Yes," Dieter answered as he buttoned his tunic and pulled on his field cap, "it is." He stopped and looked at her. There seemed to be little warmth in his face. Elsa suddenly saw a part of him she had never know before. He had never spoken much about the war. Dieter had told her about the places and people he had seen, and even the injustices. But he had never spoken about his actual experience of combat, death and killing. Now that she saw him preparing for this dangerous journey, she could see how he shut part of himself off from her. There was a sternness in his jaw that showed determination and commitment, where she was used to seeing an easy and gentle smile. She involuntarily took a half step back from him.

"Elsa, you have to stay here right now. It's too dangerous out there. Once I warn the Americans, Jost and Hans will bring you over with everyone else. But now you have to go back to your room and stay there."

"How will we know if...when you reach the Americans?"

"I'm bringing a field radio, a small unit tuned to a special frequency. Hans will listen for me, and then he and Jost will bring everyone over."

"What about Remke?"

"You just have to worry about staying away from him while he's here. Jost!" he yelled over Elsa's shoulder. "Coming," came the answer from down the hallway. Dieter reached out to Elsa, taking her hand in his.

"I have to do this. And I have to know you're safe while I do it. We just need to get through this and make sure this war doesn't go on forever." He kissed her, softly but quickly, afraid to lose himself in her warmth and softness. Jost stood in the doorway, waiting respectfully.

"Jost, please take Elsa back. When Remke gets here, tell him I went out to check on the patrols."

"Which way are you headed?" asked Jost.

"I'm going up to the observation post on the hill first, then decide from there once the patrols report in. The Americans have to be over the Mulde by now." He turned to Elsa.

"Please, go with Jost. Now." His eyes pleaded with her. She squeezed his hand and looked into his eyes, deeply. She leaned in and whispered to him. "Find the Americans. I will find you. I love you." Then she turned abruptly and ran out of the room. She didn't want Dieter to see her crying, not now when he needed all his strength and concentration. There would be time for tears of sorrow or joy later.

Dieter put on his pack, slung his Schmeisser over his shoulder and walked down the hall to the radio room. Hans von Schierke was testing the radio, setting it to a different frequency than Operation Gambit used to insure that Remke would not overhear their communications.

"Remke just called in. He asked for you but I told him you just left. Hurry, he'll be here soon." Hans gave him the hand-held radio. Dieter slung it over his shoulder as Jost came back from bringing Elsa to her room.

"She's not happy, but she's staying put for the moment."

"Take care of her for me, Jost." Jost knew Dieter meant more than caring for Elsa while he was gone.

"We'll see you across the river. Now go put an end to this."

"I'll stay by the radio. Let us know whatever you need," Hans said, "and God go with you."

"We've been through a lot together," Dieter said, as he made for the door. "We'll get through this, too. If not, well, I have been honored to know both of you." With that, Jost and Hans came to attention and saluted Dieter, not with the required Hitler stiff-arm salute, but with the regular and now proscribed traditional military salute, arm bent and the flat of the hand brought up to the brow. Dieter snapped to attention and returned the salute. He felt a lump in his throat and great pride in his men. He couldn't think of a single thing to say. He turned and walked in brisk, long strides, out the castle courtyard and towards the looming presence of Hill 182.

Back in her room, Elsa put on a pair of warm coveralls and a paratrooper's loose rainproof smock from among the clothes Jost had gathered for her. She pulled her brown hair up and tucked it under a blue *Luftwaffe* field cap. She checked her Luger and put it in her front pocket, and tucked extra bullets in the coverall pockets, picking up a small pack with food and a canteen. She looked in the mirror, and hoped that in the dark, she could pass for a man if need be. Going to the window, Elsa looked down. There was one floor below her, about a ten-foot drop if she hung by her hands outside the window. Praying that the ground was soft, she sat upon the window ledge, pulled her legs up and swung around, gripping the ledge and hanging down the side of the castle wall. She let go and dropped, hitting the ground hard but rolling. She got up quickly and looked around, then started running in the direction Dieter had headed.

Elsa understood that Dieter would only be distracted and worried if she went with him. He needed to think he was alone, not responsible for anyone or anything but stopping Operation Gambit. Elsa also understood that she was not about to sit idly by and wait, especially with a clearly insane Erich Remke in the same building. She would follow Dieter as best she could. At least there would be two of them heading to warn the Americans.

~

Lt. Colonel Howard Sadler stood on the hood of his jeep, binoculars to his eyes and scanning the horizon, which was broken by rolling meadows and lightly forested hills.

"I told you Barney," Sadler said to his intelligence officer, "I told you, damn it, that there was nobody in front of us!" Sadler smiled broadly down at Captain Barney Canfield, who was studying a folded map in the passenger seat of the jeep.

"Colonel, there's not much of the map left. Looks like this area has only a few main roads and lots of tracks and dirt roads like this one. If we stay on this road it looks like it will bring us out near Pretzsch, on the Elbe River."

"Then that's where we'll go to meet up with the Ruskies. We'll be in the history books, Barney!" Sadler had given up on a major battle to clinch his reputation, but he saw this as a lightning raid deep into enemy territory to link up with the Russians. Whatever the brass might say, the public back home would love it, and that's what counted. He clambered down from the hood and looked back on the line of vehicles backed up behind him.

Sergeant Johnny DeAngelo sat in the back of the jeep, leaning against the .50 caliber mounted machine gun. He lit a cigarette with his Zippo lighter and looked down the road as Sadler had. "Kinda bunched up back there, Colonel," he said as he exhaled.

"Now don't worry, Johnny, we haven't seen a German plane in days. No reason to waste time spreading out and getting lost out here." Sadler turned to the map Canfield was holding, and began pointing out the route he planned to take. Over his shoulder, from the northeast, there came a high-pitched, long drawn-out screeching sound.

"What the hell is that?" asked Sadler, incredulous. DeAngelo swung the .50 caliber around and up, yelling, "Take cover!"

Two Me 262 jet fighters banked in a graceful arc above them, lining up to attack the bumper-to-bumper trucks, jeeps and halftracks below them. The noise from their jet engines was strange and alien to the GIs below, some of whom froze for a critical second, staring up at the swept-wing shaped forms. DeAngelo saw their hesitation. He began firing the machine gun, even though the jets were not yet within range. The rapid fire sound jolted the men into action. They piled out of vehicles and ran away from the road for cover. The jets came in low, firing their four 30mm cannons at the line of vehicles. Shells and explosions chewed up the line, as gas tanks exploded and men who were too slow were caught in the deadly fire, their shattered bodies twisting in midair from the force of the impact.

DeAngelo and several other men stood their ground and kept their heavy machine guns chattering after the jets. In seconds, the attack was over. High-speed jets were excellent against other fighters, but as ground attack planes, they were simply too fast, unable to slow down enough to inflict total destruction.

As the two jets climbed away from the attack, DeAngelo saw a wisp of smoke trailing one of them. "I think I hit one, Colonel!" he yelled, excited at the thought of damaging one of Hitler's wonder weapons. He looked down and saw Sadler crawling out from under the jeep, dirt on his face and his mouth opening and closing, sound barely escaping as he looked down the column at the burning wreckage.

"Oh no, no, no…"

Captain Canfield and two lieutenants ran along the column, ordering undamaged vehicles to pull out of line and away from the burning wrecks. Medics tended to the wounded and the dead were pulled from the wreckage and laid in a row alongside the road. When everything was under control, Canfield went back up to the front of the column, where DeAngelo was giving Sadler a drink from his canteen. The Colonel's hand was shaking, but his face was cleaned up and he looked like he had pulled himself together.

"How bad is it, Barney?" he asked shakily.

"Twenty-six dead, about twenty-nine wounded, some pretty bad. Two jeeps, six trucks and three halftracks destroyed. And the Germans know we're here." Sadler looked stricken. At that moment, the walkie-talkie in the jeep squawked, and a tinny voice said "Eagle Leader, come in. This is Base." Sadler reached for it, suddenly embarrassed by the heroic call sign he had given himself. He had chosen it for how it would sound in the history books. Now he was certain it would go no farther than his own court martial. Base was the radio post he had left behind after he crossed the Mulde, not wanting to be within reach of headquarters in case they ordered his return. The walkie-talkie had a short range, and could reach only back to his radio vehicles.

"Come in Base. This is Eagle Leader," he answered despondently.

"Eagle Leader, HQ has ordered me to contact you ASAP and tell you they order your immediate return. The order reads 'All 537th RCT units must return to area west of Mulde River without delay.' Want me to read that again, Colonel?" Sadler could hear the nervousness in the radio operator's voice as he told him the bad news. He held the walkie-talkie away from him, as if it were diseased. He knew that his entire future was at stake, and he had to make a choice now. Determination returned to Sadler as the news from headquarters seemed to snap him out of his shock and depression. There was only one way to go home a hero, and it was not back across the Mulde.

"Base, please repeat. Cannot read your transmission. Please repeat." With that he tossed the walkie-talkie on the ground, pulled out his .45 automatic, and fired one bullet into it. The walkie-talkie jumped and came to rest with the case cracked, pieces of metal and wire jutting out. Now they were on their own. He turned to his stunned subordinates.

"Alright. We're not going to let these men die in vain. The 537th is going to be the first unit to contact the Russians, Germans be damned!"

"But Colonel…" Canfield broke in.

"No buts, Captain. We're moving on. Get a detail to take the wounded back in the trucks. From here, we walk."

"Why walk, Colonel?" DeAngelo asked.

"Because the Germans know we're here. They'll be looking for us on the roads. We'll move the remaining vehicles into the woods and hide them. Then we go cross-country towards the Elbe."

Within thirty minutes the undamaged vehicles were hidden in the woods, the wounded were being driven back to Wolfen, and over 600 men were advancing on foot, directly towards Hill 182 just ten kilometers to the east.

~

"Benedikt!" Remke yelled as soon as the paratrooper walked into the radio room at the castle headquarters. "Where are the Panzers?" Benedikt was momentarily taken aback by the crazed, fierce look in Remke's eyes. Remke had always been highly focused, even driven, but Benedikt had never seen him like this.

"Speak, man!"

"Sir! They are in position two kilometers to the rear. They are camouflaged in a small ravine. They can move up the slope into a firing position that covers this entire front when ordered. Most of my company is deployed around them."

"Good. Wendel just reported the Americans to the west, about 12 kilometers from here, headed in this direction. We may need to lay down some fire to nudge them in the right direction if they go off course. He had to make a strafing run at them, since they obviously spotted him also. He thought there were at least two battalions of infantry."

"Then your plan is working," said Benedikt flatly.

"Of course. It will work. By this time tomorrow there will an entirely new conflict begun right here. If everything goes well, the Russians will have to pull their forces away from Berlin to fight the Americans. The war will not end! And you, Benedikt, will be responsible, along with your comrades. Your name will go down in history." Remke smiled at the compliment he was bestowing upon Benedikt, waiting for a suitable response.

"I have only you to thank for that, Colonel Remke."

Remke's eyes glowed with anticipatory glory. He foresaw everything going perfectly in the morning, and the opportunity to keep killing Russians expanding days, weeks, months, even years into the future. A perfect existence, with all these men serving his own need to keep the blood flowing, building a sea of death around him. He needed to be sure they were all doing their part, acting out their assigned roles perfectly.

"Where is *Hauptmann* Neukirk?" he demanded, turning to Jost and Hans. "You, *Feldwebel*," he snapped. "Where is he?"

Jost stood to attention. "Colonel, he went out a while ago to check on the incoming patrols. I don't know where he is right now."

Remke didn't like one of his key officers out of touch. He turned back to Benedikt. "Go out and find him. Now."

As night fell, Dieter looked out to the east from the observation post on the hill. Hans had called him earlier on the radio saying, in a hurried report, that the Americans were closer than they had thought. Dieter decided to wait for another contact report in order to be sure he headed out in the right direction. Even though Wendel's jets flew over the area for the rest of the afternoon, searching for the column on every road and track, the Americans had simply disappeared. Dieter was forced to wait until dawn to leave, not wanting to run into the Americans at night, when any soldier was likely to shoot first and forget about asking questions. He had ordered his men at the observation post to return to their unit, telling them he would stay until their replacements came up. He was now alone, and as the stars came out he thought about how peaceful the dark countryside was. He had no way of knowing that he was at the center of a web of events that were, at that very moment, drawing powerful forces towards him. Or, that the woman he loved more than life itself was huddled up only meters away, having heard his discussion with Hans, and waiting with him, in spirit at least, for the dawn.

CHAPTER THIRTY-ONE

18 April 1945
Hill 182
Outside of Bad Schmeideburg, Germany

Benedikt gunned the BMW up the dirt and gravel road that led up to the top of the hill. Instead of following Remke's order to find Dieter, he had gone back to his men last night and gave them their final orders. He told them that the coming day's events might leave them separated, and that they should follow his orders explicitly, even in his absence. He shook hands with every man in his company, said his farewells, and departed just before dawn. Leaving his men, some of whom he had been with since the beginning, he felt both sadness and relief. As he drove away, he had felt a freedom he hadn't felt in years. He had done everything he could for them, and now they were on their own, with just one final duty to perform. He had something else to do, beginning with Dieter. Benedikt thought he knew what to do next, but he had to be sure of Dieter first.

Jost Brunner had gone out to the observation post during the night. He and Dieter were sharing cold rations as they heard the motorcycle ascend the hill. They stood apart and casually held their Schmeissers at the ready, not knowing who or what to expect. They exchanged glances as they saw it was Benedikt. He turned off the motor and got off the BMW.

"I thought I'd find you here," Benedikt said obliquely as he walked towards them. His StuG 43 Assault Rifle was slung over his shoulder, not held at the ready as he noticed Dieter and Jost's weapons were, however hard they tried to look like they weren't.

"Why is that, *Herr Hauptmann*?" Jost asked as he stepped forward between the two men. "Colonel Remke sent you out yesterday to find *Hauptmann* Neukirk. Last night he was wondering where you were."

Benedikt took a deep breath and looked both the men in the eyes. If he were wrong, it could all end here, and he would die a traitor's death at the hands of two loyal German *Soldaten*. He smiled inwardly at the thought of loyalty. Who was he being loyal to now? There was only one answer, and it was to himself. It was not how he had lived and fought the past years, but it seemed the only path left to him now. It was not perfect, but it was enough.

"Because, my Bavarian friend, this is the perfect jumping-off point for warning the Americans and stopping Remke before he succeeds."

Jost was too protective of his officer to believe Benedikt immediately. He didn't move from in front of Dieter and did not lower his Schmeisser.

"What about your oath of loyalty to the *Führer*?" Jost asked, trying to sound angry, "does that mean nothing to you?" Every German soldier had taken an oath of honor, pledging total loyalty and obedience to Hitler.

"I have lived by it. And now our country is broken between the Russians and the Western Allies. I cannot obey an oath that will turn Germany into a battleground between them. Remke must be stopped, now! If I am right, we can do this together. If not, shoot, damn you!"

Jost did not move or speak, waiting for Dieter. Dieter walked around him, patting him on the shoulder. He extended his hand to Benedikt.

"You're right. On all counts." Jost watched them another moment, then finally moved his submachine gun away from Benedikt. "Well, my *Hauptmanns*, if that's all settled, we had best contact Hans and find out where the Americans are this morning."

~

Hauptsturmführer Hugo Raalte had been ignoring repeated radio calls from SS headquarters demanding another report. He had sent in several, including the fact one of his companies had found Remke's hidden headquarters, almost deserted. The calls had become more frantic, until he decided he couldn't ignore them any longer.

"Karl!" he called for his aide. They had found a small farm and spent the night there, monitoring various *Wehrmacht* radio transmissions to find out the location of the nearest American units.

"Yes, sir!"

"Anything new on the radio?"

"Not since last night. It seems certain the Americans are halting at the Mulde River line. The Russians are closing in around Berlin and heading for the Elbe River."

"Then it's time for us to make our move. The Americans won't get any closer, and the liquor's all gone anyway," he said with a smile, adding more seriously, "so send a message to Headquarters. Tell them we've had radio trouble but it is now repaired, and that we have located Remke, and plan to capture him today. That will keep them busy for a while!"

"Excellent, sir. And then?"

"Destroy the radio and get the men moving. Towards Bad Düben, the Mulde, and a nice American POW camp. We'll let Remke and these other idiots around here kill themselves or get taken prisoner by the Russians if they want."

~

"I make three of them," Billy whispered. He kept his binoculars on them as Rose brought his sniper scope up to his eye. They had crawled up a small streambed to within 50 yards of the base of Hill 182. On the west side of the hill, near the crest, Billy had spotted three Germans. No other movement showed anywhere.

"Want me to take them out? I could drop two, easy from here, before they knew what hit 'em."

"No. We need prisoners. Do you think we can get up there without them seeing us?"

Rose looked up from his Springfield and studied the terrain around the hill. The ground grew rocky around the base, and thick bushes and small trees covered the lower half of the hill, broken by occasional rocky outcroppings. Pine trees covered the rest of the hill, with a jumble of boulders at the top, a wide flatter area below them. Rose could see a dirt road leading up the hill on the opposite side.

"Yeah, we should be able to make it up OK, as long as there aren't more of them up there. Hang on." Rose crawled backwards, lower in the streambed where the others were waiting.

"Kowalski, you take Luther around that hill and head up the dirt track. Wait here 20 minutes, then head out. We'll take the three Germans on the crest and wait for you. I don't want that radio damaged any more than it is climbing over those rocks."

"OK, Rosie, but I'd rather go with you."

"The radio's important, Sarge, and we might need Mandelbaum's German up there. The Captain wants those Germans alive to question." He beckoned to Mandelbaum and they disappeared out of the streambed, picking up Billy and following the folds of the land to the base of the hill. They began climbing up the rocks, slowly and quietly threading their way through the thick undergrowth. Twenty minutes later Kowalski led Luther through the same route to the base, then turned left and hugged the edge of the hill until they came to the dirt track. Kowalski stayed hidden for ten minutes, watching and listening until he was sure there were no guards posted. They darted up the track, and began walking, staying close to the edge of the road, alert for anything.

~

Raalte stood in the lead halftrack, looking back to insure every vehicle was still with them. They were descending a gradual slope on a rutted country lane, probably not used for anything but bringing cattle to the pastures below.

"Everyone still with us, Karl?" he shouted back to the truck just behind him. His aide signaled yes, leaning out the passenger door and looking back. This road came out on the main road between Bad Schmeideburg and Bad Düben. If they didn't lose any vehicles on this washed-out poor excuse for a farmer's road, in a few minutes they would turn left and head for the American lines, white flags flying, courtesy of the excellent linen chest kept by that farmer's wife.

The sound of the trucks and halftracks coming through the woods alerted the Hiwis guarding the intersection with the main road on the left flank of the line along the ridge held by Dieter's troops. The 8th Battalion had pulled their vehicles into the woods to hide them from aerial reconnaissance, covering them with netting under the canopy of tall pine trees. It was through this vehicle park that Raalte's column sped, ignoring the figures in the road ahead, signaling him to slow down. He was depending on speed and surprise if they encountered any roadblocks, but as he looked around he saw dozen of men, maybe more, in the woods running towards the road. Something was wrong.

The Germans and their Hiwis didn't expect any other units in this area, and grabbed their weapons, ready for battle if necessary. The Waffen-SS men were keyed up, also ready to fight their way through to survival if need be. On both sides, weapons were aimed and at the ready. The column didn't stop, with Raalte in the lead, signaling the trucks behind him to keep moving.

The driver of the third truck took a hard look at the vehicles under the netting, on both sides of the road. They didn't look quite right to him, and then he saw it. They were Soviet army trucks. He leaned out his window and screamed at the top of his lungs.

"RUSSIANS! RUSSIANS!"

The response was automatic. Machine guns mounted on the halftracks and on top of the trucks opened up, firing into the vehicles and men on either side of the road. Men turned in the trucks and fired their rifles and submachine guns, adding to the noise, confusion, and carnage. Raalte emptied his Schmeisser at the men standing in the road ahead of him, sure of nothing except that they had to fight their way out of this. The halftrack's machine gun began sweeping the road ahead, clearing it of anyone trying to block their way. There was only fifty meters left to the end of the woods and the entrance to the main road. Raalte looked back and saw the column still moving and firing, the surprised men in the woods pulling back behind the pine trees for cover. They were going to make it! Once on the open road, all they had to do was press the accelerator.

Then it happened. From the cover of the massive pine trees, men tossed grenades into the road, carefully aiming them so they didn't explode among their comrades on the other side. Raalte saw the grenades rolling on the ground just ahead of him. There was no time to speak or even think. The explosions threw the halftrack on its side and it slid along the edge of the road for seconds before exploding into a ball of flame. The first four trucks were taken out this way, blocking the rest of the column. At the very end of the column, the last driver tried to back up, but the rutted gravel road wouldn't allow him any traction. Men jumped from the trucks, scattering everywhere. Towards the front of the column, they were cut down as the Hiwis closed in on either side.

The firefight died down quickly. The surviving Waffen-SS men fled into the woods, leaving their dead and wounded behind. Hugo Raalte had been thrown violently from the halftrack as it exploded. He lay on the ground, his neck broken and extended at an impossible angle. Around his wrist was wrapped a strip of white sheet he had planned to hold up to the first American he saw, its sharp, clean whiteness fluttering in the breeze and mocking the blood, fire, and smoke all around him.

Rose took off his helmet and peeked up above the boulder he was hiding behind. Billy and Mandelbaum were just behind him. He turned around and held up three fingers, pointing to where Benedikt, Dieter, and Jost stood, looking out in the opposite direction. He signaled Billy to go to the left, Mandelbaum to the right, and indicated he would go up the middle. Billy made the motion of pulling out a pistol, and Rose understood immediately. He took out his silencer and fixed it to his pistol. If they had to shoot, at least they wouldn't alert every other German in the area.

Machine gun fire broke out down the road, followed by more small arms fire, which instantly increased in intensity. The three Germans looked in that direction, their attention focused on the source of the gunfire. Rose mouthed "now" and the three men stood and advanced quietly towards the backs of the three Germans, their weapons raised and aimed at each man's head. As they got closer, a series of explosions echoed along the ridge, followed by smoke billowing up from the pine forest.

"*Lieber Gott*," one of the Germans said in a quiet voice. Rose stopped and nodded to Mandelbaum.

"*Hande hoche!*" he ordered sternly, telling the Germans to put their hands up. They turned in complete shock and surprise. Benedikt had leaned his Assault Rifle against a rock by his feet and had no opportunity to go for it. Dieter and Jost had their Schmeissers slung over their shoulders.

"*Verdammt!*" cursed Jost, angry at being taken like this.

"*Amis!*" shouted Dieter, the only one of them who instantly realized the implication of the three figures who had taken them by complete surprise. He let his submachine gun drop to the ground and raised his hands gladly. Jost and Benedikt followed suit, with much less grace.

"Are you Americans?" Dieter asked in perfect, British-accented schoolboy English.

"*Ja, wir sind Amerikaner,*" answered Mandelbaum as he checked them for other weapons and moved them away from the overlook to sit on a fallen pine tree, out of sight.

"We must speak with your commanding officer immediately. How close is he?" Dieter asked breathlessly.

"Slow down," Billy said to him. "We ask the questions here." He looked them over. One was a *Luftwaffe* paratroop officer by his uniform. The other two wore the Brandenburg cuffband and the *Feldwebel* wore those brown pants, although none of them carried Russian weapons.

"No, no," Dieter insisted, "you must listen to me. There is no time to lose."

"First, *Hauptmann,*" Billy said, taking in Dieter's rank, "you tell us a few things. Such as why your Brandenburgers are wearing Russian uniforms, what is Operation Gambit, and where is Erich Remke?" Mandelbaum repeated the question for the other two in German. The three Germans looked at each, stunned, then each of them began talking at once. "*Ruhe!*" Mandelbaum said, commanding them to be quiet.

"My name is *Hauptmann* Dieter Neukirk, and I will tell you everything you want to know, and more. But we must hurry."

For the next ten minutes, Dieter spoke as calmly as he could, describing everything about Operation Gambit. He was very curious about how these Americans knew about it, but he forced himself not to ask any unnecessary questions and waste precious time. He told them about Remke and the Hiwis, and the overall plan, explaining that they were about to leave and contact the approaching American forces themselves.

"What was that fighting we just heard?" Rose asked Dieter, studying Benedikt as he did so.

"We have no idea. Are your other patrols this far out?"

Rose had been staring at Benedikt and did not answer him. Instead, he snapped his fingers in sudden recognition. "Now I got it, this is that tall paratroop officer we saw that night, Captain, taking the American uniforms when we went out on patrol!"

Billy studied him as Dieter translated for Benedikt. They spoke and Benedikt gestured towards Rose. "*Hauptmann* Benedikt wishes you to know that the prisoners were well-treated, except for being relieved of their uniforms. They were given adequate replacement clothing. And he congratulates you for twice observing him unnoticed." Rose half-smiled and nodded at Benedikt in return, then beckoned Billy to step a few paces away with him.

"What do you think, Billy? Are these guys on the level?"

"I dunno, Rosie. Everything they told us matches up with what we know, and you're right about the Benedikt, he was the guy that night. It does all add up. I just don't know if we should tell them we're the only Americans east of the Mulde."

"Why not? They're our prisoners. Let's see what their reaction is." Before they could continue, Dieter spoke up again.

"Please, do you have a radio? You must contact your commander and warn him!" Billy walked over next to Dieter, and indicated to Mandelbaum to translate for the others as he spoke.

"Listen, you've got nothing to worry about. I don't know what that shooting was about, but it wasn't any other Americans. We're the only Americans east of the Mulde River. We do have a radio, two of our men are bringing it up here now, but it doesn't work, at least not to transmit." When the translation was complete, the other two Germans broke out in a chorus of "*Nein, Nein*" and Dieter shook his head empathetically.

"Captain, you must believe me. There are two battalions or more of American infantry somewhere close by. If they wander into this area, Remke will attack them. Without a radio to warn them, he may succeed. And who knows what is happening along the Elbe with the Russians?"

"Rosie, go hustle up Kowalski and Luther. Let's see what we can hear on that radio," Billy said.

"We have a radio, but it is only short range. I can contact one of my men and get a situation report. If you trust us," added Dieter quickly.

~

"Over there!" DeAngelo spied the smoke first. The sounds of gunfire and explosions seemed very close, but from within the woods it was difficult to pinpoint the direction. They kept moving forward until they reached the edge of the woods. From there, they could see out over open, rolling meadows that slowly rose until they reached a road that ran parallel to a wooded ridge on the horizon. To their left a large hill dominated the landscape.

"Sir, if that's Hill 182 on this map, then that's the road to Pretzsch right there. We get on that and it's a maybe a ten mile hike to the Russians," Captain Canfield said. He was beginning to get excited, after he overcame his initial shock at Sadler's disregard of a direct order. After all, Sadler was the C.O., so he would take it on the chin if things didn't work out. Why not be the first GIs to contact our valiant Russian allies?

"Or," Sadler answered, looking through his binoculars, "that could be the Russians right over there, trying to fight their way through to us!"

"Want me to take a patrol out, Colonel?" asked Sergeant DeAngelo.

"Hell no!" growled Sadler. "We need that road and we need to help the Russians if they're there. This is no time for half measures. Reconnaissance Platoon up front, then each battalion advance in skirmish formation. I'll close up the rear with the Headquarters Platoon." Sadler looked at his watch and back to the men still in the woods.

"We move out in ten minutes. Get ready, men, this is how history is made!"

~

The three Germans and five Americans huddled around the malfunctioning radio as Luther tuned into different frequencies searching for a signal. Rose and Billy had conferred about using the German's radio. They claimed another trusted soldier was on radio duty and could tell them how close the American forces were if they had been spotted again. Billy was inclined to try, but Rose wanted more proof before giving their prisoners access to their radio. It still could be some kind of trick.

"Nothing yet, Rosie," Luther said, listening to the earphones and tuning the dial, "just some routine rear-area stuff. Ya know, these here Jerries shouldn't even be lookin' at this radio. It's top secret!"

"Don't worry, Corporal. I know this must be the latest version of your OSS field radio," Dieter said with a smile. "I see some very nice improvements!"

"God damn!" Luther said, chagrined. "Wait a minute…Rosie, Captain, listen to this!" He held the earphones away from his head. A small tinny voice could be heard, repeating over and over "Eagle Leader, come in. You are to return west of your line of departure immediately. This is a direct order. Acknowledge."

"Holy shit," said Billy. "Whoever Eagle Leader is, he's obviously east of the Mulde. That's the line of departure. Sounds like we have a fucking unauthorized operation here." He looked up at Rose, who nodded back at him.

"Get on your radio, *Hauptmann.* We need to know where that American unit is!"

~

When the shooting started, Remke raced up to the castle tower. He saw the smoke and heard the firing die down. Reports began to filter in that it was a collision with the Waffen-SS. He knew that Raalte and his men were too concerned with surrender to try and interfere with him. He came back down to the radio room, and instructed Hans to send out an order to all units to take off the *Wehrmacht* tunics. It was time to go on full alert.

After he had done so, Hans leaned back in his chair, stretching weary limbs. "Not too much longer now," Remke said. "Do you need a replacement?"

"No sir, I am fine." said Hans suddenly, not wanting anyone else operating the radio. Changing the subject, he said "Too bad about that tangle with the SS. I hope we didn't loose too many men."

"Actually," Remke answered, "it was quite instructive and useful. It showed what can happen when two groups of soldiers, wearing basically the same uniform, meet unexpectedly in a front line area. Imagine what will happen when our men meet the Americans!"

"Yes, sir. I understand."

"I am going down the road to inspect the units. I should be back within the hour, unless the Americans show up first. Contact me with any news, immediately."

"I will, sir."

"And remember, you are not to take any orders from *Hauptmanns* Neukirk or Benedikt. If they show up here they will be put into custody until they can explain themselves."

Remke went out to the Puma armored scout car that he had taken from Benedikt's unit. With its radio he could stay in touch with most Gambit units. He instructed his personal guard on what to do with Neukirk and Benedikt if they showed up, then climbed aboard the scout car. He reached into his pocket for his goggles, remembering he had left them in the radio room. Impatiently, he stepped back and walked back into the building.

Hans heard the call come in on the frequency he and Dieter had agreed upon for any emergency. He gave the pre-arranged signal that it was clear to talk. "Oak Tree, all clear." The response came back, "Linden Tree, all clear." Hans listened as Dieter told him they had made contact with the Americans, overjoyed at first and then despondent when he heard they had no radio.

"There has been no sign of the American column, Dieter. Remke has just gone out to inspect the units. Watch for him. He's given the order to remove the *Wehrmacht* tunics and make final preparations. Can you make it to the American lines?" As he asked this last question he saw something out of the corner of his eye. Remke's goggles, sitting on the side table by the door. He then felt a pair of eyes watching him.

Remke was walking down the hall when he heard Hans give an unfamiliar call sign. What was "Oak Tree"? He stopped his rapid walk, suspicious now, and slowly and quietly came to the edge of the door. He clearly heard Hans speaking to Dieter, telling him to watch for him and talking about the American lines. Now he understood. He was surrounded by traitors, just like the *Führer*. And he would deal with them the same hard way.

Hans heard a sound behind him, metal on leather. Before he could turn or speak, Erich Remke calmly pointed his Walther at his back, to the left slightly to hit the heart, and fired. In the small stone room the sound was tremendous. Hans pitched forward in his seat, slamming against the radio and sliding to the floor, a pool of blood spreading underneath him.

Remke was trembling with rage and wanted to tell Neukirk he had killed his traitorous friend, but he stopped himself. He didn't want Neukirk to know he had heard anything. *Watch for him*, he had said. There was only one place where he could be then. At the observation post. He ran out to the courtyard and signaled to three of his guards.

"With me, on the scout car!" They climbed on the armored vehicle and held on as Remke opened the passenger door.

"Colonel Remke!" A shout came from the castle tower, followed by the face of a guard leaning over and waving his arms. "Colonel Remke, the Americans!"

Remke took the stairs two at a time. From the top of the tower he could clearly see figures advancing out of the woods opposite the road, coming right at his men. For the moment, he forgot about Dieter. The actual sight of them stunned him for a moment. He brought up his binoculars and looked at the first group of men. American helmets! Yes, those were Americans!

Remke took the scout car unseen around the back of the castle, into the rear of the first unit of the 9th Battalion. The men were all ready, in full Russian uniforms. He walked among them, telling them they were about to save the Reich, or beginning the first step in the liberation of Russia from the Communist yoke, depending upon whether they were Germans or Russian Hiwis. He recognized one of the German non-coms.

"You. Feldwebel Schmidt, correct?"

"Yes sir."

"Are you ready to do your duty, Schmidt?"

"Always have been sir, and so have my men."

"Then when I fire this red flare, you step off with your men and set a good example. Pass the word down the line. Red flare, advance and attack. Remember to let any radio vehicles you see escape."

"I know sir. I don't see any out there though."

"Exactly. Which is why I want both battalions to advance at once and push them back onto their headquarters. They must be in the rear somewhere. Understand, Schmidt?"

"Understood, sir." Remke clapped him on the back and returned to his scout car. He got the flare gun and went back to the edge of the tree line to watch the Americans advance. Soon, very soon they would be in range.

Dieter heard a loud noise over the radio and then silence.

"What…Hans! Oak Tree, come in!" Benedikt was standing on lookout while they were listening, as was Rose. Suddenly he saw hundreds of men move out of the forest to their right.

"Amis! Hier! Hier!"

At first Rose thought he was calling him to come here, but when he walked over he saw what he meant. "Captain, I think we got Eagle Leader right here."

They all ran over to the outlook. Perhaps two kilometers away, the line of Americans came out of the woods and advanced in skirmish formation. Billy didn't have to watch for long.

"Luther, stay on that radio! Find out what's going on! *Hauptmann*, get that man back on the line!

"Hans, come in now!" Dieter pounded his fist in frustration. "Where are you?"

"Captain, I got somebody else. 'Base' is calling Eagle Leader, saying HQ is ordering him back, and asking if he should return. He's getting no reply."

"Who the hell is Base?" asked Billy.

"It's an old trick," answered Rose. "When you don't want to receive a certain order, you leave your communications back in your rear, close enough to get to if you need them, but far enough back that you can claim to be out of touch."

"You mean those guys got no radio?" Kowalski asked.

"Not that I can see," said Rose. "That means we have a little time before someone gets on the horn to Army HQ and tells them the Russians are attacking us."

"How long, Rosie?" asked Billy.

"Can't really tell. They could be behind the next ridge or just over the Mulde. Sounds like Base is getting nervous, though."

"Well, I think he just got some backbone," interrupted Luther. "He just radioed that he's coming looking for Eagle Leader to deliver the return message in person."

They all looked at each other in frustration. Mandelbaum explained to Jost and Benedikt, who began to talk between themselves. Dieter stayed on the radio, calling for Hans.

"OK," Bill said, turning to Mandelbaum and Kowalski. "You guys head back towards the Mulde, in the general direction that unit came from. See if you can find whoever Base is, or any radio unit. It's a long shot, but it's worth it."

"Should we send up help for these guys?"

"Listen up," interjected Rose, "the most important thing is getting a message through that these are not Russians out there. A hell of a lot more guys will get killed for a long time to come if we don't do that. That's the top priority. Do whatever you have to do to get that message back, but…" he stopped for emphasis and pointed at each of the men, "…but do not let Base contact Eagle Leader. If he broadcasts this to the world, it's all over. Understood?"

Mandelbaum and Kowalski looked at each other, assessing the impact of what Rose had told them. If they found Base, and the radio operators didn't believe them, stop them from going forward to Eagle Leader. By any means necessary.

"Got it, Rosie," Kowalski answered for the both of them.

~

Remke judged the Americans to be close enough. He didn't want them annihilated, just pushed back. He lifted the flare gun and fired. Even in daylight, the red flare burned brightly, floating slowly to the ground. True to his word, Schmidt was the first man out of the woods, firing his submachine gun. Others followed and within seconds, over seven hundred Russian-garbed soldiers were pouring out of the woods, a deep-throated "*Huzzah*!" coming from the Hiwis.

~

Sadler was at the rear of his men, glad to see them all spread out before him, feeling like a powerful military commander, ready for anything. Then he saw something he had never seen before. Enemy soldiers, charging straight at him, yelling terrifically, all headed straight for him. Germans! It couldn't be!

His Recce Platoon was out front by fifty yards. They dove for what cover they could find, firing back at the waves of men coming at them. The two battalions behind them took cover as well, taking advantage of the dips and swells in the meadow. Sadler watched in terror as his Recce Platoon was overwhelmed within minutes, with everyone killed. Then he saw the attackers go to ground as well, as heavy return fire stopped their assault.

Sadler was down on the ground when he noticed that DeAngelo was calmly standing and watching the battle through his binoculars.

"Colonel," he said, "those ain't Jerries. Those are God damn Russians!"

"What? Are you sure? There must be some mistake. Give me those!" DeAngelo gave him the binoculars and he saw for himself. He had seen enough newsreels and photos to recognize a Russian uniform, and there were hundreds of them right out there.

"Canfield! Get something white for a flag of truce and get out there! This is some kind of terrible mistake!"

"Out there, sir? Walk out there?"

"Get your ass in gear, Canfield, that's an order."

"This is an international incident sir. Shouldn't you as commanding officer go..." Sadler pulled his .45 and pointed at Canfield.

"Either you go now or I shoot you for disobeying a direct order."

Canfield didn't answer. He turned and pulled a white handkerchief from his pack, and then some white field bandages from his medical kit. He tied them to a stick, and with the small handkerchief and bandages fluttering from the stick held above his head, he walked out onto the killing ground.

"Cease fire! Cease fire," Canfield called repeatedly as he walked by his men hiding under cover. As he got closer and closer to the Russians, he could hear their fire slacken also, in response. Several times he fought the urge to duck, but kept walking on. Soon he was to the front line of his troops, still holding to white flag of truce above his head. He didn't know what to do next.

"Amerikanskki!" he yelled, in imitation of what he thought was Russian.

Across from him, one of the Hiwis said the man next to him, "We're not here to take them prisoners, are we? What are you waiting for?" They both stood up and fired long bursts from their submachine guns, sending Canfield backwards in a shower of blood as the spray of bullets ripped him apart, the tiny white flag flecked with red before it hit the ground.

~

Remke watched his men push the Americans back. The rearmost group withdrew into the woods, and the other units pulled back slowly, using cover fire from those behind them to withdraw. He could see the battle was going his way. The Americans had taken first losses, and since it appeared he had a numerical superiority, it was only a matter of time. He went back to his scout car and ordered the driver to go up the hill to the observation post. It would be a fine place to watch the battle from and settle accounts at the same time. He could also order in a few well-placed artillery shells if he needed to give the Americans another reason to fall back.

~

"Captain, we have an idea to propose," Dieter said. Jost had taken over for him on the radio after he and Benedikt approached him.

"I'll take anything you've got right now," answered Billy.

"*Hauptmann* Benedikt proposes that he and your Lieutenant attempt jointly to stop the battle."

"How the hell can they do that from up here?"

"Benedikt has a motorcycle up here. If he and an American go together, they might be able to order a halt to the fighting. On foot, it would take too long. With the BMW, they might stand a chance."

"Jesus, Dieter, that's a swell idea. Ride a motorcycle in between a few hundred men trying to kill each other." Billy shook his head.

"Let's do it."

Everyone looked up in surprise at Rose. By Rose's tone, the Germans needed no explanation. Benedikt got up and said "*Gut, kommen Sie hier.*"

"Wait a minute!" Billy ordered. Both men stopped. He walked over to Benedikt's StuG 43 assault weapon. He picked if up and looked at Rose. "What do you think?"

Rose looked at Benedikt. "As long as he's driving he can't shoot me with it. Sure." Billy tossed Benedikt the weapon and he slung it over his head and arm. Benedikt and Rose went off without a word between them, to the BMW parked behind a row of boulders. Benedikt kick-started the motorcycle and it roared into life. Rose took his Springfield rifle and slung it on his back, pulling out his grease gun and holding it in one hand. As he straddled the back of the BMW, Benedikt turned and raised a quizzical eyebrow at his new-found ally.

"Don't worry, buddy," Rose said over the rumble of the engine. He pointed his finger at the small submachine gun. "Remke."

"*Ja, sehr gut,*" Benedikt said laughing. He looked back at the American and used one of his few words of English. "Cowboy, *Ja*?"

"Yeah, I'm the lone fuckin' ranger, Benny. Let's ride."

Benedikt accelerated, his rear tire spraying dirt and rocks behind them. Rose gripped onto his belt with one hand and kept the grease gun at the ready with the other, thinking about what a crazy war it had turned out to be.

~

Remke's Puma scout car raced over the meadows toward the hill, three of his men still clinging to the top. To his left, small arms fire continued as the Americans were slowly but steadily pushed back. Satisfied that the battle was still going well, Remke focused on the hill looming ahead of him.

The driver slowed to cross a small stream, and once up the sloping bank he gained the dirt road that led up to the top of the hill. Remke signaled him to stop, and got out to check the battle one more time through his binoculars. Satisfied that he could leave it for the moment, he told his driver to continue. The road began to bank upwards as the meadows turned into a rocky field at the base of the hill. Just before they were about to begin their ascent, a motorcycle flew past them coming down the hill.

"Turn around!" Remke commanded. The driver threw the scout car into reverse and floored the accelerator. Remke had caught a glimpse of olive drab as the motorcycle sped by, and he knew the other person driving it was Benedikt. If that really was an American, his worst fears were confirmed. As they gained on the motorcycle, Remke could see clearly that it was an American riding on the back. Suddenly the rider turned, brought up his arm and sprayed the scout car with submachine gun fire. The bullets hit home but *pinged* harmlessly off the armored plate. One of the men riding on top of the vehicle yelled and rolled off.

"Fire!" shouted Remke. The machine gun atop the Puma began firing, bullets digging up the road all around the motorcycle. Benedikt saw they were gaining on him and would have a clear shot within seconds. He swerved to the left, going off the road and swerving among the rocks for a bit of cover. Quickly he turned around a large boulder and came back at the scout car head on, ducking his head and pulling to the left so the motorcycle could pass close by the passenger side of the car. The gunner was thrown off by this quick maneuver and his fire went high.

Rose understood immediately what Benedikt intended. As they passed close he slowed and Rose raised his grease gun again and emptied a long burst as they passed into the window ports, hoping to get Remke.

Remke saw them coming and pulled his pistol, about to thrust his arm out and add his fire to the machine gunner's. Then he realized Benedikt was targeting him. He ducked down in his seat, keeping the armor plate between his body and the motorcycle. The burst of fire, when it came, caught the driver in the head and chest, and the bullets ricocheted around inside, cutting into the legs of the gunner in his turret, another slicing through Remke's left arm. The two remaining men on top of the scout car ran off as Rose sprayed a final burst at the rear of the car.

Benedikt braked violently and spun the BMW around as Rose rammed a full clip into the grease gun and they both waited a moment, watching the halted car, waiting for movement. Benedikt turned to Rose and shrugged. Rose gestured for him to go forward, and he nodded in agreement.

Remke hardly noticed the pain in his arm. He heard the motorcycle coming again, and looked back at the gunner, who was grimacing in pain.

"Fire at them, you idiot!" Remke pointed his Walther at the man, "Kill them now or I'll finish you off!"

The gunner was white-faced from shock and loss of blood, but the pistol aiming up at him cleared his mind. He swiveled the gun around and aimed at the motorcycle speeding towards them. He pulled the trigger.

Benedikt and Rose saw the movement of the gun at the same time. This time the gunner knew they were going to come in close, and wouldn't be fooled again. Rose fired straight ahead, peppering the vehicle with fire, in hopes of at least distracting the gunner's aim. Benedikt swerved right, seeking shelter in the boulder field again. He opened the throttle and jumped the bike, heavy with its extra load, over a low jumble of rocks. The machine gun fire followed him, getting closer as he raced to a large boulder just ahead. Expertly he darted and swerved in the boulder-strewn field, Rose holding on and leaning in with him at every turn. Just before they reached cover, the chattering machine gun caught up with them. The bullets came in low, just ripping into the rear wheel. The BMW collapsed as the tire and wheel were shot out from under them, sliding forward and then smashing into the boulder they had been raced so desperately for. Benedikt and Rose were thrown from the bike, hitting the boulder and tossed to the rocky ground. The bike began to burn as leaking gas hit the hot metal of the exhaust.

Remke opened the door of the scout car and looked over at the two men and the burning motorcycle. Benedikt tasted blood in his mouth, his jaw felt broken and there was a terrible pounding in his head. He saw Remke in the distance and tried to lift his weapon, which lay on the ground next to him, only to find that his arm was broken. He felt dizzy. He looked over to Rose, who was also trying to get to the assault rifle. He was crawling towards him, dragging one leg broken at the ankle behind him, his face contorted in pain. He reached the stock of the weapon, pulled it towards him and tried to sit up. He turned his fractured leg as he tried to get up and Benedikt heard him gasp in pain, as he then faded into unconsciousness himself.

Remke went to the driver's door, pulled the dead body out and got in. The gunner was now dead also, his blood thick on the floor of the car. Remke drove off, back up the hill, ignoring Rose as he squeezed off a few wild shots before the pain and shock rendered him unconscious as well.

Remke drove up the hill enraged, with the smell of blood thick around him. The instrument panel and windshield were sprayed with it, as was the inside of the vehicle. Remke's arm and hand were sticky with his own blood and in his eyes everything seemed to be covered in light red flecks of blood. He looked around in horror, not knowing if it was real or not. Then he laughed, long and hard, as he downshifted and accelerated around a hairpin turn as he neared the top of the hill. So be it! Nothing could stop him now, nothing could wash away the blood he would spill. *Perfect.*

~

Hans von Schierke could feel his lifeblood leaving his body. He cursed himself for his stupid mistake, letting his guard down for a moment. He wondered why Remke didn't finish him off after one shot. He didn't know that Remke had been certain he had killed him with that single shot to the heart. Remke's aim had been off just slightly, and the bullet hit Hans' shoulder blade and veered downwards, missing his heart but tearing through a lung before exiting his chest. Red froth bubbled out of his mouth with every painful breath. As he lay on the floor, soaked in his own blood, Hans waited to die. Then it occurred to him that he could move, still breathe, although his body seemed to weigh an enormous amount. He tried to lift himself up onto the chair with his left arm, but the pain was too great. Slowly, he turned onto his right side and got himself up on one knee. He had to steady himself, and almost passed out twice. Finally, he was up, leaning on the radio table, and fell into the chair. He breathed heavily, and the pain in his chest was like nothing he had ever felt. He keyed the radio.

"Oak Tree," he gasped. "Come in. Oak Tree..."

~

Remke pulled the Puma over before he arrived at the very top of the hill. He got out, made sure his Schmiesser had a fresh clip, then headed up to the summit, off the road and through the rocks and pine scrub.

~

"What's that?" asked Billy. Faint sounds came from Dieter's radio. Dieter lifted it up and asked expectantly, "Linden Tree, is that you?" Jost came closer to listen.

"...yes."

"What happened, what's wrong?"

"...shot...did you stop...Remke?" The anguish in Dieter's eyes was painful to see. He couldn't think how to tell his friend that they had no way to stop Remke.

"How bad is it, Hans?"

"Don't...worry..."

"Hans, stay with me, we'll get help to you!"

Dieter handed the receiver to Jost and turned to Billy, explaining that Remke had discovered Hans talking with them over the radio and shot him.

"Damn!" Billy erupted in frustration. "Rosie and Benedikt are probably dead down there, who knows where Kowalski and Mandelbaum are, and that radio unit is getting closer! Shit!"

"We meet again, Captain Boyle," spoke a voice in accented but good English. Billy turned to look. Surprise and anger stormed over his face.

"Remke, you bastard," he said through gritted teeth.

Erich Remke stood with his Schmeisser aimed squarely at them. A slow drip of blood splattered on the ground from his left arm, but he gripped the Schmeisser tightly, showing no sign of weakness. Jost and Dieter were kneeling by the radio, in no position to resist.

"Captain Boyle! What a surprise! I never thought I would be again honored by the presence of General Eisenhower's errand boy."

Luther sat about fifteen feet away, hunched over his own radio, which he had set up on a flat rock, which abutted a larger boulder. He heard but did not see Remke, and was sure Remke couldn't see him. His Thompson was leaning against the boulder, just out of reach. He thought about grabbing it, but that meant he would have to move into Remke's line of vision for a split second before he could bright the weapon to bear. Instead, he quietly pulled his .45 automatic from his holster and prepared to stand up.

Remke caught a movement to the right out of the corner of his eye. He saw a man, an American by his helmet, standing up and raising a pistol towards him. He swiveled slightly and fired a burst, aiming from the hip. Bullets ricocheted off the rock, but not before several found their mark and Luther collapsed backwards, his pistol firing off one wild round into the air. Within seconds Remke again covered the three other men calmly and walked toward them.

"I made a mistake not being sure the Count was dead," Remke said. "I will not make another such mistake today. As you can see, everything is going according to our plan, *Hauptmann* Neukirk. Your last thought should be of how much you have contributed to the success of Gambit, instead of what a miserable failure as a traitor you turned out to be."

"Remke," Billy said, almost begging, "think about this. This isn't Paris, there's thousands of lives at stake. You can't hope to win, just to prolong the killing."

"Exactly, my dear Billy, exactly." said Remke with an anticipatory delight. "It is such a bonus to have you here to see my success, although I cannot let you live to tell about it. I am so glad you were able to let me know that a radio unit is making its way up to those poor Americans fighting our Russians for their lives. I was beginning to worry."

Remke grinned evilly and let out a short, harsh laugh. He raised his Schmeisser and aimed it at Billy's chest. A few short bursts and the three men would be dead.

Crack!

A single shot rang out. Remke stood looking at them with a stunned look on his face. The small group of men looked at each other, frozen in the moment, waiting for the end. Remke's look changed to one of determination, and his finger tightened on the trigger.

Crack!

Remke stumbled forward, the Schmeisser slipping from his grip. He fell to one knee, his mouth gaping open as if he were trying to form a question. He tried to turn, and collapsed. Beyond him, standing at the edge of a large tree, was Elsa Klein, her arm extended and quivering. She was holding a smoking Luger.

"Elsa!" Dieter stood and ran to her. She dropped the Luger to the ground and fell into his arms. Billy began to walk over to them, a million questions forming in his mind as he stopped to look down at Remke, whose eyes showed some slight movement. Jost put his hand on his shoulder, shaking his head, telling him silently to leave the two alone for the moment.

All Remke could see was sky. White billowy clouds drifted overhead as he tried to take in what had happened. Why couldn't he move? He couldn't feel his legs or make his arms move. He felt helpless, and there was still so much more to do. He wanted to get up, feel a gun in his hands, and take his revenge, but he could do nothing. Nothing. All he could do was to watch the clouds roll overhead, until the last one passed and bright sunlight arced out from behind it. It bathed him in a pure light, shining down on his broken body lying in his own blood, seeping into the ground beneath him.

Anna?

It's all right, Erich. Come to me now. It's all over.

He saw her. The bright sunlight seemed to change into her long blonde hair, caressing his face as she held out her hands to him.

I can't, Anna. I can't...

He tried to rally one last time, to answer the bugle call of destruction he had so carefully planned and organized. Then it was over. The best part of him, the part that had fallen in love with her and always cherished her memory in a secret part of his destroyed heart, smiled up at Anna and took her hand, leaving all the rest behind, lifeless on that desperate ground.

"Elsa, how did you get here?"

Dieter held her close. She was shaking, and Dieter could see she was exhausted as well as terrified.

"I followed you. I was going to follow you to the Americans, so we could be together and you wouldn't have to worry about me." She began to cry softly. "I was hiding in those bushes since yesterday, waiting for you to go. I didn't want you to know I was here because you would leave me behind."

"You saved our lives, all of us. Come and sit down." He led her around Remke's body and they sat near the radio. Billy came back from checking on Luther, who was dead. Dieter quickly explained to him who Elsa was and how she had gotten there.

Billy took Elsa's hand and said, "Thank you very much. *Danke.*" She smiled faintly back at him, nodding her head in understanding. Jost came over and gave her a drink of water from his canteen, watching her with fatherly concern.

"Dieter," Billy said evenly, "I hate to interrupt this reunion, but we still have to stop Gambit and we've run out of options."

"Jost," Dieter said in German, "see if you can get Hans back on the radio." He turned back to Billy and spoke quietly, even though Elsa and Jost couldn't understand them, as if what he had to say must not be said out loud.

"There is one way left. We can only do it if we are sure that this," he gestured to the battle still raging below them, "will become something far worse. Only if we are certain Gambit is succeeding."

"I don't know what you have in mind, Dieter, but I'm pretty damn sure it is succeeding. First, that Base radio unit won't have a hard time reaching Eagle Leader. They can't be that far behind, and the fighting won't be hard to find. Second, the Russians are ready to believe the West would attack them. They are absolutely paranoid. I know. I've dealt with them."

"I agree," Dieter answered. "Gambit is actually working even better than we planned it. We have to act now." He looked over to Jost, who nodded in the affirmative as he talked to Hans on their radio.

"So?" asked Billy.

"If Gambit succeeds, do you think more men will die than all those fighting here, now?"

"Definitely. Many many more, soldiers and civilians. Tell me what you're talking about."

"I can stop that battle. Now." Dieter looked grim and fearful, as if he couldn't bring himself to say how aloud.

"How, damn it?"

"I can call in artillery and air strikes. We have significant forces in reserve."

"But they're all so close together…" Billy started to say. He suddenly realized what Dieter meant.

"Everyone down there?"

"Yes. It would stop everything."

"You're crazy! Those are your own men down there! And you're asking me to wipe out a couple of American battalions!"

Dieter drew in his breath and tried to speak calmly, "What I am proposing is that we jointly agree to stop this battle in the only manner possible, and to save tens of thousands of lives on both sides, if not more."

"Oh my God." Billy felt like he had been punched in the gut. The realization that Dieter held the key to the only possible way to stop Operation Gambit from reaching its final goal made him physically ill. He half walked and stumbled over to the outlook that gave them a view of the battlefield. Gunfire and grenade explosions rippled across the meadows and woods as the fight continued.

Noise from the field radio lying next to Luther surprised him, as he heard another frantic message from Base. "Eagle Leader, come in. This is Base. I hear gunfire. We are moving towards the sound of gunfire to make contact. Repeat..."

Billy reached down and shut off the useless radio. He looked up at Dieter.

"Oh my God, we have to do it. Now."

"Yes." He turned and spoke quickly to Jost and Elsa. Jost's face was stern and betrayed no emotion. Elsa's expression was one of horror.

"No, no, you can't! All those men!"

"But Elsa, it's the only way. If we don't, ten, a hundred times more people will die, another new war will start right here!"

"But they are here, now! How can you be so certain?"

"Because, God help me, I helped plan all this, and it is working, perfectly. I know what will happen next. The Americans will radio back that the Russians are attacking them. Other American forces will come forward in support. All along the front, British and American forces will go on alert as word of the attack spreads. The Hiwis will pull back here, and allow the Americans to counter-attack, right into the oncoming Russians. There will be incidents all up and down the front, until suddenly it is a new war. And Hitler and the Nazis will still be in power in Berlin. I will not let that happen."

Dieter turned from her, wishing he hadn't inflicted the brutal logic of his decision on her. Elsa buried her face in her hands and wept. He held out his hand to Jost for the radio and looked at Billy, who solemnly shook his head and said simply, quietly, "Yes, and God help us."

"Hans, are you still there? Listen very closely..." Within a few minutes, Dieter had given precise map coordinates to Hans for artillery and air strikes. He promised his friend he would come for him soon and get him a doctor. He ended the transmission with tears flowing down his cheeks. No one spoke.

As the ten Arado AR-234B jet bombers took off from the Wittenberg airfield and formed up with their twelve Me 262 jet fighter escorts, the two *Maus* Super-Heavy *Panzers* were moving into position to fire. Their giant tank treads slowly labored up a sloping hillside to get into firing position, and the two *Jagdtiger* tank destroyers moved up with them.

The *Jagdtigers* were ready first, and opened fire with their 128mm guns, sending high explosive shells in an arc to the map coordinates over a mile away. The *Maus Panzers* fired next, their 125mm and 75mm guns adding to the deafening noise. The fire kept up steadily, with the fifty supporting *Panzergrenadiers* around their flanks covering their ears and hugging the ground as it shook from the powerful recoils. The remaining men of the *Luftwaffe* paratroop company left the area when the firing began, following Benedikt's last orders to the letter.

Billy heard the shells screaming in overhead and instinctively ducked as the noise passed over him. Explosions marked the field below as the *Jagdtiger* shells found their mark. The shelling increased in intensity as the *Maus* joined in, and the meadows and forest erupted violently as more shells tore into the ground shared by the combatants. No one was firing anymore, every man on the field was struggling to make himself as small as possible, to hide in the folds of the land and avoid the rain of death.

The sound of approaching jet engines drew Billy's attention. In the distance, rapidly approaching, he could see the low-flying forms of a stream of jet aircraft. The ten bombers came in five groups of two aircraft, staggered to cover the killing zone. The Arados visibly slowed as they came in on their bomb runs, releasing their bomb sticks exactly over the battleground. Large explosions blanketed the ground with fire and death. Four of the Me 262 jet escorts flew high cover, circling overhead and keeping watch as the Arados departed and the eight other fighters descended and strafed the battlefield for several runs. Billy could see two peel off and swoop down on a target to the west. Smoke billowed up from where they struck. Base was destroyed. Billy soon realized he was the only American alive and unwounded east of the Mulde River.

They watched in astonished fascination and horror as the aircraft and shelling put a quick end to the battle. After the last strafing run, the shelling continued for a while, slowed, then stopped. The landscape was ruined. Where minutes ago there had been meadows and woods, now there was only smoking craters and shattered, burning trees. Nothing was recognizable and nothing moved. It was over. Gambit had failed, but only at this price.

Billy and Dieter looked at each other. They wore no expression and had no words. Jost was holding Elsa, comforting her in his arms as she cried. Dieter knew instinctively that he was not the one to give her comfort now, not after what he had just done. He hoped that one day they would be able to comfort each other, and that this had not ruined what was between them. He felt immense relief, but no joy.

"What do we do now?" Billy asked.

"I must try to help Hans. And we must find Benedikt and your Lieutenant Rose."

With Jost supporting Elsa, they began walking down the hill and found the Puma scout car. Billy and Dieter removed the dead gunner and they got in, the stink of drying blood washing over them. They agreed that they would take Dieter and Elsa to the castle and leave them there to care for Hans. Jost would go with Billy to help look for Benedikt and Rose. Jost took the driver's seat and started the engine. They rode in silence, the destroyed, smoking landscape muting any attempt at forming words, or even coherent thoughts.

Jost pulled into the courtyard. Acrid smoke filled the sky beyond the castle as the sun struggled to shine through. Dieter helped Elsa out of the scout car and turned to Billy with his hand extended.

"Captain Boyle, good luck to you. Perhaps we will see each other again." Billy took his hand and shook it.

"*Hauptmann* Neukirk, I..." Billy felt a lump in his throat. This man, who he had only come to meet this day, had shared with him the most difficult decision of his life. And perhaps saved the world from another war. He gripped his hand tightly, let go, and stared at the sky.

"Jost..." Dieter began. The two men looked each other in the eye, memories of their years together flashing between them. Words were useless. Jost smiled, and gave a slight nod. Dieter turned, holding Elsa tightly in his grip, and walked towards the castle entrance to find Hans.

Jost drove off with Billy sitting silently beside him. They found Rose and Benedikt not far from the road at the bottom of the hill. Both were alive but unconscious. Rose's leg was badly broken, and Benedikt looked even worse off. His jaw was dislocated and he was bleeding from the ears. They loaded them carefully into the Puma, and Rose stirred, his eyelids fluttering open.

"What..."

"Don't worry, Rosie, it's all over. Remke's dead and so is Gambit."

"Good. What about..." In the cramped quarters of the scout car, there was no way to keep a man with a broken leg comfortable. Rose grimaced with pain, and Billy jabbed a shot of morphine into his thigh.

"Don't worry, Benedikt's here, and we'll get you both to a doctor soon."

Billy looked at Jost, and signaled that he should leave. There was no need for him to end up in a POW camp when he could just disappear. The non-com looked at Benedikt and back at Billy. He shook his head and stayed in the driver's seat. He pointed to the road west and said simply, "*Los.*"

Billy didn't need to understand German to know that the veteran *Feldwebel* was not about to leave one of his officers alone in enemy hands, even if that enemy was a recent friend. They drove off towards the American lines, leaving hundreds of dead behind, and the certainty of an end to this war in the coming days.

****

Five days later, on April 23, 1945, 1st Lieutenant Albert Kotzebue of the 69th Infantry Division led a patrol of seven jeeps east of the Mulde River and made peaceful contact with Russian 58th Guards Infantry Division, at Torgau on the Elbe River. Germany finally surrendered to the Allied Forces on May 7, 1945.

EPILOGUE

23 April 1995
Torgau, Germany

Flags snapped in the sharp spring breeze as yet another speaker approached the podium on the platform overlooking the calm waters of the Elbe River. The morning festivities were about to conclude, and the audience was restless. They had been sitting for over an hour, and most were ready to move on. They were a mixed group, mostly elderly, tourists mixed in with the local Germans. There were other events planned for today, and it was getting close to the mid-day meal.

During the past year, there had been many observances marking the fiftieth anniversary of the Second World War, starting in Normandy and working eastwards, following the campaign that they commemorated. It was only logical that the last of these occur here, along the Elbe River at the juncture of the meeting of Russian and American forces. It was, for all its historical importance, a small event. Many veterans and government officials had already made their pilgrimages to the beaches of Normandy, to Paris, the Battle of the Bulge, and other major events. Just as the men who fought to this point arrived exhausted and wishing only to go home, those here seemed eager to get the job over and be done with it.

There were representatives of the U.S. Army, including a band and a color guard. There was a Russian uniformed contingent present, but the Russian armed forces of the former Soviet Union had little interest in an event that, while it celebrated a victory, also markedly pointed out how far they had retreated since the fall of the Wall and the downfall of

Communism. There were perfunctory speeches and a brief re-enactment of the meeting by soldiers in World War II-era uniforms.

The German government and armed forces were of course absent, having no interest in celebrating anything to do with Soviet domination so soon after the reunification of East and West Germany. The local population though, took full advantage of the tourism possibilities and had welcoming signs out in the town square, and publicized other planned local events to persuade visitors to linger a few days longer. Torgau itself was not a tourist mecca, but the countryside was beautiful, and the attractions of the *Dübener Heide* were highlighted as a worthwhile destination.

The speaker concluded, and the U.S. Army band began their last number. There was a restless shifting in the seats, as if the audience was eager to get on their way, either bored, hungry, uncomfortable, or all three. Looking out over the audience from the back row, there were a lot of white-haired heads.

There's a lot of old men here, thought Billy Boyle, *including me.*

He stood up slowly, putting his hand to his back as a help to straighten up. He held onto the chair in front of him for a moment to steady himself. He smoothed back his thick white hair and put his Boston Red Sox cap on, and zipped up his jacket against the chill. His ruddy Irish skin was wrinkled, but he was proud of still having a full head of hair and a trim and wiry body. He just had to take his time with everything now. He turned and walked slowly, in short steps, to the rear of the seating area. He really didn't care what these fellows had to say. What did they know?

So what the hell are you doing here? he asked himself. *You're a seventy-six year-old widower, and you should be at home in Boston, not looking for answers here. Or forgiveness, or God knows what.*

He shook his head, as if disagreeing with himself. He really didn't know why he came. He had not been back to Europe since the war, and never had any desire to. Fifty years had passed since, as a young man, he had made a momentous decision here, with another man he had known only for a few hours. Since then, he had gone long periods of time without ever thinking of that day. But it always came back, sooner or later. He could see Dieter Neukirk as clearly as if he were standing in front of him now. He could see Elsa standing there with a smoking Luger in her shaking hand and he could still see Erich Remke's eyes, looking at something that no one else could see, as the life ebbed out of him.

He realized he was weeping, and took out his handkerchief to blow his nose. *Damn! Why am I standing here bawling like a baby?* He stomped one foot in frustration, wishing he knew what to do now that he had gotten himself here. He had taken this trip on impulse, alone, over the objections of his children and grandchildren. They had not wanted him traveling alone and he could have had their company if he wanted. He actually had wanted someone to come with him, but he was afraid. Afraid that he would have to explain something he had not talked to another human being about in fifty years. Afraid that if he did, they would think he was a monster. Afraid, as he looked towards the last years of his life, that once he really had been a monster and would be called upon to account for it.

Dieter Neukirk sat holding his cane in front of him and as the last speaker went on and on, his head dropped and his eyelids grew heavy. The wind tousled his thinning silver hair, which still showed some traces of blond. He had gained a little weight over the years, and sat solidly in his chair, a respected, well-known local retired official. The *Burgermeister* had asked him to attend today, and he had agreed, although for his own private reasons he would have anyway. Now, fighting off the desire for a quick nap as the speaker droned on, he wondered what had drawn him here. By the time the speaker finished, he had lost that battle, and it was only the first loud notes of the band that woke him, with a slight startle.

What foolishness this is, thought Dieter. He frowned, and decided to leave before the crowds made movement difficult. Using his cane, he hoisted himself up with a wince and began shuffling down the aisle.

He saw the other man, about his age, and recognized another veteran immediately. He knew the man was lost in a memory as he saw him blow his nose and wipe his eyes. He had seen it before in many other unguarded moments. As he neared him, he looked away so as not to intrude. When he came closer, something nagged at him. The man was obviously an American by his dress, but he looked familiar, especially the eyes. He stopped and looked directly at him, his eyes searching for recognition. Could it be?

Dieter could see the face of the young American from fifty years ago quite clearly. He tried to imagine what the years would have done to that face. Before he could collect himself, he realized that he had been rudely staring, and the American was returning his gaze. He felt embarrassed, and stammered, "Please excuse me, I thought…"

The other man cocked his head, as if to hear better. He pointed a bony finger at Dieter. "Is it you…Dieter, Dieter Neukirk?"

"*Mein Gott, ja.* Yes, Captain Boyle, Billy!"

"You remember me?" Billy asked stunned. By the look in Dieter's eyes, he knew immediately that the German had never forgotten a thing either.

"Of course, of course," Dieter said smiling as he grasped Billy with both hands. "Come, let's walk away from all this *quatsch*." Billy didn't understand the term, but agreed with the tone. He nodded and followed Dieter.

They walked down a gravel path that led along the river, leaving the park where the commemoration was being held. Here it was quiet. Ducks swam in the water among the reeds at the riverbank, breaking the silence with occasional flurries of quacking and flapping. Dieter pointed his cane to a bench alongside the path, and they both sat down, gratefully. Dieter straightened his leg out, and Billy saw a slight wince as he did so.

"Arthritis?"

"No, I was shot in the leg. After the war. It was not serious at the time, but it bothers me more as I get older."

"How did you manage to get shot after the war?" Billy was glad to have something else to talk about, even though he had so many other things he wanted to ask.

"*Ach*, it is a long story. They made me a police inspector after the war. I didn't want to, but there was little choice. This happened in 1949," he said, tapping his leg.

"They? Do you mean the Russians?"

"Yes," said Dieter resignedly. "The Communists, Russian and East German. They wanted anyone with Intelligence experience who was not a Nazi. I refused to work for the security police, so they made me a criminal inspector for this province."

"So you stayed here, with Elsa?"

A smile played across Dieter's face. "Yes, we stayed here. We always said any life together was a good life, even in East Germany. There were many times during the war when we never thought we would both live through it all. We were married two days after you left. She died six years ago. I still miss her."

"I know. I know."

Dieter looked at the wedding ring on Billy's hand and felt the shared weariness of love lost. For a moment, each old man lingered in his own thoughts and memories.

"I must admit, I came here hoping to see someone from back then," Dieter said sadly. "I never saw Jost or Benedikt again. I thought that if any of them were still alive, they might come here. Tell me, what happened to them and to your Lieutenant Rose?"

Billy was glad to be able to tell Dieter what he knew, smiling at the memory.

"Old Jost refused to leave Benedikt, who was in pretty bad shape. Rose had a bad broken leg, but was OK other than that. I got them to a field hospital, and the doctor wanted to treat Rose first. He said Benedikt didn't stand much of a chance anyway with a fractured skull. Rose pulled out his .45 and told that doctor he wouldn't have any chance at all if he didn't treat that German right away."

"What happened to them?"

"Benedikt pulled through. Rose surrendered his pistol to the M.P.s after the operation was over. The only reason he didn't get court-martialed is that my boss showed up."

"Someone fairly high up in Intelligence, yes?"

"Yes. I worked for Eisenhower at SHAEF headquarters."

Dieter raised an eyebrow in surprise and admiration. He now had many questions to ask, but still wanted to know more about Jost and Benedikt. Billy told him how they had kept Jost out of the POW camp by assigning him orderly duties at the hospital where Benedikt was recovering. His skull was badly fractured, and it took weeks to heal. After the surrender, Colonel Harding helped Billy get papers that allowed Jost to travel with Benedikt to Bavaria, back to his farm. Rose made the arrangements for them, and the night before they left, they all had drinks together. In broken English, German, and sign language, the four men promised to never speak of what had happened. To Billy's knowledge, none ever did. That was the last time he saw any of them.

"The day after we left you, Colonel Harding sent in a patrol to gather up dogtags from all our guys. There was a standing order for no American units to cross the Mulde for another five days while they cleaned that up. They hushed up the whole thing. It just never happened."

"I am glad to know, finally, that Jost got back to his farm. He was my *Feldwebel* since the start of the war. He was a fine man."

"You were all fine men, Dieter, to work from the inside like that to stop Operation Gambit. Now you tell me, what happened to Hans, why was Elsa there, and whatever happened to the Germans in American uniforms?"

First Dieter told him the story of Elsa and her work hiding Jews at St. Ludwig's Hospital, how Jost helped her there, her arrest and rescue. That was why the Russians never put him in a POW camp or shipped him back to Russia to die in a labor camp. They had awarded Elsa a medal as a "Hero of the Anti-Fascist Struggle", and it would have been inconvenient for her husband to be a prisoner, so Dieter was left alone after the surrender. They had cared for Hans and kept him alive, nursing him for a week. When the Russians came, he disappeared into a POW camp and was never heard of again.

"Didn't Benedikt tell you about what he ordered his men to do?" Dieter asked, in response to Billy's question about the American-uniformed group.

"No."

"When he left them with the tanks, he ordered them to go to Strauch, the commander of the unit in American uniforms, and order them to another location. Once they got them loaded on their trucks, they simply surrounded and disarmed them. There were less than forty of them, so it wasn't difficult. Most of them were happy to be relieved of their suicide mission, and melted into the countryside. A number of the paratroopers came by the castle on their way to surrender to the Americans, which was the last part of Benedikt's order to them."

"Now it all makes sense. As much sense as it can make." Billy hung his head and both men were quiet, content to let the time pass and watch the river flow by them. Finally Dieter spoke, looking out at the river and the sky beyond.

"I don't think you traveled all this way, after fifty years, to wrap up loose ends, my friend."

"Dieter, I don't know what I expected to find here. All I know is I keep seeing old men like us who have had good lives, families, and careers. But we left over a thousand men dead out there somewhere, men who never had that chance. They haunt me still, those young boys. Americans, Russian Hiwis, and Germans, too. They never had a chance at life, and nobody remembers them."

Dieter laid his hand on Billy's shoulder. "I have something to show you. First, where are you staying?"

"I don't know yet. I came straight here from Leipzig this morning."

"Then you will stay with me, no arguments. Come, follow me in your car." Dieter got up, and with a quickness in his step he had not felt in months, he led Billy to his car.

Billy followed Dieter out of Torgau, onto back roads that led through meadows and pastures. The landscape looked very familiar to him, and he remembered walking cautiously through this country with Rosie and the others. It seemed surreal to be driving out in the open, as if on a Sunday ride back home. He saw the sign for Bad Schmiedeburg, and recognized the small castle that had been the Gambit headquarters. It was now a restaurant and café, and a colorful sign read *Gasthaus zum Schloss.* He left his car there and got into Dieter's. They drove a few minutes, and with a shock Billy realized they were crossing the scene of the battle. He hadn't been prepared for this. The woods that he had last seen blasted and burning had grown back. The meadows that had been full of craters were now cultivated fields, with farmers turning over the soil for spring planting. It was beautiful and quite normal.

"I had to drive by here almost every day when I worked," said Dieter. "In one way, I became quite used to it. In another way, I have never gotten used to it." He said nothing else. They drove to the hill.

"Hill 182. That's what we called it."

Dieter just nodded and drove up the road. It was a nice, wide paved road now, instead of the rutted gravel path that Billy remembered driving the scout car down as if it were yesterday. At the top, there was a small parking area and a path leading to the outlook. Billy looked at Dieter questioningly.

"After your Colonel's men left with the American remains, we went down and buried ours quickly in common graves where they laid. Several years later, when they began plowing the fields, the remains started to surface. We didn't have time or the men to bury them too deeply. I petitioned the Soviets for permission to exhume them and give them proper military funerals."

"Did they allow that?"

"The exhumation, yes. But since there had been persistent rumors about Russians in this area, since many of the locals had heard Russian spoken by our men in the course of daily routine, I had to manufacture some sort of story."

"What did you tell them?" Billy was intrigued by what Dieter was going to show him, but also admired how his re-discovered friend had survived the Soviet occupation and obviously manipulated the authorities.

"I told them that there was a large group of Russian POWs working as transport laborers with a German column that got hit by an Allied air attack here. Since the bodies were mixed together and not identifiable, they didn't give permission for an official military cemetery. But they did allow us to remove the remains- just bones by then- to a common grave and maintain it as a local cemetery. Come."

Dieter lead Billy towards a path where a sign marked *Denkmal*, or memorial, pointed in the direction of the outlook. Dieter walked quickly over the familiar ground, while Billy took his time, age and curiosity keeping him to a slower pace as he looked around, trying to remember where they had climbed up the hill and first observed Dieter and the others. Everything had changed so much. Then the path turned and emptied out to a large flat area. Encircled by a low stone wall, a cemetery of sorts sat in the middle of the area. An iron gate opened into it, and the cemetery extended to the edge of the outlook. Inscribed in the stone by the gate was simply "1945". Inside was a single large rough stone, ten feet high and four feet wide at the bottom. There was a German cross on it, and Billy read the inscription, slowly, understanding just a few of the German words.

> Hier ruhen 99 Deutsche Soldaten die in April 1945 bei den
> Kämpfen im Dübener Heide gefallen sind, und unbekannt

Russische Soldaten die als Kriegsgefangene in Transporten ums Leben Kamen.

Dieter translated. "Here lie 99 German soldiers who fell fighting in April 1945 in the Dübener Heide, and an unknown number of Russian prisoners of war who gave their lives as transport workers."

"Do you know how many?" Billy asked.

"Over 400 Hiwis and more than a hundred Cossacks. I never could admit the real number or the Soviets would have been suspicious." He walked over to one of three squat German-style military crosses that were the only other monuments within the walls. It read simply *Die Unbekannte Russische Soldaten*, the unknown Russian soldiers. There were fresh flowers at the base. Opposite it, there was a similar stone cross commemorating the unknown German soldiers at rest here, also decorated with fresh flowers.

"I came here before the Torgau ceremony this morning," Dieter said, explaining the flowers.

"Is this all your doing?" Billy said, gesturing at everything.

"Well, yes. But mostly Elsa's. She insisted on an adequate memorial, within the constraints of what the Communists would allow. My being the Chief Criminal Inspector didn't hurt either. No one asked too many questions." Dieter paused, thinking of Elsa. The same sad smile played across his face again. "The fruit trees were her idea also. She said the blossoms always gave her hope in the spring."

On two sides, apple trees had been planted, flanking each side of the cemetery with rows of white flowering blossoms. Combined with the view, it was a beautiful spot. Billy felt a lump in his throat. He drank in the air, the scent, the blue sky above, and the soft green grass under his feet and the flowers under each cross. He put his hand against the hard rock, wanting to remember everything, to have this peaceful place firmly in his mind, to lay to rest the other memories of a lifetime ago. Billy felt Dieter take him by the elbow.

"Come, there is one other thing Elsa did before she died, just after reunification." They walked over to the third cross, at the far end of the cemetery, near the stone wall. It was smaller, and newer than the other two. In small letters, inscribed in the stone, it read *für der Amerikaner*. For the Americans.

Billy put his hand on Dieter's shoulder, to steady himself, and to say all he could not say. He closed his eyes and prayed, tears welling beneath his eyelids.

Finally, he thought, *finally*.

A strong gust of wind, traveling up the *Dübener Heide*, hit the side of the hill and swirled the branches of the apple trees to their right. A flurry of thick, white petals blew across the cemetery and played about the feet of the two old men, scattering across the grass and drifting against the stone marker in front of them, cushioning and blanketing the ground with their pure whiteness.

The End.

Author's Note

Erich Remke, Billy Boyle, and Dieter Neukirk are fictional characters. Operation Gambit is also, fortunately, a product of the author's imagination. The historical context within which these characters are found is not.

The movements of American, Russian, and German units are accurate and follow the course of the final battles in the last days of the Second World War in Germany. The meetings with Hitler, at which Remke and Guderian are present, did occur on the dates shown. Fegelin did propose recruitment of British POWs to fight against the Russians, an idea denounced by Hitler as fantasy. Remke's more ambitious plan for Operation Gambit is grafted onto those historical events.

The Russian volunteers, or Hiwis, serving unofficially with the German army, were commonplace on the Eastern Front. Whatever their motivation for fighting against the Soviet Union, they had everything to lose and little hope of gain. Their actual numbers are undocumented. German commanders often did not report them as part of their combat strength, since the Nazi High Command did not approve of their use. The Soviets dealt with them when captured by instant execution, and did not wish to acknowledge the large number of their soldiers who went over to the enemy.

St. Ludwig's Hospital in Berlin is the fictionalized version of a real hospital in that city, Saint Hedwig's. At Saint Hedwig's, which is within sight of the New Synagogue, a social worker named Marianne Hapig did actually coordinate medical care for hidden Jews in wartime Berlin. Elsa Klein is the fictional counterpart of this real-life hero. Using documentation from bombing victims as described in the book, she saved hundreds of lives. The smuggling out of Berlin, with the unwitting assistance of the

German Army, of young Jewish girls as nurse's aides, did indeed happen. The author visited Saint Hedwig's during a walking tour of Berlin. Standing on the steps to the hospital entrance, one could easily imagine the fear and terror that an ill or injured person would feel, leaving the relative safety of a hiding place to seek out medical services during the depth of the Nazi terror. The bravery of those who survived, and of those who helped them, can only be considered in awe.

Finally, the inscription on the monument described in the Epilogue really does exist. Hiking through the Harz Mountains in central Germany in 1999, the author and his wife came upon a small German war cemetery, with this marker, or *Denkmal.* A memorial to Russian dead in a German military cemetery was thought provoking, to say the least. The graves all showed the soldiers, mostly very young boys, to have died during the last week of the war. The German dead had their names, birth and death dates listed. Stones engraved with "Unknown Russian Dead" marked the Russian burials. What was incredible was that on that day, fifty-four years after those final battles, there were the fresh flowers on the Russian graves. That moment provided the inspiration for the climax of this story.

But what of the truth? Is it stranger than this fiction? Who hiked up that mountain trail that day, and gently placed a bouquet of flowers in a small glass vase at the marker for a long-dead Russian soldier? Why? Mysteries, large and small, from the most devastating conflict of the 20th Century are still with us today, challenging us to consider how we would act under circumstances of which we can barely conceive.

And wondering, perhaps, what would I do, and what price would I be willing to pay?

James R. Benn

Printed in the United States
16749LVS00001B/100-105

9 780974 408484